Some Kind of Wonderful

GIOVANNA FLETCHER

PENGUIN BOOKS

PENGUIN BOOKS

UK | USA | Canada | Ireland | Australia
India | New Zealand | South Africa

Penguin Books is part of the Penguin Random House group of companies
whose addresses can be found at global.penguinrandomhouse.com

First published by Michael Joseph 2017
Published in Penguin Books 2018
001

Set in 12.96/15.3 pt Garamond MT Std
Typeset by Jouve (UK), Milton Keynes
Printed and bound in Great Britain by Clays Ltd, Elcograf S.p.A.

A CIP catalogue record for this book is available from the British Library

ISBN: 978–1–405–93266–0

www.greenpenguin.co.uk

For my dear friend Chuck, who knows just how much life can change in a matter of months (Hello, Phoebe)!

I

My phone bleeps at me via my headphones, interrupting the sound of Ryan Adams as he tries to calm me down with his soulful voice and the skilful bell-like picking of his guitar. I'm sitting on a sun lounger, on the beach of a swanky hotel in Dubai. I should be relaxed and care-free already. I should be dreamily looking over at my wonderful fiancé and cracking into a foolish grin as I think about the way in which he popped 'the question', while excitedly thinking through all the things we need to arrange for our wedding day. I should be wondering whether it's OK to sit Mum and Dad together on the top table or if I should include Mum's other half too, before deciding to buck the trend completely and sit with our mates. I should be debating with myself whether I have to ask all three of my future sisters-in-law to be bridesmaids, even though, back in 1995 when we were just munchkins, I promised my best mate Connie that she'd be my one and only. I should be thinking about whether I'll wax or simply shave before the Big Day to prevent me getting a rash, whether heels would make me look too tall next to the groom in our wedding pho-tos and if I have to get myself something 'old, borrowed, new or blue' or wait for someone else to think of it. I have absolutely no idea why it's a tradition, but I'm not one to take chances on superstitions so I obviously wouldn't wait in hope that someone else has the foresight to save my marriage from doom. No, no! I'd get those goodies myself, to be sure. Get myself a nice blue silk garter that's for Ian's eyes only.

I should be thinking these things with a lightness in my heart as I gaze lovingly at him across our sun loungers, because these are the worries and concerns I've been longing to ponder over for as long as I can remember.

That's what I *should* be doing, but I can't look at my fiancé in that way. I literally can't look at him. Because the man sitting beside me, the man who has been sitting beside me for over ten years, is not my fiancé. He's just my boyfriend. Just. I can't bear to look at him any more because every time I do a feeling of disappointment swells through me and I have to fight back big fat tears. Tears that confirm I am not good enough to be Mrs Lizzy Hall, even after all the legwork I've put in. Tears that confirm he doesn't want to commit, even though we've bought a flat together and that he seemed delighted when we wrongly thought I was pregnant last year. We were gutted to realize I wasn't. I thought our reactions let us know we were ready for more, for things to progress.

I don't understand.

I know he does want to marry me. I know that because he's asked my dad. He did that years ago and told me he was doing it so he could 'bank it' ahead of the right time. That's how he worded it to me. So I've been living with this air of expectation, of it being the inevitable, of it being on the horizon ever since. But the horizon seems to be getting further away from me and harder to see. I feel like I'm on a dinghy desperately trying to get to that line in the distance but to no avail.

I don't want to be on a dinghy.

I hate the things. I fail to see the point of them.

I used to think I was a sturdy cruise liner, heading into the future with purpose and direction, yet my transportation has shrunk over the years and so has my certainty of getting to where I was confident of going. Any longer and I'll be like Rose on the *Titanic*, holding on to a piece of debris and willing it to keep my hopes and dreams alive, while selfishly watching my lover freeze to death (Jack could've fit, FYI).

Sometimes I want to say something drastic, like, 'If he doesn't propose by the end of the year then I'm off,' but I love him and would hate for things to end up that way. Plus, I've dedicated ten years to this relationship and I've invested so much into us. We both have. Flippant ultimatums must stay in my head, because if they were uttered out loud, I'd be horrified at having to follow such a thing through.

Maybe marriage isn't so important anyway.

Yeah right. My repetitive drawing of wedding dresses when I was a little girl would suggest I felt, and still feel, somewhat different. And it's not just the marriage part. I'm not obsessed with the idea of a big white dress draped in the rarest lace, the massive marquee with a fifty-foot dance floor, the bridal bouquet made entirely of cream roses or the Jo Malone Peony and Blush Suede candles I'd love to put on every table to ensure the place smells divine. No. That's not it at all. I'm driven by the thought of marrying Ian. That's what I want. I want to be HIS wife – and I want him to want that too.

My phone bleeps again through my headphones. Bringing it up to my face and shielding it from the glare of the sun, I see it's my mum. She's phoned every day since we've been here, which is more than she'd usually phone me at home. She's getting ahead of herself, as usual. I had to have a word with her before we left for this very reason.

'It's happening. It's happening!' she continuously shrieked when I went over to drop off an onion that she'd asked me to pick up for her on my way to visit my sister Michelle. I'm sure it was a ruse to get me over there as Ted was walking in with fish and chips for them both when I left.

'Pardon?' I asked, frowning at her manic expression and hysterical excitement as she hopped from foot to foot. Even her own divorce hasn't been enough to dampen her joy at the prospect of marrying me off. Neither has the fact my younger sister Michelle is getting married to Stuart next week – and that Michelle's about to drop Mum's first ever grandchild shortly after – been able to distract her. None of that is enough to wane her interest in me and my future nuptials.

'He's going to propose! I know it!'

Obviously I knew what she was getting at. Every time I've mentioned this trip to friends or family they've had the same reaction. Even the cashier in the local supermarket, who usually rattles through my basket of nutritious shopping without even acknowledging me, gave me a certain look when she spotted my suntan cream along with my usual collection of organic vegetables and asked where we were off to.

But this is nothing new. Whenever we go away it's the same. People suppressing their grins as though they know something I don't, or adamantly declaring Ian's going to propose while we're away, just like Mum did.

I'm used to batting away their predictions, something I've realized I do for three reasons – one, because it's a little embarrassing having people speculate over my love life and whether Ian thinks I'm The One. Two, to stop myself feeling disappointed when the question doesn't come, because what these people don't realize is that they're feeding into my own hopes of that teeny tiny question being asked. And three, to stop them feeling sorry for me when I come home sans ring or fiancé. So I swipe my hands in front of my face, knocking their assumptions out of my aura (is that how they work?), and screw up my face while I give a strained 'Nooooo . . .' Making it look like I'm not ready for that stage in our relationship anyway. Commitment from the love of my life is not what I'm after at all. Don't they realize I'm super hip and happy not to be a Mrs? I'm a feminist, don't you know . . .

Hmm.

Don't believe a word of it.

The issue is I've been here so many times before, and each time it gets that little bit more humiliating. My heart literally skipped a beat when we were up in the Peak District and I turned to find Ian on what I thought was one knee. He'd simply tripped. Not only that but he'd landed in a cow pat so I had to listen to him moaning (and smelling) the whole way back to our tent while I held in the tears of disappointment that were stinging behind my eyes. Then there's the time he insisted we travelled into London on New Year's Eve so we could watch the fireworks. Ian has no interest in New Year's or fireworks, so I thought it was his plan to get me somewhere romantic under false pretences. Nope. He actually did want to watch the fireworks while being squished and pushed by thousands of strangers, all elbowing each other out of the way to secure the best view above The Eye. Then there was Paris. Oh Paris, how you failed me! The City of Love turned into the City of Nothing. A big project came in at work that urgently needed Ian's attention, so he spent the whole time on his computer bashing away on his emails or with his mobile phone pressed firmly against his ear. I don't even think he'd have noticed if I were there or not – well, apart from the one horny bonk we had when we first arrived which ended abruptly thanks to another ruddy phone call. There wasn't a hint of '*amour*' in the air, apart from the love affair Ian had with his electronic devices.

I've had years of feeling excited and then disgruntled when the longed-for question hasn't been popped. Yet despite giving myself a stern talking-to over the black hole of self-pity I will fall into when Ian doesn't get down on one knee in Dubai, I found I was smiling to myself as the plane took off from Heathrow. A feeling of anticipation flitted around my insides. At that point I *did* look to Ian with an expression of complete and utter love, feeling like we were on the cusp of our forever promise.

But here we are. Thirteen days into our two-week holiday, ready to fly home tomorrow, and the all-important finger is as bare as it was when we arrived.

I thought it might happen on the first night, but then Ian announced he was shattered from travelling and wanted an early night. Then, when that didn't happen I had high hopes for the second day – we were out on a boat trip after travelling to Khasab by bus earlier that morning. As soon as I saw the idyllic spot where we'd be spending the majority of the day I knew a proposal was about to be gifted. The sea beneath us was so turquoise it was almost fluorescent, and surrounding us were gigantic, barren rocks, as high as they were wide. I'd never seen a spot more magical. It was beyond stunning. As was the little sail we took to the nearby beaches, which saw half a dozen dolphins swimming alongside us as we went. It had all the makings of a movie-perfect proposal. Literally, Richard Curtis couldn't come up with anything better.

On the third and fourth day we were just by the pool so I didn't think it would happen then, so I spent the majority of that time wrestling with an inflatable flamingo. But on the fifth day we went out to the desert and rode camels. It was exactly as you'd imagine. Perfect.

But, no.

Nothing.

He didn't even seem to be enjoying spending time with me. He was as grumpy and humpy as the camel I was riding. I couldn't work out what was wrong with him.

Each day has been the same since, with me questioning every little detail and him seeming almost indifferent towards me. The past few days I've given up hope. It's not going to happen this time. It's made me angry and annoyed at Ian, which I know has caused me to be a snappy bitch. I would be inclined to say that my foul manner isn't fair on him, but I wouldn't be feeling this way if he'd just declare some lifelong commitment.

I see Ian sit up next to me and look out at the picturesque sea in front of us. His dark blond hair is far shorter than it was when we first got together at eighteen. It used to be longer than mine. He was rocking the man bun before it was even a thing. It's the first thing I noticed about him. He looked so exotic while he leant on the student bar and ordered a snakebite from the barmaid. I couldn't fight the urge to go over and have a little flirt. I batted my eyelids, made him laugh, made myself laugh, and loved how he took me in. His eyes slowly moving over me as he listened intently to what I was saying, and absorbed all I had to offer.

I couldn't believe it when he revealed he also lived in Essex – and only twenty minutes away from the family home in Ingatestone that I'd moved out of the day before. I'd gone all the way to Sheffield and somehow found myself being enticed by a local boy. So he wasn't as exotic as I'd imagined, yet there was still an incredibly sexy and mysterious air about him. I felt drawn to him. He was magnetic.

A decade on and he's lost the man bun. It was something that happened before we left Sheffield and rejoined the real world. He decided to chop off his golden locks so that he would be taken more seriously and get a 'decent job'. It turned brown for a while, but his sacrifice worked. He was offered a cracking job in recruitment a month before we left university, thanks to a graduate training scheme. He's never once had to worry about the possibility of unemployment. The haircut paid off and I've slowly got used to the slightly darker-haired, more grown-up, version of him.

Along with the loss of hair went all air of mystery. Although I'm not suggesting it's a Samson and Delilah situation – rather that the titillation that comes with the unknown can only last for so long before it becomes annoying.

I look at his tanned bulging arms and along his muscular back. Physically he's nothing like he once was either. At the start of uni he was tall and slim – quite pole-like. Most of the guys were. Then he got a bit porky by the end of the first year, which was clearly down to the copious amounts of pasta I cooked us, and the fact we'd often get raucously drunk with our mates before chomping on a greasy feast from the kebab shop. In the second year he started riding his bike to lectures. Over time he started having less pasta and food dripping with fat and oil. By the time we graduated he had rock hard abs and ten times more stamina – in every way.

Since then he's bounced between bulking up and slimming down into more of an athletic frame. It's always led by whatever he's currently obsessed with. Once it was weight training, then it was spinning classes. Now he varies what he does and has a body that looks capable of doing anything as a result. By comparison my body doesn't look quite as competent, but at least it's gorgeously tanned right now. Plus, I've been religiously body-brushing before showers in the lead-up to this holiday so the cellulite situation is looking a little less garish.

Keeping his eyes trained out front, Ian turns his head to me.

I press pause on my phone so I can hear him.

'I'm going for a dip,' he says, before swiftly getting up and walking off.

He didn't even ask if I wanted to join him.

I swallow the hurt, remembering that I was pretty mean at lunch and snapped at him for food pressuring me. I had wanted a burger, he ordered a salad. Yes, I know I should've just had what I wanted because I'm on holiday and a flaming grown-up so can do what I sodding like, but I find it difficult to enjoy such treats when I'm sitting opposite someone who's eating a smug salad. Not that Ian ever eats salad in a smug fashion, but rather that the lettuce sits there calling me a fat cow and I can't deal with it. It makes me angry.

Anyway, I barked at him in front of the waiter and then begrudgingly ordered myself a salad because I knew it was 'the right thing to do'. To be fair it was a delicious non-talking bit of rabbit food, but I had to grit my teeth when a plate of burger and chips went by and I got a waft of it.

As a result my chat wasn't the best, but neither was Ian's. We pretty much sat there in silence while we munched on the plate of health.

I look out to sea at my gorgeous boyfriend and let out a heavy sigh.

If only he'd pop the question, I know I'd be an absolute delight.

2

As much as I'm trying to avoid thinking about the reality of Ian not proposing, it seems the outside world wants to keep reminding me of the possibility. Yet again the sound of my phone bleeping cuts through the music, although this time it wakes me up too. Thanks to my sodden chin I can tell I've been dribbling. Attractive.

Glancing beside me and then out to sea I notice that Ian hasn't come back. Or maybe he took one look at me with my droopily drooling mouth and decided to sit elsewhere.

I look at my phone and see that this time it's Connie, my best mate. Part of me wants to blank her call too, as though the lack of Ian 'putting a ring on it' has turned me into a failure of life. But she hasn't phoned the whole time we've been away and I miss her voice.

'Babes!' I say quietly, aware of the other sunbathers catching cheeky naps, having consumed copious amounts of cocktails in the midday heat. Thankfully the sun's getting lower now and it's a tiny bit cooler as a result. It also casts a gorgeous orange glow over everything in its reach. It's a great time of day, when everything starts to wind down and feel calm. There's a lull in the air, as though the temperature drop has allowed everyone to truly relax. The scent of coconut suntan cream fills the air – or maybe it's simply another cocktail being delivered to a lucky hotel guest.

'All right, Doll?' she replies, her husky voice unable to conceal a smile. It's a sound that has always soothed me and I can't help but dissolve as I hear it.

'Just about,' I sigh, rearranging the black triangles of my bikini so that my boobs sit more evenly. Evidently they've tried to escape while I was snoozing, and decided to give passers-by a right eyeful.

'Whoa!' she gasps at my lacklustre tone. 'Anyone would think you were the one sat at your desk with a ridiculous hangover while pretending to get shit done.'

'I heard that,' booms a voice in the background, presumably her boss Trevor.

'I'm on my lunch. Don't make me complain to HR for harassment!' she heckles back. If I spoke in that manner at work I'd get sacked, but that's Connie for you – endearing, blunt, bold and kind all at once. 'Anyway,' she says, her voice becoming soft once more as she turns her attention back to me. 'Hit me with it. What's up?'

'It hasn't happened?'

'Yet,' she says firmly, instantly knowing what I'm talking about – she's the one person I have spoken to (at length) on the topic. I might want Ian and everyone else to think I'm chilled out about it, but Connie has always been my sounding board. I need her. She makes me less neurotic.

'He's not going to do it,' I state.

'Liz. The fact you think he won't makes me think he might.'

'That's ridiculous,' I mumble, although willing to hear more. Her suspicions are much more alluring than my own.

'Think about it. You've always gone on about how so many proposals are predictable or naff,' she reminds me.

'So he won't do it here?' I preempt, remembering that I have been very vocal and judgemental about others' romantic gestures in the past. Like when Syd from up the road took Clara to a local restaurant and arranged for the ring to be put into the dessert. I don't think he expected her to order a chocolate mousse, but still, no one wants to be presented with a sloppy brown diamond. Or when Darren basically suggested marriage to Tanya rather than asking the question, leaving her bewildered as to whether she was engaged or not. I mean, it's pretty simple really – find a meaningful, romantic spot and drop to one knee before asking the love of your life to marry you in a clear and concise manner. And don't even get me started on Henry who asked Adrian while they were on the train from a boozy night out in London. There are no words for the lack of imagination, planning or even care put into that one.

Yes, OK. I can understand what Connie means. It's highly likely my noisy opinions have been detrimental to our own situation and left him confused. I thought I was offering clear guidance on what not to do but maybe that's made the whole thing too restrictive. The truth is, as I've watched my mates, who have been in fresher relationships – like Henry and Adrian who'd only been together a year when the proposal took place – walk up the aisle and declare their 'I dos', a part of me has felt a little frustrated and hurt that they've overtaken me. I've felt like we've been superglued to our current boyfriend/girlfriend set-up and I've obsessed over pulling us free and getting in front of that altar too – before another mate announces they're getting hitched to someone they met a week ago. I spend more time thinking about it than I should, but I can't help it when everyone else seems to be growing up without me. I hate to say it, but I should've been first. Admitting that makes me an awful person, I know.

'I'm saying the holiday isn't over,' Connie says calmly. 'He probably thinks you would've been disappointed with a straightforward first-night attempt, so he knows he has to do things a little differently. You are high maintenance, after all.'

'I am not,' I gasp.

'Are you suggesting you're laidback? Because I hate to break it to you but—'

'OK. Fine,' I huff, cutting across her before she breaks down my flaws: impatient, critical and finickity. I know I can be anal about how I'd like the big question to be asked, but it's a huge deal. I've waited long enough to hope for more than a dirty ring, a half-arsed attempt or for the question just to be blurted out when we're munching on a Big Mac, surrounded by a bunch of wasted passengers. Not that Ian would ever be crazy enough to do that. I know how much he detests a (tasty) burger, and a night out raving.

'Look, don't get disheartened and don't waste the last

day of your holiday brooding over this. You know you get weird when you think about this stuff. You get all possessed and cray cray,' she says in the bluntest of tones.

I would interject and argue otherwise, but I know she's right. I've obsessed over this milestone in our relationship for far too long and have often found myself daydreaming about it at the most inappropriate times – his grandmother's funeral being one of them. Don't judge me! I think it was just because we were in a church with all of his family. I couldn't help wondering whether the next time we all got together like this would be for our wedding, and if it might be nice to honour Ian's grandmother in our celebrations somehow. Like incorporating her wedding flowers into ours, or putting a picture of her up somewhere to show she'd still be with us. OK, maybe I did find myself thinking about it for far longer than I thought I did.

'I don't even think he likes me any more,' I feel myself whine.

'God, you're annoying, I can see why.'

'Oi!'

'I mean it!'

'He's acting weird.'

'Do you remember what Fiona said about Mike before he asked?' she quizzes me about her older sister who got engaged after just six months of dating – without even being up the duff.

'He was being a right knob. Cagey and distant,' she prompts.

'I remember.'

'Well, then! Enjoy the rest of your holiday and we'll mull over it as much as you like when you get back. Preferably over wine, because I can't handle all this wedding chat sober.' I imagine her rolling her eyes theatrically as she gives a little chuckle.

'How's it going?' I ask.

Connie is a serial dater. Ian and I used to joke that going on dates was how she could afford to eat, buy the latest Topshop 'must haves' and live in London. It was fun to joke about, even if we knew she'd be disgusted over the mere thought of being paid for.

Regardless of the bill arrangement, while Ian and I would be tucked up with a boxset back in Essex, she was out almost every night on a quest to find Mr Right. She's still looking. I would say she's had a string of bad luck, but actually, she's incredibly picky and isn't afraid to cut ties when someone shows a hint of possibly having the potential to, one day in the future – possibly decades down the line – annoy her.

'I have a date tomorrow night. Tinder,' she tells me.

'Funny name.'

'Ha ha ha. Very funny. He's called Matthew and he's a mortgage broker,' she states. Long gone are the days where she'd be excited or nervous at the prospect of making small talk with a total stranger. Now it always sounds like she's being a martyr, checking out all the available men London has to offer on behalf of all women everywhere. It's a tough job, but she's willing to sacrifice herself for the good of the sisterhood. She blogs about her experiences under the pseudonym Vix Bishop on the blog *You're Just Not The*

One and her exploits are just as legendary as she is. One thing's for sure, she's wasted in marketing.

'Interesting job,' I comment, wondering whether she'll be praising or condemning him in her write-up. I always look forward to her posts. A few of my favourites would be the one with the guy who turned up in his gym kit after doing a HIIT class. The guy who came along with his mum – I'm not even joking. And then, the bloke who attempted to flirt with a gentle nudge, only to use too much force, causing Connie to fall over on the cobblestones in Covent Garden and fracture her elbow. All three failed to secure a second date and one thing's for sure, her accounts of modern-day dating make me relieved I'm not single too. I'd be useless.

'Hmm . . . well, if nothing else he'll be able to give me some financial advice about getting on the property ladder. It's hard for us single folk but we're almost thirty, Lizzy. It has to happen.'

'We're twenty-eight,' I remind her, an itchy feeling creeping over my newly tanned skin at the thought of reaching the end of a decade.

'I'm thirty next year,' she says, as though the number isn't crashing down on her too.

'Fuck,' I say, just as Ian comes back and frowns at my choice of language. He plonks himself on his sun lounger, stretching out with his arms above his head, his ribs and muscles doing a little dance, before settling with his eyes shut.

'Exactly,' Connie says gravely. 'Now on that bombshell I'd better go. Lunch is over and Trevor's vein's popping out while he tries not to shout at me to get back to work.'

'I'm just here!' Trevor says indignantly, as though he's standing right next to her – honestly, it's a good job she's well liked and ridiculously talented at her job.

'I'm going to the loo before I even *look* at my emails,' she tells him.

'You're terrible,' I giggle.

'It's a shame I'm too good to get rid of,' she says, laughing to herself. 'Right, promise me you'll make the most of the last night there. Ring or not, you know it's coming at some point. You and Ian are meant to be.'

'Yeah,' I nod to myself while looking at his hairy legs lying next to mine.

'Just enjoy being away from your ruddy desk with the love of your life,' she orders.

'I will, I will,' I smile.

'Call me as soon as you're back. We need a girls' night!'

'Agreed.'

'Bye, Chick,' she says, blowing a kiss down the phone before hanging up.

I breathe out a sigh as I take the phone away from my ear and hold it to my chest.

'It was Connie,' I say to Ian, extending out a pathetically bare olive branch.

'I guessed,' he replies, not bothering to look over at me.

'Sorry I was a bit of a grump earlier,' I continue, knowing there's no way I'll enjoy my last night here if I remain pissed off, and that I should apologize for being so irrational over some green leaves.

'You should've just had a burger,' he says, pursing his lips as he looks over, his brown eyes squinting at me. 'I just wasn't hungry, but it doesn't mean you had to eat what I had. You're a grown-up, Liz. You can do whatever you want to do.'

'And you wouldn't judge me?'

'As if,' he laughs, his face scrunching up into a frown. 'It's just food.'

'Thank you . . .' I say, feeling stupid for even turning it into an issue.

'Cocktail?' he asks, sitting up and looking around for our regular waiter, Sahid, who's been on the beach with us every day – it's like he never leaves.

'Always!' I cheer.

'Two pina coladas please,' he says when he grabs Sahid's attention. We've been here long enough to not only know the cocktail list, but also what we love.

Sahid nods in acknowledgement, a smile forming on his dark mouth, his big brown eyes glistening with joy at the same order we've placed over the last few afternoons.

As he walks away I turn to Ian and see him staring ahead at a family who've been building sandcastles since I woke up. The young girl is pushing her younger brother out of the way because he keeps knocking down her pristine work, and the mum has to go over and sit between them, starting a new game to keep them amused.

'It's wonderful here . . . We're all so very lucky,' I say, my mind wandering off into a little daydream of loveliness where we revisit the hotel in five years with two little children to frolic on the beach with.

Ian turns to me then and purses his lips into a tight smile.

'Yeah . . .' is all he manages back.

No doubt he's sharing my daydream of what our future will one day look like.

3

Almost every night since we arrived we've done the same thing, and that's chill out in the hotel. There are six different restaurants, each specializing in various cuisines, and one has a different themed buffet each evening with a dozen or so desserts to choose from. To be honest, I could've spent the whole holiday in that eatery and been one very happy lady as a result. Whether I'd be able to fit into my aeroplane seat on the way home is a different matter.

Tonight the theme is Italian. I thought Ian might suggest going elsewhere rather than being faced with an evening of heavy carbs but he shrugged along with my plans earlier so I booked it regardless. We did only have those salads for lunch so we've earned this indulgence. My mouth is practically salivating at the thought.

'Are you ready yet?' I call hungrily.

Ian is still in the bathroom, he's been in there for ages – and Connie said *I* was high maintenance. I've literally had a shower, thrown on my favourite white off-the-shoulder cotton dress, scrunched some mousse into my long caramel-coloured hair, dabbed some gold highlighter on my already bronzed cheeks and brushed some dark brown mascara through my lashes. I've been ready for about half an hour. During that time I've been perching on the end of the bed, watching some naff American reality TV show about wedding dresses that I've suddenly found myself hooked on.

My tummy gives an almighty growl, alerting me to the fact we're fifteen minutes late for dinner already. I go to the bathroom door and give it a little tap.

'Babe?' I prompt, trying not to nag while simultaneously vocalizing an air of urgency.

The door opens and Ian, with a tiny towel wrapped around his waist, steps out looking a little pink-cheeked.

'You OK?' I ask, as he walks past me to grab a white shirt out of the wardrobe while barely giving a glimpse in my direction.

'Yeah. Fine,' he shrugs, a frown forming as he drops his towel and starts doing up the buttons while slipping on his boat shoes and kicking the balls of his feet on to the beige carpet to help get them on quicker.

'Erm,' I say, confused by what he's doing.

'Huh?' he murmurs, raising an eyebrow at me.

I point at his nether regions and the fact he's sorting out his footwear before putting on either his pants or shorts, his little friend and two wingmen gaily swinging freely between his bare legs.

'Oh,' he says, shaking his head, cupping his manhood before going back to the wardrobe and locating some underwear. He settles for the black Calvin Kleins I bought him for his birthday six months ago – I've wanted to get him a pair ever since David Beckham did their campaign and looked sexy as hell. Justin Bieber nearly ruined my love for them when he took over from him. But then he turned cool again, so all was good. Plus the cast of *Moonlight* have more recently taken over the job – which I think is why Ian has gone with my underwear choice rather than snivelling at it.

I watch as he pulls up his pants and cotton shorts without taking off his shoes first. It's a lazy move that clearly isn't making the task any easier.

He's being odd, distant and flustered.

My heart feels heavy at the realization. Is there a possibility he is actually going to do it?

A knock on the door makes us both jump.

'Who's that?' I ask him.

'Why would I know?' he asks, eyes wide and looking at me questioningly, frustrated at having caught one shoe in his pants with his ridiculous antics. His bits are still flopping everywhere.

I wait a few seconds, until he's finished hopping himself into decency, before going to the door.

'Hello?' I ask as I swing it open, only to be greeted by Sahid. 'Oh. Did we leave something?' I ask, looking around the room as though I'm going to spot the missing item. I always double-check that I've not left anything behind whenever I leave somewhere. Sometimes, if I'm feeling super-meticulous, I even triple-check. It's a habit. 'Hang on, did we not sign the bill?' I ask, turning to Ian. 'Did you sign it, babes?'

Rather helpfully he looks back at me blankly.

'Ma'am,' says Sahid, with his impossibly polite and soft voice, while a bashful smile spreads across his face. 'I've come to take you to dinner.'

'But we know where we're going. We've been there before. Some days for breakfast, lunch and dinner,' I laugh, my tummy angrily protesting at the thought of the copious amounts of delicious pancakes, waffles and scrambled eggs I've eaten for brekkie during our stay. I'll be sad to say goodbye to it all. Let's face it, Shredded Wheat accompanied with the greenest juice our Nutri-bullet can muster doesn't quite have my taste buds rejoicing in the same way.

'Sir?' Sahid says, looking past me to Ian, who's just finished sorting out his attire and is now standing staring at us both.

For a moment I'm not sure if he's going to speak or not.

'We thought you'd like a bus tonight,' Sahid informs us.

They say bus, but they really mean golf buggy. They're forever zooming past us on those things at a ridiculous speed. I don't understand why people that *can* don't just walk. It's a pleasant little wander through the gardens and it doesn't even take that long, five minutes tops. That said, we've just been offered one, so why not! We can take in the scenery a little later when we attempt to walk off our pasta, pizza and bottomless Tiramisu.

'Darling?' I encourage Ian, who seems to be a little startled by Sahid's gesture.

'Dinner?' he says, the same tight smile as earlier forming on his lips as his eyes skim over me.

'Fab,' I shrug, happy that he's finally getting a move on.

Sahid looks just as confused as we are, but doesn't say anything. He waits for us (Ian) to gather our crap together and then leads us down the one flight of stairs and on to the awaiting four-seater buggy. Ian doesn't sit next to me. Instead he sits next to Sahid who's driving.

I hover for a bit, my brain confused as to why Ian's chosen to get into the passenger seat over sitting with me. We're a couple. It would've been courteous and loving, right?

'Come on then,' Ian says, gesturing for me to get on as though it's me who's kept us waiting all this time.

'Right,' I nod, walking around and climbing into one of the rear-facing seats, feeling rejected while my mind debates whether this is a little tactic to throw me off the track. Could this be the start of a proposal? Perhaps he thought the golf buggy is a tad too obvious so is choosing to be distant and aloof. If that's the case then I'm sure we'll have a right giggle over this in years to come once we're happily married, old and sitting in our rocking chairs by the fire.

'Hold on,' calls Sahid, before he puts his foot down and we start moving down the stony path.

My body sways from side to side as we make our way through the gardens, the path cutting across the bright green grass that's been watered to perfection. Exotic plants sit in well-maintained flowerbeds at the side of us, while overhead baskets of dainty white, pink and purple flowers have been placed in iron archways for us to drive through. A sweet floral scent fills the air and makes the atmosphere even more enchanting. I've loved walking through here during our stay. It's peaceful and romantic. My thoughts skip to us walking back through here later on. I have a ring on my finger and am giggling girlishly as Ian has his arm draped across my shoulder and gazes at me with intense love.

Further along we pass families who are only just calling it a day and returning to their rooms from the swimming pool and beach. I spot a little girl struggling to carry a giant pink inflatable before her dad swoops them both up effortlessly. I can't wait for that to be us. If he were sitting with me, I'd give Ian's arm a little squeeze right now. He'd understand immediately and lean over to kiss my nose. I hope, anyway.

The light dims as we move further away from the main gardens and buildings and down a route I've not been before – Sahid must be taking us a different way to the one we usually walk. Maybe he's decided to take us on a little detour to show us more of the hotel to ensure we come back again. It's beautiful after all. The palm trees above us have been decorated with fairy lights, and the pretty purple, pink and white flowers continue to follow us, lining the pathway while giving off their intoxicating scent, which I'm happy to have wafting over me.

As we start to slow down I realize I can hear waves crashing. We're nowhere near any of the restaurants. We're somewhere else, somewhere back by the water.

When we come to a complete stop I turn to look at the beach and see a glow of orange creating the black silhouette of my own shadow next to me. I crane my neck ever so slightly, it's all my sudden nerves will allow me to do, and see fire torches lined up, leading to a wooden gazebo on the sand. Sheer white drapes cascade from the sides, blowing in the gentle sea breeze.

'Shall we?' Ian asks coyly, coming to my side and gesturing to help me off the buggy.

His hand seems just as shaky as mine as he guides me from my seat and around the vehicle so that we're facing the beach and the romantic setting before us. We keep walking along the sandy path laid out for us, and end up underneath the thatched roof of the wooden frame. A table and two chairs are set up for dinner. Cream candles have been lit and grouped in various heights around the edges of the room as well as on the table, while pink blooms are scattered beneath the crockery and our feet. The same flowers are used in a daisy chain pattern, which trails prettily along the beams – the delicate against the sturdy.

Ian's hand grips tightly on to mine and I feel his body stiffen as we stand and take it all in.

My breath catches in my throat. This is it, I think to myself. Without doubt, this is the moment I've been dreaming about for as long as I can remember. He's finally doing it. I'm about to become the future Mrs Hall.

A smile spreads across my face. I'm so ridiculously happy, even though he hasn't asked yet. I feel as though my heart is going to burst, as though I could break into song at any moment and it wouldn't even be weird if I did. This is so enchanting and magical that no one could possibly judge me for whatever my excited mind decides to do.

'Er . . .' Ian mumbles, his eyes going from me, to the setting, to Sahid and the waitress who's currently serving champagne from an ice bucket beside the table.

I mean, champagne practically shouts proposal when

poured on any night that's not Christmas, a birthday or anniversary. And a bottle of it too. Not just a glass. That means we're about to have something big to celebrate.

My breath catches in my throat as I feel Ian's body start to lower, thinking the obvious. But then I hear the scraping of a chair and see that he's decided to sit down, not kneel.

He lets go of my hand and faffs around with his swan-shaped napkin, as though he's trying to kill it rather than unravel it, while I swallow the lump in my throat and try not to look too disappointed that he didn't drop down on one knee straight away.

I know it's coming. Tonight. We've been a couple for over ten years and, although Ian has had his odd romantic moment, he's never done anything on this scale. He's clearly made a plan of when he'd like to ask, so I just have to enjoy every second, and wait patiently for him to make my dreams a reality. All at once I feel a tidal wave of love swoosh over me and crash into Ian. I knew he'd get there at some point and right now I love him more than I ever have.

'This is amazing,' I gush, giddily grabbing hold of the chair across from him, only for Sahid to pull it out for me and help me into my seat.

'Hmmm . . .' he sounds, while more frantic swan-bashing ensues.

He's nervous, I realize. The thought makes my heart flutter. This obviously means as much to him as it does to me. This would've felt completely different if he'd have been forced into it all those years ago, or if the wicked side of my brain had issued an ultimatum, but here he is after being given time to do it his way. He's doing this because he wants to. Because he wants it as much as I do.

'Here,' I say cheerfully, taking the folded napkin from him and calmly unravelling it before handing it back with a smile so big I'm unused to the sensation it creates in my cheeks and the back of my head.

'Thanks,' he mumbles, looking over at the waitress and giving her a little nod as he lays the napkin on his lap.

I copy the gesture, excitement bubbling away in my tummy at what's going to happen next.

'I'm starving,' Ian declares, as food starts finding its way in front of us.

'That's what you get from just eating a salad,' I joke.

He gives a stilted laugh, so I'm unsure whether he's actually taken it in good humour or annoyance that I've brought up what happened earlier. Either way, as two plates of bruschetta are placed in front of us, and a platter of carpaccio, cheese and bread is wedged in the middle, I don't have time to ponder on it.

'This looks amazing,' I say as I dive into the delicious beef in between us. 'I mean it. This is incredible,' I continue, full of joy as I place the loaded fork into my mouth and feel it practically melt. A pleasured sound comes from my mouth, but I can't hold it back. It's divine.

I stuff my face and happiness makes me do it. Sitting here, knowing what's about to come, I feel more content and secure than ever before. It's only when I realize that I've eaten most of what's on my plate and a large helping of what's in the middle, that I notice Ian has barely taken more than a few mouthfuls.

'I thought you were hungry,' I say, although not feeling the shame of earlier when comparing my indulgence to his health-mad restraint. He's chosen this food for us to eat on this special occasion, therefore, it's my first duty as 'wife-to-be' to eat it in its entirety and enjoy every single bite.

'Yeah . . .' he says, screwing up his nose and taking a deep breath. 'I feel a bit dodge.'

It's the nerves, I think to myself. Bless him. I don't know why he doesn't just spit it out. This is already more than I ever wished for in my proposal dreams.

'Oh babes,' I say, cocking my head to one side sympathetically.

'You only ever call me babes when you've been talking to Connie,' he notes, an edge of annoyance in his voice that I'm hoping is to do with his tummy not feeling right.

'Really?' I frown, wondering what he's going on about. 'I always say babes.'

'You don't,' he says, matter-of-factly. His shoulders shrug in disagreement as he shakes his head, his bottom lip giving a defiant pout.

'I do,' I state calmly.

'Don't.'

'Ian?' I protest, not entirely sure what he's getting at but feeling irritated nonetheless.

'What?' he shrugs.

'Well, it's an odd fact to bring up now . . .' I say, gesturing at the gorgeous al fresco setting we're in, and subtly referring to the fact that this is the night we're about to become engaged. There's no need to ruin it. 'Don't you like it when I call you that?' I ask, popping a bit of stinky blue cheese into my mouth – I might as well eat it if he's not going to.

'Not particularly,' he says, his lips pursing together. 'It sounds a bit common.'

'Ian!' I shriek, unable to contain my laughter.

'What?'

'Did you just call me common?'

'No. *Connie*'s common,' he says, a chuckle rising from his throat.

'Now that's not very nice,' I reprimand him, torn between smiling at him and being loyal to my best mate.

'Chill your boots, babes,' he mocks, shifting in his seat. 'I didn't mean anything by it.'

'I thought you liked me calling you that,' I say, taking a sip of my champagne and telling myself to, as Ian has suggested, leave the conversation there. He's joking with me about a stupid word. It's fine.

'There are other things about you that I prefer,' he says. The words are sweet but his voice is shaky. I wonder if it's nerves creeping in.

'Like?' I say slowly, my voice low and inviting, wondering if this might be his segue into the moment I've been waiting years for. It's not ideal that it's going to come straight after him dissing my bestie, of course, but I'll take it. He's already said he didn't mean anything by it, and despite what he says I know he loves it when I call him babes, and that he thinks Connie is far from common. Surely he knows that she's from the posher end of the village that we grew up in back in Essex – although

I guess she does still carry that twang in her voice, even though she's moved to London.

'Erm . . .' Ian stumbles, clearly thinking about how to answer. 'Things like . . .'

Ian's face freezes and I can't help but laugh at the awkwardness of him trying to work out something he likes about me. Surely it can't be that difficult when we've been together this long? He knows everything about me – there must be some good qualities in there.

'You know I love everything about you,' he says while giving a little cough and clearing his throat with champagne.

'Clearly not everything,' I tease.

'Enough, though,' he says meekly.

'Enough for what?'

He looks at me as though I've caught him off guard. Am I steering him into a proposal with a shameless leading question? Part of me is expecting him to come back with 'Enough to ask you to be my wife', or something similar, but he's been force-fed the line. I cringe at myself and back away from the table slightly.

This has to come from him.

In response he breaks protocol and picks up the champagne bottle himself, topping up his glass before downing it in one. He's not a particularly heavy drinker. In fact, I can't recall the last time we got hammered together.

It's good to know the thought of marrying me has, quite literally, forced him on to the bottle though.

Oh babes . . .

4

The rest of the bottle is gone before the main course is brought out. I've only had the one glass, but that isn't an issue as Ian has just asked the waitress, whose name is Maya, we've learnt, to bring out another bottle. I'm hoping to get more of a look-in during the next round, although I am concerned at just how much Dutch courage this proposal is clearly requiring.

'Do you think you should slow down?' I say quietly, not wanting to embarrass him in front of Maya or Sahid. I'm sure they've seen worse.

'Ooh, Mummy!' Ian cackles, curling his finger up to his mouth like he's in an *Austin Powers* film.

I can't help but laugh. He's never this silly, or this out of control.

'You know what I love about you, Liz?' he asks, gesturing at me with his empty glass.

'What?' I ask, trying to make my eyes as smouldering as possible as I look at him.

He looks at me confused for a minute, as though I'm meant to be giving him the answer to his drunkenly slurred question. His gaze drops downwards to the plate in front of him, as though he's only just noticed what was placed there a few minutes ago. We've been treated to a delicious platter of grilled seafood – lobster, tiger prawns, red snapper, scallops, baked oysters, Alaskan king crab legs, mussels, all served alongside a sweet chilli sauce and mixed vegetables and jasmine rice. A noise of surprise sounds from him before he picks up the whole lobster, yes, the whole thing, and eats it with his hands.

'You are wonderful,' he mutters, although I'm not sure if he's saying it to me or the dead crustacean in his grasp.

'Ian?' I try again.

His eyes find mine, sort of, and a huge breath is expelled. 'Oh Liz. Lizzy, Lizzy, Lizzy. You are the best.'

'Thanks,' I laugh, starting to feel embarrassed for him. 'I'm just going to pop to the loo,' I add, shifting from my seat just as Maya gestures where I have to go.

'Don't be too long. You might miss the best bit,' Ian chortles to himself.

It's not that I especially need a wee, but I feel we need a moment. A breather. As soon as I'm away from the table I pull my phone out.

'Lizzy?' Connie says excitedly after just one ring, clearly expecting my call. I wonder if Ian had run his plans by her. Maybe that's why she was telling me to enjoy myself earlier, and being so reassuring.

'He's drunk,' I hiss.

'Pardon?'

'Blind drunk,' I say, realizing she needs more detail to understand what's going on. 'Con, it's such a romantic setting. We're on the beach, the food's amazing, there's flaming Champagne—'

'Oh my god,' she squeals.

'– but he's wasted.'

'He can't be that bad.'

'He is.'

'As bad as when you came to stay with me?' she asks, causing me to laugh.

A few years ago we decided to go to some club in London with Connie and stay over for the weekend. Well, Ian got so wasted in the trendy little cocktail bar we went to before the club that he ended up puking his entire liquid intake over the bouncer's shoes. Luckily we dragged him away, whilst begging for forgiveness, before things turned nasty. We didn't all get beaten up, so it must've worked. The next morning he insisted that his drink was spiked, but I knew he'd been doing some weird fitness research online and had decided to live on nothing but caffeine and a single banana all day. I'd say that was the root of the issue.

'OK, he's not as bad as that,' I concede.

'Then this is salvageable,' she encourages. 'Let me know how it goes.'

The line goes dead.

I take my time going for a pee and checking on my make-up before returning to Ian and what should be our heavenly spot beneath the stars. When I get there he is slumped over his dinner, this time using his fork but still managing to look more caveman than I'm used to.

Hearing my footsteps on the wooden decking, his head jolts up to look at me, his brown eyes wide and soft. He takes a deep breath and then sighs, his hands going up to his face.

'Babes,' he says, looking embarrassed as he gently mocks me.

'You're such an idiot,' I say, sitting in the seat that Maya pulls out for me.

A gentle chuckle escapes his mouth. 'I'm sorry.'

'That's OK,' I tell him, calmly placing my dead swan of a napkin back across my thighs. He might be playing this all wrongly, but my heart is weak for him and I don't want him to think he's failed.

'I wanted this to be perfect,' he says sadly, his words evoking more softening from me.

'It is. You're there and I am here. To me it doesn't get more perfect than that.'

'Well, isn't that the sweetest thing,' he says, his hand reaching into his pocket as he clumsily slithers out of his chair and lands on one knee beside me.

One knee!

'Oh my god,' I say, petrified, nervous and excited at what he's doing, even though I've wanted it for so many years and suspected it since we arrived tonight.

Ian fiddles in his pocket before extending his arm out in front of me and holding out what's in his hand. A beautiful, glistening, stunning, diamond ring, cut into a cushioned halo, with smaller diamonds extending out across the band. It is beyond anything I've ever Pinterested.

'It's beautiful, Ian,' I hear myself say, my hands flying to my mouth as tears spring to my eyes. For the first time ever I feel like I'm floating on air. Ian wants a life with me.

My head is spinning as I look up from the wondrous sight before me to my beloved Ian. His expression doesn't quite match mine. Instead I find him frowning as he gawps from me to the ring, as though the whole thing has caught him entirely by surprise. As though he's woken up from a dream and found himself in this position. Clearly the joys and consequences of inebriation.

'I. I. I . . .' he stammers, painfully.

He makes a gesture with his hands, as though he's proffering the ring to me once more, but then he holds it back into his chest, his fingers tightening their grip around the delicate band.

I feel for him. He wouldn't have meant to drink as much as he did, but it's done now and will give him comedy-gold material to use in his groom's speech at our wedding.

Our wedding!

'It's OK, darling,' I say, placing my hand around the back of his neck and pulling him into me so that I can kiss him on the forehead.

'No!' he says, squirming away from my touch. He leans back into his heels and clumsily slips on to his bum as a result. He doesn't try to get back up. He sits there, stooped over. Looking at the ground, at the ring in his hands, at the rose petals scattered delicately on the floor, anywhere but at me.

'Ian?' I prompt softly. Having never seen him like this I'm unsure what to do. I can usually read him like a book but this is so far from our norm.

He takes a deep breath and rubs the back of his head

aggressively, making his hair stand on end. I resist the urge to flatten it out. 'I'm so sorry, Lizzy,' he says meekly, his hand coming around to pinch the bridge of his nose, his face wrinkling up in torment.

'Honey, this is fine. You don't need to worry,' I tell him, hating the fact he's clearly feeling foolish for letting himself go for once. I get off my chair and join him on the ground, my hand cupping his knee as my arm drapes across his broad shoulders, giving him a little shake.

'But I do,' he sniffs, rubbing his eyes.

Is he crying?

'It doesn't matter how you do this, Ian. You don't even have to do it right now, if you'd rather not. It can wait. *I* can wait,' I say, swallowing at the words I never would've predicted myself saying, ever. I'm not even entirely sure I mean them, but I'm hoping it'll help him relax.

'No, Lizzy,' he says, shaking his head dramatically. 'I can't.'

I look at my drunken love and try to ignore the disappointment growing inside me, the urge to tell him how long I've waited for this perfect moment, and how bereft I am that he's ruining it, but I know I can't. Also, I don't want to. I want this to be perfect too and perhaps now isn't the right time.

'Let's just enjoy the rest of the dinner then,' I say, getting to my feet and lifting his arm to help him up off the ground. 'We haven't seen dessert yet and I bet it's going to be incredible,' I encourage, noticing that Maya and Sahid have kept themselves busy (and away from our dramatics) by clearing our mains and bringing out the next course – a quick glance tells me it's not going to disappoint and that it might just get me through this mess.

'I'm not going to ask you,' Ian says quickly, resisting my help and opting to stay sitting on the floor.

'All right, don't rub it in,' I laugh with as much cheer as I can muster. 'I've said it doesn't matter.'

'You don't understand what I'm saying. You're not hearing me,' he scolds, his voice getting stronger and louder. 'Not tonight. Not ever. I can't. I don't even . . . This isn't what I want.'

The words hit me like a slap, sharp and full of sting. Slowly they trickle their way through my body and leave me frozen on the spot.

'You don't want to marry me,' I whisper back.

Ian's eyes come up to meet mine. 'No.'

It's the most forceful and clear he's been all evening – and all holiday.

'But . . .' I start. But what? How can I possibly finish that sentence? I can't force him into changing his mind or beg him to want what I want.

'I'm sorry,' he sighs from the floor.

'Why did you bring me here then?' I ask. I'm surprised to hear no anger in my voice. There's nothing. Not even sadness. It's just a voice that's trying to understand how we've reached the point where Ian is jilting me at the proposal – worse, halfway through it. 'You bought a ring. That must've meant something. You organized *this*,' I say, my hands grabbing rose petals from the table before letting them fall to the ground. 'You must've wanted this at some point.'

'I thought I did.'

His voice is, heartbreakingly, as calm as mine. It's measured. All slurring has gone. I know he's now in control of what he's doing here. This isn't a drunken mistake. He's sobered up in an instant. He means it.

'Thought you did?'

'It's what everyone's always told us to want. And then with your sister about to get married too, and having a baby ... It's been hard,' he shrugs. 'I'm always being asked when I'm going to do the honourable thing.'

'And this is honourable?' I ask, feeling tears prick at my eyes but clenching my jaw so that they can't escape.

'They asked all the time,' he says, his shoes scraping along the floor as he crosses his legs. 'People at work, our families, friends – strangers in bloody shops who we're just buying sofas from, they all expect it from me. They practically told me I had to do it.'

Our families and friends are one thing (I can only imagine what his mum says to him as she's as forthright as my own), but I vividly remember the female shop assistant he's referring to. She was younger than us but had just got back from her honeymoon. She asked the question as we were deciding between an L-shaped sofa and an oversized chair, but she certainly wasn't piling on any pressure.

'Ian, I doubt she even cared. She was just making conversation. We've been together for ten years. When people find that out it's understandable that it's a go-to question,' I say, suddenly defensive of everyone who's ever pried. 'You can't blame everyone else for this.'

'OK, what about you?' Ian asks, his arms gesturing at me as though I'm one giant problem.

'Me?'

'Dropping hints all the time,' he continues, even though my face has fallen and I know I can't contain my death stare any longer. It's hitting him in full force, but his piercing eyes are unwavering.

'I wanted to marry you! Is that a fucking crime?' I ask, my voice rising.

He has the decency to bow his head and not bite back, to even look a tad apologetic.

'You could've just said you didn't want to.'

'But I didn't know that's how I felt until tonight,' he says pathetically. 'I thought it was nerves. Then I thought it was the champagne.'

'You had enough of it,' I scoff, picking up the second bottle and swishing it around to show that it's half empty. 'So what changed your mind?'

'Is this really what you want?' he asks imploringly, his lips pursing together as his eyes fill with a woeful look.

'An explanation? Yes!' I nod with certainty.

'No.' His voice is low and steady, rising up from the depths of wherever this doubt about us has been hidden. 'Us.'

'Us?' Call me stupid, but I hadn't pieced together the whole puzzle. No popping of the question doesn't just mean no longer becoming Mrs Hall, it means no longer being Ian and Lizzy. It means saying goodbye to our life together.

A pain – an actual *physical* pain – shoots across my chest, burning at anything in its way before it compresses and constricts, threatening to squeeze everything out of me.

'So it's not the wedding you don't want. It is actually *me*?' I say with a shake in my voice. 'You're done. After all those years together, after everything we've been through, that's it?'

'I love you, Lizzy,' he sniffs, getting to his feet, holding his hands and grabbing on to mine, his thumbs making small circles on my skin just like he normally does when he has to comfort me. The problem is it's not usually him that's caused my sadness and heartache. 'I don't want to hurt you.'

'Don't give me that shit,' I glare, my anger blasting out. It's one thing to cast me aside, but acting like he's worried about my feelings is laughable. 'Don't try spouting some kind nonsense when you're breaking my heart. You don't mean it, so don't fucking bother.'

'Lizzy—' he begs, as though I'm being unreasonable and overly sensitive towards the man who's plucked out my heart and stamped on it. As though I should be taking his feelings and hurt into consideration too.

'What's wrong with me then?' I ask, interrupting whatever rubbish consolation chat he's attempting to give me and getting to the nitty gritty I know is going to haunt me for years to come as I sit and dissect tonight. Pondering over what I did to ruin such a good thing. 'Have I become boring? Fat? Is it because I don't make our bed in the right way? Is it because I refuse to make a pizza with a cauliflower base? Or did I cook your favourite dish too many nights on the trot? Did I iron your sodding shirts with too much starch and leave them too stiff around the collar? Clean your football boots too vigorously? Or is it because I didn't give you a blowie when I *legit* had a headache last week?'

'There's no need to be childish.'

'A ring!' I shriek, bashing my hand on the table, the loud bang making Maya, who's been standing helpless at the serving table for the entirety of this shit-show, yelp. But I don't stop. I want my words to hit home and let him know exactly what he's doing. What he's already done. 'You held a ring in my face, Ian. You organized this romantic night with champagne, and then instead of offering me a lifetime of commitment you dumped me. While you still had that ring in your hands. Do you really want to start hurling names at me? Because if that's the case you're about to get a serious earful.'

'No, Lizzy. I'm not trying to justify this,' he whines pathetically.

'Good, because you can't.'

'Right,' he nods, taking a pause to breathe. 'I'm a total arse and you deserve to hate me for the rest of our lives.'

'I will,' I agree, feeling like my wounded heart will do anything but. All I really want right now is for him to hold me and retract it all, but he's already freed himself of me and my troubles, and part of me wouldn't know what to do if he attempted such a kind gesture anyway.

'And it will kill me knowing you feel that way about me,' Ian says, having the decency to look suitably lugubrious. 'Surely you can see it's better to do this now rather than when we're in the church on our wedding day? Or worse, when we actually have a family together?'

A sob escapes my mouth as I see all my dreams of our lives together being shredded into streams of useless nothing.

'I want you to go. Now. Leave me alone,' I say, knowing there are more emotional outbursts to come, that I'm about to break beyond repair, and that I don't want him to be here for it.

'It doesn't have to be like this.'

'I can't see how it doesn't.'

'We can talk about this. Be reasonable with one another,' he says, his arms stretching out as though he's going to hug me. Although now I don't want them anywhere near me.

'I said, leave me alone. Just fuck off!' I say, a guttural sound escaping. 'I don't want to look at you, Ian. All I see is how I've failed us.'

'We failed. This isn't all on you, Liz,' he says, this time sounding genuinely sad, but I won't hear it.

'No, it is. It really is. Because I would still marry you in a heartbeat,' I cry, aware of the tears tumbling from my cheek to my collarbone.

'Liz . . .'

'Please go.'

I can't look at him any longer, but I see his body hesitate, unsure what to do. He hovers on the spot, no doubt wondering whether he should stay or go. He's always loved to do the right thing. Whether it was getting to lectures after a night out, making sure he saw his mum once a week or opting for a salad over a fucking burger. He's done it. But what is the right thing in this situation?

An intake of breath is followed by a large sigh.

'I'm so sorry,' he mutters, sounding like someone who's lost the battle, even though he's definitely got what he wanted – to get out of having to spend a lifetime with me. 'I'll be in our room if you want to talk.'

'No, you won't,' I bark, shocking us both as I stop him in his tracks. 'You'll go to reception and book yourself a separate room for tonight. I'll let you know when I'm out in the morning and you can pack all your stuff.'

'But we're going to be travelling to the airport and flying home together.'

The thought crushes me further.

I don't say anything. I can't. I don't want to think about having to spend time with him. I don't want to be anywhere near him when he's clearly fallen out of love with me.

We stay in limbo for a while, neither of us talking. Just little sniffles and the catching of breath becoming our miserable soundtrack.

Finally he concedes and I am left alone.

5

I wait until I hear the golf buggy drive off, and then I walk out on to the beach, keel over and sob. I wail uncontrollably, my face squashed against the sand as I cry out in despair. I want it to bury me, to part aside and drag me under so that I no longer feel what I'm feeling. The heaviness. The darkness. The grief that's only just started to show its face, but it's there. I know it's coming for me. I know it'll consume me and that makes me fearful.

This can't be happening.

The person I now am seems so far from who I thought I was when I came to dinner tonight. Broken, not whole. Weak, not strong. Desperate, not content. I am not me. I am a stranger.

When the sobs threaten to suffocate me I have to force myself to calm down, to stop letting the black infuse its way right through all of me. I dig in my heels and stall, catching my breath, recharging my fight.

Life as I knew it has ended. It's dramatic, disastrous and catastrophic yet everything is as it was before. Turning on to my back, I open my eyes to see the sky still glittered full of stars. Stars that on any other night I would've deemed magical or otherworldly. The sea still moves, its waves crashing into shore. The mosquitos still hum, the air still breathes. It's the same as before.

This is my pain and mine alone. Nothing else has changed.

The breath in my chest slows once I've finally been able to regain control of my bodily functions from my heart. Already I feel physically bruised thanks to the emotions trying to beat their way out of me. It was a futile attempt. They needn't have bothered. They won't be going anywhere for a while, no matter how hard they fight.

I've no idea of the time. Everything seems to have halted, as though I'm living in an altered universe. But then again, it has and I am. The man I thought would love me for ever has left me. He's deserted me – and not, I hope, because someone else has tempted him elsewhere, but because he doesn't see a future with me. He doesn't want *me*. He literally doesn't desire *me* any more. I'm unneeded. Surplus to requirements. Undeserving of future attachment and love . . .

I get up before emotion grips hold of me again, physically moving away from the grief. Sand sticks to my legs, but I can't be arsed to wipe it off. It's everywhere, and my life is now messy enough as it is. I don't need to swipe at my skin aggressively to get it off. It'll dry and fall before long and my legs will go back to normal. If only the same could be said of my heart.

I feel sluggish as I wander back to the spot in which I should've become the happiest women alive. There's no sign of Maya and Sahid, yet everything has been left as it was. The candles are still burning, the petals are still scattered, and the champagne (what's left of it) has remained on ice.

I pour myself a glass and take a seat. Only once my bum has landed do I notice my napkin has been placed over a loaded plate. I lift it up to find a giant selection of desserts – mini lemon meringues, brownies, cookies, little bite-sized toffee eclairs, chocolate bombes and tiramisu. It all looks delicious.

I've never been one to starve my way through something painful. Never have I said the words 'I'm not hungry' or lost my appetite. Thankfully, the same is true now. With my champagne in one hand, I lift a fork with the other and tuck into the meringue, the top crunching as I fork through it, the bottom crumbling as I lift it away. I bring it to my lips and feel a deep satisfaction as I eat it.

It's a fleeting feeling, so I repeat the action. I do this again and again, stopping occasionally to take a gulp from my flute. Eventually the plate is clear and my tummy is aching from being stretched so much. I'm full but empty all at once. I no longer feel at all satisfied, so I top up my glass, resolving to sip at it this time.

I try to gather my thoughts, to make sense of what's happened here tonight, but I can't. I'm lost and I'm fearful I'll never be found again.

My phone rings. I retrieve it from my bag, wondering who's calling to investigate this time, but I can't look. I can't cope with my failings and the pity I'm going to receive. Instead of answering it, I throw it on the floor, stand up, grab the chair and crush it with a wooden leg.

It shatters instantly.

Silence wins.

Silence takes over.

Silence numbs me.

A fog descends, clouding any thoughts from forming and before I know it the sky's getting lighter and the birds are chirping at one another. When a young woman arrives to clean our wooden hut and prepare it for the next lucky couple, I decide it's time to leave. Slowly I walk along the paths, past the restaurant and through the gardens.

Once inside our room I grab our suitcases and start packing away our things. I do it for both of us. It's habit and something I've always done. It's strange to know this is the last time I'll be doing it for Ian – although I take little care over his belongings. I bung it in, mixing in the clean with the dirty and not bothering to wrap up his toiletries to prevent them from leaking and ruining everything. It feels rebellious.

Sitting on top of the cases to force them shut with a click and a bang, I'm finally done and ready to go home. I collapse on to the bed and close my eyes.

I'm startled awake by the bedroom door being opened and catching on the lock, causing a clatter. I must've put the chain across when I came in earlier.

'Shit,' I hear Ian mutter from the hallway.

I go to call out, to say 'babes' or ask him what he's up to, but then I remember what happened a few hours ago and the fact we're no longer together and decide against it. I'm no longer meant to care.

Glancing across our hotel room I see that everything

has been packed away and that it looks spotless. I do this whenever we go away. Ian's always taken the mickey out of me for it – apparently there's no need for housekeeping to come in whenever I check out because I leave it impeccably clean. I thought it was a good quality to have, but perhaps that's just one of the little things that have irked Ian and forced him into abandoning me when he should've been marrying me. Saying that, I have many idiosyncrasies. This is merely the tip of a rather large iceberg, I suspect.

Annoyed that my decluttering task is complete, my eyes land on the clock on the telly.

'Fuck,' I gasp as I jump off the bed, realizing we're meant to be leaving in ten minutes.

'Lizzy?' I hear Ian call desperately, the door still ajar.

I really don't want to see him, but I have no choice. I shut the door so I can unlock the chain before reopening it fully.

There he is. My heartbreaker. The crusher of my dreams. The one who wants to disentangle his life from mine.

Ian has the decency to knit his brows apologetically, his brown eyes looking at me in his own sorrowful way. There might be no tears, but I can see he's hurting too, or maybe this is for show so that I don't hate him too much for ending things. Deep down I know Ian wouldn't do such a thing. He doesn't give in to social pressure and would rather his face reflect exactly what he's thinking. He doesn't put on a show, whether that's faking happiness to see someone or sadness because someone's cat has died. He doesn't deliver an emotional expression unless he's feeling it. His inability to fake enthusiasm for evenings out is part of the reason we've found ourselves such homebodies. It's easier than feeling like he's pissed off whenever we go out and having to apologize for him. Clearly I should've known that him 'not feeling it' and freely cutting ties related to me and marriage as well.

He looks dishevelled. Although I don't need a mirror to tell me he doesn't look as shitty as I do.

'I'm going to shower,' I mumble, lowering my gaze to my feet as I shuffle away.

'Liz, are you OK?' he asks, coming after me and stopping the door from closing with his foot, his hand resting on the glass panel between us. 'I'm so sorry things have ended this way. I never meant for it to all spiral out of control like this. I thought I could make it work. I wanted to. You deserve so much more than I could've given you. I should never have done this to you.'

'Ian. Please don't even pretend you care about my feelings,' I say, my voice sounding firm and vulnerable all at once. There's a finality in his words that brings home the reality of our situation. There's no turning back. He regrets the way in which this has all happened, but not the act itself.

'But I do.'

'Then care enough to leave me alone and let me deal with this without you,' I say, pushing the door firmly while feeling him lift his foot up and away. It closes.

The win is crushing. If this were a movie he'd fight for me, push harder on the door and saunter into the bathroom so that I couldn't resist before sweeping me up into his arms declaring he's made a mistake. But this isn't a film.

I shower quickly and throw on the travel clothes I'd piled up earlier – jogging bottoms and an oversized top. I brush my teeth and roller some sea-salt stick under my pits, but don't bother with make-up. I don't see the point or have the drive.

Once the last of the toiletry items have been gathered up I take a deep breath with my hand on the door handle, calming myself before going back in to where he is. Ian is lounging with his feet up on the bed, watching some reality TV show about airports and looking pretty chilled out.

'Thanks for packing for me,' he says, scrambling into a sitting position as soon as he sees me come in.

Normally I'd be grateful for the acknowledgement and recognition, congratulating myself on having found such a kind and thoughtful partner. Today I'm not.

'I'm leaving in five,' I say, turning my back to him and placing my wash bag into the smaller suitcase we're sharing. 'With or without you.'

I hear his shoes thump on the floor as he gets off the bed and heads into the shower.

My teeth grind together as I fight away the tears. Soon enough I'll be home and things will be easier to cope with.

Home.

Our home.

The home we co-own.

Sadness engulfs me and takes away any solace home was holding for me.

The whole journey to the airport I plan to beg the airline staff to move our seats so that we're sitting separately on the plane. I can't bear the thought of our elbows and thighs touching for seven hours and forty minutes. Obviously we wouldn't talk – I'd put on my eyemask and feign sleep the whole way – but feeling him next to me would literally be the worst kind of torture.

Nervously handing over our passports to the chirpy check-in assistant, who's dressed in red with her brown hair effortlessly swooped up into a French plait, I notice her glancing between the two of us. My request is lost in my throat, as my mind wonders what she sees. Is our heartache apparent? Does my sunkissed skin betray my sadness? Has she noticed how far we're stood apart? How I flinch when Ian brushes my hand in an attempt to help me find our paperwork? Does she notice that we're all wrong?

'Good news!' she sings, looking from her computer screen to me. Me. Not Ian. 'We have some space available in Upper Class today. Have you flown Upper before?'

'No,' I croak.

'Oh, actually . . .' she says, picking up a pair of glasses from the desk in front of her, her face concerned as she puts them on and inspects the screen closer. 'I can't get two seats next to each other but I could always—'

'No. No. That's fine. Yes. Yes please,' I blurt, not caring that my eagerness to sit separately isn't hidden.

If last night had been an actual proposal and this lady (who is clearly an angel) had offered us the same upgrade, I'd be feeling completely smug right now – I wouldn't even bother trying to suppress it. I'd be heading straight to the Upper Class lounge to take a picture of me with some bubbles for Instagram and Facebook, while simultaneously giving another flash of my new bling – just in case someone missed the gushy post I'd inevitably have posted the previous night. I'd be declaring that I was the luckiest girl alive.

As it stands, I still feel lucky. Although now it's for not having to be anywhere near someone I still love wholeheartedly. It hurts to look at him, to feel his touch or get a whiff of his aftershave. I don't want to hear his voice or catch his gaze.

I don't want to come to the realization that all I actually want right now is to curl up into his arms while he tells me it's all going to be OK.

That is not my reality. Therefore, the further away he is from me, the better.

6

When Ian suggests he goes straight to his mum's from the airport rather than home with me I don't protest. In all honesty I enjoyed the free champagne a little *too* much on the flight. The air stewardess just kept bringing it out, so who am I to refuse? Perhaps the lady who expertly read the situation and upgraded me put a little note next to my name saying something along the lines of 'alcohol needed – has a twat of an ex on board too'. Maybe. Whatever the reason, my head is pounding when we reach London, leaving me even more irritable than before. Plus, I haven't said a word to Ian since we were in the hotel room so I'm not about to start. Buggering off to his mum's is the least he can do while we try to figure out how the hell we move forward from here and start unpicking the many ways we are so tightly stitched together.

To add insult to injury, when I get back to our block of flats I find the lift has a great big 'out of order' sign stuck across its closed doors, meaning I have to drag and heave my suitcases up four flights of stairs. I'm a sweaty mess by the time I get to the top. I'm now in the foulest of moods.

I thought walking into the flat would offer some sort of comfort, the familiarity of the walls and belongings, the smells and textures giving me some sort of warmth and friendliness. Instead, the memories start flooding back as soon as I get my keys out to open the front door. There we were five years ago, excitedly hopping from foot to foot, about to walk into our first proper home after years of renting and dreaming it would happen, before Ian swooped me into his arms and goofily carried me over the threshold.

'We're not married,' I laughed.

'One day,' he replied, kissing me in a way that was full of promise.

The memory mocks me.

I push forward, turning the key in the lock and stepping over the post that's gathered while we've been away. Our first bit of post was a 'new home' card from my nan. We all thought she was going to lose her rag about me moving in with a man out of wedlock, but she was rather cheery about the whole thing and not as old-fashioned as we'd feared. In fact, she's the only one who has never really pushed the idea of marriage on to any of us, even though she and my granddad got married within a few weeks of meeting each other. She didn't even flinch when Mum told her about Michelle being up the duff out of wedlock, which I know Mum found difficult because, apparently, Nanny had been quite strict with her when she was younger. Getting older has clearly made her less conservative and more liberal.

Struggling through the narrow doorway with our two suitcases, I place my key into a small wooden bowl on top of the console table. We'd bought the bowl while travelling around Africa seven years ago. We found it at a huge market in a town square that was mostly for the locals rather than frivolous tourists looking to buy a cheap souvenir. I wanted a larger fruit bowl at first, or one of the colourful woven rugs with bold geometric patterns arranged in panels and executed in the interlocking-tapestry weave, but Ian, rather sensibly, pointed out that neither would be the easiest thing to carry as we trekked around – we were heading from Cape Town to Cairo and we were only at the start of our trip. I agreed and we then compromised on the smaller version of the fruit bowl, which was just as beautiful but meant I wouldn't have to dump any of my possessions to make room for it.

I toyed with the idea of moving it elsewhere last year and getting something new in its place, but Ian insisted it held special memories so we had to keep it where we could see it – even though it doesn't really go with the décor in the flat, which is made up of mostly glass furnishings, copper accessories and Farrow & Ball Borrowed Light-painted walls – a classic pale blue that makes the space feel nice and airy, even though it's a one-bedroom flat.

It's been a while since I looked at that bowl and thought of our travels together. It seems like such a long time ago and the pot has just become a pot. Back then, we'd only just left uni and knew that we had to return by a certain time so that Ian could start his new job, but we wanted one big adventure first. The people we met, the cultures we stole glimpses of, the animals we encountered and the beaches we bathed on were beyond what we'd hoped.

We stayed in an orphanage for a week, sleeping in the village chapel at night, then played games and taught the children the Hokey Cokey in the daytime. One of my fondest memories is of us getting ready for bed and hearing the hundred children, who must've been crammed in their single dorm, happily singing the song they'd learnt from us. We grew closer on that trip and knew we were ready to head home and become proper adults.

As it does whenever we come back from any trip away, the flat seems darker and smaller than when we left. Like a Cadbury's Creme Egg, it's as if someone's made the whole thing smaller while it's been out of our sight.

Yet it's the same. Posters, pictures and postcards adorn the walls, capturing special memories of places we've visited and moments we've had.

Our belongings share stories too; an ebony figurine – another treasure from Africa – of two people in a tender embrace, their hands placed on each other's hips, their heads solemnly bowed. Then there's a mask from Venice, a silly road sign from our trip along Route 66, a pot of jam I took from a posh spa in the Lake District. Pillows we picked out together, a rug Ian loves but I've hated since the moment he brought it home. There's our huge DVD collection, even though we now watch most things on Netflix or iTunes. The gramophone Ian bought me one Christmas along with a Tracy Chapman vinyl that hasn't been played since that day because I simply forget about it – other than to be annoyed with how much dust it collects. Shelves of books we've both read and debated, a sofa we've fallen asleep on many a time, usually with our arms and legs wrapped around each other. A breakfast bar we've eaten every dinner at since we moved in, even though there's a proper dining table a few feet away. A bed we've had sex in numerous times – I mean, not millions, or thousands, or possibly even hundreds of times – but it definitely has seen some action . . . I mean if that bed could talk I'd rather not think about what it might say.

My eye, rather tragically, lands on a trophy I made Ian last year because I'd forgotten it was our anniversary and panicked myself into super-gluing various household objects together and spray-painting it gold. In Tippex along the bottom, on a wooden ice lolly stick, I wrote the words 'My better half'. If that's the case then what am I left with now? The rubbish half? A below par human being who no one will ever want to marry? Wonderful.

Tearing my eyes away, I drag the suitcases into the bedroom and dump them on the bed. I lean against the side of the mattress and look around, feeling uncomfortable in my own home. All this stuff, stuff that I thought held so much sentimental value, means nothing to me any more. Now it symbolizes empty promises, broken hearts and me not being good enough. I thought this was us building strong foundations for the future; turns out we were playing with sandcastles.

I'm tempted to grab scissors and cut up Ian's shirts, or at least cut holes in his socks so that his toes poke out. Something tells me it would help to feel like I'm doing something, as though it'll help me gain control of the situation. In reality I know it would only be a moment of weakness and that I'd feel wretched and stupid afterwards for doing it.

I can't stay here and do nothing though. The realization is strong and sudden. I can't be surrounded by 'us' when 'us' is no longer an option. The sense of loss and grief is too overbearing.

Grabbing hold of the bigger suitcase, I undo the clasps and flip it over so that my neatly folded clothes land in a heap on the floor. I'm not going to be needing my array of brightly coloured skimpy clothes for the foreseeable future – the thought of wearing any of it causes my skin to feel itchy. No. A bright red kaftan with gold beaded embroidery that shows my bare thighs and a classy amount of cleavage isn't what I want in my life right now.

Stepping over the dumped clothes I go to my wardrobe and throw open the doors.

Black.

I want to take anything that's dark, miserable and comfortable with me. I rip clothes off hangers and grab them off shelves, not even looking at what I'm packing, just taking note of the colour. I pack it all, then retrieve my wash bag. Once the essentials are done I go back into the lounge and look at all of our belongings. What on earth happened to *my* stuff? How has it all been left with memories of Ian smeared all over it? I don't want to be reminded of a person I wasn't enough for, so anything we bought together can stay here. Although what here is mine? What possessions have I bought without the two of us in mind?

The CDs! I think with relief, even though I can't remember the last time I listened to one of them. I go to the shelf unit in the corner of the room and trace my finger along the pile. They're all either Ian's or bands Ian's taken me to see. Likewise the DVDs are none I came here with.

I remember taking a load of my stuff to Mum's when we moved in here; they must be there still.

I look down at the books. I know I haven't got any of my favourites from Paige Toon, Adele Parks, or Lindsey Kelk here either because they all live on my Kindle. I wouldn't want my go-to reads dampening Ian's high-brow collection of the classics he likes people seeing when they come over. He used to like telling me all about them, of course, but I tended to zone out and tell him I'd read the darn things. Having someone explain a book to you is neither entertaining nor interesting.

In the drawer of the wooden coffee table I find my laptop and charger. I place them into a blue Ikea bag along with some photo frames containing pictures of my family and a fluffy pink pillow I bought when we went to a market a few miles up the road. It was cheap and Ian hated it. I loved it. I could leave it here to spite him, but seeing as I'm leaving so much behind already I feel like I want something to put in this pathetically empty bag. Plus, it'll protect the minimal things I have taken with me from breaking on the way.

I hoik my bag over one shoulder and grab my suitcase

with the other arm and attempt to exhale some of the anxiety running through me.

I know this isn't the last time I'll see these walls, but I know I'll never live here again or refer to it as my home. It's never been mine, it's been ours, and I need to get 'ours', 'us' and 'we' out of my head before I drown in despair. Ian doesn't want me, I understand that – but now I have to realize that I don't want to be with a man who can so flippantly go from proposal to break-up. Whatever I thought we had we didn't. I'm not going to stand here and mourn. I'm not going to wait for Ian to come home and beg for him to reconsider us being together, declaring I never wanted to get married anyway. I'm not going to waste my time on someone who doesn't want, or deserve, my love and respect. I'm leaving and moving forward.

I step out of the flat and stride along the corridor, feeling a little lighter for leaving everything behind. Then I realize the lift is broken and that I have to shift everything down four flights of stairs.

Why is nothing ever easy?

7

Why I decided to smash my phone up when the love of my life pulled our cosy life from under me is beyond comprehension. I've not been able to get in touch with anyone since, which is quite ironic seeing as I spent most of the holiday avoiding calls and texts. It's been a blessing in one way as I haven't had to have an awkward chat with my mum yet, but it also means I've been unable to sort out my life or seek solace from Connie. And I so need my mate.

I get the bus to Chelmsford station and then a train into London. I don't travel into town that often. I used to when we were younger and we had mad nights in Fabric, buzzing from caffeine pills (we were so cool), but that was years ago. If it wasn't for the heaviness that already exists in my chest, I'd be finding this journey overwhelming, but it's a Monday night and the train isn't too busy. I look through the window and get lost in my thoughts as I watch the Essex countryside zooming by – fields, forests and towns becoming nothing more than a hazy blur.

It's only when a young girl comes over and asks me if I'm OK that I realize my face is soaking wet with tears.

I am not coping.

This is not OK.

But of course it isn't.

'I'm fine,' I snivel, looking back out of the window.

The girl rubs my arm sympathetically a few times (no doubt she's rightly assumed this is because of 'some guy'), and backs away.

It takes me an hour to scramble my way to Connie's and now I'm here I'm back to being a fully fledged emotional mess and far from the independent woman I thought I'd magically turned into when leaving the flat. Getting through this isn't going to be that easy.

I ring the silver buzzer but am greeted with silence. I ring again, just in case she is in the loo or something.

It's a Monday night, I was sure she'd be home.

Fuck!

Her date!

She's out seeing Tinder or whatever his real name was.

Shitting fuck.

I drop my suitcase by her doorstep and slump on to it, cradling my head in my hands. I've really not had the best twenty-four hours.

The tears rise and blind me so I shut my eyes as tightly as possible, willing the pain away. I curl up into a ball, trying to protect myself from the torture of life and stop the chilly November air getting through to my bones.

I want to block it all out.

'Babes,' I hear, as the tapping of shoes moves closer to me.

I groan as she shakes my shoulder.

'Liz?'

I open my eyes to see Connie staring at me in sheer

panic. I start to wonder what's worried her so much, but obviously it's the sight of me asleep in the foetal position on her doorstep, still in my travelling clothes, with a face that's swollen to ten times its usual size thanks to all the tears it's cried.

In comparison, she looks gorgeous. Her dark brown bob is effortlessly styled, her fringe just the right length to appear sexy as it flirts with her eyes, and her lips are a gorgeously deep red. She looks like she's stepped out of some trendy magazine in her retro white Calvin Klein tee that's cutely tucked into her emerald pleated midi skirt, the look finished off with a grey boyfriend coat and some black Converse. I've no idea how she manages to pull off such an eclectic style so effortlessly. I'd look a shambles in it.

I glance past her and see her handsome date shifting uncomfortably behind her, not quite sure what the deal is with the emotional friend they've encountered and whether he should back away now. He really is very good-looking and stylish with his tailored grey coat, skinny black jeans and turquoise t-shirt that gently grips on to the muscles clearly hiding underneath. He's tall, broad and looks like a lovely fit for Connie, therefore I feel awful for the date-ending words I'm about to utter.

'He's left me.'

'What?'

I nod my head.

She pulls me up on to my feet and into her arms for a hug. It's so tight I can barely breathe.

66

'I'm so sorry. What a shit,' she whispers, burying her lips in my hair.

Connie breaks away but keeps her arm under me, propping me up. She turns and looks behind her.

'Do you think you could carry this in for me, Matt?' she asks sweetly, her head tilting towards the worthless crap I've carried here.

'Yes, yes. Of course,' he says.

'If you could make us a tea as well, that would be great,' she says, holding me close and guiding us all indoors. It's as though she thinks I've lost the ability to walk, but maybe I have. I've lost everything else.

'Are you OK?' she asks once I've been placed on her mustard Chesterfield sofa and helpful Matt has put a cuppa on the wooden floor next to me.

Connie's only been living in this flat for six months, and I've only been here a handful of times, but already this feels more comfortable than my own home. Maybe that's because I know Connie so well and this place totally encapsulates the woman she is without someone else coming along to water it down – it's like being completely engulfed by my best mate.

'I don't think I am OK . . . It's all a bit crap,' I say honestly, managing to keep the emotion at bay this time. I'm tempted to say I'm all dried up, that I've cried myself into dehydration on the tear front, but I know I shouldn't jinx it. It's a wobbly time, but right now I'm empty and numb, which is far better than fragile, weak and broken.

'Agreed,' she sighs, joining me on the sofa and shifting my feet about so that my legs wind up over hers.

'Erm, I'm going to leave you to it,' Mr Tinder says, hovering in the doorway, helpless now he's completed his dictated tasks.

'I'm so sorry,' I mutter. 'I've ruined your date.'

'Nonsense, the dinner was perfect and Matthew was just walking me home. He wouldn't have been getting his end away tonight anyway,' Connie states unashamedly, without even cracking into a smile.

'Connie!' I shriek, but the laughter that follows feels good. 'I'm sorry about my friend, Matt.'

'Don't be. She's made me laugh all night,' Matt smiles, looking smitten at Connie before snapping out of it and turning back to me. 'I'm sure he'll regret this soon enough,' he says kindly, his face becoming sympathetic.

'I think it's too late for that,' I sniff, the fact he's talking about Ian catching me off guard.

Matt purses his lips at me.

'I'll call you,' Connie says, not even attempting to get up off the sofa and see him out.

Matt smiles to himself as he leaves.

'Good night?' I ask, pleased to be thinking about something else.

'Yes. A really good one.'

'Until I came along.'

'Stop apologizing,' she tuts.

'Good material for *You're Just Not The One*?

'Not yet . . . I'm definitely going to see him again,' she coyly shrugs, taking a sip from her mug. She never writes about people before she knows for certain that it's not going to go any further. She's got quite a back catalogue

68

of failed dates with Mr Wrongs to delve into though if, like in situations like this one, she actually likes a guy.

'You're so blunt with him,' I tell her. 'And bossy.'

'That's who I am. You should know that by now,' she laughs, patting my leg. 'I didn't see him complaining.'

'No. He accepted you just the way you are,' I note, although I'm aware of the tinge of sadness that's present as I say it.

'It was a first date, babes. There's time for him to find me overbearingly annoying – which I know I am,' she declares without a hint of regret.

'I don't know who I am,' I tell her, voicing what's been slowly dawning on me since the proposal that never was.

'You're Lizzy,' Con says, very matter-of-fact. 'We've been best friends for as long as I can remember and you once stole my boyfriend.'

'I did not,' I splutter, even though she's veering us away from what I'm trying to talk about.

'James Healy,' she sighs, jogging my memory.

'I was six!' I exclaim, although I do know exactly what she's talking about and I will admit it was very shady behaviour on my part.

'It still counts. I've been haunted by it ever since. I think that's why I can't commit,' she says, a smirk appearing on her beautifully rouged lips.

'I mean it. I don't know who I am,' I sigh.

'But none of us do.'

'I thought I had it figured out, though,' I say, nodding and shaking my head all at once. Nodding because I was so certain of it and shaking because I now realize I was deluded. 'One half of Lizzy and Ian, Ian and Lizzy. I'm not sure I know how to be just Lizzy. It's been ten years.'

'He's robbed you from the dating game for ten years? He ought to be shot. There are plenty of guys out there who'll want to heal your wounds.'

'I couldn't think of anything worse.'

'Not yet.'

'Dating is a minefield and I'm not ready for that.'

'It's fun. You watch, you'll be on Tinder in no time.'

I don't reply, although my insides shudder at the thought of me on a dating app swiping left and right. It's something I dare not think about. It's too soon to be thinking of other guys when the last ten years have been focused on being with one guy for ever. I can't flick a switch and start acting differently. I can't suddenly stop loving Ian, even if I know that I should.

'Why do you think he did it?' I ask.

'He's clearly gay,' she states. We both know it's not the case, but it stops my mind for a millisecond while I ponder the suggestion.

'Why do any of us do anything?' she continues, swivelling herself around so that she too is lounging along the sofa, her feet by my face, mine now by hers. 'Liz, you're wonderful. You always have been – whether you were with Ian or not.'

'Have I changed?' I push.

'We all have,' she says dismissively.

'But have I changed since dating Ian?' I ask, starting to sound desperate.

'You were only eighteen when you met, so I would hope so.'

'But have I become who I should be?' I whine.

'Are any of us who we should be?' she frowns.

'You're sounding very cryptic,' I tut.

'And you aren't?' she asks, raising an eyebrow at me. 'You want me to say something, to tell you what you want to hear. Feed me my lines. Or, better still, why don't you just say what's on your mind.'

'Fine, it's simple really,' I say, grabbing a cushion and hugging it into my chest. 'I don't know whether I'm me because this is who I should be, or if I'm this version of me because of Ian.'

'You're you,' she says firmly. 'Just a slightly modified version because of your time spent with him.'

'Oh crap.'

'Babes,' she says, scrambling up on to her elbows. 'Everyone who comes into our lives leaves their mark. That's how we grow, mature and evolve as humans. There's nothing wrong with that.'

'But I don't want to be the me he made me. I want to be just me. My me.'

'Darling . . .' Connie whispers. I know she's trying to bring me back from the never-ending pit I'm falling into, and I want to stay with her, I really do, but I'm struggling.

'Do you know the last time I listened to a Bananarama album?' I ask.

'Enlighten me.'

'On my way to uni for Fresher's week. Then Ian came along with his cool music and I didn't want to admit to even having it in my collection. I didn't even have my favourite band's album in our home just in case it made him look at me differently – even after we'd been together for years,' I say, disparaging of the realization.

'I don't know when I last listened to East 17 . . .' Connie ponders to herself, sitting back as she looks up at her living-room ceiling. 'And I was properly obsessed with Brian and his stupid hats. We just drifted apart, you know? I'm sure you no longer singing 'Venus' in the shower was more a natural progression.'

'I still sing that in the shower, just very quietly. I can't use my razor without humming it.'

'See? You're still a proud fan.'

'But I never made Ian sit and listen to them like he did with me and Damien Rice. I knew he'd hate them. I thought he'd think I was stupid for liking fun pop when his preferences were so deep and meaningful. I made him think I was someone I wasn't.'

Connie laughs at my confession.

'I mean, hiding a secret kid or the fact you've murdered someone would be a bigger deal,' she suggests, playfully nudging me in the side with her knee.

'I'm not saying I hid who I was, had an overhaul of my personality, or that Ian changed me,' I explain. 'I just adapted little bits to suit what I thought would work for us.'

'You compromised.'

'Exactly,' I nod, pulling my bottom lip through my teeth. 'I can't help but wonder if I'd be happier right now if I hadn't done that.'

'Babes, your man just dumped you and you look like shit. Of course you'd be happier. I expect any alternative would be appealing in comparison.'

'True,' I agree, hugging the cushion a little tighter into my chest.

'I'm going to get the wine,' she says, scrambling to get off the sofa before travelling to the kitchen on all fours.

Fab idea, I think, rubbing my fingers over my forehead, my musings proving to be a little too much to deal with sober.

I get up from the sofa and move to Connie's iPod that's docked on her oval-shaped speaker. My finger swipes upwards as I wait for an album that's going to grab my attention and demand to be played.

I laugh to myself when I find it.

8

I wake up in Connie's bed with a stinking hangover.

'Eurgh,' I groan, my mouth dry and metallic-tasting, my head rhythmically pounding. It's been throbbing for a couple of days now, but alcohol has added to the pressure of it once again. I feel gross.

'You're awake!' Connie sings, chucking my discarded tee over to me. She's just stepped out of the shower and has a blue towel wrapped around her, and a floral shower cap on her head. Somehow she still makes this look stylish.

'Why am I—'

'Starkers? After a few wines you decided to sing the entire back catalogue of Bananarama — which you had on repeat the entire night. It started off quite mellow but by the time we reached 'I Heard a Rumour' for the third time, it had escalated dramatically with you full on acting out the lyrics while dancing around the flat. For some reason you thought taking your clothes off would improve your performance,' she states, wearing an expression that tells me it clearly didn't.

'Shit . . . Did the neighbours knock?' I ask, a recollection of an angry fist bashing on the front door swinging through my foggy memory.

'Several times.'

'I'm so sorry.'

'They'll get over it. I've had to listen to them swearing at each other at three in the morning – they can handle a little party,' she laughs, walking over to her chest of drawers and putting on matching pink knickers and bra.

For a split second I wonder when was the last time I wore a two-piece like that. I tend to just chuck on whatever I find first – which usually turns into the same bra being worn again and again until the wire pops out, the elastic gives in or stubborn grey circles appear around the armpit area. Although even then I know I've kept a comfy bra's boob-holding dreams alive despite it falling to pieces and looking ghastly.

Connie chuckles to herself while dabbing concealer under her eyes and quickly buffing in some foundation. 'You were so funny. Eighteen-year-old Lizzy was back. And there you were thinking she was dead and buried. Turns out you *can* resurrect her.'

'Shame I can't remember much of it,' I say, sitting up and pushing my head through my top even though I haven't located my bra yet. 'What are you doing today?'

'Work,' she states, skilfully swiping a black eyeliner pen across her top lids to give the perfect flick.

'It's a Tuesday!' I note.

'Yep.'

'I'm meant to be at work in an hour,' I say, the thought of it making me feel sick with anxiety. 'I can't go. I can't face it yet.'

'No one can force you,' Connie shrugs, grabbing a white t-shirt and black maxi dress from a pile of clothes next to me and throwing it on before locating ankle socks and Converse, the notion of being sacked for not doing my job genuinely lost on her. 'You can stay here for as long as you like. There's food in the fridge and you've got Netflix on demand. I won't be home late. I'll grab us dinner on the way.'

'I'm going to go to my mum and Ted's, actually.'

'Oh?'

I can understand the confusion. All I wanted last night was my best mate, all I want now is my mum and my childhood bedroom.

'I don't want to put you out,' I tell her.

'Seriously, you wouldn't be. I want you to stay,' she says, pushing me so I fall back on to the pillows.

'You are fantastic and you know I'll be back here soon enough,' I say, managing to smile. 'I've got to go break the news to Mum. I should probably pick up a new phone too, before she starts panicking that she can't get in touch with me. She might think something awful has happened. Oh wait. It has.'

'She texted last night to see if you were with me, actually,' Connie admits. 'I was going to tell you. She did want to talk to you but you were swinging your bra over your head at the time so I thought it was best not to.'

'Do you think she already knows?'

'I imagine so. If she tried me then she must've tried Ian first.'

'I guess that makes things a little easier,' I say, as the realization of my crumbling life dawns once again.

'This is going to be the shittiest bit, babes. But it will get better. I promise.'

'It has to.' I half smile, half want to cry.

'Get your head around it and then just get it out there.'

'I don't want people to know,' I whimper.

'Because it makes it more real?'

'I'm not ready.'

Connie scrambles on to the bed and wraps her arms around me.

'You'll get through this,' she says, kissing the top of my head and looking me straight in the eye, hammering the message home.

The thing is, deep down, I know that at some point I will. I'll wake up and be happy again, I'll wake up and won't feel so hurt, betrayed and humiliated. But right now the journey ahead seems bleak, lonely and hostile. This wasn't a road I ever envisaged seeing myself on and I'm in no shape and no way prepared.

'You'd better go before you're late,' I say, looking around the room for more clothes.

'Have you met my boss?' she asks, raising an eyebrow at me, making me feel sorry for him again. 'I'll wait for you and then we can walk to the station together. Give you a hand with all of this.'

'You sure?'

'Absolutely. Trevor won't mind too much. I'll mention periods or something. That'll keep him quiet.'

Connie cackles as she gets off the bed and heads towards her bedroom door.

'I moved your suitcase and bag to the bottom of the bed for you. Your clothes from last night are in there too . . . Get dressed, you little nudist.'

I pull the duvet up over my head, close my eyes and take a few deep breaths, preparing myself for the day ahead – because that's all I can focus on at the moment. A day at a time. Or maybe that should be an hour at a time, or minute or even second ... I'm not sure I'm ready for what lies ahead.

9

I get a new phone. The nice man in the shop even sets it all up properly for me so that all my apps and music store are running by the time I leave the shop. I'm now completely contactable.

The first thing I do is put it straight on airplane mode. Later.

I'll deal with everyone later.

I don't listen to music on the way to Mum's, because I know I'd gravitate towards something depressing and solemn. Seeing as I'm already consumed with such a heavy sense of foreboding, I don't think I need something to drag me down further. I might've listened to Bananarama last night when I was drunk, but I'm not in the mood for them now. I can't force happiness upon myself. I'd rather just sit in silence and listen to the sound of the train roaring its way back into my home county.

Ingatestone is the little Essex village I grew up in, which is only a twenty-minute drive from the place Ian and I bought together. It's quaint, picturesque and has a real sense of community thanks to the club down one end and the many pubs scattering the High Street. Mum and Dad moved here before I was born and Mum still lives in the same house now, just with someone else. Mum was there on her own for years before Ted came along, and Michelle and I had moved out as soon as we could, so it doesn't feel weird to have another man in the house we all used to live in together. I guess other people might think it's strange, especially when Dad still comes over for dinner with them both, but it works for us.

I've got the key in my hand and am about to put it in the lock, when the door flies open and Mum comes leaping out, grabbing hold of me and causing me to drop everything I am carrying. I've never had as many hugs as I've had over the last twelve hours, and it's starting to make me realize that I have had a real lack of physical interaction in my life lately, and that's including with Ian. It seems like such a natural thing, yet it feels so alien. Saying that, I've needed and wanted each and every one. They don't take away the pain, but being enveloped in someone else's arms for that little moment makes me feel safe, as though I'm not having to face the scariest chapter of my life alone.

'I've been so worried about you,' Mum says, grabbing hold of my hands and kissing me on the cheek before kissing my hands.

Mum is never one to step out of the house without 'her face on' and her hair done, yet here she is in all her natural beauty with her honey-blonde hair in a scrunchie on top of her head.

Oh, the sweet woman.

I might've been freaking out about her quest to get me married off, but I just see the love and concern pouring out of her and am floored. Granted, I'll probably be annoyed with her again in half an hour, but that's the way we are. She loves to protect and mollycoddle me while I protest her love, but beneath it all, knowing she has my back, no matter what is a huge comfort.

'Come on, before they all start yapping,' Mum says, picking up my dropped items and shooing me inside before the neighbours come out and have a nose at her heartbroken daughter.

The place has hardly changed since we all lived here. Most of the furniture is the same – it's just been reupholstered umpteen times by Mum, who loves giving herself little projects to do. I might not have lived here for over a decade, but it still conjures up the feeling of going home to the place I belong. It's my little cocoon and as soon as I step inside I realize I never want to leave it again.

'Take all this up so we're not tripping over it, Elizabeth,' Mum orders of my life possessions as she hands me the items she has picked up. 'I've made you some lunch.'

'Thanks, Mum.'

She purses her lips together sadly before making her way into the kitchen. God knows why it's me feeling sorry for her.

I trudge upstairs and dump my stuff on my old bedroom floor, although now it looks nothing like it did as it's been transformed into a guest room. No longer do posters of Take That adorn the walls; it's stripped and fresh and painted in a mellow yellow, with white bed sheets and curtains, and little soft teddies lining the windowsill.

It might sound horrifying to see your childhood bedroom stripped back to its bare bones, but I got the good end of the deal so I can't complain. Michelle's old room has been turned into a mini home gym by Ted. She was pretty pissed the day she came back to find a treadmill where there used to be a bed, but it's not like she ever stays over. She only lives five minutes up the road. In fact, I suspect this was all done long before we even realized, as we never usually have any reason to come up here.

Before heading downstairs for lunch I go over to the mirrored wardrobes that line one side of the room. Sliding open one door, my throat constricts at finding it completely empty, except for a dozen empty hangers waiting for guests to use them. Swiping the door back to where it was and opening the second one, I breathe a sigh of relief. There it all is. Stacked up in a variety of cardboard boxes I pillaged from the local Budgens before I left for uni, is my stuff. The bits and bobs I need to help me find out if I've become the person I'm meant to be, or grown into a complete fraud who was willing to lose herself for love.

Who is the real Lizzy Richardson? I guess we'll find out soon enough.

My mum will be shouting up the stairs for me to go down soon enough, so I decide to leave it all where it is so that I can start my quest properly after lunch. Knowing that I'm so close to the old me is enough to lift my spirits. Not so much that I bounce gaily down to Mum, but enough to ignite a little excitement as I close the door and head towards the dozens of questions I'm sure she is going to be firing at me.

They don't come.

Instead, when I walk into the kitchen all of my favourite Mum-inspired delights are laid out on the kitchen counter – torn roast chicken, a mini shepherd's pie, a massive crustless quiche, baked eggs, sausages, bacon, muffins and crumpets. It's a feast and, as far as I'm aware, it's only the two of us eating.

'I didn't know if you'd fancy anything so thought I'd see if I could tempt you,' Mum shrugs shyly, her lips pursing together and twisting.

'Oh Mum . . . you shouldn't have.'

But that's what she does. That's the sort of mother she is. If I think about anything I went through in my early life Mum was always the first one there trying to sort it out for me. She was made a bit redundant in that role when Ian came into my life because he was always there to pull me through instead. Plus, I largely kept any struggles from Mum – not because I didn't want to share it, but more because I didn't feel I had to. But now that I need her again, here she is – with an army load of food that she's slaved over.

I sit at the wooden worktop and take in her offerings.

'I'm sorry,' I blurt out. It catches both of us by surprise.

'Elizabeth?' Mum says softly, her shoulders dropping. Only now do I realize she was doing her best to stand strong and be the one in control. I might be the dumped fool, but I know her dreams for me have flitted away too – dreams she must've wished for before I was even born. Hopes of my happiness, contentment, and meeting the love of my life before settling down to give her grandchildren. 'You don't need to be sorry.'

'I don't know what happened.'

'And that's life,' she says, popping serving spoons and forks into the dishes laid out before sitting down opposite me. 'Sometimes things just don't work out and there's no real reason for it.'

'But there's always a reason.'

Mum smiles at me as she picks up a knife and cuts into the quiche. 'The next few weeks are going to be rubbish. You'll wallow, you'll cry, you'll wonder why this has happened to you and what you could've done differently. You'll mourn for the future you thought you were heading towards and be angry that it's not materialized. Then it'll all stop. You'll accept that you have a new version of life ahead of you and, more than that, you'll start living and loving again.'

'Said by a woman who knows what she's talking about.'

'Amen to that,' she nods.

I never interfered when it came to Mum and Dad's divorce and I have to say, it was a total shock. There were no arguments or doors being slammed. No sign that they weren't getting on aside from the usual squabble over something meaningless. We were on holiday on the coast when they sat us down and told us, together, that Dad was moving out. We thought they were joking. We'd just spent five days laughing and being silly together as a family and couldn't fathom how they'd reached that decision. Sure enough, though, the day after we got back, Dad packed up his suitcases and a couple of boxes and moved into a flat at the back of Budgens. Waving him off was incredibly bizarre. Mum shut the door and got on with making us dinner, but we noticed her slipping into the sadness that lay underneath her cheery exterior. It wasn't what she wanted. It was clear it was Dad who'd initiated the whole thing, yet she never spoke badly of him.

I was fourteen at the time, and Michelle was twelve. We were aware of what was happening and Mum knew we were looking to her for reassurance that life was going to be OK. And most of the time it was. There were emotional times when I was a total shit and back-chatted too much, which led to her screeching and sobbing at me (I felt awful), but we made the situation work and we got through it. We recovered enough to be able to pull together again. I won't lie, there were times when I called them both from uni, calling one after the other, and hated the fact that they were both on their own. It was surely better to be together than lonely and bored.

Still, they only lived a few streets apart in the village. It took time, but soon enough, once Mum had started dating Ted and her heart was on the mend, she started inviting Dad over for dinner and they started seeing more of each other, making birthdays and Christmas one hundred times easier. Ted didn't mind or feel threatened by the presence of an ex-husband, and so a firm friendship was formed.

I know Mum knows all about heartache and having to rebuild the foundations beneath her. I'd go as far as to say she had it far worse, because she had to consider my and Michelle's feelings too. It's funny how things happen when you get older that give you a newfound respect for the adults you were sure were only out to ruin your life when you were growing up. Mum, more than anyone, knows what I'm going through, and that must be tough on her to witness. I feel shit for having to put her through it, to be honest.

I look out to the garden and see Ted banging about in his shed at the far end, the flat cap on his head making his ears look even bigger than normal. Grabbing a hanky from his pocket, he gives his nose a blow and wipes his crystal-blue eyes with the back of his hand. It's freezing out there. Mum probably banished him from the house so that she could have some alone time with me to fully assess how I'm doing. Ted's a good man. A solid example of how being broken doesn't necessarily mean you'll never be fixed again.

'Can I stay here for a bit?' I ask. Connie's does sound appealing, but I have my own room here, my mum and a heap of clues as to who I was when I left for Sheffield.

'This is your home for as long as you need it to be,' she says, flashing a smile that doesn't quite reach the softness around her eyes. She's hurting because I'm hurting and while that pains me, it makes me realize there's nowhere else I'd rather be right now than with the woman who has nothing but unconditional love for me.

'Thanks, Mum,' I say, piling some sausages, shepherd's pie and a crumpet on my plate before tucking in.

Mum looks delighted at her success.

Half an hour later, and probably a full stone heavier, I decide to revisit my wardrobe of stuff, pulling out boxes and placing them in the middle of the room so that I can tackle them one at a time.

Each box is carefully taken to my bed and opened with trepidation, expectancy and excitement. Slowly I unfold the cardboard flaps, as though by respecting the vessel filled with my old toot, they'll be more likely to respect me back and provide me with the answers I desire. I feel like I'm in some cheesy 90s movie, or an episode of *Eerie Indiana* – a throwback to my childhood of weekend morning TV viewing.

There's a lot of crap. Seriously, there are things I can't even believe Mum has bothered saving from a trip to the dump. Did I really put my foot down about keeping a lopsided clay bowl I made in junior school? Or my old maths books that are void of any personality or individuality? To be fair, the answers were probably copied from Connie's anyway – she was the brainy one, I was the more creative one. Even the two-times table left me feeling a bit sick with anxiety, but a pencil and an idea left me enthralled for hours. My imagination knew no bounds, whereas my maths skills were highly limited.

Flicking through an old folder of my classwork

entitled 'The World of Work', I find a drawing. It's of what I wanted to be when I grew up, or what I assumed I would be. I'm playing tennis. Yep. That's right. Tennis. My feet are the size of cruise ships against my skinny (one pencil-line worthy) legs and I'm wearing sweat bands on both my wrists and ankles, as well as around my head. I was clearly very focused on catching all the sweat I would be perspiring. My hair is tied up in a huge red bow and I have the biggest grin on my face as I hold my racquet in the air and people throw flowers at my feet. Some appear to have fainted – clearly in awe of my brilliance.

As the date on the art piece tells me it was birthed early July, I'm guessing Wimbledon was on and it was all people were talking about. That must be the case, as I don't remember ever wanting a sporting career. I'm not putting myself down but I don't have the drive, determination, self-control or self-discipline it takes to be a sporting hero. I also love my food too much – and I'm not talking organic kale and broccoli. Not without Ian around to scrutinize.

Come to think of it, I do remember begging Mum and Dad to get me a tennis racquet one summer, and then me dragging Michelle down to the tennis courts behind the community club for the majority of the holidays. It must've been nothing more than a summer romance, though, as it was quickly forgotten once I got back to school and realized that I was indeed shit at it. One of my classmates actually played for the county and I knew I didn't look quite as fierce as she did when attacking that ball. She also made these guttural grunting sounds as she worked the court and I simply couldn't master them. Sadly, tennis wasn't for me.

The picture might not tell me anything about the person I could've been now, had I dedicated myself a bit more (I am not athletic, but Ian has got me more into my overall fitness – which I'm obviously thankful for), but it's a reminder that not everything written or stored in these boxes is going to enlighten me beyond having a little chuckle to myself. I clearly had no idea who I was at just eight years old, and that's fine. I'm obviously no better off now!

The next box I ceremoniously open contains my CDs and DVDs. Turns out I don't have as many as I thought I did, but my absolute favourites are there. From Bananarama to Take That and So Solid Crew, from *Sleepless in Seattle* to *Fifty First Dates* and *Harry Potter and the Philosopher's Stone*. I breathe a sigh of relief as I pop my So Solid album into my laptop and let it play while I continue to sort and search, hoping that the sound of '21 Seconds to Go' will make me feel like the boss of my own life.

The items start becoming more recent, evolving from an older version of Lizzy Richardson, and I soon locate a stash of photographs. I absolutely adored disposable cameras and usually had one on me to capture special moments, although I was careful not to take more than one picture of the same thing for fear of wasting the film. It was evidently a love affair that extended far longer than my non-existent tennis career, as I go from finding pictures of me and Connie dangling off my bed upside down, our big pre-brace teeth being shown in all their hellish glory, to us downing Sambuca shots in Dukes with a bunch of our other mates. The skirts we're wearing are so short we might as well not be wearing them, and I have a cigarette in my hand.

In one particular image that's been captured on another night out I appear to be wearing my top as a skirt and nothing but a bra to cover the top half of my body. Connie is rocking a similar look to mine.

A smile spreads across my face as I remember the night this picture was taken. It was a Thursday and we were only meant to be heading into Chelmsford to make use of happy hour in one of the pubs at the back of Debenhams. We got a message from a group of male friends, who were a few years older, saying they were going into Dukes so we decided to go last minute. We were literally on our way to the station to go home when we changed our minds. Only, when we got to the club we discovered that particular night was beach-themed, and they had a strict no-jeans policy, which was a disaster as we were standing there in skinny jeans and vest tops.

In a moment of abandon I grabbed Connie's hand and led her to the other side of a big wheelie bin, where I managed to convince her that we strip out of our jeans, lower our tops and treat our bras as bikini tops. We were allowed in, and at no point did anyone query the fact that we were both a year underage, or that we were indirectly being forced into getting our kit off so that we could go inside and have a flirt with some older men. Back then I was so set on a night out that I'd do just about anything to make it happen. I was a sociable little thing.

I can't remember the last time I acted like that. Yes, it might've been a bit reckless and slutty (I will never show my mum and dad this particular pic), but I was having fun. You can see in the picture that I'm laughing my head off and that we all seem like such a tight bunch of fab people.

At what point did I drift so far from that image that I forgot about it? If I think back, Ian and I did go out a fair bit in the first year, although it was rarely to clubs. Ian hated them with a passion. He was more into his bands, so we went to a lot of gigs and listened to live music instead. It was because he harboured this great passion for and knowledge of music that I became disengaged from my own love of dancing. I thought I could rock my body to anything with a musical beat. However, Ian's preferred musicians wrote songs that made heartache sound like it was something to disparagingly wallow in, rather than shake off and dance about. There was no room for me to strut my stuff underneath an imaginary glitter ball, close my eyes and see where the music took me. I guess I could've done so if I were starring in an episode of *Girls* – Lena Dunham would've had Hannah experimental dancing across the stage – but I wasn't. So I didn't. Instead, I'd do as Ian did and quietly sit nodding my head appreciatively. His love was an art form. Mine focused on carefree fun. His seemed cooler, and I guess at a point in life where I was desperate to fit in and be accepted, I was happy to absorb his preferences. I wanted to please him and for him to know I was totally right for him. I was his 'one'.

How have I got to this point in life, where I'd rather spend a night in on the sofa watching *Making a Murderer* than getting dressed up to go out with mates? Because this isn't just about a difference in musical taste, it's not even about having more self-control and keeping myself fully dressed at all times. It's the social element that really causes me to take a moment and ponder the difference between me then and me now. I was a social butterfly, whereas now I'm more likely to turn down an invite to go out (they have become few and far between), with some silly excuse about work or lying about already having plans.

Perhaps putting myself out there once more is the way to paddling my way back to the girl I once was, and saving her in some way.

The picture is enough to get me thinking in a more detailed way of the changes I've undergone since meeting Ian – some little, some big. Changes that I made, not because he necessarily asked me to, but because I chose to for one reason or another.

I jump on to the bed, grabbing an old notepad in which I'd written a few lovesick poems over Henry Collard, my first senior school crush, and start writing everything I know about the girl who left for Sheffield ten years ago.

'*She . . .*' I start writing, realizing that I feel so far removed from the girl I once was that I've automatically started talking about her in the third person. She seems like someone I used to know, rather than am.

What a scary thought to begin with.

She . . .

. . . was eighteen years old.

. . . loved going out with her mates and would regularly be carried home or bundled into the designated driver's car after one too many.

. . . would go out on a Monday, Thursday, Friday and Saturday.

. . . would dance literally like no one was watching (they probably weren't anyway), and let the music transport her somewhere else. She didn't care if it was some cheesy 80s tune or hardcore drum and base — if it had a beat, she was there.

. . . saw mates every night.

. . . loved an Archers and lemonade.

. . . used to socially smoke.

. . . had killer legs.

. . . could wear heels all night and not complain.

. . . loved her body.

. . . loved the greats like Bananarama and the Spice Girls but wasn't afraid to mix it up with a little R'n'B or drum and bass.

. . . listened to Kiss FM.

. . . loved Kiss FM because it made her feel naughty and sexy.

. . . had a huge crush on the actor Billy Buskin and had his poster on her wall.

. . . loved quick and easy food. Pasta, fish fingers, waffles, chicken dippers and frozen lasagnes (the ones we've since found contained horse meat) when Mum wasn't around to cook.

. . . *used to wear multi-coloured eyeshadow.* (My eyelids were a disco ball of fun at all times. Even my eyeliner was blue.)

. . . *was useless in the kitchen as Mum used to do it all.*

. . . *could devour a tub of Häagen-Dazs ice cream in one sitting and not feel sick.*

. . . *wore thongs.*

. . . *wore miniskirts, tops as skirts, bras to clubs.*

. . . *also mixed it up with her daytime look of baggy jeans and cute little character tops.*

. . . *loved singing!*

. . . *watched MTV.*

. . . *loved* Big Brother *and* Friends *and watched them religiously.*

. . . *was a soap slut.* Emmerdale, Hollyoaks, Corrie, EastEnders *– she loved the lot.*

. . . *shaved her legs every day – just in case.*

. . . *was very handy with DIY, although a little haphazard in her approach.*

. . . *would whip off her bra and get into her PJs as soon as she got home.*

. . . *used to swear like a trooper. Every sentence contained the f-word.*

. . . *used to write poems about anything and everything – e.g. Henry Collard.*

. . . *was a big-time lover of cheese.*

. . . *weighed eight stone two and wondered if that was a little chubby.*

. . . *drank tea with milk and two sugars.*

. . . *made the meals she could cook (pasta sauce, curry and chilli con carne) with copious amounts of garlic. She loved garlic.*

. . . *used to wear a crazy amount of make-up.*

. . . *never used to dye her hair.*

. . . *used to work in the home department in Debenhams and enjoyed making the displays look pretty while harmlessly flirting with the guys in Electricals on the upper floor.*

. . . *wanted to travel the world.*

. . . *had been in a three-month relationship with Richard — which felt very long term and committed.* (Clearly I revised this thought when I met Ian and subsequently broke Richard's heart.)

. . . *thought we'd live in a trendy area of East London together and be super cool.*

. . . *was extremely excited to be moving up north and gaining a bit of freedom from 'The Parentals'.*

. . . *thought anything was possible.*

I sit back and look at the list, wondering if there's anything else I should add to it. It's funny how quickly the words have been tumbling down and on to the page; she's clearly an unforgettable character.

Deciding it's a solid start I turn the page and start a new list, accessing how far I am away from where I once was.

Now I . . .

. . . *am twenty-eight years old.*

. . . rarely go out with my mates, and always make excuses as to why I have to pull out of arrangements. So much so that people have stopped asking me to join them on nights out.

. . . can't remember the last time I was so drunk I literally had to be carried home.

. . . drink sensibly or not at all.

. . . drink organic red wine — unless on holiday and can make full use of the bar for cocktails. I would personally prefer white wine at home, but seeing as Ian is a red wine fanatic it didn't make sense to have two bottles open at once.

. . . quite fancy an Archers and lemonade.

. . . don't smoke at all.

. . . on the rare occasions we do go out, rarely dance. I've lost my mojo and therefore feel awkward and silly. I feel like I'm being watched and judged.

. . . still have killer legs. Seriously. They're my best asset.

. . . couldn't think of anything worse than having to wear high heels. I wear an inch to work and that's enough. My back, feet, knees and shins can't take the strain — plus I look like Bambi on ice as I cautiously totter about.

. . . am dubious about my body. I see its flaws glaring back at me whenever I look into a mirror.

. . . try to tackle those flaws in the gym, three times a week.

. . . still love the greatest bands of all time but now have an even more diverse love of music, especially the live stuff.

. . . hate Kiss FM. Yes, completely contradicting the statement above but it's just noise.

. . . *feel old if I listen to Kiss FM. I've even outgrown Radio One. I'm now on to BBC Radio Two!*

. . . *have a profound respect for the very talented Billy Buskin . . . and am currently contemplating putting a poster of him back up in my old room.*

. . . *never eat processed foods as I know they contain too much sugar, salt and unknown ingredients, like horsemeat. We got a bit obsessed with food documentaries and after seeing what I've seen there's no going back.*

. . . *cook! And I'm great at it. Everything is fresh and prepared from scratch.*

. . . *would settle for a tub of Booja-Booja (a sugar- and dairy-free ice-cream alternative) over Häagen-Dazs.*

. . . *wear more natural make-up and usually neglect my eyelids altogether.*

. . . *wear big knickers and don't understand why I ever tortured myself with thongs, or thought they were sexy.*

. . . *wear clothes as they're intended and in the manner they were designed for — to cover me up!*

. . . *can't remember the last time I wore baggy jeans or a top that had a character on it — superhero or otherwise.*

. . . *rarely sing. Not even in the shower.*

. . . *binge watch* Friends, New Girl, Gossip Girl *and* Girls *(lots of 'girls' in there) whenever Ian is out (this will no longer be an issue).*

. . . *don't watch any soaps at all.*

. . . *never shave my legs unless I'm wearing a dress or shorts. What's the point if no one is going to touch them?*

. . . haven't had to do a DIY project for a few years. Ian has been in charge of the tools since we moved into the flat.

. . . would never let my boobs swing freely without a bra on. Ian once (rather innocently) referred to them as my udders, which led to me keeping them in my balcony bra until bedtime so they looked more pleasing and I felt more attractive.

. . . try my best not to swear as I realize it's not big or clever. However, I still secretly believe there is nothing more satisfying than dropping 'fuck', 'fucking' or 'fucked' into a conversation.

. . . never write poems — although maybe lists can become my new thing.

. . . rarely bother buying cheese because Ian hates it and it goes to waste. My intake is usually limited to Christmas when I can eat it with family.

. . . weigh ten stone. Fuck. How'd that happen? I think my bones got heavier. Come to think of it, my clothes have shrunk too.

. . . am caffeine free and usually drink fresh mint tea.

. . . never cook with garlic because Ian said it gave him migraines. Food is bland without it. I'm pretty sure it's psychological on his part as there's always garlic in the dinners we eat outside of the house.

. . . work for a small interior design company here in Essex called Home Comforts. Being Essex-based we largely add bling and garish prints to people's homes. It's not to my own taste (I'd say it borders on tacky),

*but the clients are always super happy with the work
we do.*

*. . . still want to travel the world. (Seeing Africa, having a
fleeting trip to Venice and driving across America on
Route 66 was great, but it didn't quench my thirst for it
at all. I always wanted to see more, but our jobs have
prevented it from happening.)*

. . . have been dumped by the person I dumped Richard for.

*. . . have moved out of my flat in Chelmsford (not a cool
part of town), and back in with my mum.*

*. . . don't crave the freedom I did when leaving for
university, but rather need some parental support.*

. . . miss my friends.

. . . wonder when life stopped being so fun.

. . . no longer think anything is possible.

. . . actually think 'life' is a bag of shit.

I feel pretty het up as I place the pen down and look at
the two lists side by side. I mean, I've gone a bit depressing at the end, but my hand took over on that one and I
didn't bother stopping it – a spot of free-flowing writing
is supposedly meant to be good for the soul.

So now I know who I was and who I am. I'm not suggesting for a minute that Ian was the sole cause for me
adapting my ways and becoming someone new; I'm sure
a lot of it was because I grew up in the time we were
together, but some of it is a direct result of our relationship and I have to think about whether I want to be the
person Ian helped create.

I don't.

I want to peel back the Ian layers and find me again.

I start by bringing my hand around to my back, unhooking my bra through my top and whipping it out of my sleeve.

It's a step in the right direction.

11

'God, this is depressing,' I hear, as Michelle waddles into the room and looks over the boxes surrounding me on the floor, one side of her upper lip curling in disgust as she leans back against the wall. Her face is somewhat similar to mine but also nothing alike at the same time. Our eyes, noses, mouths and even ears are different from each other, but it's the way we use them that anchors us together as sisters. Maybe it's the characteristics we've inherited from our parents I can see reflected in her face that remind me of myself. Little mannerisms we've picked up from the environment we grew up in that'll always give our connection away. She's always been blonder than me, although this has been heightened thanks to her obsession with bleach. She's two inches smaller and far rounder, with curves that seem to go out and in at just the right points. Her eyes are bigger and brighter, her nose smaller, though with the same sloped tip. Her cheeks are rounder, pinker and plump – as are her lips. Mine always seem rather deflated in comparison, especially when she's pouting them in the manner she is right now.

Michelle has come upstairs wearing her Ugg boots. A trail of mud follows her in, along with a waft of freshly washed clothes. Mum said she's been frantically washing before the baby gets here, but I didn't realize that applied to her own clothes too. Her navy wrap dress is covered by a chunky grey knit cardigan, yet even through the layers I can see her bump has really grown in the two and a half weeks since I've seen her. She's popped out. She doesn't look as comfy any more either, although that could be a direct result of hauling herself up Mum's narrow stairs, and she's still got a fair way to go. I won't be pointing that out right now though, as she tends to be quite sensitive about anything and everything I have to say about her pregnancy, or upcoming wedding. She's feistier than me, always has been.

'Thanks,' I mutter, continuing to sort the boxes into 'keep', 'charity' and 'dump' piles. Unsurprisingly, the 'dump' pile is growing the quickest. I'm no longer feeling attached to some of the things I once loved and cherished.

'Seriously though, I did not see this coming. I thought you were going to totally eclipse me with some engagement news, and that everyone would be yapping on about that next week,' she frowns, disbelievingly shaking her head while simultaneously scratching one side of her bump. 'I didn't expect you to steal the attention by letting your life fall apart twelve days before the biggest moment of my life.'

'It's not like I planned this,' I say, telling myself not to argue with a pregnant lady, even if she is being an absolute moron.

'Stranger things have happened,' she pokes, inspecting the ends of her hair and picking at a split end before dropping it on the floor.

'That's not very nice,' I reprimand, feeling like our mother.

She stares at me, declining to retract her cold statement as she sweeps her hair over her shoulder and places her hands on her hips.

She's two years younger than me, meaning most of our childhood was spent with me doing things that she couldn't. She constantly whined and bitched, but I thought that all largely ended when I left home for Sheffield. I didn't realize she was still harbouring feelings of resentment over the fact I passed through our mother's fanny before she did. I mean, that's hardly my fault and not something I've ever wanted to, or felt I needed to, apologize for.

'You're about to get married and then give birth. I think it's safe to say all eyes will, well and truly, be on you,' I say curtly, hoping she'll see sense.

'They won't,' she strops, flapping her arms by her sides. 'As if they will be now you've gone and done this.'

'Don't be a twat,' I sigh, dropping my eyes to the useless box of magazines by my feet – mostly *Sugar*, *Sneak* and *Bliss*, but with the odd cheeky *More* thrown in too (bought for Position of the Fortnight, even though I most definitely would not have been having sex at the time). It might be interesting to see familiar faces of long-forgotten celebrities on the cover, but I don't need to be hoarding them for the rest of my life.

'Mum and Dad are going to be constantly looking at you to see if the strain is too much. "Oh no, Michelle is content and happy, how must our Lizzy feel?"' she mocks, her hands over her chest as she looks painfully worried.

My mouth drops in response.

'It's not a competition,' I manage to say.

'No,' she agrees. 'You wouldn't feel that way, because you've always been the winner. But as soon as I was set to trump you you've gone and derailed the race and set it on a completely different course.'

'Seriously? Are you actually being fucking serious?' I gasp. I'm all for a spot of healthy sibling rivalry, but this is ridiculous.

'A little,' she shrugs.

'Fuck off, Chelle,' I say, picking up a *Sugar* from next to me and chucking it into a box that's sitting next to her to hammer home my point. The bang makes us both jump.

'No, *you* fuck off,' she hisses with such a strain that she causes a vein to pop out on her forehead. 'I'm getting married. This is *my* time!' she shrieks. 'This should be the happiest time of our lives. Mum and Dad should be fussing over me and gushing about how wonderful the whole thing is, but instead you're here with your broken fucking heart and my feelings are going to be a mere second thought.'

'I think you should calm down before you harm the baby,' I say, lowering my voice while trying to be a responsible adult – something I always fail to be when I'm around Michelle.

'Are you saying I'm a bad mum already?' she says, her face clouding over and turning thunderous, almost murderous.

Oh fuck.

'Of course not,' I say, trying my best to reel it back in while feeling my patience wane. This is not OK. I really don't want to be arguing with her, but equally she's gone a bit *One Flew Over the Cuckoo's Nest* on me and I can feel my heart angrily pumping in response to her unsympathetic attitude towards me.

'Are you saying I'm not putting my baby first?'

'Chelle!' I say, trying to stop her falling further into the hormonal pit of pregnancy.

'You are something else. Coming in here and stampeding all over my—'

'I've been dumped!' I practically shout, jumping up on to my feet and interrupting her mid-sentence. 'The man I thought I was going to grow old with, who has had my heart for the last ten years, has decided I'm not good enough. *He* stampeded over *me*,' I blast, banging at my chest like I'm Tarzan of the fucking jungle.

She doesn't try to cut in, just stands there in disbelief. She's the fiery one usually, something we've always put down to her being the youngest (and most immature) and therefore this is an odd turn of events for us both.

'Believe it or not, your nuptials haven't even entered my head until now,' I continue, feeling the wind beneath my sails guiding me upstream towards my point being well and truly made. 'Although all I can say is that the sight of you getting married is all I'll be able to focus on that day because anything else is just going to be too painful to bear. No, I don't want to talk to our grandparents, aunts, uncles or any of your friends about how severely I've been shat on. I'd rather dig a little pit for myself and slowly starve to death. I'd rather stay in bed until a load of maggots come and eat me. I'd rather tie a giant weight to my legs and jump into a river and drown.'

Point. Made.

'Are you suicidal?' she asks quietly, her voice wobbling along with her chin.

'Oh shit, no,' I declare, the question taking me aback. Maybe I went a step too far and hammered my point a bit too ferociously.

'Really?'

I take a moment or two to think about it. I know I've just given three pretty horrific slow-death preferences rather than having to converse with people at my sister's wedding (people who are actually decent folk), but I don't think that's where my head is at. This is my rebirth, not my funeral.

'That would be one way to fully upstage you, though,' I joke, as if it's worth contemplating. It isn't, FYI. I am not there. Not yet.

'Don't you fucking dare,' Michelle sobs, running at me with her arms open wide, her body hitting mine with a soft thump as she takes me into her arms and squeezes me tightly. 'Bridezilla and pregnancy hormones do not mix,' she adds, nuzzling herself closer.

'It's an overwhelming time,' I say, rubbing her back, which seems further away than usual thanks to my niece or nephew growing between us.

'It is,' she sniffs, nodding her head. 'But enough about

me. I'm sorry for being a shit. You know I didn't mean all that.'

'Not all of it,' I half smile at her, giving her shoulder a slight push.

My little sister is one of my top two friends along with Connie, and although I'm sure Michelle would tell me I'd marginally scraped it on to her top ten list, really I'm probably in her top five, maybe even three. Regardless, I know we love each other unconditionally and that our bond, even if I'm not her best mate, is unbreakable. I'd do anything for her.

Michelle bows her head bashfully. 'I can't imagine how you must be feeling right now having been brushed aside and forced to move back in with Mum and into this room.'

'It's not that bad. The situation is obviously pretty dire, but the room is fine,' I shrug. 'It's comforting being back in here.'

'I guess . . .' she says, giving it another look. 'I mean, if it were me, I'd be sleeping on Ted's flipping running machine,' she says, her pitch rising as she points her thumb in the direction of her old bedroom, AKA Ted's home gym. 'They got rid of me good and proper, didn't they.'

We both laugh at that.

Michelle chuckles while rubbing at my arm. 'Sorry, bubs.'

'Don't be,' I say, pursing my lips together to stop myself getting emotional.

I often wonder if all siblings are like this and able to

switch between love and hate so easily – not that I could ever hate the girl who has continuously been one of my greatest allies and my scariest antagonist all at once.

'Although you have truly buggered up my seating plans,' she mutters before pulling me in for another hug.

She really can be an absolute bitch.

I 2

I know I can't lock myself in my old bedroom for evermore, but I do so until the end of the week. If anything I take a few steps back in my mending-heart process after doing too much too soon; however, by Sunday night I'm back to being fired up and ready to leave the house.

So this morning at eight a.m., after having a whole week off – I called in and explained very honestly that I wasn't fit for human interaction – I decide to go into work. I'll admit that it was also a slightly selfish move as Michelle is heading to Mum's today to sort out wedding favours. I didn't want to get in the way or make her feel like I was intruding on a special moment she should be sharing alone with Mum, so thought I should leave them to it. I have no desire to stir things up again now that I've finally managed to convince her that my break-up wasn't meticulously timed to ruin her wedding plans.

Mum said getting back to work would help take my mind off everything and she was right. It's amazing how looking at endless catalogues of sparkling tat can make you hate life just that little bit more than you already do.

I've always heard that big life events can cause you to look within and question the things you hold dear, enjoy and even put up with – that the stark reality of them can make you question the fibre of your being and force you to see the world around you clearly for the first time. Well. On the walk here a guy shouted lewd remarks at me out of his van window and then followed them up with 'go fuck yourself, you uptight bitch,' when I didn't seem grateful for his attention, I stepped in dog muck just outside the shop and then a box of sequins fell from the top shelf straight on to my head – causing a bump to pop up. I'm pretty sure I've cut it, but I don't feel too dizzy so I'm sure I'm fine, although the words 'fuck my life' have been uttered more than once.

Thankfully, my boss Stephanie is out with a client most of the day and has taken the assistant Pippa out with her. Seeing as it's only us who occupy this shabby chic (and ridiculously expensive) showroom in the heart of Chelmsford, I don't have to worry about small talk – and she's already grilled me over the phone on the ins and outs of our break-up, so it's not like she's going to be rushing back for gossip. The only thing is, I'm not feeling too inspired to dream up ideas for the homes and spaces of other people right now, and seeing as that's my job it means I'm being very unproductive.

At lunchtime, just as I'm tucking into a KFC bucket with garlic mayo and have oil dripping down my chin (fuck you, Ian and any clean-eating food doc we've ever watched), Connie calls.

'Babes, the craziest thing has just happened!' she trills, diving straight to the point.

'What?' I munch.

'Well, I didn't want to say anything in case nothing

came of it and I'd just be left feeling like a tit, but I submitted something to a publisher,' she says, her grin apparent in the cheeriness of her voice.

'You finally did it!' I say, my mouth still working its way around a tasty chicken leg while simultaneously shoving in an extra chip for good measure – I'm close to popping in a spoonful of baked beans too but decide against it.

'Yes! But I changed the idea from when we talked about it,' Connie sings.

'Mmm . . . ?' I manage, finding it hard to swallow now that I've jammed too much food into my mouth. Connie has been thinking about turning her blog into something more tangible for a while. She did try and get one of the monthly magazines to take her on as a dating guru or new 'girl about town' columnist, but that proved pretty tricky, as it tends to be a 'one in, one out' policy and a case of 'who you know'. The second thing we talked about was trying to turn her work into a self-help guide – almost a *Dating for Dummies*, but in a way that tells the reader we're all in this together and that it's all right not to have met the love of your life even though you might be turning thirty next year.

'I sent in a fiction idea,' she carries on. 'I figured I'll have more scope with that and won't need to worry about being sued by wankers of yesteryear if vanity gets to their heads. Anyway, Karl at work's wife's friend is a literary agent. I managed to persuade her to get her friend to read the book and send it on to some of her publisher mates if she thought it was any good.'

'And . . . ?' I say, certain of what's to come.

'She did. Then three editors came back interested.'

'No!'

'Yes. That all happened while you were away, actually, but I didn't want to bother you with it.'

'Oh, bless you,' I say, knowing why she wouldn't have told me the other night either and risked being insensitive. She has the ability to be a blunt powerhouse when she wants to be, but never when things are serious.

'I've just been in to meet the final editor and hear what she has to say,' she says excitedly, which is funny to hear as she's usually so nonchalant about most things life has to offer. 'I'm in love. I accepted her offer of a two-book deal right there on the spot. I'm going to be a fucking author! Well, I say me, but really Vix Bishop is – I'm the researcher, she's the one with the words and the loyal readership.'

'This is amazing! Congratulations!' I squeal, throwing my chicken bones in the tub and wiping my mouth with the back of my hand, which I then wipe on my black jeans.

'Who knew cavorting my way across London and beyond would actually lead to something of actual substance. The fuckers were worth it,' she shouts.

'I've always told you how good you are,' I praise.

'At cavorting? Oh yes, I'm very good,' she says devilishly.

She gives a dirty cackle and I join in.

'Have you told work yet?'

'Trevor knows. He's heartbroken – aren't you?'

'Heartbroken that you're *staying*,' I hear him say, making Connie laugh louder.

'Staying?' I repeat, surprised she hasn't already packed up her desk and given an Oscar-worthy kickass exit speech to the rest of the office – Bridget Jones-style.

'Yeah, I'm not going to be leaving this place any time soon. It turns out books don't pay that much, and I still have my rent to pay. One day I will be saying adios to this bunch of twats and not coming back, though!'

'Is that a promise?' Trevor calls, making Connie howl.

I know he doesn't mean it. Even though Connie tends to find happiness at the expense of others, her humour is always seen for what it is. Light-hearted fun. She's well loved and, as she always points out herself, an asset to the team. There's no doubt in my mind that the prospect of losing her to a new career is a saddening one.

'We should get together and celebrate. What are you doing tonight? I could get the train up as soon as I'm done here,' I offer, wondering if this is my chance to venture out and reclaim my sociable days. It certainly would be the first Monday night out I've had in years. Just thinking about the spontaneous fun we could possibly have sends a tremor of excitement across my tummy.

'Oh, I have a date,' she says, sounding sorry and pleased all at once.

'The same guy as the other night?' I ask, trying not to sound too disappointed over the fact Connie has her own exciting life to be living still even though mine has gone kaput.

'That's the one. I saw him Saturday night too,' she admits, her voice dropping.

'This is serious,' I exclaim.

'No, it's not like that. It's just a few dates.'

'Yeah . . . Maybe another night then,' I say, trying to push through the murkiness that's creeping over me. 'Oh, I'll see you at the wedding, anyway.'

'Of course! Little Chelle is getting married,' she sings. 'Should be a good one.'

'Ooh Con, Steph's just on the other line,' I lie, feeling guilty instantly. I never tell her porkies. 'I'd better go. Enjoy tonight. Let me know how it goes. I promise I won't be sat on your doorstep waiting for you when you get home this time,' I joke, laughing as I hastily put the phone down while Connie is cheerfully saying goodbye back.

I lower my forehead on to my desk before banging it on the wood a few times. Not heavily, not enough to draw blood or even make a mark, just enough for me to feel it. The repetitive drum attempting to knock some sense in there or shake me out of this fog that's blowing into view.

What just happened? Here I was, hating life, and then my best friend phoned with some great news and I've been left feeling even crappier.

I'm happy for Connie, let's not jump the gun and pretend I'm anything different (OK, I'm slightly jealous too), but how have our lives completely flipped on their heads? How have I become the single one in a dissatisfactory job while she's just bagged her dream occupation and potentially a man too?

My best mate is reaching and achieving and I'm just sitting here doing the same thing I always have while the world around me falls apart. I'm twenty-eight and living back home with my mum. I'm single and working in a job that I don't particularly like. I know I'm going through a tough time and all that, but I don't want to start getting used to the way things are. I don't want to stop dreaming and achieving. I don't want to start coasting. I need to stop failing. I need to start making changes to my current situation.

I've looked over my lists from the other night again and again, not knowing how to bring back the girl I once was, or even if I have the energy to do so. But maybe that's the wrong way of looking at it. Maybe seeing how much I changed during my relationship is enough to show me how adaptable I am. All this phase of life is doing is giving me a chance to adapt again, although this time my new discoveries will be solely because of my own tastes and preferences. I don't have to parade down the street in minimal clothing, but I do have to put myself out there and see what life has to offer.

With my phone still in my hands I go on to my notes and start a fresh one. At the top, in capitals, I type 'THE PROGRESSION OF LIZZY RICHARDSON', and then set about writing a list of the things I am going to change or do something about to be the best *now* version of me. I need to give myself options so I can find out who I am.

> *Sort out what's happening with the flat. Rent it out or sell it. Get it done.*
> *Get dolled up and go out with Connie — or whoever offers.*
> *Join a group — get a hobby?! Look at what's on in the area.*
> *Start writing poems again.*
> *Sing more (could be part of new hobby?).*
> *Buy a pack of thongs.*
> *Job . . . think about whether I'm happy here.*
> *Travel?*
> *Music. Find a love of my own.*

I stop mid-flow to switch on the radio. It's tuned into Radio One because Stephanie refuses to concede to the fact we're too old for it now. I turn the dial until Kiss FM appears on the little digital screen. The old me used to love it, so it's time to see what I think of it now.

Bruno Mars booms out of the speaker with 'Uptown Funk' and a smile spreads across my face. Despite myself I drop my phone and jump my way around the room, punching at the air as I go. I'm knackered by the time it finishes but feeling pumped. I'm ready to jump some more to the next song but the mellow strumming of a guitar comes in and the sound of a man and woman soberly singing about a raining utopia kills the mood.

Funny though, I thought Kiss FM was a bit more vibrant than that. I look at the radio screen before turning some more. KISS comes up again, but this time a dance track beats its way into the room. *This* is the KISS I know. I didn't realize there were now spin-offs to everything life has to offer.

I haven't voluntarily (or happily) listened to music like this for a long time, but the fact it's full of feeling, desire and a beat that keeps giving stops me from turning over. Instead I sit back down, my heel tapping along to the bass drum, as I grab my phone and see if there's anything else I can add to the list or an old habit I can 'crack' immediately.

Without thinking too much I pick up my bag and lock up, taking another trip to the shops, this time to buy some new underwear. I giddily power walk my way through the busy High Street, but find myself feeling stupid as I eye up the display of knickers in front of me. It's shameful how bashful a set of Marks & Sparks briefs can make me – and most of them are black, white or nude. It's not like I'm in Ann Summers next to a bunch of sex toys, eyeing up the crotch-less knickers, yet I feel as though I might as well be. I think Sisqó's 'Thong Song' has a lot to answer for here. I'm literally standing in front of my normal high-leg variety and looking at the skimpier sets out of the corner of my eye to avoid drawing attention to myself. The result is that I probably look like a shoplifter.

My eyes fall on a pack of multi-coloured lace thongs and water a little at what seems like an unforgiving fabric choice. Two rows down things get a little simpler with a plain black set that promises to have extra stretch. I grab what I assume is my size and head to the counter. I feel like I did when I bought tampons for the first time – embarrassed and cross that I'm being made to feel this way because of my gender. I'm aware no one else is actually forcing that emotion on me; it's something I'm doing to myself.

The checkout woman, a miserable-faced Indian lady who's already frowning before I drop my pack in front of her, scans it without even looking.

'Would you like a bag?' she asks, her voice nothing more than a monotone drone.

'Yes. Yes, of course,' I say, horrified at the thought of going out in public with my new undies out on display. I could bump into someone I know.

I snatch up the bag and hastily scurry off.

I get back to the office unscathed, but feel childish for my lack of feminist pride. I am choosing to try on this underwear in a quest to see if they're something I like. I'm making informed decisions and not doing something just because someone, a man, has told me whether or not it's their preference. Although, I must say, when it came to undies Ian was never particularly vocal about what he liked. On the rare occasion we did have sex (ten years . . . ten years! The sexual passion did unfortunately trail away from time to time) my knickers would be off within ten seconds anyway – without him grabbing so much as a glance as to whether they were lace, crotchless or full-on Bridget Jones.

So this is about me, and what I prefer to have cuddling my lady garden.

When it comes to me and my list, this tiny action is achievable right now, therefore it carries more weight than it would if I were usually trying on undies, which I'm starting to realize rarely happens. Part of me wonders whether slipping into them is going to automatically rewind me into the girl who used to wear them while standing in clubs wearing her top as a skirt.

There's only one way to find out.

With the place still empty I go into the bathroom and have a quick change. I was expecting a string up my bum, like the ones I wore when I was young and foolish, but these actually have some meat to them. Yes, they're up my arse and feel like a comfortable wedgie, but I'm going to see out the rest of the day and assess how I feel then.

That's two things from my past that I thought I would never revisit. Both have surprised me. I know switching off KISS in the past would've definitely been led by Ian's taste, but the thong situation was a choice made by me and the fact I was sick of pulling fabric out of my butt crack.

Neither of these little acts is going to change my outlook on life or lead the way to finding the person I was or will become, but they're little stepping stones, and I have to start somewhere.

Inspired by my balls and 'go get 'em' attitude, I pick up my phone and go to messages. I'm not sure I'll ever press call when it comes to Ian ever again. His voice is the last thing I'll ever want to hear. So I start texting instead.

The flat. Either you can buy me out or we sell it. Can get an
estate agent in ASAP if it's the latter. Elizabeth.

OK, it's ridiculous me writing my name, but my given
name is just pathetic. I should just write Lizzy. Or not
sign off.

I press send anyway, before I have a chance to over-
analyse further.

Within thirty seconds my heart constricts as a reply
pings through.

Whatever you think is best.

Cock.

13

Before I can conjure up more expletives towards my ex, the office phone starts ringing.

'Home Comforts, Lizzy speaking. How may I help?' I say serenely into the handset, the words spilling out automatically as I push aside my frustration with Ian for the time being.

'Lizzy, it's Cassandra,' the caller replies. Cassandra has been one of our most loyal clients. Or rather, someone who's constantly asking us over to tweak things in her stunning home. She's younger than me, lives in a gorgeous manor house outside Braintree and is married to Jake – who's hilariously funny and witty, but who's always travelling abroad for work. They don't have children, although I know they're planning it soon (we've already been asked to 'think' about the nursery), and in the meantime Cassandra is making the most of keeping the house in order and putting her desired stamp on the place, with our help.

'What can I do for you, Cassandra?' I ask.

'Can you come over?' she asks, her voice thin and nasally.

'Now?'

'It's a total disaster.'

'What is?' I ask.

'You need to see it. Can you come?' she asks, sounding desperate.

'Stephanie's out, but I'll give her a ring.'

'No, no, I need this sorted now. Can't *you* just come?'

'OK . . .' I say, confused. We're all part of one team, and I know her house intimately, but Cassandra in particular usually deals with the big boss first. However, there's no point bothering Stephanie with this until I know more anyway. 'I'll be there as soon as I can.'

'Thank you.'

I leave the office and run round to the taxi rank, deciding it sounds like a big enough deal to put this one on expenses. Cassandra has always been happy with the work we've done and constantly emails over praise she's received from her mates, so I'm unsure as to why she's in such a panic – but it's good to be out of the office. I didn't realize how claustrophobic it would seem after being away for a few weeks.

Thirty minutes later, after sitting in the back of the car wondering what could possibly be wrong, I'm finally being buzzed through the house's huge iron gates and riding along the silver-birch-lined gravel driveway that winds through its gardens and parkland, the house slowly coming into view after a few false reveals along the way.

It never fails to wow me with its beauty. It looks traditionally English and imposing, with small burnt-orange bricks, white beaded windows and a set of chunky, solid and inviting radius-top-shaped double doors sitting within a classical pillared and pedimented porch. The whole thing is topped by what looks from afar to be a thatched roof, but is actually very thin slate tiles, which have been put under a conservation order by the council. Apparently it's something to do with the aesthetics of the house with the surrounding countryside, though they own several acres of land and can't be seen from the road. Whatever the reason, it costs Cassandra and Jake a small fortune to maintain. The fragile tiles are continuously failing to withstand the weather, but at least they look pretty.

The grounds are equally stunning, with the team of groundsmen managing to keep it colourful no matter the season. Every time I come here I'm surprised to find my eye is drawn to something new. Today I spot a splattering of deep-purple bushes in the turning-bay island, their wispy and elegant branches spilling up and over like an umbrella.

The taxi drives around the turning circle in front of the eight-bedroom house and comes to a slow stop. I've barely had a chance to step out of the taxi when I hear the front door opening.

'Thank god!' Cassandra sighs from the porch.

'Everything OK?'

'Come in,' she pleads, storming back into the house, her arsenic-green stilettos still clomping as she goes.

The interior of the house has been largely designed by Cassandra but executed by us. She was very headstrong about what she wanted, and while it's great to have a client who at least knows their preferences and doesn't look at you gormlessly between swatches, her ideas were no different to the other places we've worked on. This was not helped by the fact we'd been recommended by a friend of hers and she literally just wanted an altered version of the same thing.

In my opinion the interior of this house with its modern sparkly furniture doesn't match its traditional exterior or tell me anything about the owners. It's a thought that always occurs to me when I'm here, but even more so now as she walks me through to the living room, an area we've recently redone for the third time. Its zebra-print wallpaper and pink diamond-encrusted furnishings leave it perilously on the edge of looking tacky, although Cassandra loves it, and at the end of the day my job is purely to make her happy and help her execute her ideas. I don't have to live here. It's not meant to be a reflection of my personality, I'm merely meant to make the client's vision a reality while secretly hoping they take on some of my ideas. That being said, I'm hoping the reason she's asked me over is because she has had a sudden urge to revamp the whole place and make it into something far more elegant and classy.

'I've been looking at this for days and it's been really bugging me,' she says, pinching the top of her perfect button nose as though she's finding the matter difficult to talk about.

'What is it?' I ask, concerned.

'The whole room,' she sighs heavily, looking at me from underneath her fake eyelashes.

'Oh?' I sound, my heart beginning to race at the thought

of finally getting our hands on this room and decorating and furnishing it to perfection. 'Any specifics?'

She looks at me blankly.

'OK,' I say, nodding my head enthusiastically, willing myself to get this right as I might only have this one chance to pitch my thoughts. 'It's fine not to have new ideas, that's why we're here.'

Cassandra sighs again, her bright pink lips pouting out as her eyes scan across the room. 'What would *you* do with it?'

Her question sends a bolt of excitement through me. I look around the room, taking it all in again as I think about how I word my thoughts. 'Well, like you, I love colour, so I think I would mix that love with more neutral tones to really help them pop? For instance, a yellow sofa against a soft stone-grey wall would really help infuse so much fun into the place without it becoming overbearing. Or pink could work,' I say, knowingly appealing to her taste. 'I'd keep a variety of textures and patterns, too, as I think that's quirky yet sophisticated, but use them in specific areas rather than everywhere – like with scatter cushions, maybe. In fact, I'd collect fabrics and art pieces from places I've visited to give it a really personal touch. By doing that I'd be ensuring the room was unique to me and a true reflection of my own loves and tastes and know it couldn't really be meaningfully replicated by anyone else.' I think of all the colourful rugs I saw when Ian and I were travelling around Africa and couldn't bring back and how great a small one would look under a coffee table in the middle of the room. The thought conjures up a longing pang for my old walking boots and the sheer joy of getting to a hostel after a day's travelling. It startles me.

'Interesting,' Cassandra says curtly.

'Also,' I continue, focusing on the room once more and walking towards the huge bay windows lining one side of it that have always bugged me thanks to them being completely covered up with trendy white wooden shutters – a silly design as they block out far too much light. 'It's such a beautiful room and these windows could really unlock another dimension. The view of the garden could be framed so nicely if we got rid of these shutters. The difference in light coming through would really lift the space and make it even more inviting.'

I stop myself from blabbering on and turn to Cassandra, seeing if anything I've said has tickled her fancy or ignited a thirst for simplistic yet classy interior design. It's hard to read the expression on her face because, thanks to her love of Botox, her frozen features display none.

'I was so happy with it,' she mutters forlornly, as though she hasn't listened to a word I've been saying.

'Yes, I guess the issue with such a statement room is that they can lose their appeal and novelty once you're living in them every day,' I say regretfully, deciding not to add that it was something we forewarned her about. 'They project so much into your atmosphere it can be overwhelming at times. Really you want a space to lend itself to your needs but give way for you to live in it comfortably.'

'I'm very comfortable in it,' she states, playing with the cuffs of her aqua-coloured jumper.

'You are?'

'Extremely!'

'Well, it's easy to get bored—'

'Not bored either!' she snaps, cutting me off. 'There's so much to look at, so many colours, shapes and textures.'

'OK . . .' I say, sounding as confused as I feel. 'I'm sorry, Cassandra, but what seems to be the issue if you still love the room?' I ask, stopping myself from guessing again and annoying her further.

'This,' she says, pointing to the wall behind her. Painted in Farrow & Ball's All White (I wouldn't usually go so stark but Cassandra hated the idea of going for a delicate grey), there's a collection of nine black square frames, which have been hung closely together to make a bigger square. Like a screengrab of Cassandra's busy Instagram page. The frames have been filled with pictures of her and Jake on private yachts, at lavish parties and sunning themselves on a secluded island in the Caribbean. It might be a reminder of bling-filled times, but it's probably the calmest area of the room, which is probably why I like it. That being said, she clearly has an issue with it, so I stare and try to see what our client is seeing, giving a little 'hmmm . . .' to let her know I'm thinking about it.

'It's dull!' she exclaims dramatically.

'You think?'

'There's nothing going on,' she huffs. 'Look at all the bareness surrounding the prints. Look . . .'

I do as she says. OK, I can see how to her eye it might seem a little bland. She loves things to be vibrant and crazy, but on a personal level I completely disagree. Then again I disagree with the whole idea of this room. 'What about . . .' I start, feeling myself trying to clutch at straws in the air and hoping a wonderful idea is about to appear. Seeing as she hasn't leapt on any of my earlier suggestions it's clear we have entirely different tastes. I have to be more Cassandra. 'Well, we could change the pictures frequently to keep it fresh.'

'I'm not sure it's enough. Honestly, I can't bear to bring anyone in here. It depresses me too much.'

Jeez, that's quite a statement. Though a part of me can sympathize at needing a room to represent the person you are, and taking from it what you need, to make it your sanctuary, your haven. I couldn't be in my own home any more, the one I shared with Ian, because it filled me with sadness. OK, it's not on the same scale, and I know Cassandra is probably over-exaggerating her feelings, but I still hate the thought of our work not filling her with complete joy. And, quite frankly, I'd rather be alone in my current misery.

'I think we need more zebra,' she says, nodding in agreement with herself. 'We should wallpaper the whole room. It's too good to be wasted on just one wall. It needs more.'

I look around the space that's bigger than the whole downstairs of Mum's house and imagine the safari madness that could take over if I don't take control of the situation. Before we know it I'll be in charge of buying stuffed giraffes, lions and zebras to complete the look along with an indoor rainforest and sprinkling water feature. However, the business side of my brain is telling me not to go in too forcefully with my opinions. Rather I need to compromise to keep her happy so that she feels supported, but also make sure the project isn't going to completely derail and make potential future clients, Cassandra's mates or anyone who might come into this house, see our work here and think we're absolutely awful at what we do.

'I know!' I say, unable to believe I'm even suggesting it. 'The frames. Let's change them. We can get chunkier ones and wrap them in the wallpaper. If we reprint the pictures in black and white too it should look quite classy.'

Cassandra squints at the wall as though trying to imagine it.

'I love it!' she sings.

I hate it, I think, while beaming at Cassandra. I am happy she's happy, but really the whole thing saddens me. It's yet another beautiful space ruined by too much faff. As a result, I already know a part of me will be silently weeping when it comes to painfully hanging the new frames on the wall.

14

A grey cloud is not looming over me when I wake up on Michelle's wedding day – metaphorical or actual. It might now be December but the sun is shining brightly, and I find myself waking with an actual grin. Today is not about me and what might be happening in my own life. It's all about being there for my little sister as she commits to the man who wants to stay with her to the grave and not be a douche by failing to admit that. Hurrah to my little sister for finding a good egg!

I let Michelle have my bed last night while I slept on the sofa. Not only is she the bride but she's also heavily with child, so it seemed like the right thing to do. Plus she pretty much kicked me out of my room and hung her wedding dress and other bridal paraphernalia over my wardrobe doors and on my chest of drawers, so I didn't really have much of a choice. I honestly didn't mind though, I took it as my first official wedding day duty as chief bridesmaid.

I'm woken by the smell of bacon and sausages sizzling in a pan. Easily tempted, I throw off my duvet and investigate. In the kitchen I find Mum sitting in her dressing gown, her rollers already in (God knows how long she's been up), Ted skimming over the sports section of the *Mirror* and my dad standing over the hob with a spatula in one hand and frying pan in the other.

'Hello, angel,' Dad beams at me, holding his hands as far away as possible as he bends in for a kiss. I wrap my arms around his neck and give him a good squeeze, his grey stubble tickling my cheek. I get my height from my dad. Obviously I'm not as tall as he is at six foot four, but I've always been taller than any of my female friends. I also inherited his sloped nose, albeit a daintier version, and his big brown eyes. Although, his contain a wisdom I can only hope to inherit one day.

'Morning,' I say, kissing Ted on the cheek and sliding in next to Mum on the bench opposite while looping my arm around her waist and placing my head on her shoulder. She kisses me on the forehead.

'Is she up yet?' Mum asks.

'I'm sure we'll know when she is,' I say, prompting the others to laugh.

'I heard that,' Michelle says, wobbling into the room with a massive grin on her face. 'I'm getting married!' she shouts, her hands fist pumping the air multiple times.

We all cheer in unison as Dad bashes the spatula against the frying pan to make a clanging sound as if making a toast. Seconds later we're gathered around the table munching on sausage and bacon sandwiches, slathered with ketchup, on glorious white bread.

White bread was severely frowned upon when I lived with Ian. Most processed food was, actually. I understood when it came to McDonalds, but was silently miffed when it came to my bread and pasta choices. At first I refused to believe it was that terrible for me when the rest of the population seemed to be happy enough eating it. But my reluctance to budge meant Ian started to refuse eating food I'd cooked. He wasn't being mean. He just wanted to stick to a set diet while training – although training for *what* I could never quite understand. It's not as if he was Greg Rutherford and about to one-and-a-half hitch-kick his way into becoming a long-jumping Olympian. Not even close. He simply liked being fit – which was fine, but I couldn't cope with there being no heaven-sent carbs in my life, so decided to compromise. As soon as I tried the bread alternatives of wholemeal, sometimes rye (the fresh loaves, not the odd little packets that fall apart when you look at them and never ever seem to go mouldy – what is actually in it?) and wholemeal or brown rice pasta, I realized I was going to be OK. We were going to pull through. That being said, even in Dubai I found myself longingly looking at the spread of delicious white bloomers, rolls, ciabatta and focaccia, and begrudgingly thinking of Ian's disapproving judgement if I were to take any back to the table with me. God forbid I would be that gluttonous . . . which I obviously was. My top drawer at work is stuffed with naughty treats. Whenever I'm there on my own, I slowly open it, my body instantly reacting in a shameless manner. I don't slowly nibble and savour, I actually scoff. Without chewing. The phrase 'it didn't even touch the sides' was made for me in those moments of pure greed. The sad thing is that I didn't enjoy any of it. Instead I'd feel rotten and guilty as my tummy automatically bloated and gurgled at me in pain, wondering if Ian would notice I'd caved in to my longing.

Well, not any more. As I sink my teeth through the spongy white bread and crunchy, salty meat, I feel positively orgasmic.

'This is flipping great,' I say to Dad as he slides in next to Michelle, which isn't an easy feat, given her current girth and his long legs.

'Thanks, Larry,' Ted says, licking ketchup off his fingers. He's a dopey thing is Ted. Or maybe I should say docile. My dad wouldn't be sat here with us if Ted was less of a man than he is. He's not threatened by Mum's past, and that's why he's slotted in so nicely. It feels natural to have him here with us now.

'This is the perfect start to my magical day,' Michelle grins, looking around the table at us all with tears in her eyes.

I do the same and love what I see. Life might sometimes be shitty and startling, but nothing will ever surprise me more than this sight – my dysfunctional family being more functional than some of the supposedly functional families I know. Whatever happens in life, I know I'll be lucky to have this crazy bunch there with me every step of the way.

'You'd better not screw up my hair, Elizabeth,' Michelle suddenly warns me, interrupting my pleasant thoughts while wiping her mouth and throwing a warning look my way.

'Oh, crap. That's exactly what I'd planned to do,' I say, my voice thick with sarcasm.

'Well, jealousy does funny things to people,' she tells me.

Whether she means it or not, there's an air of smugness to her voice that riles me.

'Like the time you put a cigarette burn in my prom dress half an hour before I was due to leave?' I ask, wanting to smack the look off her face.

'Exactly,' she nods over the sound of Mum gasping – she was there when I cried off my make-up in a major meltdown. I told her it was Michelle who did it but little Chelle acted all innocent, telling Mum she'd never do something as foolish as smoke, even though I knew she always had a pack of menthol Silk Cut hidden in her school gym bag.

'Or the time you hid my car keys so I missed Jason Solomon's party?'

'I think you'll find the police turned up that night and Jason got arrested for possession of Ecstasy,' she shrugs.

'No!' grumbles Dad, the bubble of our innocent childhood bursting.

'I did you a favour that night. It's a shame the same can't be said for Connie who got caught high as a kite.'

'You said she was drunk,' says my poor mum, who I had persuaded to go with me and get my best mate in the middle of the night so that her own mother didn't find out and go mental.

'OK, what about when you tried to snog our maths teacher!' I stammer.

'What of it?' she asks, giving me a defiant stare while

not denying it. Clearly not willing to address the inappropriateness of being found with her hand on Mr Howell's shoulder while her eyelids fluttered in his direction. She laughed it off as soon as she saw me and thankfully, although he looked ridiculously uncomfortable and fearful (probably for his job), nothing went any further. I still feel sorry for Mr Howell as I am adamant the whole thing was entirely orchestrated by my little sister.

'Michelle!' Mum squeals.

'You knew I had a passion for maths,' she says candidly. 'It's not my fault Elizabeth didn't possess the same talents.'

'You were being a slut!' I blast.

'Girls,' says Ted, who's never really had to live with us or tell us off before. 'I think you should stop now.'

'I didn't start it. The dumped one did,' snarls my wonderful sister.

'Michelle! Go to your room now!' Mum reprimands, her voice booming louder than I've heard it do in quite some time.

'My room? My *room*? I would, but Dumbo here has his running machine in there and all my stuff has been shoved into the loft.'

'Wh—' starts Ted, looking speechless.

'I don't know what we're all playing at here but—'

'OK, OK, OK. Stop it,' I shout over Michelle, who's still carrying on with her spree of insults. 'Shut up!'

Thankfully she does so. The tamed beast tenses her jaw as she looks down at her empty plate.

'Right. You're stressed because it's your wedding day

and emotionally unstable thanks to the rather large loaf you're currently baking. Let's stop though. This is going to be a magical day for all of us. Got it?' I say forcefully, surprised at myself as I take control of the situation. I might've helped start it, but there's no way I can continue.

'Oh fuck, I'm so sorry,' weeps Michelle, her demeanour changing in an instant as her bump bounces up and down with each sob.

Pregnancy hormones are lethal. After seeing Chelle's rollercoaster of emotions in action last week and now, I vow never to leave the house, for the security of the nation, whenever I do indeed get pregnant – which seems like another dream that has sailed up the river to Not-going-to-happen-any-time-soon-ville thanks to me being a newly spun spinster. A further heartbreak.

'Don't be soft, darling,' Dad says, giving Michelle a little nudge.

More sobs.

'Hey,' he soothes, putting an arm around her shoulder and kissing the top of her head.

'I've already ruined the day,' she sniffs, covering her face with both hands.

'Far from it,' Ted tries, pursing his lips.

'We're all a little bat-shit crazy here – that's why we love each other,' offers Dad, his face deadpan.

'Couldn't have said it better myself,' Mum nods, the sides of her mouth curling even though she hates any of us swearing.

'Go have a shower and I'll come up and get everything

ready for you,' I tell her, gathering up the empty plates as I get to my feet.

'Thank you,' she says sheepishly, nibbling on her lip as she leaves the room.

We don't breathe a sigh of relief as she leaves the room. We don't all look at each other wide-eyed and joke about what just happened. We don't mock her outburst. Today is her day and we're behind her every step of the way.

We are united.

I cry when I first see Michelle in her wedding dress in my childhood room, the organza lace flowing wonderfully over her womanly shape.

I cry when I see the look of pride our parents and Ted give her when she's walking down the stairs.

I cry in the back of Ted's Ford Mondeo when I hear the bells ringing at the church ahead of our arrival.

I cry when Dad takes hold of Michelle's hand and kisses it while preparing to lead her up the aisle.

I cry when I walk into the church, which smells heavily of incense, and see their families and all of their friends staring back at me with expectant faces, eager to see the bride. One hundred and twenty-three faces looking at me and through me all at once.

I cry when I see Stuart, who is usually devoid of any emotion, welling up at the sight of his bride behind me.

I cry when Mum gives a delightful reading of Corinthian's Love poem – the opening line always being one to make me assess how I'm letting my own love rule my emotions.

I cry when Michelle stumbles over her vows and gets the giggles, causing her bump to shake beneath her dress.

I cry when the elderly choir start singing a questionable version of 'If I Ain't Got You' by Alicia Keys, and my elderly nan starts joining in even though she has no idea of the melody.

I cry when Stuart fist pumps the air once they've been pronounced man and wife, a relieved look falling on both their faces.

I cry as they hold on to each other and laugh their way out of the church towards their future as a married couple.

I cry, and every single one of my tears is for my sister on her incredible special day.

Pride, happiness and joy.

All for her.

Just as it should be.

15

'I thought she'd bump me up, not move you down,' Connie grumbles in my ear as we look at the seating plan in front of us.

I know there was a standard top-table set-up until I became a solo entity. Since joking (not joking) about my inconsiderate heartbreak ruining her plans, Michelle decided to rip the whole thing up and start again. Rather than me being sat with my family, I've now been shoved on what appears to be the singleton table.

Yaaaay . . .

I'm so thankful Connie is with me right now, even if she has come in her black Dr Marten boots and canary-yellow lace midi dress and looks utterly cool while I'm standing in an unforgiving floor-length lavender brides-maid's gown that longs to hug in all the wrong places. I seem to have grown a sympathetic pregnancy bump in the last couple of weeks or, more accurately, a gigantic food baby. I did say I wasn't the sort to starve myself or go off food in the name of love, so it's not too surprising I can see the results of my indulgence.

'Wait! Before we go over there,' I say, holding on to her arm to stop her, grabbing two glasses of bubbly from a young waitress's tray and thrusting one in her direction. I haven't had a proper chance to talk to her and know the day will only get more manic as it progresses.

'Huh?' she sounds, accepting the drink.

'Congratulations,' I beam, touching our glasses together. 'You did it and I'm so proud.'

'You are the sweetest,' she says, grabbing my face and planting a big kiss on my cheek. 'I'd be nothing without you, Elizabeth Richardson.'

'Don't make me laugh!'

'I mean it,' she says, her eyes wide as they look lovingly at mine. 'I'm so glad we fought over that doll when we were younger and our mums split us up and forced us to be friends.'

'That's not what happened!' I laugh, screwing up my face.

'Isn't it?' she giggles. 'Come on. Let's go see what riff-raff we've been lumbered with.'

We get to our table to find a couple of guys (lads might be a more accurate description) hovering by their chairs while goofing around. One girl is in her seat already, although currently glued to her phone, her petite frame hunched over and her brow creased as she frantically taps away on the screen that she holds just inches from her eyes.

'Oh, you win Mrs Sociable,' Connie whispers in my ear, pointing at the name cards that confirm I am indeed sitting next to her.

I sneak a glance at the card next to mine in the hope I'm next to someone else I know and see I've been left with Paul Short, Michelle's ex of three years. Wow. She really is trying to punish me for the inconvenience of my life. Paul wasn't a particularly friendly person, so I'm surprised he's agreed to come to this. That being said, I'm sure they both have their reasons for the inviting and accepting. Michelle probably liked the thought of smugly rubbing her marriage to a really nice guy in his face, and I bet Paul's intrigued to see the man who's agreed to put up with Michelle for the rest of his life.

Regardless of the reason for his presence, it means I'll be eating between a guy I could never stand and a woman who could be lost in the deep dark comment section of the *Mail Online* for all I know.

I hope the grub is going to make this worth it.

Kicking out the bottom piece of fabric on my dress that keeps gathering at my ankles, I pull out my chair and shuffle into a sitting position. My tummy bulges against the fabric, so I squeeze my chair in as far as I can, unfurl my napkin and place it in such a way that it covers it up. My concern dissipates instantly.

'You're Michelle's sister, right?' the girl next to me asks in the sweetest of voices, no longer having an intimate moment with her phone. She's gorgeous. Her long brown hair frames her olive face beautifully and those big brown eyes are divine.

'Yep,' I smile, proud to be sister of the bride regardless of the unflattering attire she's put me in and the table she's placed me on. 'I'm Lizzy.'

'Natalia,' she says, putting her hand on her chest. 'You guys look nothing alike.'

'Sometimes we do,' I shrug. Funny how people do

that – hear you're of the same gene pool and set about dissecting your features, habits and quirks, as though you're a puzzle to be conquered. 'That's my bestie Connie over there,' I point, just as Connie elegantly downs the rest of her Prosecco.

'Oh, do you want to swap?' Natalia asks, starting to get out of her seat as she takes my words in the wrong way.

'God no!' I say, pulling her back down. 'Michelle would kill me if I started playing around with her plan.'

'She really would!' Connie heavily nods from across the table, her lips pouting outwards.

'OK . . . Well, it's lovely to meet you,' Natalia says, smiling in Connie's direction.

'Hello!' Connie grins back. 'What about you? How'd you all know the happy couple?'

'To be honest we haven't got to know your sister too much yet,' Natalia replies, looking back at me regretfully. 'We went to secondary school with Stuart. Me and that bunch,' she says, glancing over at the group of guys who are just starting to take their seats.

'Oh, nice.'

'You must have loads of gossip on old Stuie then,' Connie whispers conspiratorially while placing her elbows on the table and sitting forward, eager to hear what Natalia has to offer.

'Loads,' she laughs in reply. 'But if I spill what I know so might he and I'd rather keep those skeletons in the closet where they belong.'

'I hear you!' Connie cackles. There's a reason why

142

everyone loves Con as soon as they meet her. There's no awkwardness with strangers, just this warmth that's instantly genuine.

'This is such a treat. We rarely see each other,' she says, smiling wistfully at the guys in front of her who are pouring themselves wine and tucking into the bread and butter.

'Funny how life changes,' I say.

'Exactly. You know what it's like. Life moves on but it doesn't mean you don't love the people who used to be in your life every single day. People you meet at school help sculpt who you become,' she says, hesitantly looking at her phone before placing it face down on the table. A split second later, changing her mind in a decisive manner, she picks it back up and puts it in her clutch bag before dropping it on the floor between her feet.

'We've been friends since we were tiny,' I share, my finger wagging between Connie and me. 'Even though I went up north to uni we remained as tight as ever.'

'That's rare! With me my uni mates took over really.'

'Well, I got into a relationship straight away,' I say, kicking myself for talking about Ian, but deciding not to dwell on him much longer. 'Connie was the only mate who didn't require loads from me or get shitty over how much time I was spending with my ex. Our friendship is effortless. Always has been.'

'I can't get rid of her!' Connie laughs, pointing her thumb at me. 'I've tried.'

'She's even moved to London to try and shrug me off,' I join in with a smile, knowing she doesn't mean a single word of it. 'But then I just turn up unannounced and ruin dates.'

'She really does,' she smiles, reassuringly winking at me.

'So whereabouts in London are you now?' Natalia asks, picking up her glass of white wine that one of the guys opposite, the cute one with the brown shaggy hair, has silently poured for her.

'Bethnal Green?'

'No way! I used to live just round the corner but have edged slightly closer to Shoreditch.'

'Fancy.'

Natalia doesn't bat away the compliment. Instead she nods her head at it. 'All of my mates live around that way so I couldn't go too far, but I set up my own business a couple of years ago and the time just felt right to make another bold move.'

'You clearly don't do things by halves,' I say.

'Work hard, play hard,' Connie nods along, impressed.

The bread basket is being proffered by Shaggy Hair guy, who I think is called Chris. We all reach in for some. It's been a long day and we're only just getting started.

'What do you ladies do?' Natalia asks, putting some butter on her knife and spreading it thickly on top of her cut roll.

'I've just signed a two-book deal,' Connie chimes, rightfully looking delighted as she says it.

'Oh my God! That's amazing. Congratulations,' Natalia says, picking up her glass and clinking it against Connie's.

'Eesh. Don't congratulate me until it's out on the

shelves,' Connie says in a way that would make her seem bashful and modest. I know she's neither and the thought tickles me. 'Anything could happen in that time. I could completely fail at it.'

'I highly doubt that!' I tut, wanting to boost her in case she is having a genuine moment of self-doubt. I've been pretty caught up in myself lately and haven't asked her much more about the book. We really do need some more time together. You'd think that would be easy nowadays, but it seems as difficult as ever. It turns out that while I was spending each and every night with Ian, Connie was building quite the life for herself in London – which I've always known, but didn't really think about the fact that I wasn't the only one whose plans were preventing us from meeting. Now I'm back to being just me with loads of time for her, she still has her own plans to honour. Not that I would ever complain. As she points out – I'm the one who left her to go up north for uni.

'And you, Lizzy?' our new friend prompts.

'Oh,' I say, my mind on Connie. 'I work for an interior design company in Chelmsford. Have done for years now,' I say with a little shrug. I used to announce my chosen profession and occupation with joy in my voice, even though the actual job is far from what I thought it would be, so my downbeat tone of voice catches me off guard.

'Did you study it at uni?'

'No. I actually went for English Language and Literature,' I laugh. 'I didn't really know what I wanted to do but knew I leant more towards something creative. Uni was brilliant for lots of reasons,' I say, trying to disconnect the fun I had in Sheffield from all the memories I shared with Ian, but failing miserably. Try as I might, thoughts of him keep creeping up on me. 'Long story short, I ended up coming back here because of my relationship, but was limited with the work available. Everyone was leaving uni and applying for jobs at the same time.'

'We all know that feeling,' Natalia nods.

'It did me a favour as I was pushed into trying something different, and then one thing led to another and I started working at Home Comforts,' I admit, remembering how excited I was about starting my job there.

'Do you love it?' Natalia asks, clearly expecting me to gush about it.

'The past week has been shitty because I'm going through a break-up—'

'I'm so sorry,' she interjects.

'Ergh,' I sigh.

'It's the same guy,' pipes in Connie.

'Eesh!' Natalia responds.

'But it's totally fine,' I say, trying my hardest to push through and answer the question without letting emotion get the better of me, because I know deep down that it really isn't fine and that my heart is still as raw and hurt as it was. 'I have loved my job for a long time, but everyone who comes in at the moment seems to want the same thing. We get a lot of customers who've seen the work we've done on a friend's house and they basically want us to replicate it with the slightest variation.'

'Recommendations are massive,' Natalia says kindly, looking genuinely impressed. 'And knowing what your client wants to the point their friends then take their business to you is a sign you're doing something right.'

'Sounds tedious.' Connie says it like it is as she screws up her face and tops up her glass.

'It really is. I long for the day someone walks in with a Pinterest board that doesn't contain some sort of animal-print pattern, or a mirror on every surface – even the loo seat – and a ridiculously oversized TV hung up on the wall.'

I'm over-exaggerating but it's totally worth it for the laughter that spills out of the girls.

'Just don't get me started on the need for bling,' I smirk. 'I've put sparkles in places only the mice will see! And I never want to see a zebra again in my life. Which is a shame because they're actually quite cute.'

Thankfully, Zebragate has been resolved. We mocked up a frame the following morning and took it over. Cassandra fell in love with it instantly, as I knew she would. Meaning the risk of a real-life jungle appearing in an Essex living room was narrowly avoided.

'Sounds awful,' declares Connie, her face screwed up in disgust.

'I have no qualms if that's what a client genuinely loves – but I hate the fad. I long for clients to think of their houses as an extension of themselves and a place to show glimpses of their dreams, ambitions and inspiration. It shouldn't be the same as Joan Jones' next door.'

'I couldn't agree more,' says Natalia passionately. 'And

sometimes the real crux of a room comes in the smaller details or the heart behind them.'

'Exactly!' I shout with excitement. 'Like cushions that give a subtle nod to a sunset they once saw in Namibia or a wall colour that matches the exquisite cornfields they were standing in when they received a life-changing call – maybe hearing they'd got the job they'd always dreamed of, or maybe it was the spot their partner spoke of love for the first time. Personal little touches . . .'

'What a beautiful idea,' smiles Natalia.

'She's got lots more where that came from,' Connie says with a big grin on her face. 'So what does your business do, Nat? Can we call you Nat, Nat?'

'You can,' she smiles, looking at me. 'I also work with interiors.'

'Shut up!' I gasp. 'In Essex?'

'No, no, no,' she says, shaking her head, looking relieved that she's not putting up with my particular clientele. I know they don't represent the whole of Essex; they're just this little trendy niche that's thriving at the moment thanks to certain TV shows. 'I mostly work in Mayfair, Kensington, Chelsea . . .'

'You mean, the posh parts,' Connie suggests cheekily, her eyes widening at me, practically shouting at me to 'get in there'.

'I wouldn't disagree,' Natalia shrugs, taking a bite of her bread.

'Wow,' I say.

'Although you'll be surprised how much the animal

print, big TVs and bling live on,' she chuckles, covering her mouth as she continues munching.

'Well, if you're ever looking for new staff or anything,' I say without thinking, cringing as I prepare myself for a super eggy moment. We've only just met and this is highly inappropriate.

Natalia reaches down for her bag and pulls out her phone. Ignoring the dozens of emails she's had in the last ten minutes, she clicks through to her contacts. 'Put your deets in there,' she tells me.

I do so as quickly as I can before she changes her mind. Or I do.

'Now, on a more serious note,' she says, looking around the room like a little meerkat. 'Does anyone have any idea when the food is coming out? Because I am fucking starving.'

Oh, I like her!

16

I have such a ball. Connie and Natalia have me howling with laughter on numerous occasions. So much so that waking up in my room this morning, I'm doing so with a lightness in my heart, just as I did yesterday. I feel surprisingly good considering I've had a heavy night!

I thought being at a social event without Ian for the first time would be unbearable, that part of me would be longing to get out of there even though it was my sister's special day. Or that loneliness would eat me up from the inside out as I realized I didn't know how to function without my plus one by my side. That I'd be uninteresting and pathetically moping around aimlessly without the security and confidence that comes with being in a social situation with someone who's already firmly on my side.

Looking back on it now, I realize I didn't feel at all like that. If anything, it was nice to just be in the room enjoying the day without having someone else to think about. I didn't have to worry about Ian being bored if I left him alone too long, or whether one of my uncles was going to say something rude and offend him – which is a situation that's happened numerous times before because they seemed to like winding him up. I didn't have to include him in conversations he might not particularly care about; for instance, I know he would have been shuffling beside me and clenching his jaw to stop himself yawning during the fifteen-minute chat I ended up having with my darling nan about her front garden, which looks exceptionally good all year round – she trims it up a right treat. I could have that chat and not worry about someone subconsciously tapping their foot beside me. I could dance the night away without a care in the world, all the while throwing the craziest dance shapes I could conjure and not caring about the fact I looked like an absolute plonker. I could stay as long as I wanted and didn't have to worry about him preferring to leave early. I could drink what I wanted, have shots with the girls, and not worry about him thinking I was silly for getting a little tipsy.

There's something quite wonderful about only looking after myself. I know Ian and I had a great relationship (perhaps that thought is laughable now it's fallen apart), but he had a lot of control over our relationship and me. He wasn't controlling, I'm not suggesting that. I don't think it was ever done in a purposefully negative manner or with him demanding to be the alpha male, but right from the start I handed over the responsibility of decision-making. Early on I realized that what made him happy made me happy in return – and that was all I ever wanted. I wonder if I'd still be in the same position I've found myself in if I hadn't done so. Whether I would feel quite so lost and unsure of who I am without Ian in my life. We could've been married by now or perhaps we'd have broken up much sooner, me declaring we weren't compatible and that I wanted different things.

Obviously it was strange to be there, at an event we've been talking about for so long, without him. I felt like my right arm had been savagely chopped off and fed to starving wolves, but last night I became aware of my left arm swinging loyally by my side. I'm capable. It's more a case of me learning how to function without the missing limb.

Well, I fucking did. What's more, I had the best time ever doing so.

I mean, there was a pretty sorry moment in the loo when I had my head against the cold toilet door and found myself on the edge of a wobble. We'd just been dancing to Beyoncé and I was boiling hot, so I loved my face being against the metal sheet. The sudden stillness became my weakness as thoughts, feelings and emotions came flooding in unexpectedly. I had a silent sob to myself over the romance of the day and my lack of man, direction, purpose and confidence. But then I gave myself a stern talking to.

What would Beyoncé do, you twat?

I took a deep breath, flicked my hair back over my shoulders, and walked back on to that dance floor like a champ. I'm so glad I did!

I think back to the numerous shots that were consumed and am hit with a complex wave of groggy regret and utter joy. I had fun. I laughed, danced, drank and was very, very, very happy.

My phone bleeps beside me. My heart stops when I see it's a text from a number I don't recognize.

How's the head? I'm at the gym trying to sweat out the bad stuff. No one is standing next to me. I think I still stink of alcohol. Blaming you! N.x

I would've been sad, and surprised, if Natalia never got in touch after the amount of fun that we had together last night. That said, I'm delighted that she's got in touch so quickly. I know there's a three-day rule when it comes to dating, so I'm thrilled to see the same pathetic rule doesn't apply in friendships.

Gym? Are you for real? ;-)

I hit send, attaching a selfie of me in my current state – in bed with leftover make-up smeared across my puffy melon of a hungover face.

You're so funny! x

You say funny, I say normal and realistic. x

I wish I was like her and in the gym. In fact, Ian's version of me would probably have stopped drinking a lot sooner last night and still have been in the gym first thing this morning. I haven't actually exercised since the holiday (yes, we were *that* couple who worked out while on a relaxing 'break') and I'm starting to feel it. I don't weigh myself, I don't think scales are a true reflection of what's going on with my body, but there's a reason my dress was so tight and unforgiving yesterday and for all my clothes to suddenly be giving me muffin tops. Mum hasn't shrunk my garments in the wash. I've ballooned. My holiday and heartbreak diets are catching up with me. I haven't been working out, and my body knows it. Not just in its size, but in the fact it just doesn't feel as good and able. I think I underestimated what that time in the gym was giving me. I haven't been in the mood to work out, not only because it means pushing myself out of the fog that has been consuming me, but also because fitness and the gym are so heavily linked to Ian and his hobbies. The reality, though, is that I'm currently rebelling against Ian's ideals as a human and for our bodies by doing the opposite. No exercise and eating anything I fancy. Which is everything I see.

There might have been certain aspects of our relationship that were led by Ian, but that doesn't mean they were bad for me. For the first time ever I crave the terms 'clean living' and 'emptying the bucket' to be bandied around – and not because of Ian, or the fact Natalia is impressively up and going for it already after a heavy night out, but for me.

As far as I can remember there isn't a gym in Ingatestone, and I really don't want to travel back to the one I am a member of because I don't want to run the risk of bumping into Ian there. The thought of seeing him anywhere is horrendous enough; I've boycotted everywhere we've ever been together to avoid it, so doing so while I'm sweaty, knackered and as red as a beetroot really would be an atrocity.

The gym is out of the question. However, thinking

about it, I don't want to be boxed into a gym right now anyway.

I look out of my window – the curtains are already open because I was too drunk to close them last night – and see that it's a nice crisp winter's day. I locate some leggings, a baggy t-shirt and some old trainers that were hiding at the bottom of the wardrobe. Obviously I didn't bring any of my workout gear with me, so I'm less Sweaty Betty chic and more Primark throwaways, but it'll do.

I lean over, touch my toes and feel my body stretch. It's uncomfortable and comforting all at once. Before I can talk myself out of it, I jog down the stairs, straight out the front door, up my road and out of the village. I push myself to run further into the real countryside of Essex, which is full of farmers' fields and forests. The scenery helps get me going, but I know this is harder on my body than it should be. My legs feel heavier as I pull them along and my chest doesn't want to expand as much as I know it can. It's fighting the movement, rather than welcoming it. I've allowed it to become lazy. How crazy that all those hours in the gym can be undone so easily with a month of overindulgence and neglect, thanks to all the emotional turmoil after my holiday.

The sweat drips down my face as a stitch attacks my right side, but I don't stop even though so much of me wants to. My brain hits override, and I tell myself to run through it. Somewhere deep down a determination takes over, a desire for achieving and getting the run done.

An hour later I return to the house red and puffy, with

last night's make-up now streaming down my face. I'm shattered, my body hurts to the point of burning, but I feel amazing – amazing because I can finally stop, of course, but amazing because of what I've just done, too. I felt an urge, albeit a feeling that was inspired by Natalia's fitness efforts, to get out of the house. I ignored any excuses my mind threw out about not having the correct attire, running on an empty stomach and being mightily hungover, and just went for it.

Best of all?

It was entirely for my own benefit and not to impress someone else . . . although I will be boasting about my efforts to anyone who'll listen, for at least a week.

I take my phone out of my pocket and text Natalia.

I see your gym session and raise you a run in the countryside. Feel like death. It's amazing! X

Totally trumped me. ;-) x

Seconds later I message Connie – who I last saw when I was begging her to stay at mine, but she insisted on getting the last train home, meaning she missed the end of the party.

You left at the right time. More shots. More dancing. Just had to run it off. At least five miles! Xx

An instant reply bounces back.

Bugger off, you smug bitch.

Well, I can't deny it. I cackle as I make my way upstairs for a shower.

I'm still buzzing later that day when I answer the door to Dad. Everyone's coming over for a post-wedding gossip, a takeaway, followed by wedding cake and some tea and coffee . . . Ian would say it cancels out the good work I put in this morning. I say, I've earned it so can have what I please!

'You're looking fresher than I thought you would,' my dad sings to me as he strides in, giving me a kiss on the forehead as he does so.

'I went for a run earlier!' I exclaim proudly, shutting the door. 'Went for miles. I didn't stop once.'

'You look great for it,' Dad says, his face beaming as we venture into the lounge. Mum turns to greet Dad with a wave. She's sitting with her feet up, watching some nature documentary while nursing a cup of tea and a packet of biscuits.

'Haven't you wanted to start running again?' she says to him, her eyebrows raised expectantly.

He looks between the pair of us, caught a little off guard – his mouth gawping just enough for me to notice.

'Yeah . . . that's right,' he says with a slow nod of his head.

'Remember when you were younger, Elizabeth?' she asks. 'You two used to run together.'

'Really?' I ask.

'It wasn't that often. Maybe three or four times,' Dad shrugs.

'Nonsense. You did that 5K race together. Remember? You got a little plate for it and everything.'

Now that she's saying it, I do have a very vague recollection of struggling through the countryside with Dad next to me.

'I think I actually found the plate thing,' I say, remembering an item I picked out of a box the other day. It was absolutely filthy, but you could just about see 5K engraved on it. I had no idea where it had come from. I'm pretty sure it went on the dump pile.

'You should take your dad out with you next time, love. For old times' sake,' Mum says, placing a Chocolate Hobnob in her mouth, and crunching down on it while looking mighty pleased with herself for coming up with the idea. 'It'll be a nice thing for you two to do together while you're back here.'

I look at Dad. He looks as baffled as I feel. It doesn't appear that he's thought about going out for a jog recently. He's not overweight, but he's not exactly the fittest man I know, either. If he were to start running again, I'm not sure he'd choose me as his partner.

'Everything's OK, right? You haven't had a health scare?' I ask with a panic, wondering if that's the cause of this chat.

'Don't go killing me off just yet,' he laughs, the lines around his eyes crinkling up and showing his age. 'Right,' he says decisively, almost to himself, as he jabs his fist in the air. 'Sign me up to your new running club.'

I have to laugh at the concern on his face. He doesn't look like this is something he actually wants to do, so I can't work out if he's just saying he'll come because Mum has sprung it on him and he doesn't want me to feel upset if he turns the idea down. If he's not sick then I imagine this is another way for Mum to keep an eye on me to make sure I don't cut myself off from society and become a wallowing mess.

'I'm a pretty shit runner to be honest, Dad,' I say, attempting to let him off the hook.

'I won't be any better,' he shrugs, stealing a telling side-glance at my mum. 'Just let me know when you're next going and I'll try to come with you. It'll do me good to loosen these old bones a bit.'

'What a lovely idea,' Mum says, shoving in yet another biscuit.

An awkward silence that I can't quite decipher falls upon us.

I open my mouth to see if I can figure out what's going on when the doorbell rings and startles us all.

'Has he forgotten his bloody key again? Honestly!' Mum tuts to herself, before turning to me. 'Can you get it? It's Ted with Michelle and Stuart.'

I wander off down the hallway, wondering what's going on with my mum and dad, because something clearly is. It doesn't feel like they're not getting on, but something has clearly happened. It's a thought I don't have long to ponder over. When I get to the door, Ted is in the middle of tripping over. He's literally mid-air while a white box, presumably containing the top tier of the wedding cake Michelle was hoping to save for the baby's first birthday, does its own little flying spree.

In my direction.

It might be happening in slow motion, but as the box opens, the cake reveals itself and propels out. My arms stay firmly by my side, failing to block the cake from its final destination.

Me.

The white buttercream icing hits me with a splat, covering my face and chest. It's not as light as it tasted last night and hits with quite an impact.

There's a moment where no one says a thing. I stand there frozen, feeling their eyes on me. Then a deafening laughter spills from Michelle and Stu, the pair of them cackling hysterically.

I feel my emotions flounder. Either this moment is mortifying, even though it's only my loving family here to witness it, or it's one of the funniest things that's ever happened to me.

Laughter wins. It rises up and bubbles out of me as I wipe the delicious-smelling goodness from my eyes.

The very worst has happened to me lately. I can handle a bit of smashed-up cake on my face.

I scoop it from my hand to my mouth and enjoy the sugary goodness.

'I want some!' Michelle giggles, leaping over poor Ted who's still on the floor rubbing at his ankle. She uses her finger to swipe a bit off my face and licks at it.

'Mmmmmm . . . As good as I remember,' she smiles at me.

'That's gross,' says Stuart, screwing up his face in disgust.

'What's going on?'

'Are you all OK?'

Mum and Dad come wandering down the hallway. They take one look at me and fall about laughing. Quite literally. Mum actually collapses down the wall, clutching at her tummy. She can't even stand through the laughter.

'Oh, Elizabeth,' she wheezes.

'Try a bit,' Michelle says, helping herself to more of my cake face and shoving it in.

'Seriously, if I were marrying Ian this is how we'd have served up the cake,' I laugh, tears springing to my eyes. 'Plates are so overrated.'

'I'd better try some,' smiles Dad, helping Mum up.

'Me too,' sniffles Mum, giggles still spilling from her mouth.

They both join my little sister in picking bits from my face and eating them. I feel like I'm a monkey being checked for lice, although I don't think they could ever feel as good as I do right now.

I embrace the silly moment and feel joyous from it.

Joyous and sticky!

I need another shower!

17

In the two weeks since Michelle's wedding I've been working on 'THE PROGRESSION OF LIZZY RICHARDSON' and looking up clubs in the area. Group activities that'll get me out of the house and meeting new people, but also developing a new skillset or reigniting a passion for an old hobby I've completely forgotten about. I've had to look further afield for some, as the village is pretty limited in its options, but not too far beyond the neighbouring villages as I want to keep it local. I've found a lot of churches or community clubs I could join and immerse myself in, but I don't think I'm looking to be that involved. I just want to find out who I'm meant to be whilst engaging in some fun activity. That shouldn't be too difficult a task.

The week before Christmas I find myself alone in the office at work. Stephanie has been called out to put up an old client's Christmas tree and make the rest of the house look festive. She's taken Pippa with her.

No one really thinks about redecorating at Christmas because the houses always look so magical and full of charm (and highly blinged up here in Essex), so it's dead in here. No phones ring, no emails pop up. As we've already put plans in action for a few properties to start their makeovers in early January, nothing much else can be done. For that reason, I'm looking back over my whittled-down list of possible hobbies and making notes.

I could join a choir. Absolutely! I also want to sing more so this could be a two bird, one stone situation. I've found a couple of different sorts of singing groups so far. There's obviously the one at church, but there's also an all-women a cappella ensemble who meet every Thursday night here in the village. It sounds great, but the thought of having no music to follow scares the life out of me. I know I can sing, but I need at least the bashing of a piano to bleat along to. It's the only way to ensure I remain in time and some sort of key! It won't be easy to become part of something like that, clearly. I'm sure there'd be auditions, identical to those in *Pitch Perfect*, but it might be worth investigating. Especially if it means meeting someone like Rebel Wilson – my ultimate female crush for so many hilarious reasons.

On the list there's bell-ringing of *The Hunchback of Notre Dame* variety, not the bells on a table sort (which is weird). Seeing as I hear them all day every day when I'm at home, and they go berserk at the weekends for weddings and services, I'm pretty intrigued to see how it all works. Only downside, I might have to be a member of the church to be allowed to take part. I don't think I'm going to find myself by turning to God, but this might be worth keeping in mind if other options fail me along the way.

Juggling is scribbled on my list, but I don't know why I've written this one down, to be honest, as I'm below average when it comes to throwing and catching a single ball as it is. This option is clearly my own version of running away to live with the circus. I'm pretty sure the circus wouldn't want me.

Cheerleading is written in capital letters, showing my enthusiasm for this particular idea. It's even followed by five exclamation marks. Basically I want to be in *Bring it On*, but I'm not in high school, college or America. Only a slight problem though as, after lots of Googling, I have found just one class for 'senior' participants (ouch) that is half an hour away. It's a drive but it could be worth it – as long as I don't have to be the one thrown in the air. I couldn't handle that, and neither could the ones catching me! Haaaa . . . maybe this one requires further thought.

I've written down 'starting a book club', but I know Connie won't read what I've suggested, so it would probably end up being just Mum and I having a chat. We swap books and do that already so there's no point faffing about with this one.

Then there's the local drama club that I was a part of as a kid. If I'm honest I think I'd cringe at this one now and am better off with the choir idea.

Karate could be fun, and it really would be a useful skill to have now that I'm single and mostly alone, with no one to protect me. Ever . . .

Fuck me, that's depressing. I don't want to feel weak and dependent. Karate is definitely a firm contender.

Aqua aerobics, tennis, badminton and gardening have been brainstormed next, but suddenly I'm not so keen. Purely for the fact they make me feel twenty years older than I am – and terribly British country bumpkin. That said, I have also thought about horse riding. It's something I did when I was five or six, but I've not been on a horse since. I loved it though.

For the completely absurd, I've written down 'Hula hooping club'. I don't even know if such a thing exists, but I can remember seeing some article a year or so ago about hoop love growing thanks to a contestant on *Britain's Got Talent*, so you never know. I'm not saying I'd be good at it, but I'd give it a go and I'm sure I'd have a laugh doing so if I ever managed to find a class.

I look back at my list and the scribbles I've just penned over it. I think joining a choir might be the best way to ease me in gently.

As I'm about to suck it up and email the a cappella choir, I remember an old school friend had posted something ages ago about starting some sort of singing group which seemed like fun. I've not seen anything pop up of hers for a while, so I imagine she's one of the lucky ones Facebook has decided to mute from my page. As soon as I type in her name and get directed to her account I find a post about not forgetting to bring sheet music to the next 'Sing it Proud' rehearsal.

I remember her well, Jodie Craig. She always seemed lovely. I mean, we never really hung out or anything as we were in different forms and our paths never truly crossed due to our friendship groups. In fact, I'd say I've found out more about her from a Facebook stalk after we left school at eighteen than I ever did when we were at school together. All I knew back then was that she smiled a lot, was always in the school shows (invariably the lead), and usually won the talent show. She was bubbly, fun, and didn't care what people thought of her. I might not be looking for a friendship to start up, but just remembering her passion and joy makes me want to get in touch.

I click on 'message' and type out a little note saying that I'm back in the village and wondering if there is space in the choir and if I have to audition or anything.

A few minutes later a reply pings through.

Oh, it's lovely to hear from you, Lizzy! My mum mentioned you were back so I thought I might bump into you at some point. We meet at the church (the one near the park, not the one your sister got married in) at seven PM every Wednesday night. There's no size limit and absolutely no need to audition. I'm not looking for the perfect choir (although I happily remember you can hold a tune very well). We want to spread the happiness singing can offer.

Tonight is our final session before Christmas. We won't be rehearsing but rather going straight in and running everything we can remember – there'll be lots of festive numbers and mulled wine in the break if I can locate enough flasks to get it there. There'll also be some mince pies from one of the members. Would you like to come in and watch to see if it's your sort of thing? It's really quite remarkable.

Oh, isn't she just a delight?! As I type out a message telling her that I'd love to go along, I feel excited about the prospect of meeting new people and doing something I used to love. The only difference is that this time I'll be doing it for the sheer joy factor, and not because I think I'm going to be the next big pop star (yes, I did once think that).

I text Connie.

I'm going to be in Jodie Craig's choir!

Three hours later she replies with a laughter emoji.

18

At precisely seven twenty-eight I walk into the church, figuring that if I were to arrive any earlier I'd have to make small talk with strangers or people I've not really spoken to in years. I know mingling with others is a huge reason for me taking on this new class (and the hope is that I might learn something about myself through their questions), but I want to just observe today without any pressure being added. They're singing, I'm listening. That's it.

While walking through the huge wooden doors, doors I haven't entered since primary school when we were made to come here for celebrations like the Harvest Festival, I steal a glance at the altar to see a bunch of roughly twenty people standing around in a semicircle next to a black grand piano. They're visibly waiting for the stragglers to join them while flicking through their sheet music, quietly singing lines to themselves and getting prepared. The stragglers are less focused on what they're about to do and are making the most of seeing their mates. Their bags have been dumped on chairs lining the right-hand side of the church behind where the congregation sit when it's particularly heaving, like at Christmas. They look like they're in no rush to get into their formation with the rest of the team.

Instead, they're perfectly happy cradling their cups of tea and having a gossip.

I fleetingly wonder where I would fit in here as I nervously slip in on the end of a pew right at the back of the church. I'm fiddling with a loose piece of thread from the end of my shirt.

I want to be here but I also want to be hidden. I don't want to make eye contact with anyone who might chuck a glance in my direction. Part of me wants to shrink away. Another part of me wants to actually leave. The feeling of being the new girl is intense and unlike anything I've experienced before.

I've been so comfortable with our cosy little life at home for so long that this feels totally wrong. This is not sitting down and hardly talking to my partner while we happily munch on (vanilla-powdered and coconut-oiled) popcorn and watch a Netflix series together. This is out of the house and conversing. I'm still in actual clothes past seven o'clock. I still have make-up and a bra on!

I bite the inside of my cheek to steady myself. I want to be here. I really do. I've never been one to suffer with social anxiety in the past, but I know this is the result of Ian and I shutting ourselves away and not venturing out to anywhere other than the gym. I don't know how to talk to people in a social capacity. I've forgotten how to be me.

I didn't realize trying out something new as an adult would be this tough! It's far more overwhelming than doing so as a kid. When I was twelve I'd have been straight up joining in without a care in the world. I don't understand how changing the way we interact with others can have such a lasting effect on how we might react in social situations, but it makes me angry that I've allowed myself to feel this way in a scenario I'd have previously thrived in. But it's the anticipation of the unknown. I don't know what's expected of me, even though I'm meant to be here just to watch.

'You made it!' Jodie says, cutting into my thoughts while sliding in next to me and placing an arm around my back. She's exactly as I remember her. Her blonde hair is still long and down to her waist, and her smile is just as big, warm and inviting. She's wearing a yellow t-shirt with 'Sing it Proud' printed across the front, along with some blue skinny jeans and white ballet pumps — the uniform of the group, although everyone is wearing t-shirts in different colours.

'I'm so glad you came,' she sings, her hand rubbing along my shoulders.

'Thanks for having me. It looks great,' I say, pursing my lips together sweetly, looking up at the people before me, seeing the individuals rather than the daunting group. The sight is comforting. It's such a collective bunch of men and women of all ages and sizes, all wearing the same happy and contented faces Jodie displays. It literally is a case of everyone being welcome. Clearly this makes it less *Pitch Perfect* than I'd hoped, but I'll reserve my judgement for now. I'm sure this lot can give some attitude when the song demands it.

I notice a few other people occupying the pews in front of me who also aren't wearing the Sing it Proud tees; some are on their own like me, others are little families or sitting in couples. They're possibly spectators too, seeing as it's the last rehearsal. Perhaps they're here to see what their loved ones have been getting up to while out of the house on a Wednesday.

'Like I said earlier,' Jodie continues, while still rubbing my shoulders. 'I'm happy for you to sit here and watch so you get the gist of what we do, but really it's all about fun. Song-wise it's a case of anything goes. As you'll see, we can do anything from Bieber to Disney, Little Mix to Stormzy.'

I laugh when she says that as my eye lands on a man who must be in his seventies, who isn't even the oldest in the group. He looks like your average elderly man, although there's something about the way he's standing, looking around the room with a cheeky expression on his face, that makes him look like quite a character. That said, I can't imagine him spitting out some rhymes Stormzy-style.

'Stormzy?' I repeat, wondering how I would even cope with doing something like that, never mind Grand-dad over there.

'OK, we keep him for the younger lot once a few others have gone home,' she laughs, leaning forward and smacking her thigh as though she's in a pantomime. 'My point is that anything is up for grabs. You hear a song you want us to do then bring it in and let's do it. We even do musical theatre stuff sometimes.'

'It all sounds great,' I say, mustering up a huge smile to hammer home my excitement. It does, but I just want to see them now.

'Proof's in the pudding,' she laughs, getting up. 'We can catch up some more in the break.'

'Fab.'

'OK, everyone. Places, please,' she says, clapping her hands together.

The sound booms around the church, the incredibly high ceilings causing an echo. I love churches. I mean, I might not venture into them aside from weddings, christenings and funerals, but I find something calming about them. I don't think I believe in God specifically. I'd agree that there is a greater being, but I think that's actually the spirit of the universe rather than one giant man looking down on us and casting judgement and doling out challenges, joy and punishments. I don't know what that classes me as, but I do know that I like being in here. Knowing that people congregate in this beautiful space and channel such love and devotion through their prayers leaves an atmosphere in the room that's enchanting. Not enough for me to convert or become devout, but enough for me to respect the sacramental aspect of faith.

The pianist starts playing as the stragglers become silent and join the more eager members of the group. All eyes are on Jodie as the assembled group begins to focus. She leads them through a warm-up, her arms waving around enthusiastically as they go up and down scales.

'Brilliant,' she praises, ending their finishing note with a twist of her hands. 'We'll end with all the festive numbers, of course. First though, seeing as this is the last session of the year, and we have an audience for once,' she sings, looking over her shoulder to me and the others sitting in front of me. 'Let's kick off with some of the favourites.'

A bubble of excited whispers spreads through the four rows.

'Let's start with Becky's favourite,' Jodie instructs.

'Ooh . . .' the happy group reply in chorus, the elation building as they flick through their folders to locate the right page, shuffling their weight from foot to foot, getting comfortable before giving their leader every ounce of their attention.

The piano plays a few notes individually but gives nothing more. Then Jodie's body bounces in front of them, leading them into the song. 'Ahhs' are sung out proudly, and even without the help of violins, I know exactly what the song is.

It's Elbow's 'One Day Like This', but not as I've ever heard or seen it before. My body sits up a little straighter at hearing the huge sound being created. It's wholesome, engaging, heartfelt and uplifting – and it's only the intro. The piano kicks in at the start of the verse as the choir break into the emotional lyrics, all harmonized and brilliant.

I'm smiling, literally grinning at them as they tell me to throw my curtains wide. Being here, watching them, it feels like I'm doing just that. And it's not perfect. It's full of quirks, personality and mistakes. I watch one lady, who's standing on the end in orange, unable to stop grinning as she does her 'bum, bum, bums' slightly out of time, an older guy at the back singing with so much gusto he almost falls from the step he's standing on, and there are questionable notes being sung out left, right and centre, but it's the feeling. The emotion. It's amazing. Electric.

I'm so happy I came.

How crazy that thirty seconds can make such a difference to how you feel towards something. I take in each warm expression before me, each lyric, ooh and aah, and let it fill me with a feeling of exhilaration.

I want to be here.

Never mind having one day like this a year. Just having one little moment like this, one that gives me hope that new beginnings are here. That's what I need.

Yes, it's a love song, of course it is. But love has many guises, one being self love. It's been rubbish lately. Life has been shit. My soul and heart have been crushed. But being here, watching them, hearing them . . .

I want to be in their team!

As the song comes to an end my body propels forwards, standing as my hands find themselves clapping so hard they almost ache. No one else joins me, and the eyes of the choir are on me as a result.

Surprisingly, I don't feel like a total tit as I sit down and get ready for the next number to start.

I'll be honest, on my way here I told myself that I didn't need to stay for the mulled wine or mince pies. I thought I could nip out beforehand to stop myself feeling awkward for gatecrashing their rehearsal. Yet here I am, with one hand holding a plastic cup filled with warm festive goodness, while the other shoves a whole pie in my gob.

'I remember you!' says Mr Higgins as he too shoves a whole mince pie in. I recognize him instantly. He used to run the pet shop at the far end of the village and I visited at least once a week to longingly pick up the hamsters and gerbils. He never once got shirty about the fact I never bought one. I think he felt sorry for kids like me whose parents wouldn't let them have pets.

'That's good,' I smile, brushing away loose crumbs from my top.

'You've not changed one bit! Did you leave for uni or something?'

'Yes, that's right. Sheffield,' I smile, touched that he remembers the details. 'Then I moved back down to Essex but bought a place in Chelmsford.'

'And now you're back here?'

'For now,' I nod. 'Staying back at Mum's.'

'Oh,' he says in surprise, his eyes widening at me. 'And why's that?'

'Ah. Erm,' I struggle, my mind not giving me the words to share what's happened with a near stranger. When things like this happen you instantly think everyone knows all the details straight away. This is meant to be the downside of social media, village life and gossiping, but at least it gets the news out there quickly so that you don't need to explain it to everyone you see. 'Just . . . you know,' I shrug, looking down to inspect my plastic cup.

'A man,' he rightly assumes.

'Yep,' I blink.

He purses his lips knowingly, looking down at his own drink. 'We're not all bastards. Just keep that in mind.'

After offloading his words of wisdom he winks at me, his green eyes sparkling in my direction.

'Thank you,' I smile.

'Whoever he is, he's clearly a fool. I wouldn't let a fine-looking thing like you slip by,' he says, a grin now appearing on his lips.

'Albie, I heard that, you rotten swine,' a woman of a similar age playfully reprimands as she bats his arm lovingly. I recognize her from the pet shop too.

'Nothing to see here,' he says, chuckling naughtily as he takes a mouthful of his drink.

'Honestly, sixty years of marriage and he's still seeing what else the world has to offer,' Susan Higgins says kindly to me, clearly not offended.

'Keeping my options open,' Albie laughs.

'I'm Susan, this is Albie,' Susan says, ignoring him completely.

'I know. I'm from here. I used to be in your shop all the time.'

'I knew I recognized your face. You're Linda's daughter!' she exclaims, looking happier than ever. 'Yes, I'm terribly sorry about what you've been going through,' she says, shaking her head as she remembers what she's heard. 'This one did the same to me, you know. Came running back two weeks later though, didn't you.'

'I said we're not all bastards,' he says, referring to our

previous conversation as he shrugs apologetically. 'I'm not one now.'

'It was a blip!' nods Susan.

'Quite,' says Albie, putting an arm lovingly around her waist. 'I wouldn't change it though. I think losing you made me realize how special you were.'

'You big softy,' she smiles.

Love wins.

Sometimes.

I find myself getting lost in the chatter. Before long I'm sitting again, the Christmas carols have been sung and I'm saying goodbye to everyone as I'm leaving with a bounce in my step.

Walking home I think about Jodie. All of the people in that church, doing something that clearly gave them a buzz and filled them with joy, were there because she decided to put a group together. How wonderful that she's able to do that for others. It must be so fulfilling for her. So satisfying.

I feel more like me than I have in months. Years. Thanks to such a positive experience even after being probed by Albie and Susan, I have no doubt that I'll be starting properly with the group in January. In fact, I decide to take my phone out of my pocket and message Jodie so straight away.

19

'You've joined Jodie Craig's choir?' Connie laughs the next afternoon.

I'm walking back from the station after work and thought I'd give her a buzz. She's been a bit shit lately at picking up her phone when I call so we've been relying on texts, but even they have been sporadic. It could be that I'm noticing how little we actually manage to speak now that my attention isn't focused on trying to be a domesticated goddess. Either way, I'm surprised when she actually answers with this statement, which she practically shouts down the phone.

'That's correct,' I say proudly, still thrilled with myself for doing something on my list. The buzz from last night is still humming away in my tummy and I'm excited about getting involved with Jodie's tribe of melodic excellence.

'This is exactly why I said for you to come stay with me,' Connie sighs, as though my life has taken a tragic turn for the worse – which is comical because it's basically already become as bad as it could get thanks to Ian's shunning of me as a bride, or having me in his life all together for that matter. 'You've been sucked back into village life,' she continues. 'I think it's already too late to save you . . . a fucking choir?'

'It was fun!' I admit, her horror at the thought of group singing putting a smile on my face. I do love it when she's like this – fiery and humorous.

'Fun? Oh babes! You're already in too deep,' she gasps. 'Oh shit – you're going to forever be singing in my face like you're in some godawful musical, aren't you!'

'Calm your boots,' I chuckle, turning off the busy high street and up towards Mum's. 'Anyway, my first rehearsal isn't until January because of the Christmas break. Oh my gosh, you should so come with me!' I blurt, before really thinking about it.

'What?'

'Come with me! Join the choir! Be a part of the singing tribe,' I say, feeling excited at the thought of us having a regular thing to do together. 'We've never joined a club.'

'Have you forgotten all we went through in Girl Guides? We worked incredibly hard to get as many badges as we could, as *quickly* as we could so that we could fill up that dreadful sash. You know what, I think the hard work paid off. I now know crap about nothing much,' she declares.

She might rubbish it now but I know how much we loved those weekly club sessions. Although we did disappear quite a bit to play Knock Down Ginger on the nearby houses – banging on doors as loudly as we could, then running away before getting caught by the owner. Come to think of it, I don't think Connie has always brought out the best side of me. But then, it could've been my idea. It's hard to remember who dragged who into what when we have so many years of friendship behind us.

'You know how to do some proper knots now,' I offer, remembering how we painstakingly studied a manual while sitting on the Christy Hall floor for hours on end, trying our hardest to wrap and loop as instructed in the hope we'd impress our leaders.

'When was the last time you had to do a sheet bend double knot?' she retorts.

'That sounds more like a sexual position than something you'd do with a bit of rope.'

'Pah!' she breathes, taken by surprise, having not heard me talk like this in quite a while. Funny, we used to talk about sex all the time, but when I was in a relationship and actually having it (well, at least at the start when we were like two hungry sex pests), it felt wrong to share the intimate details.

'Is this what I've got to look forward to now that I'm a spinster? Someone sheet bend double knotting me?' I ask, making her laughter rise a notch further.

It's nice having that reaction from someone. I haven't felt funny for a long time – but looking back at the old me who left for uni, I was always in a huddle of laughing people. Laughter was once a big part of my life. How can you lose something as simple as laughter? I fail to believe my life had become void of a giggle, chuckle or cackle. Maybe I was too blind to see the truth that our love and enjoyment of one another was fading, that we were more miserable than happy.

'Come on, Con,' I beg. 'Come with me.'

'Have you heard me sing?' she sniggers.

'It doesn't matter,' I declare, remembering that Connie is probably the most tone-deaf person I've ever met. 'Jodie says anyone's welcome. Really, you should've seen some of the people last night. She's managed to pull in such a diverse bunch. She's amaz—'

'Jeez,' she says, stopping me. 'You used to talk about Ian non-stop. Then a few weeks ago all you were going on about was Natalia. And I imagine, now that she's gone quiet on you, all I'm going to hear about is Jodie. You fickle beast.'

'Oi!' I say, taken aback. I'm used to her taking the mickey out of everyone, but usually she's on my side – and she's never complained about me talking about Ian before so it hurts to think she might've thought I went on about him like an obsessed groupie, albeit one who actually got to keep the guy for a while. 'That's not fair.'

'Just an observation,' she mutters.

'You're making it sound like I flit around like an idiot. Leeching on to people who don't want me,' I tell her.

'I didn't say that.'

'You basically did,' I shrug, not willing to back down even if I know she probably didn't mean it in the way it sounded. The point is she's said it, and knowing Connie, that means she's felt it, but what am I meant to do when her diary is the busiest it's ever been? 'I can't just sit around and wait for you to have time for me, Con.'

'Babes,' she sighs. 'I don't expect you to.'

'What *have* you been doing?' I poke, lowering my voice as I pass an elderly couple, who are shuffling along while holding hands. I smile at them, and quicken my pace to move me out of earshot. I have a feeling this conversation with my best mate is about to turn ugly.

'Working on the book.'

'Just that?' I ask, perturbed that she has a bona fide, adult, her-life-is-on-course-for-greatness reason to be absent from my life. In the last six weeks, where I've done nothing but watch my tan fade, she has been achieving and reaching for the stars in a way S Club 7 would be proud of. 'Or have you been going on your little dates too? Because I have to say, you were there for me at the start of all this shit, because I left you with no choice, but you've been pretty shoddy since,' I hiss, suddenly angry at her – my whole face screwed up as I speak. I know I have felt this way, but it's still a surprise to me to hear the words spurt out of my mouth. Even as they spill down the phone line between us I'm aware of how unreasonable I'm being, but I can't stop. 'So where have you been? Whose bone have you been busy with, huh?'

'I have a boyfriend,' she replies matter-of-factly, rebuffing my childish remarks as though she hasn't even heard them.

The words stop me. Literally stop me in my tracks as I'm turning on to Mum's street. Telling me I'm a twat for being rude to her would've hurt less than this – and that makes me feel like a failure of a friend.

'Is it Mr Tinder? When did this happen?' I ask, trying to make my voice light and cheerful, attempting to do a complete U-turn.

'I haven't wanted to say anything because it felt like

an insensitive time to tell you,' she says softly, a tone she rarely uses, even with me.

'So now I'm single you're coupled up,' I say, my constricting throat making the words come out more like a squeak.

'It looks that way,' she says quietly.

'Wow . . .'

'It's early days still,' she offers, as though the thought of her also going through a break-up might console me. Clearly it doesn't. I don't want her to feel how I do. 'Who knows, I might be back on the boning market soon enough . . .' she continues, with a feeble laugh.

A silence invades, which is something that never usually happens with us on the phone. More often than not we're yapping away until one of us has to go or we get cut off when Connie hits the underground and runs out of signal. This uncomfortable void isn't like us at all, but then we've never been struck by these complex emotions. Even when Connie was footloose and fancy free in London while I was in Netflix and chill land with Ian, I never felt jealous of her. Maybe that's because she was always my single friend, who wasn't about to overtake me into marriage like the others. Maybe I was attracted to what I considered imperfections when compared to what I was striving for in life. But the world has shifted.

I shake my head, annoyed and ashamed at myself. My best friend has bagged a boyfriend. I should be nothing but thrilled for her. This isn't about me at all, and I'm an idiot for making it otherwise.

'Did you actually like the choir?' Connie asks after a while. 'You're not just saying it to wind me up?'

I'm not sure she's particularly bothered, to be honest, but it's her way of moving the conversation forward and away from the weirdness, and I have to credit her for that.

'Yes,' I say simply.

'I can imagine you in a choir.'

'They have t-shirts,' I say quietly, perching on Mum's brick wall with my back to the house, not wanting to go inside until I'm off the phone and have collected my sanity. 'You know, don't feel bad about not wanting to come with me.'

'I won't,' she laughs.

'I should've guessed that.'

'It's my idea of hell – but you'll love it. You're a great singer.'

'I'm not sure about that.'

'Remember "Girls Can Too"?' she asks, prompting a memory of us standing on the playing field as seven-year-olds, performing our very own version of Gina G's 'Ooh Aah . . . Just a Little Bit' to anyone who was interested. Occasionally the older boys would even stop what they were doing to come and watch. Not that we cared – they were gross, obviously.

'Our pop career was legendary,' I chuckle.

'Your voice was. I just did forward rolls next to you,' she says, and I can hear the smile in her voice.

'Or the occasional handstand.'

'While flashing everyone my knickers,' she laughs.

184

'You don't need me beside you flashing my undergarments, Lizzy.'

'When you put it like that . . .'

'Exactly, I don't think Jodie Craig would be impressed.'

'More fool her,' I smile, relieved that we're having this light-hearted banter. 'Plus we rehearse in a church.'

'Oh, churches hate me,' she declares regretfully, following it with a laugh. 'That would never work.'

'In all seriousness, though, I imagine it'll be good for me to have something that's mine. I need to start doing things on my own without relying on someone I know being there with me,' I say honestly, aware that I've gone from begging her to come with me to being relieved that she isn't. Because her words, no matter how pointed or flippant, do hit home one truth – I'm happiest when I have someone by my side, whether that be a best friend or a lover. I feel more content with Connie or Ian with me to plod through life together. In fact, ten years ago I literally left Connie, the mate I was inseparable from, to go to uni and have my first real solo experience, only to find myself fully immersed within days in another pairing with Ian. Perhaps breaking that pattern and actually taking time to be on my own in situations will be good for me, no matter how far out of my comfort zone I'm pushed.

'Yeah . . . exactly. You don't need me for this. You have it covered,' she encourages.

'I was thinking actually, what are you doing on Christmas Eve?' I ask. 'I thought we could do what we used to do and head into Chelmsford or something. Remember how much of a big deal the countdown was in Dukes? I mean it's a shame we can't go there – I still can't believe they got rid of it, but I'm sure there's somewhere else we could g—'

'I'm so sorry, Lizzy,' Connie butts in. 'I've made plans with Matt . . . I can get out of it. I'm sure—'

'No, no! It was just an idea. That's all,' I say quickly, sadness creeping up on me.

'I'm coming back to see Mum and Dad the next morning and have promised to stay for a few days. Why don't we hang then? You could even head back into town with me for New Year's,' she says, her voice jolly and hopeful.

'Eesh, I was planning on hibernating for that one. Pizza, duvet and bed by ten o'clock,' I share. I really don't want to celebrate the passing of time right now, not when I don't even recognize my life as my own.

'Babes, you love New Year's!'

'When the year ahead is full of hope . . .'

'It is!'

'For you!' I state.

'Lizzy, you're starting again,' she says, the soft tone returning. 'Surely the hope, promise and knowledge that anything could happen this year makes it more exciting than ever? Don't be sad about what wasn't. Look forward with excitement to what might happen! There are so many possibilities.'

'I'm just not where I thought I would be,' I sob, covering my mouth in a bid to stop myself. It's no use, the tears come fat and heavy and my breathing turns erratic as a result. 'Oh shit. Sorry, Con. I'm fine, I've just got to go.'

'Lizzy, wait!' she calls, but it's too late.

I'm already hanging up.

I sit on Mum's wall a little longer, trying to calm myself down. Eventually I wipe my eyes and take a deep breath, looking at my feet as the heels of my boots bash against the bricks behind them. The December sun has already faded and set, filling the street with darkness. I'm not quite ready for a night in front of the telly with Mum and Ted, so before going into the house I call my dad. He picks up instantly.

'Want to go for a run?' I ask straight away, before he's had a chance to say hello or ask me how I am.

'Now?' he practically chokes. Clearly he's been looking forward to this call ever since he missed out on my previous run.

'Yeah! You said you wanted to come along some time . . .'

'It's a bit late.'

'It's only six. Have you had dinner yet?'

'No . . .'

'Well then, we can grab something together after.'

He takes his time responding, which makes me wonder if he's trying to find a good excuse to get out of it.

'I'll be at yours in ten,' I say, before he can wrangle his way out of it.

'OK,' he sighs.

I rush inside to get ready.

20

I decide against going out on Christmas Eve. It was a nice idea when Connie was part of my nostalgic plan, but it quickly lost its appeal when she told me she was busy. Instead I go over to Dad's for a takeaway curry and then we walk up the high street to the church for one of the two services being given tonight – we didn't fancy the Midnight Mass. If I'm not going to be off my face in a club screaming a countdown before singing along to Slade, I'd rather be tucked up in bed hoping Santa's going to bring me something great down the chimney. What that is, I really don't know. A time machine? A lobotomy? I probably shouldn't even suggest that in jest . . .

We aren't a religious family even though I keep finding myself in places of worship lately. There's something incredibly welcoming, exciting and otherworldly about being there for the celebrations of Jesus's birth. I like the feeling of community it brings, and I really love singing along to the hymns and Christmas carols that never fail to transport me back to my childhood.

Dad walks me home afterwards, even though I'm in my late twenties and perfectly capable of escorting myself through a sleepy village that probably has a zero crime rate other than naughty adolescents stealing penny sweets from the newsagents. Although as some penny sweets are now ten pence a pop, I can understand their fury if their pocket money can't fill a white paper bag with sugary goodness.

The thought takes me back to shopping in Woolworths with Mum when we were younger. I'd go straight for the vanilla fudge and live in fear of Mum telling me to put stuff back when the cashier weighed it. Michelle used to go for foam-based sweets. Mushrooms, flumps – anything filled with air that meant she could have plenty of them. She'd then eat her collection as slowly as possible to wind me up, as I'd invariably have gobbled up my one piece of fudge in five seconds flat – like a Hoover gathering up dust.

'I know this has been a tough couple of months for you, Elizabeth,' Dad says, giving me a hug as we say goodbye. 'But I've really enjoyed having you here more. It's been nice.'

We're both wearing Father Christmas hats that a little girl was selling for a pound at the church. Dad's is far too small for him and he looks hilarious as he pulls the most sincere of faces.

'Thanks, Dad,' I smile, squeezing his arm.

'I liked Ian.'

'I know . . .'

'A lot,' he adds, nodding as his brows furrow seriously.

'Don't rub it in,' I smile, not entirely sure where he's going.

'He was all right,' he winks, placing his hand on my shoulder. 'But, what I mean – what I want to say, is that it's great having quality time with you. Just you. When your children grow up, move away, meet that special someone and create a place for themselves in the world, they become preoccupied with living their own lives. And that's what you want as a parent. You want your child to thrive in that way . . . but I've missed you.'

'Luckily for you I'm single, have somehow handed over the place I had of my own and am no longer thriving,' I tell him in a sarcastic manner that's strangely upbeat. Obviously I'm not feeling happy about the situation, but rather realize that humour is one of the only tools left at my disposal.

'I wouldn't say that,' he tries.

'I think it would be hard to convince me otherwise,' I admit, pursing my lips together.

'You're young,' my dad says. 'This isn't the end, Lizzy. It's the beginning of something new. Don't be scared of new. New can be wonderful.'

'How's the *new* that you left Mum for? Is that working out well for you?'

His intake of breath shocks me, as though the words I've blurted have become a physical punch that knocks him backwards.

'I didn't mean it like that,' I say, grabbing his elbow, cringing at myself for being so stupid.

Dad opens his mouth as if to say something, but stops himself, shaking his head.

'I'm sorry, Dad,' I whisper, feeling awful.

'I have nothing but love and respect for your mum,' he sighs, looking behind me to the house. Rather than disowning me on the spot, he pulls me in and kisses my forehead. 'One day I'll explain it . . . I'll see you in the morning.'

I feel shit watching him turn and leave. I realize I don't

know the details of their split, just that Mum was heart-broken and we were left to see that every day. I also know how incredibly lucky Michelle and I are to have divorced parents who actually like each other now. They don't simply tolerate each other at family gatherings when they're forced to be in each other's company. In a bizarre way they're more connected now than they ever were. Who the bugger am I to question something that seems to work so well for them? Especially as they've probably tried to get to this point in their friendship to make things easier for Michelle and me. It can't be easy dividing a family unit – no matter how old your children are.

'Dad!' I shout, running towards him.

He's rubbing at his eyes when I catch up, with his cheap Santa hat sodden in his hands.

'I love you. I love you so, so, so much,' I say, wrapping my arms around his broad shoulders and pulling him into me.

'I know you do, darling,' he sniffs, accepting the hug and returning one even tighter.

We stand holding each other for ages. I feel his body rise and fall with each breath and feel his heart beating through the thickness of his winter coat. The night is cold around us, but a warmth spreads through me as something between us stills.

It occurs to me that I'm not the only one who needs to feel loved.

God, I really do love him.

I squeeze him again.

21

When it comes to celebrating Christmas, I feel I have two options – embrace it wholeheartedly and enjoy spending time with my family (while not having to worry about sharing the day with Ian's clan), or sleep for the whole day and refuse to acknowledge it at all – it's another day that's targeted towards being with loved ones, highlighting my painful single status even more. As the latter is my plan for New Year's Eve, I've decided to make the most of having my family together with zero plans other than to watch trashy festive TV, eat enough food to feed the five thousand (which has started with a fry-up courtesy of Mum, even though I'm still full from last night's curry) and drink myself into oblivion. The first two plans are going well, but Mum raises an eyebrow at me when I attempt to add Baileys to my morning coffee. Champagne breakfasts are 'a thing' in a lot of households, so I fail to see how this is any different, but I decide against it anyway, smiling cheekily at Mum as I pop it back on the Christmas alcohol table.

Yes, we have a whole side table dedicated to booze at Christmas. Quite simply, if you're not feeling festive enough, downing some liquid Christmas spirit might help. That's the hope. And if not then there's always the table next to it, which is slightly bigger and holds all the snowflake-adorned, Santa-decorated, sparkle-encrusted snacks we could find in Budgens. These are essentially all the normal sugary crap we'd love to eat all year round but refrain from doing. However, the fact they're repackaged in all things Christmas, sprinkled with magnificent pine trees, twinkling stars and angelic angels, gives us permission to indulge. As Dad and I have been on a run (we only managed three miles and were ridiculously slow) we're feeling pretty smug about tucking in. We've announced we're going for a Boxing Day run tomorrow too, so that gives us extra self-righteous we-can-eat-what-we-like credits today.

While Mum bangs away in the kitchen there's no point asking her if she wants help, she prefers to be in there on her own – Michelle, Stu, Dad, Ted and I are all snuggled in the lounge watching *Home Alone*. I wanted to watch *The Holiday*, but no one else shared my desire, so instead we're watching a spoilt brat wreck the house of his neglectful parents while setting booby traps for the dumbest burglars in film history . . . it's blooming great!

Just as eight-year-old Kevin McCallister cuts the homemade zip-line, sending Harry and Marv crashing to the ground below, my phone vibrates with a text. Usually I send a chirpy message out to everyone I know on Christmas morning, even people I haven't seen in years. But the news about Ian and me has seeped out into the rumour mill, meaning I've been avoiding most people and tried to limit my time spent on social media, which has been full of pitying inbox words of wisdom, shock or sorrow.

I realize our *news* had to be shared at some point, but I'd rather have stuck my head in the sand for a bit longer. I wish I were like Liana Jarvis who three years ago declared her boyfriend had dumped her with some kick-ass Facebook status and a picture of her soaking up the sun in a gorgeous part of Ibiza. I can still remember the sight of her standing butt naked, with her back to camera, as she stood in front of the most amazing view in what, I can only assume, was a private villa. It was an empowering image. I can remember liking the photo and seeing everyone else's words of encouragement at her being such an inspirational woman.

I'm not Liana Jarvis.

I've never been that kickass.

That's not actually true, I realize. Eighteen-year-old me would be going one better than Liana Jarvis. She'd be partaking in some full-frontal nudity, with her arm playfully placed across her pert breasts, her sun-kissed, wavy beach hair blown over her face, with the biggest grin imaginable. The picture wouldn't tell a story about a girl who's being dignified, strong or defiant in the midst of a break-up, but rather one about a girl who's still living. One who's celebrating the fact that life goes on . . .

But that's not me now. The reality is that I'm lounging on the sofa in my Christmas pyjamas at two o'clock in the afternoon, nestled in my dad's armpit, having not messaged a single person I know.

No message of defiance or self-celebration from me. Just silence. And not because silence is golden, but because I have nothing to say. My life isn't a status update or a nicely filtered photo. It's real. I keep trying to pick myself up, to gee myself along, but it's a slow process. Every time I take a step forwards it feels like I take another one backwards, with grief, sadness or anger creeping up on me. I never expected a break-up to feel so much like a death. Ian has been ripped from my life, and that hurts.

I clench my jaw, annoyed that my ex is still such a huge part of my thought process. Over time his presence in my heart and brain will fade away. I know it will, but that thought doesn't comfort me right now. Not when I know he's probably been out with his old buddies enjoying the single life. They'll all be standing around at some undiscovered talent's gig while Ian's exchanging flirty glances with some fitness fanatic, heavily-tattooed rock-chick. He'll fleetingly think of his recent ex and wonder why he wasted so much of his life dating me when there were others out there more suitable.

Funny, when we were together people would occasionally drop in comments like, 'I don't know what he'd do without you,' or, 'Before you came along he didn't know his arse from his elbow,' blah, blah, blah. He clearly can now and he must be coping. He must be thriving. He's not tried to contact me other than to respond to that one text, so I doubt he's sitting at his mum's right now thinking about me. He won't be wondering how he's going to continue putting back together the fragmented pieces of his soul that have been so carelessly given away. Ian will just be getting on with it. But of course he will, he knew it was coming. And why on earth would he want to contact me anyway? He doesn't want me.

I sigh to myself as I pick up my phone, although my mood is lifted by seeing Natalia's name on the screen. It's been a couple of weeks since we last spoke, but she genuinely is an intriguing character who I'd love to see again. I just really clicked with her. Since the wedding we've messaged numerous times. I know that she has a love of Nutella (who doesn't?) but only allows herself to eat it on her Sunday-morning toast. She swims three times a week, after doing either a spinning or HIIT class. And she, like me, has amazingly close relationships with her parents. She knows all about my mission to find who I'm meant to be, and has been sending me hilarious groups to consider trying out. A couple of her suggestions are a laughter club and doga – which is basically yoga but with your dog sniffing at your crotch the whole time you're in downward dog pose. For once I'm really not sorry that I don't have a pooch.

I haven't heard from her for a while though – I did message her once I got home from the choir session the other night, but she didn't respond. So it means a lot that she's bothered to message today.

Merry Christmas to you and yours! I hope you're having a wonderful day filled with mulled wine, lots of turkey and a gigantic tub of Quality Street! Xx

OK, it's highly likely this is a round robin text, but she didn't have to include me in her list of recipients so I appreciate the gesture.

And Merry Christmas to you! Hope you're having a good one. Xx

She surprises me by messaging back instantly. I'm sure she has lots of other people contacting her who she knows better. Plus, I imagine her family are all getting ready for a Christmas Day walk. I've never understood how families fit it all in. A Boxing Day walk makes sense, but not on actual Christmas Day when Mum's having fun in the kitchen peeling and prepping enough potatoes, carrots and Brussels sprouts to ensure we have the leftovers as bubble and squeak for the next fortnight, there's trashy TV to watch, and two tables loaded with guilt-free alcohol and treats. But Natalia strikes me as someone who'd manage to pull on her Hunter boots and warm but trendy double-breasted khaki parka jacket from some swanky yet chic designer label, before heading out with her huge family while the Christmas dinner slowly cools in the oven.

I've been meaning to message you. It's been so manic with clients wanting me to magically transform their homes before Father fucking Christmas leaps down their chimney. Anyone would think this day was a last-minute plan and not the first date everyone pins in their diaries each year. Seriously, my fingers ache from the amount of bows I had to put on one tree yesterday. Now I just have to look forward to taking the whole thing down and working on what's left. This one client has redecorated his lounge every January. I'm talking complete overhaul of curtains, wallpaper, furniture, fixtures and fittings. Once the bows are gone he thinks the magic goes with it. Gosh, can't believe I'm messaging you about work on Christmas Day, but you know what it's like! Xx

I chuckle as I read it, knowing exactly how she feels. Pausing to think before I type.

Sounds like you need to get yourself an assistant . . .

I take a deep breath as I await a reply, wondering whether she's going to jump on the idea or think I'm a cheeky cow who's overstepped the mark after one drunken night on the dance floor together.

Tell me about it. Know anyone I should approach? Ha! Just out with the family – Mum's dog needs a serious walk. Let's talk in the New Year. I promise I won't go AWOL this time. Xx

Looking forward to it. Have a fab day. Xx

I type out my reply and press send before I allow myself to fully digest and revel in what she's said. She's thinking about hiring. This is a big deal. After we met I decided to Google Natalia and see what I could dig up. I didn't have to look very far and it turns out I've seen her work many times in magazines and online. After years of working for a huge company she decided to set up her own business and is now renowned in the London circle as the designer everyone longs to collaborate with. Not only that, but it turned out that I already followed her company on Instagram. She kept my hope alive that interiors should be about more than how many crystals and sequins you can fit on a lampshade or whether eight mirrors in one room is too much (it is!). Her work is insane.

I can't help but grin as I put my phone down. Merry Christmas to me, I smile, opting to treat myself to a little something from the drinks table after all. It's past mid-day now and I decide to spread the love (it'll ease any judgement from Mother) by pouring a little port for her, Ted, Michelle (just a centimetre) and Stuart, as well as a Guinness for Dad.

The drinks are received with gratitude, meaning I can hide my face in my glass and let my mouth give way to a huge smile. Another one.

'What you smiling for?' asks Happiness PC Michelle, always ready to sniff out a whiff of joy and stamp on it.

'Nothing,' I shrug.

'Is it too soon to do Christmas gifts?' Michelle grins, clapping her hands together excitedly like she did when she was a little girl, bouncing around at the foot of the tree. We used to open our presents as soon as we opened our eyes on Christmas morning, but over the years, thanks to hangovers setting in and us not always being together on Christmas Day due to the chore of having to see in-laws, the whole present thing has stirred up less and less enthusiasm. It's not that we're over the day – not at all. But rather we usually wait to open our presents at a more reasonable time. Not at six in the morning, or straight after people have walked in the door. One year Michelle was sitting on the porch step waiting for me to get back from a drunken Christmas Eve with Connie. She insisted on ripping paper off gifts before I was allowed to take my coat off or get rid of my rancid Tequila-shot breath. It wasn't a pleasant experience for anyone.

Nowadays we usually know what we're getting too, as we do a family secret Santa – one where we tell each other exactly what we want. Some might say it sucks the joy and fun out of the whole thing, but I have to say, it's brilliant opening a gift and finding something you completely love, or need. I haven't put in my request this year, though, as I haven't really been able to muster the enthusiasm.

'Mum!' Michelle shouts, straining her neck as she attempts to call around the door. Her big bump prevents her from moving more than a few inches in her seat. 'Mum!'

'What? What is it? Is the baby OK? Are you having contractions?' Mum breathes excitedly as she darts in, chopping knife still in hand, her mind instantly skipping to the thought of the best gift of all time arriving – her first grandchild.

'Can we open presents now?' Michelle pleads, her palms placed together as though she's praying.

'Mi-chelle!' Mum whispers, her face looking cross for the briefest of moments before looking at the gifts under the tree. She glances back to the kitchen, debating whether she has enough time between steaming (carrots), sautéing (Brussels) and roasting (everything else) tasks. 'Come on then. It's not like there's much,' she tuts, putting her knife precariously on the coffee table – an action she won't be able to do once her grandchild arrives. We've already been briefed on baby safety by Michelle, and blades at reachable heights was definitely mentioned along with the suggestion we all start drinking our teas and coffees at a lukewarm temperature to avoid any burns, and the placing of a coin jar by the front door. The idea is that we'll empty our pockets when we arrive so that no coins can roll out unknow-ingly and become a choking hazard.

Knowing Michelle, I imagine she'd do us a favour and kindly keep hold of our loose change, too. Unbur-dening us of our heavy money. She's thoughtful like that, my little sister.

'Lizzy first!' Michelle sings, elbowing Stuart in the ribs before giving him a firm push in the direction of the tree.

'Really?' I laugh, feeling dubious as to why she's so happy to be gifting, it's clear either she or Stuart are my secret Santa. She's never like this. The last few Christ-mas gifts have most definitely been recycled from work, no matter who she was buying for. The last time she was my Santa, she hadn't even removed the previous tag. Sally, who works alongside Michelle in the Council's accountancy department, had given her a hugely gener-ous gift box from Lush. I almost messaged her to say thank you myself! I mean, it was gorgeous, so I didn't grumble, but still, it would be nice to receive something from my sister that she actually bought with me in mind.

'I can't wait to see what this is,' sings Mum, looking as excited as Michelle. 'Your Santa had nothing to go on.'

'That's because I really didn't want anything,' I tell her, although I whole-heartedly agree that it was easy for me to be Mum's secret Santa as she'd even sent a link to her desired label-maker on Amazon. It arrived the next day without any fuss. All I had to do was wrap it.

'You just didn't know what you wanted,' says Michelle, giving me an over-exaggerated wink.

'Clearly not,' I frown, taking the rectangular-shaped box from Stuart, who can barely contain a grin himself.

'Open it then,' says Dad.

'I have a feeling this is going to be the best present of your life,' declares Michelle.

'It's that good?' asks Ted, tearing his eyes away from *Home Alone* to engage with the rest of us.

'*That* good!' beams Michelle.

She's even managed to get me excited.

Everyone is watching as I pull off the red ribbon and start ripping at the brown wrapping paper to find a black box inside inscribed with an aqua-coloured letter R. Whatever it is, it seems like a luxury item. I'm impressed with her. She's clearly gone above and beyond to be extra nice to me this year after my break-up, and I strongly suspect she's gone over our usual spending budget of fifty pounds to buy me something special to cheer me up.

One more tear of the paper causes my mouth to drop. As I read the snappy list of features down the side of the box I'm left in no doubt about what the gift is. Words like 'waterproof', 'silicone', 'quiet', 'ears', 'pulsing' and 'speeds' jump out at me and fill me with embarrassment. It's a vibrator. Michelle has given me a sodding vibrator, while we're sitting with our parents on Christmas Day. If the ground could swallow me up right now and send me all the way to Australia, that still wouldn't be far enough to shield me from this horror.

'What is it, love?' Mum asks, craning her neck to have a look, her fingers reaching out to touch it.

I instinctively hold it up against my chest and cover it up to stop her from seeing it.

'Michelle told us she'd got you a bestseller,' says Ted, his eyes squinting at the back of the box. I've no idea what's there, so I arrange my fingers and arms to hide whatever writing or pictures might be displayed. Please, God, say there are no pictures showing examples of use. The thought of them seeing it makes me go queasy, the whole Terry's Chocolate Orange I ate after breakfast threatening to reappear.

'It is an extremely popular gift for young, successful, driven, independent, kickarse women,' declares Michelle, nodding.

'Ooh!' coos Mum.

I can't even look at Mum, Dad and Ted who by now have enthusiastic, yet confused, grins on their faces. Stuart looks beside himself with mirth, and Michelle still looks delighted with herself.

'It's a multi-speed vibrating, waterproof, battery-operated, Rampant Rabbit,' Michelle states, her arms extending out as though she's delivering a punchline to a joke. Sadly it's not a joke and no one laughs. Instead, the room goes quiet, even little Macaulay Culkin seems to halt his *Home Alone* trickery to ensure the moment is at the peak of humiliating.

'Did you say . . .' starts Ted, a confused look appearing on his face. Oh, poor innocent Ted.

'Yes, a vibrator, Ted. To help Lizzy get her kicks, you know. Now she's single,' she continues matter-of-factly, as though my search for an orgasm has been at the top of my list of priorities since being flung back on the shelf. 'It's the best one on the market. It does everything. I even got it in your favourite colour,' she says, her eyebrows dancing in my direction.

'So thoughtful,' says Dad quietly. I can tell he's trying not to seem mortified.

'Careful, though,' Michelle warns, leaning into me as her face becomes very serious. 'Walls are thin here . . .' She then proceeds to make vibration sounds, her head wobbling about like she's a sodding latex willy.

I cover my face with my hands, utterly embarrassed that she's talking like this in front of Mum, Dad and Ted. I don't imagine any of them have even seen one of these until now.

'Anyway, it needs batteries. I've included them but you might need a little screwdriver to fit them. Dad, can you help? Ted?'

'Ye—'

'Of co—'

'No, no!' I shout, cutting off both men as they begin offering up their services and running the risk of taking our relationships somewhere I'd never want them to go. Covering up the box, I wedge it down the side of the sofa. 'I'll sort it later.'

'Right-o,' says Ted, his eyes still transfixed by the box.

We're all still camped around, unsure how to move past the thought of me using this green penis-shaped toy.

Michelle howls with laughter, she's loving how awkward we're all being about this. 'Make the most of it. Stu won't come near me and I can't even reach down there to sort myself out. I'm living in a nightmare of frustration.'

My face creases into a grimace, trying to block out the image of my heavily pregnant sister attempting to masturbate. Too late. It's there in all its awkwardness. Eurgh! And I mean 'eurgh' because that's my sister and my unborn niece or nephew she's trying to navigate her arm around, not because I think it's an act to be embarrassed of. I simply don't want to be thinking of her in that way. Also, she's *so* pregnant. It's no wonder Stu isn't too keen on the idea of 'banging' her in her current state.

I unscrew my face, hoping it's safe to do so, but I look over to see Michelle staring at me with a huge smirk on her face, fully aware of what images and thoughts she's placed in my head. Bitch.

'Do it for me,' she mouths, absentmindedly rubbing her bump as she says it.

I mean, there's not a doubt in my mind that I will be unboxing Ann Summers' finest as soon as I get some alone time, but I'm not going to be thinking of her while I do so!

I flipping hope not anyway.

Mum shuffles out of the room along with Ted, who's offering to carve the turkey, which we know is totally ahead of Mum's schedule. Meanwhile, Dad busies himself with a box of chocolates, taking an awfully long time to decide on the deliciousness of the hazelnut noisette Green Triangle – which is always his first choice.

'Thank you,' I mutter, while tapping the box, fully aware that my face is bright red.

'You. Are. Welcome!' she smiles back.

My phone bleeps again, and I'm grateful for the distraction. This time it's Connie.

The last time we talked was so weird and, rather surprisingly, we haven't spoken since. Seeing as I was a dick to Dad last night, I'm inclined to think I might be seriously at fault with the way I reacted to her news. If I were watching myself in a film I'd say I'm stereotypically pushing away those close to me to stop more pain occurring. Severing ties so they aren't in a position to hurt me further. For instance, when Connie runs off with Matt and becomes a hugely successful author.

I'm an absolute twat face.

I open Connie's message.

Merry Christmas, babes. I hope you know I love you to the moon and back. I don't think I tell you that enough, but you should know you're the Thelma to my Louise. There's no one else I'd rather leap over the edge with. Xxx

Regardless, I'm still not joining that choir.

Seriously.

And that's why we're best mates.

I thought today was going to be a challenge to get through, but two lovely texts, a glass of port and one vibrator in, and it's actually turned out to be a huge success. It feels nothing short of a Christmas miracle.

Michelle and Stu leave just after the *Doctor Who* special has ended, and Dad decides to take up their offer of a lift home. After a busy day, Mum and Ted fall asleep side by side on the sofa, leaving me to find companionship in the bottle of Baileys I tried to flirt with earlier. The smooth, creamy, punchy liquid goes down a little too easily, so I quickly pour another one, although this time doubling the quantity.

I sit in the kitchen of the house I grew up in. It's all pretty much the same as it was when we all lived here, which is probably why I still feel so at home here. I'm so lucky to have this place to come to, but it's time to sort out what I'm doing.

It's time to be a grown-up.

Merry Christmas! Hope you're having a good one. Can we meet up next week to talk about the flat? We haven't spoken at all since the last message and things haven't moved forward at all since as a result. I'm happy for you to buy me out, but if not we should sell it. The sooner it's all done, the better for both of us.

I press send and then go on to Facebook, having a little stalk of the people I've collected over the years, some of whom I haven't even interacted with since I first became 'friends' with them.

A mate from school, who's younger than me, has just got engaged after popping the ring under the Christmas tree. Another couple, Syd and Clara (the ones with the sloppy brown proposal), have posted a video of them telling their parents they're expecting a baby. Oh joy. I'm yet another step behind.

Half an hour passes in a blur of proposals, winter sun, ski slopes and Christmas magic and slowly the excitement and happiness of earlier wanes. The same Christmas disappointment falls on me, just as it has for at least the last six years. I've held an expectation, and a hope of marriage. The same ruddy hope that's caused my heart to be butchered. All caused by the man I loved. Love. I'm not sure which yet.

Every year was the same. In the lead-up I wondered whether *our* time was upon us. Wondered so much I'd snoop around the house like Sherlock Holmes, rattling every wrapped gift I could find, trying to identify its contents. I'm not too proud to admit I unpeeled the sellotape on one occasion. I was a woman possessed. I wanted to know if my desperation was about to stop. The Swarovski earrings might've been gorgeous, but they were no substitute for an actual ring. They weren't the diamonds I was after. Instead they stared back at me, mocking my hurt heart. I felt stupid as I wrapped the gift back up, of course I did. But I was glad to get that deflated feeling out of the way before Christmas Day arrived, because I knew I wouldn't get those as well as a ring.

I'm aware that marriage isn't everything. That it should never have identified me as a person, but it's hard to be that rational when you want something so badly. I wanted the traditional set-up – marriage then kids. Now I don't know when I'll ever get either. Or even, *if* I'll ever get either.

I feel the ache of my lost dreams as I see picture after picture of happy smily couples sitting around a Christmas tree, showing off baby scans or pictures of a newborn baby dressed as an elf. Sadness once again engulfs me.

I think you were wrong, and so was I. You were wrong for not believing in everything we've built over the years. I was wrong for thinking I'd failed us. That's not true. You failed us by not believing. We could've had a very happy life together and I'm devastated that you've tossed me and our unborn kids aside to try and find whatever it was you think is missing. I gave you my all. So much so that I don't know who I am any more. You were me and I was you. Do you get that? Do you look at the key bowl and think of me? Do you imagine talking to me on the phone or go to send me a message and then remember? Do you miss me like I miss you? Some days do you wish your memories would just disappear?

At the very second I press send a notification pops up with a message from Ian.

I'm on holiday next week

He's clearly sent it before my second message reaches his phone, but him sending one line of text (without even the decency of a full stop at the end) when I've tried to be diplomatic in my earlier text grates on me. And it seems he really is moving on with his life, as he's going away. I feel a fool for the emotional slop I've just sent him and annoyed at myself for going there after weeks of restraining myself from getting in touch.

Fuck you!!!!!

I type out the two words hastily, adding more punctuation than necessary to hammer home my point.

I switch off my phone and go to bed.

22

I wake up feeling shit, and not because I downed five glasses of Baileys and ate far too many pigs in blankets, Yorkshires and After Eights. It's deeper than that. I feel sad, as though everything has hit me all over again. It's crazy how a few little words pieced together in a careless manner can cause a huge shift in how one manages to cope.

I let out a groan and look around my room. The room that was mine throughout my childhood but has since been decorated to my mum's taste. After a few days of being back in here I decided to put up some old posters that I'd found in the cupboard to put my own stamp on it. One is of the actor Billy Buskin looking smoulderingly at the camera, the other is of the Spice Girls giving their best Girl Power signs while on the set for the 'Say You'll Be There' video shoot. They all look cool and badass. They made me chuckle when I put them back up, a throwback to some other time, but now their presence makes me feel childish. Some things should most definitely be left in the past where they belong. Take thongs, for instance. They've gone now. I gave them a good bash, but they aren't for me. It's a fact. I was constantly pulling them out of my crack, and yes, I know that's where they're meant to sit, but I felt like I was living with a permanent wedgie. The last straw was when I was walking around Budgens looking for rosemary. I could feel the material snuggling its way to where it wasn't welcome and so gave a tug at my trousers and underwear underneath while performing a little leg wiggle along with a mini squat. Only when I looked up, halfway through the action, did I notice the handsome man looking at me with disgust while holding a packet of Mr Kipling mince pies. I think Sisqó was wrong. Men don't like thongs – not the realities of them anyway.

Pondering on the thought of my undies, I reach for my phone and am surprised to find it's switched off. Then I remember and a feeling of dread creeps up on me, with humiliation not too far behind. I should never have messaged Ian, not on Christmas Day, and especially not when I'd been drinking. Yes, we have to sort out the flat, but nothing much is going to be done in the next week when everyone is closed.

I bash the phone against my forehead before turning it on, my heart sinking further as the Apple symbol shines into view.

I get an instant notification that I have four messages, all of which are from Ian.

Fuck!

I also have another text ping through to tell me I've missed three calls from him.

Double fuck!

I click on his name, my eyes squinting at the screen, partly because it's so bright and my head hurts, but also through fear of what those four messages might say.

Are you OK?

Lizzy, can you just message back and tell me if you're all right?

For fuck's sake, Liz! Your phone keeps going through to answerphone.

OK, I've just spoken to your mum after calling the house phone. She wasn't too pleased to hear from me, but I made her check on you. Turns out you're just asleep. You scared me, Liz. I didn't know what to think after your message.

This is shit, of course it is. The life we thought we were heading towards has vanished. I know that was my doing, but I hope one day you'll thank me for it. Maybe not actually thank me, I know I've hurt you too much for that, but you get the point. You deserve more than being married to someone who asked simply because they thought it was the right thing to do. I'll always regret not being in the place you needed me to be, but it was for the best.

I do think of you. The smallest of things make me think of a place we've visited together or a film we've watched on our sofa. I even sat through an episode of New Girl the other day. It was on and I didn't want to switch it over. It's weird that you're not a part of my life any more. That you aren't here with me. Maybe you're right and I should've had more belief in us. I just couldn't shake off my doubts and so acted the way I did. Perhaps if I'd have voiced what was going on in my head earlier things would be very different, but what good are 'what ifs' now? They're pointless and won't help us move on.

In my opinion we should sell the flat. I'd be happy for you to buy me out, but I'm guessing that's not what you want seeing as you left rather than kicking me out, and you're offering to sell your share rather than buying mine. This place is us. But we aren't here any more. It's time to start anew.

I'll ring around a couple of estate agents whenever they're open again and organize the whole thing. I'll try and make it as easy as possible for you, unless you want to get involved, of course.

Merry Christmas to you, Lizzy. Ian. Xxx

I scroll up to my last couple of messages to him and realize he thought I'd ended my life.

I guess they could be read in that fashion. Plus, people you would never expect to take their own lives do, so you never can be too sure. The last couple of months have been overwhelming. I've struggled. Even though I've tried to put on a brave face, I've found it difficult to accept that I could be rejected so easily. It's been saddening to think that someone I invested so much in could just decide they don't love me. It has made me wonder if I'm good enough, even if at times it might seem to others that I've moved on. I'm not sure there's a limit to how long grief lasts, but I know it'll soon feel easier to cope with. It already does occasionally . . . but I've never contemplated suicide in the times it hasn't. It's not a thought that's entered my head. It's been a horrible, scary time, but it is what it is. I have to ride the storm. I wonder if I've been doing as much as I could be, or if part of me has been holding myself back and keeping things safe.

I keep looking over at Ian's message. It's the most he's communicated with me since that night – or perhaps even before. We haven't been the best at sharing our feelings and, like Ian's written, if we had things could've been different.

I wonder how he felt last night, thinking the worst. If Mum hadn't picked up the phone, would he have driven over and bashed our door down? The thought sends a chill down my spine. I hadn't sent a cry for help, like so many others do. I'm not stronger than them, or less crippled by heartache – but I know there's a way through the fog. I can already sense myself wading through it.

> I'm so sorry I scared you. I was angry and turned my phone off.
>
> I just don't understand how we got here – but here we are.
>
> It would be great if you could sort out the initial listing with an agent. The flat was still looking in good shape when I left, so it should be camera-ready without causing too much of a hassle for you. I'll come empty my stuff once it's sold.
>
> Thank you. x

I've never hated Ian as much as I thought I did. It's hard to feel that way towards someone who's held your heart for so long. Now I just have to learn to fall out of love with him and help myself move further forward. Moving forward . . .

I get out of bed, my head banging as I go, and grab hold of a pen and the notepad I used to write poems about Henry Collard in, the one containing my lists of the various stages of my life, and decide to put pen to paper.

I don't blame you as much as you think,
Even though this whole situation stinks.
It's hard to believe we are at this point now,
We barely bickered, let alone rowed.

Or maybe we did and I've started to forget,
To stop myself becoming full of regret.
For all of the things I could've done or said,
To keep you happily in our bed.

You are a fool for letting us go,
I had big dreams for us, you know.
It was more than a wedding, or gloating to friends
I longed to be with you until the very end.

But now I'm me and you are you,
Living our lives as singletons do.
Without my sidekick by my side
And no one to kiss before sleeping beside.

One day I'll be happy, and you will be too,
This is a blip for us both to get through.
Please know that I loved you with all of my heart,
And that thoughts of you linger like a bad fart.

It's not my best work, but the last line tickles me.

I'd forgotten what a great emotional outlet poem-writing was. Feelings and thoughts having to be worded rhythmically so that they fit together like a nice little puzzle. It's creative and organizational all at once – like a mental HIIT class for the mind.

I close my notepad, grab my phone and go straight to the Facebook app. I never understood people who weren't on there, letting the world know what they're up to while making themselves available to anyone they've ever come into contact with. In fact, I'm always suspicious of anyone I meet, be it friends from school, colleagues, or clients, who doesn't have an account. It's as though they have something to hide. And that's saying something when I think of the people on my timeline who share the most senseless things: like the modern-day chainmail that'll render you sexless for the next seven years if you don't copy and paste it into your own status update within a minute of seeing it (the joke's on me here because I never did); the racist videos or political statuses that make you wonder why you even befriended a particular person in the first place. It's mostly a load of time-sapping drivel that leaves me disappointed with humanity or, as I've certainly experienced in the last few years, feeling like I'm failing in life thanks to my constant comparing.

For the first time I understand.

For the first time ever I realize I don't want this vortex in my life.

For the first time ever, I decide I want to get rid of it.

Part of it is a need for privacy and not feeling like my life is being used as entertainment for others, and the other factor is that I don't need to know what people from my past are up to. If we've not spoken in the ten years since we left school – and I mean *actually* spoken, not just liked each other's posts or written an obligatory Happy Birthday once a year – then we aren't friends. Not in the slightest.

Why would I want these people seeing private moments in my life? Why would they want to see them? And why would I want to see their special moments with other halves I've never met? I don't need to see Jenna Hearne's pictures of a bride and groom I don't even know – two more people who beat me to the altar.

No, thanks.

With complete clarity it dawns on me that another love affair has come to an abrupt end: my one with Facebook. It's neither of our faults, but we aren't doing each other any favours right now. I have nothing else to give: there will be no defiant posts about my break-up, no mysterious passive-aggressive quotes, or fake 'my life is great' pictures.

I go into my settings, enter my password for the last time and press deactivate.

I don't feel euphoric as a result. Just empty. At some point I know the lack of burden will make me feel lighter. That's something to look forward to.

I roll back under my duvet. I don't really fancy moving too far from here today. In fact, I don't particularly want to do anything but sleep.

I close my eyes to do just that.

23

'Oi, get up!' Dad laughs, banging on my door as he enters my room.

I groan at him, holding my covers even closer to my body in protest at being woken up.

'You said to be here for ten!'

I notice he's in his running gear and give another whimper.

'You'll feel good when we're out there,' he says, leaning over me and planting a kiss on my forehead.

'Who on earth told you that?' I croak. 'They're liars!'

'Come on. I'll go make you a quick coffee while you get dressed.'

I let out a yawn and rub at my face, taking a deep breath as my eyes land on my posters once again. They're the catalyst I need. Before getting into my running gear, I peel back the covers and take them down, folding them neatly and putting them back in my wardrobe with the rest of my belongings from the past.

I turn back to my bare wall and finally see the potential of it.

By the time I'm dressed, Dad's standing at the bottom of the stairs, holding out an espresso cup for me, and fifteen minutes later we're jogging up country lanes and I'm at the end of telling Dad about messaging Ian.

'It might not feel like it, but this is all good, Lizzy,' he encourages.

'I'm not so sure about that,' I puff, feeling the strain of holding a conversation while we keep up a steady pace. As difficult as it might be, the action keeps the words spilling from my mouth without the luxury of allowing myself to overthink what I'm saying. 'I imagine he'll start meeting women soon. Dating again.'

'That'll be tough,' Dad nods, knowingly.

'He's probably already started.'

'Maybe . . .' Dad sniffs.

I think about him and Mum. Even though he ended things with her, Ted has come into her life and filled whatever void he left behind. She's found a new love to share her life with. Dad hasn't met anyone since leaving her. Instead he has remained alone for the last fourteen years. I don't think he's even tried to find a companion.

'*You* should start dating, Dad,' I say, quickly glancing at him so that I don't misjudge my footing and trip. 'Find someone nice to spend your time with.'

I notice his eyes widen at my words, I've clearly caught him off guard.

'It's been a while, Dad, I know. And I'm sure, like me, you're going to find the whole thing daunting, but why not? You've got nothing to lose. You might actually love it,' I say, giving him the pep talk I'm sure he'll be turning back on me soon enough.

Instead of answering, Dad pushes forward, his long legs running stronger and quicker as he rushes ahead. He's so fast I find it difficult to catch up. It's as though some external force has a hand on his back and is pushing him along.

He continues running like this for what feels like an hour, but is probably only a minute or two. All the while I wheeze behind him, struggling to reach him. Eventually I spot Dad in the distance bending over, gripping hold of his knees.

'Dad?' I shout, laughing loudly as I get closer, even though the exertion has sent a searing pain across my chest. 'It's like you had a rocket up your whatsit. That caffeine has definitely kicked in.'

'Sorry, I . . .' he says, shaking his head as he turns away and looks at the view. Farmers' fields surround us, just rolling countryside for as far as the eye can see. A light frost covers the ground, making it glisten in the low winter sun. The bare trees stand tall and strong, defiant and proud in their nakedness.

I take a deep breath and soak it all up, enjoying the fact we've stopped.

'Fancy sitting for a bit?' Dad asks, walking to a wooden fence and cocking his leg over it so that he can perch comfortably. He gestures at the space beside him.

'Yeah, all right,' I say, with a shrug. We've not been doing this long, and I'm still happy to take a rest whenever I can. 'It's going to kill starting again now we're warmed up, but on your head be it!'

I join him on the fence, rubbing at my heaving chest, which has thankfully started to forgive me. The pain is subsiding.

Now we've stopped I'm aware of just how frosty it is.

I put my hands in my hoody pocket to warm them up and find an unopened cigarette packet. After my thong dance in front of the bemused handsome stranger in Budgens a few days ago, I decided to cross something else off my list of things to revisit. Smoking. I bought a packet of menthols and a lighter before bumping into one of Mum's neighbours on the way out, so didn't get the chance to light up. Instead I left them in my pocket and forgot about them until now. I instantly feel naughty, as though I'm a teenager hiding them from my dad before a night out with my mates.

'Elizabeth . . .'

Oh shit, I think to myself. He knows! He must've seen the packet sticking out of my pocket. I was always very good at hiding my social habit back in the day, but I'm out of practice.

'This is a really difficult conversation to have,' he says, taking a deep breath and turning to me, before fiddling with his hands.

Here it comes.

'I don't know where to start,' he wavers, shaking his head as worry and concern spread across his face. 'I've had this conversation so many times in my head, even practised it in the bathroom mirror.'

He's not about to start talking about the lung cancer provider sitting in my pocket; I've no idea what's going on. The frown he's wearing and the intense way he's talking scare me.

'What is it?' I ask, feeling for him as he struggles to voice whatever it is he wants to talk about.

'I've reworded it so many times, wanting to make sure I say everything clearly,' Dad says, finding it difficult to look me in the eye, even though I can tell he's trying to. 'The problem is I don't want to upset you. But it's me. It's who I am, and although it'll be a shock when I say it, please know that it doesn't change anything between us. I'm your dad, and being a dad to you and Michelle is the most important thing in the world to me. It always has been.'

'Dad?' I say, reaching across and holding his hand. 'It's OK. Whatever it is, it's fine.'

'I need to get it out,' he says, aggravated with his own hesitation.

'OK,' I nod, calmly encouraging him.

'I need to come out,' he explains, expelling a huge breath as he says it.

'Yep,' I agree, patiently waiting for more.

'Yes,' he says flatly.

'Go on then,' I prompt, wondering what on earth is eating him up so badly. I've never seen him like this before, so whatever it is clearly means a great deal to him.

'Lizzy, this is me coming out,' he says, his eyes meeting mine.

'Pardon?' I ask, my voice going up an octave. I'm not sure I'm hearing him correctly, or whether what he's saying means what I think it does.

'Out,' he repeats. 'I'm gay.'

I sit and stare at him, aware of his own eyes doing the same back at me, reading them for any emotion or sign of how I'm taking his news. News? Confession? Admission? The words that tell me my dad isn't quite the person I thought he was. The words that imply he's been living a lie my whole life.

'Are you sure?' I ask, my voice soft and low. 'You were married to a woman for almost two decades.'

'I was. Yes. Didn't turn out how I wanted it to though . . .'

It might be said as an attempt at a joke, but neither of us laughs. I'm too confused to even raise a smile, finding his words sadder than perhaps they're intended. My mind is like thick cement, or a computer that's gone into meltdown, with everything and nothing going on all at once.

Knowing he has to give me some more information, or some guidance on how to react to what he's saying, Dad takes a deep breath before opening his mouth – his words tumbling out with great feeling, worry and desperation. 'You have to know that I adore, respect and was absolutely in love with your mum for a very long time. I still love her dearly,' he pauses, looking up at me to hammer home his point. 'Lizzy, I knew who I was from when I was six years old, but I feared others wouldn't have accepted it. I was scared of what I felt, and was scared of being lonely, of being different and isolated. When I met your mum there was an instant attraction. I knew she'd make so much of me content, and I fell for her quickly. She was fun, and a huge carer. I felt safe with her in my life. Even though I was incredibly happy for the majority of our marriage, I knew something wasn't quite right. I was continuously dishonest with myself. Trying to tell myself that the thoughts I was having were just me being silly, or even normal for a person to ponder. As if a mind wondering longingly towards someone other than your mother, a man, was a normal thing to happen in a marriage. You can't control your thoughts, they simply flit freely, of course they do. I'd try to shut them away. I spent a long time doing that. I thought if I accepted the truth I'd be letting everyone down, letting myself down. I had to be crazy for even contemplating leaving what we had. We had a happy home. Things were great. But it got to the point where I couldn't live the lie I was living any longer.'

'So you divorced Mum?' I ask for clarity.

'That was the start of it,' he says sadly, his fingers tapping on the wooden plank we're sitting on. 'It was a rather tepid attempt at learning who I actually was . . . I told your mum. I couldn't go without giving her a proper explanation. I gathered it might help her to know that it wasn't anything she'd done, that there was something inside me that was crying out to be listened to,' he says, his hands on his heart.

'And it helped Mum?' I ask, already knowing the answer having witnessed her crumble.

'It made everything far worse to begin with,' Dad says thoughtfully. 'She felt duped. As though I'd conned her. I understood, of course I did. I'd ripped the rug from under her. I didn't know who I was, but I knew I'd never be who I could become, or even be truly happy if I didn't accept myself for everything that I am.' Tears spring to his eyes as he looks up at me, his face twisted in torment. He doesn't appear to have found comfort in coming to terms with his sexuality. Rather, he's caged himself in and isolated his life further by only lightening the load by half and somehow tripling it in the process.

'You've continued to live with the lie, Dad,' I tell him, squeezing hold of his hand while pulling him in closer. 'Why not tell us at the time and do everything at once so that we all knew what we were dealing with?'

'It wouldn't have changed anything and I needed time,' he shrugs, his head shaking at the thought. 'That would've been too much. I could never have left if I had to break your hearts too.'

'But our hearts were already broken, Dad,' I say honestly. 'We would've understood and would've benefitted from the truth.'

'You say that, but you don't know how you'd have dealt with it back then,' Dad frowns, brushing off the idea. 'You were teenagers, caught up in your own dramas of boys and exams. I needed to process it on my own.'

'I guess it doesn't matter now anyway,' I say, realizing that nothing can come from this thread of conversation. Dad decided not to tell me until now. Instead he's been trying to work things out on his own. It's admirable really, although strange to think there's a whole side of Dad's life that I know nothing about – even if Mum does.

'No wonder you all get on!' I think out loud, my thoughts turning to the way Ted is so welcoming of my dad and never seems threatened by the presence of my mum's ex-husband. I don't know many men or women who'd be so trusting and forgiving. I've pondered over how lucky I am in the past to have divorced parents who are still so close, and was always short with Ian if he questioned it at all. I know it's not normal to have divor-cees live in each other's pockets, but the truth is I didn't want to start poking around into the reasons behind their bond. They'd fixed their friendship after a turbulent few years and had got to the point where it worked. It meant we could all be together, and that's all I needed to know.

'It wasn't plain sailing. It took time . . .' Dad says, his teeth pulling on his bottom lip and turning it red as he looks out at the view in front of us. 'Your mum, once the shock had decreased and once she stopped loathing me – she came to me one night and really listened. It meant so much to me. Despite the big secret I'd been keeping, she knew everything else there was to know about me. There was no one better to hear about the part of me that made me complete, for she'd already seen all the other pieces and knew how I slotted together and functioned. It was so hard. She had no clue.'

'You're pretty good at playing it straight, Dad.'

He dips his head and gives a chuckle into his lap. A tear drops on to his grey Adidas jogging bottoms. He wipes it away and looks up at me. 'That's exactly how I'd describe it – playing at being something I'm not. I didn't know how to juggle these different sides of me and turn them into one whole human. Liz, I've wanted to tell you for a long time,' he says, his head turning to face me. 'I haven't liked you not knowing, but there's never been a right time.'

'I imagine there are no guidelines for coming out to your offspring,' I offer.

'No . . . although recently I've read some great blogs and articles about it.'

'You've been Googling it? Dad!' I gasp.

'I wanted to take care over how I told you.'

'But you know us better than some sodding writer you might've found online!' I tell him, hurt that he didn't see that.

'I was procrastinating,' he says, holding his hands up to calm me down. 'Looking for the perfect way was my excuse to prolong the inevitable.'

'What about Michelle? Does she know?'

'Well, yes,' he says, his lips pursing as his throat makes a grunting sound. 'There was an incident.'

'Oh God, she didn't catch you with a man, did she?' I gasp, my mind starting to picture what she might've seen, my eyes squinting shut to stop it.

'No. No. Not at all,' Dad says, looking embarrassed at what he rightly imagines I'm thinking, which makes me feel for him even more. 'There was an app, a dating one for . . . men like me. I was persuaded by a friend to put myself on it. One of Michelle's friends used the app and saw me on there. He didn't for one second think it was actually her dad. So he told Michelle someone was using a picture of me on a fake profile. She set up a fake profile of her own and arranged a date with the person so she could address the situation,' he tells me, his fingers rubbing along his forehead.

'Of course she did,' I say, feeling myself cringe for my poor dad.

'Needless to say it was quite a surprise when I walked in,' he says, glancing across at me.

'How did she take it?' I ask, thinking of my loud,

brash, self-absorbed sister and how she overreacts to most things in life. 'She inadvertently set a trap to drag our dad out of the closet. It can't have been pretty.'

Dad thinks for a minute, one side of his lips creeping upwards. 'She laughed.'

'Laughed?' I repeat, confused. 'Surely you're not talking about our Michelle!'

'She did,' he says, beaming at the memory. I can't imagine what it must be like to carry around such a weight and then to have a large portion of that worry taken away. That's clearly what Michelle gave him with her reaction that day. She gave Dad her blessing to be himself. 'It was the shock,' Dad offers, continuing to give his account.

'I can understand that,' I nod.

'She's been great about it.'

'Dad, what made you think my reaction would be any different to hers?' I ask, because although I'm happy that Michelle has helped Dad in the same way that Mum and Ted have, I'm sad he didn't come to me and let me be a part of this with him. 'Why didn't you trust me with your secret?' I ask.

'Lizzy, please forgive me for saying this,' he says, a frown reappearing. 'It wasn't about you at that time. I needed to find out who I was before I could start thinking about helping someone I love so deeply absorb my truth. Michelle found out when I wasn't quite ready for you two to know – but now. Now, I need you to see me for who I am.'

With those words my dad's handsome face caves. He tries to compose himself, to pull himself back together, but the emotional weight is written all over his face. It's etched in his wrinkles, in the tears in his eyes and the way his lower lip nervously wobbles.

'Dad! I've always seen you for exactly who you are,' I exclaim, my words coming out with a squeak. 'You're my dad. You've been my hero for as long as I can remember. A preference for men over women would never change the love I have for you.'

I reach to put my arm around his shoulders just as he does the same to me. We share an awkward hug while still perching on the wooden fence, both cold and clammy from the start of our jog.

'Hold on,' I say, breaking away from him. 'Is this why you've been running with me? So you can find the right moment to tell me?'

'One of your mum's ideas,' he says, looking embarrassed.

I chuckle as I pull him closer.

'Dad?'

'Yes?'

'I have a packet of cigarettes in my pocket . . . would you like one?'

Sitting there, feeling my insides burn as I inhale, the two of us giggling like teenagers, I look at my dad and am hit by our similarities. Not just the physical attributes, but also the fact he was forced to look at himself and assess whether he too was who he was meant to be.

His answer was no, and he's spent the last fourteen years learning to be happy with who he is.

What an inspirational man to call my dad.

24

Dad's revelation spurs me on. I know I have to stop looking back to the girl I once was and allow myself to discover the woman I am now. I also have to move away from comparing everything to my life with Ian and wondering whether each like or dislike was led by him. I have to move on from 'us' and find myself, focusing on 'I' instead. There's no more we, only me.

With New Year's around the corner I fight off the urge to write yet another list of things I need to change about myself. Instead, I grab my Spice Girls poster from the cupboard along with a pencil case filled with felt tip pens. I turn the poster over so that I can no longer see Baby, Scary, Ginger, Sporty and Posh, and start playing with my pens.

Half an hour later I've created a brand new poster. In turquoise and pink capital letters filled with patterns and doodling, I've written:

DO, DON'T DOUBT.
DO AND DISCOVER.
DO AND FEEL THE LOVE.
DO IT FOR YOU.

I get some Blu Tack and stick it on my wall, although this time I place it closer to my bed so that it's one of the first things I'll see each morning when I wake up, a little piece of inspiration to keep me going forwards. The only direction to go in life is forwards; staying put and pressing pause is simply not an option. The sooner I get that into my head, the better. It's so easy to fall backwards and wallow, but I'm not going to achieve anything that way. I need to strive forwards so that I can see life with clarity. Although my talk with Dad has made me realize that even those you think have life figured out actually don't. So maybe not knowing exactly who I am meant to be right now is fine, although it's my duty to myself to nurture and encourage the 'me I'm meant to be' to come out and not hide away. That starts by cancelling my self-pitying plans of staying in bed on New Year's Eve and actually putting myself out there so I can mingle with people in the way I used to love doing.

I've just got to hope people haven't already made plans I can't slot into. I felt so exhilarated after my session with Jodie Craig and the choir, but over Christmas I have felt myself slowly sink back into a darker place. Dad's honest chat has given me an extra boost to continue moving forwards and finding a life I enjoy.

First up, I message Connie.

Fuck it! My bed can wait. Let's go out on NYE! Bring Matt too. It'll be nice to get to know him better so that he doesn't think I'm a complete loser for the rest of time! I'm thinking London if we can find somewhere? Might ask Natalia . . . or is that too weird seeing as I want a job from her? I mean, we have already bonded over shots so it shouldn't hinder my chances . . . right? Xx

It doesn't take too long for her to reply.

London, hey? Sounds ace. Let me have a think about where. Ask her. She'll say no if she thinks there's a problem with blurring the employer/employee relationship. But everyone goes out with their bosses these days. I regularly get drunk with Trevor and tell him all the things he's doing wrong with the company. He doesn't mind as I have him dancing along to Abba by the end of most nights out. So yeah ... invite her. We're all humans after all! X

Part of the reason I asked Connie about Natalia is because I didn't want her feeling I'm bringing someone in to replace her, or that she's become my latest obsession. I haven't had to make new friends in years, and I'm feeling rusty and awkward as a result. I am also genuinely concerned that me asking her out is pushy, but something in my head is telling me to do it anyway. So my head and Connie propel me into messaging Natalia.

Me again! Hope you're having a nice break. Connie, her boyfriend and me were thinking about heading into London for NYE. Fancy it? We've no idea where yet. Xx

Short, simple, and to the point.

Break? I feel a nervous wreck. Like there's so much I should be doing but can't because everywhere is closed for Christmas. I should've booked to go away really. Next year you'll have to remind me. ;-) Listen, most of my mates have decided to do romantic New Year's and keep it quiet, so me and my mate Alastair have booked into this club. It could be horrendous,

but it might be fun. I know the owner so will sort a few extra
tickets. Xx

I message Connie before accepting.

Natalia has sorted a club but invited us along. Xx

We're there!! Xx

I'm exceptionally happy about spending time in a club
with mates, old and new, as it ticks one of the things I
wanted to do off of my list in the quest for self-discovery.
I wanted a big night out, and here it is. I used to have so
much fun clubbing, it's bizarre to realize I haven't set
foot in one in about seven years. Not since we returned
from uni, and even in Sheffield we'd decided that clubs
weren't really 'our' thing. In hindsight, I think I'd have
gone with it a bit longer if I'd had the chance and if Ian
had been into them too, but I was too busy playing at
being grown-ups.

The main concern now is what to wear. I've no idea
what is classed as acceptable in a London club on New
Year's Eve, but decide a trip into the loft is in order.

It doesn't take me long to locate what I'm looking
for – a suitcase of clothes I'd left at Mum's when I
returned after my first year. I almost put my back out
carrying it down from the hatch, but soon enough it's
resting on my floor and I'm unzipping it.

I'm greeted by a variety of very small clothes. Small as
in there's not much to them, but also in size. They just
look tiny in every sense. I hold up a corduroy cream mini
skirt and immediately screw up my face as I take it in. I

remember it well. It was from Morgan and I'd tried it on at least three times in one shopping session before I caved in and bought it. My hand delves into the suitcase and pulls out the items I used to team it with, brown leather cowboy boots and a tight brown long-sleeved top. I was definitely going for the legs-not-boobs look. The first night I wore this outfit out I felt the bee's knees, or 'the tits' as Connie and I used to call it. Literally, it was as though this outfit gave me the confidence to talk and flirt my way through the night. I can remember chatting to Nelson James, a guy four years above me who I'd always fancied, and feeling like I was sexy as hell. We snogged that night and I'm pretty sure it was down to the outfit I'm now holding in my hands.

Holding the skirt over my hips confirms that I'm definitely not as slight as I once was (congratulations to anyone who still is – but you don't get a medal for it or even discounted clothes for using less material!).

I quickly rummage through the rest of my clothes. There is an air of nostalgia over almost every item. I didn't have streams and streams of clothes, but rather wore each piece to death as I saved up for some more. Items are dated now though or just look thoroughly lived in. There's no real point in keeping any of it. All I'd be doing is storing it back up in the loft to have this moment of reminiscence all over again in another ten years. These clothes are not me, nor are they going to be. With that realization I begin throwing everything back in the case and zipping it up.

After dragging it down the stairs and hurling it into

the back of Mum's car, I take it to the dump. Once more I drag the weight up a flight of stairs which are sitting next to a huge metal container reserved for textile goods. Laying it on the narrow landing at the top, I open it and gather a bunch of my old clothes, before leaning over the side of the staircase and stretching my arms out over the container. Letting go and watching my clothes drop to the bottom feels therapeutic, as though I'm letting that part of me go as I slowly release them from my grasp. I repeat the action until there's nothing left, because I'm not trying to revive my eighteen-year-old self. Even if it were possible to relive that kiss with Nelson James, I have to look forwards.

Grabbing hold of my empty suitcase, I skip down towards the car, feeling lighter as I go.

'Lizzy!' I hear, just as I'm about to duck into the car.

I look up and spot Ian's mum Shirley. She looks nothing like him. She's tiny with cold green eyes and bright ginger hair, which is currently scrunched on top of her head. Her eyes are wide and, most telling, she has her hand over her mouth as though wishing to snatch back the moment in which she brought her presence to my attention.

I think about going over to give her a hug, we've always got on well, but her awkwardness tells me that it might not be the best idea. Instead I retract my leg and stand up straight, leaning on the car door.

'Merry Christmas,' I offer, giving her the biggest smile I can muster.

'Yes . . . I've been doing Mum's garden,' she says, gesturing to the canvas bags of garden waste in her hands with branches poking out. 'I'm a right mess. I'd come over there but I stink so—'

'Oh don't worry! I've got to go anyway . . .' I shrug. It's a lie as my only plans for the rest of the day are going to be spent roaming the winter sales online in the hope I can get some new clothes delivered asap. But she doesn't need to know that. 'I hope you have a lovely New Year!'

'Lizzy, wait,' she calls, the desperation in her voice stopping me from leaving.

I don't say anything as I look back towards her expectantly.

'He's a good boy. Always has been . . . I don't know what he thinks he's playing at. Really, I don't,' she looks at me regretfully and I find myself smiling back.

'Take care of yourself, Shirley. It's really lovely to see you.'

And it is.

Waving as I drive away I realize not everyone is looking at me and wondering what I did wrong in this situation. Some, like his own mother, are looking at Ian and wondering if he's having an early mid-life crisis. Hell, there are probably others who don't even care.

I know I shouldn't even worry what others think about a relationship they only viewed from the outside. It's only now that I realize I probably spent too long on social media adding lovely filters to photos and writing romantic captions underneath, wanting friends and family I rarely see to know exactly how perfect we were for each other. It was for their benefit rather than my own. Their adoring comments settled my insecurities and niggles. They restored my faith in my own relationship. But they can't do that now. Sadly, their shocked reactions to our break-up are occasionally harder to deal with than the split itself, and that's something I've really struggled with.

I've prised my focus away from them and thankfully shifted it on to myself. As a result I've started to realize that, quite frankly, my broken heart is none of their business anyway. It's mine to deal with alone.

25

I decide to head over to Connie's before travelling further into town with her and Matt, to where Natalia and her mate Alastair are meeting us. This means I've been able to dump my overnight bag and now only have to concentrate on walking in my heels. I simply don't understand it. I literally lived in them from the age of sixteen to nineteen – I even went to school in stilettos because I thought they looked classy (before Mr Whittle sent me home for being inappropriately dressed) – so why are my feet acting like I've put them in a torture chamber? Honestly, you'd think my feet have never even walked down a hill the way they're behaving. It might've been nice to look back and reacquaint myself with something else I did when I was eighteen years old, but I'm so glad I thought to put a pair of flats in my handbag too, because, I swear to God, they're going on as soon as I get drunk enough not to care what I look like.

Needless to say I didn't bother hunting for a new miniskirt in the shops. I think that ship has sailed. Instead I've opted to pair my heels with some pleather (go me – Ian hated them) leggings, a white and gold cami top and a black and gold sequinned blazer. Connie has found the whole thing hilarious as I have literally been messaging her outfit options since arranging to go out. I'm happy with the outcome, even if I did continue to send Connie crazy with my frantic calls and texts.

Connie has also gone for a black and gold theme, which is something we totally arranged. However, she's wearing a swishy black midi skirt, which has gold diagonal lines that cross over with horizontal ones to make triangles, along with a sheer black vest top and black heels with a dainty lace detail. She looks like she's just stepped off the set of *Sex and the City*.

'So, how have you been?' Matt asks as we make our way through Soho, which is louder and more joyous than normal with people spilling out of pubs and clubs even though it's absolutely freezing, all singing raucously or talking over each other obliviously. There's a buzz of excitement in the air, which is inescapable and contagious.

'Fine,' I shrug, not really knowing what to say. It's taking a huge amount of effort to remember Matt's name, thanks to me continuously referring to him as Mr Tinder in my mind. But whatever his name, he's even more handsome than I remember. He's ridiculously hot, especially in this casual suit look he's currently working. I'm not at all surprised that Connie's hung up her dating shoes and given him her full attention. I'd feel a dick for saying it out loud, but 'hubba hubba'! Seriously. On top of that though, he appears to be a really decent guy. Like, properly decent. Hurrah for Connie.

'Con mentioned you might be moving soon.'

'Well, selling up and hopefully finding somewhere new,' I say, surprised Connie has told him so. 'I don't know whether I'll be buying or renting yet though. All I know is I can't stay at home with my mum for ever more.'

'Maybe you can head into town like me!' Connie sings, linking her arms through both of ours so that we flank her. I'm grateful to be held up as my shoes are already hurting. Pretty as they might look, the heels are starting to rub and I know I'm going to be nursing a blister or two soon enough.

'Ha! Well, then I definitely won't be buying,' I say, just as we come to the back door of the club as Natalia instructed, having walked past the longest queue of people I've ever seen. Our private entrance is literally a plain grey door. It doesn't even have a sign. We come to a stop and ring the buzzer, all of us looking up and down the street to make sure we're in the right place. It looks more like a house than a popular nightspot.

'You might not be buying yet. But it won't be long,' Connie says coyly.

'It might be possible, you never know,' encourages Matt, with a frown. 'I'm happy to take a look if you like? I don't know if Connie's mentioned it, but I'm actually a mortgage broker.'

'I have,' Connie says proudly, stroking his arm.

'Thank you, but you really don't have to d—'

'Well, being up here would make sense for work, too,' Connie says, her face breaking into a grin.

'Where do you work?' Matt asks.

'Chelmsford!' I declare.

'Right . . .' he says, looking extremely confused.

'Not for much longer though,' Connie trills, her eyes

widening at me as the door before us opens to reveal a stocky male bouncer. He's wearing all black, but not the kind of suit like I'm used to seeing bouncers wearing. This looks comfortable, as though he'd be able to high-kick someone out of the building without causing his expensive Italian fine wool suit to tear. His face is stern, moody and fierce. Not one part of him acts as though he's pleased to see us. If anything, he's pissed off that we've arrived, as though we've disturbed his sleep, or taken a bite out of his dinner (no doubt boiled chicken and broccoli). Perhaps we've just interrupted an episode of *Breaking Bad* and he's eager to get back to it. Either way, we're all standing and staring.

'Names?' he yaps, his voice an octave higher than I imagined it to be. More like an excited Jack Russell than an intimidating husky.

'Lizzy Richardson, and this is Connie and Ma—'

'In,' he sharply barks, knocking his head to one side to hammer home his point.

We shuffle in; I even push Connie a little so we can do as he says quicker, and we stand in the small bright white corridor to await further instructions.

As soon as the door is shut behind us his face softens into something more welcoming, making me realize the gruff exterior might be partly to keep trouble at bay. Needless to say though, I'm still a bit wary.

'Cheers, mate,' Matt says, giving him a dazzling smile.

'Bet you're glad to be on the back tonight. It's chaos out there!' Connie adds, winning him over.

'I don't mind it, love,' he says. 'Right, what you want

to do is head up these stairs here,' he says, gesturing upwards. 'Up five flights and Jasmine will be waiting to take your coats. If you're really nice to her she might take you to your table. Have a good night, gang.'

'Thanks,' we all sing. I don't know about the other two but I'm feeling relieved not to be out front queuing in the cold. I would not have been a happy bunny. In fact, more than sixty seconds and I'd have been moaning about going somewhere else. Eighteen-year-old me could queue. Sixteen-year-old me would do anything to get into a club, including removing her trousers and exposing her bra. Twenty-eight-year-old me can't even look at a queue of bustling youngsters for too long without hankering after a comfy sofa and a pair of warm fluffy socks. Why though? It's not as if I'm that much older than them . . . it's not like I've become boring.

Fuck.

Let's face it, I usually go to bed at half past ten. The fact I'm out of the house and wearing clothes is amazing, the added bonus of having done my hair and having make-up on at this hour is nothing short of miraculous. I'm here and I'm happy, even if it is taking every ounce of determination to get my butt up the five flights of stairs in these sodding heels.

When we finally reach her, Jasmine is a delight. She's full of smiles as soon as she sees us scrambling our way towards her, while holding out her hand for our coats.

Beyond her I can hear the thumping of music along with lots of cheering. The party has well and truly started.

'Busy?' I ask her.

'Heaving!' she laughs, revealing an Irish accent. 'You guys should be OK in the VIP section, but even that's cosier than usual. It's seriously mental. You will have a grand night, like, but I'm glad to be up here. That's for sure.'

'You're not going to be cooped up here at the count-down though, are you?' asks Connie, looking bereft on her behalf.

Jasmine's eyebrows shoot up in excitement before she screws her face up and chuckles. 'I don't mean to tarnish your fun, but it's just one night. I've never been one to celebrate the passing of a year. Plus, we'll all have a good time later on, don't yous worry.'

She continues laughing to herself as she leads us through the black double doors behind her and down two flights of dimly lit stairs. The whole thing is very atmospheric with the décor of rich red walls and fila-ment bulb lighting leading the way. Once we've reached the bottom and are standing in front of a rather innocu-ous fire exit door, Jasmine turns to the three of us with a wry smile before pushing it open. A doppelganger of the first security guard greets us with the same suspi-cious frown as we enter the room. I merely glance in his direction because my attention is pulled by the sight in front of me and I'm aware that if I don't keep up with Jasmine we're going to get very lost.

There's so much going on in the circular space, which is made up of three levels. We enter at the middle level, which gives us a great view over the balcony of the dance floor, which is located underneath a huge glass dome – the sort I always associate with observatories. It's so dense with partygoers that the bodies seem to move in unison as they go up and down to the beat of the music, which is bass-heavy with a catchy tune from a female singer looping over the top. I don't know the song but it must be a hit as the majority of the crowd have their heads tilted back and their mouths open wide as they shout along to the lyrics. It looks like great fun as they let themselves go under the beautiful pinks, reds and purples of the lights shining and flashing from every direction.

Around the central beacon of delight that the dance floor brings is the rest of the craziness. The bars are bustling with activity. People flirt and chatter at the various booths that are scattered around the edges, while scantily dressed girls and guys are dishing out tequila shots. And there is a lot of nudity in the place. The barmen are topless, while the female staff are in outfits my eighteen-year-old self would approve of. Instead of your standard podium dancers placed around the dance floor to encourage people to let loose (as I remember from back in the day), poles have been placed sporadically around the room and are occupied by both male and female dancers, half a dozen of whom are twisting sticks of fire in the air. It's so unashamedly sexy, decadent and majestic.

I try my best not to gawp as I follow Jasmine up a staircase and into an area that's filled with beds. Not the freestanding variety, but shaggy-covered mattresses that have been sunken into heavily detailed carved oak frames that follow the curve of the balcony, giving an amazing view of the room. Pillows have been piled in the middle of each bed, and the guests cradle them in their arms or recline on them as they talk to their mates or attempt to make new ones.

'You're here!' I hear Natalia shouting as she lunges off one of the beds and comes towards us with her arms open wide. I'm so glad she looks happy to see us and that this isn't awkward. Obviously we had an amazing time at the wedding and have messaged a lot since, but we haven't actually talked properly or managed to meet up, so this could've fallen flat on its face. She looks prettier than I remembered. Her long hair has been curled to look beach-swept and she's had a fringe cut in. She's wearing a skirt like Connie, although hers is a midi-length tulle in mauve, which she's teamed with a white off-the-shoulder bodysuit and cute kitten heels. Her skin has an olive glow that I wish I could bottle up for my own use. She looks stunning.

As Natalia says hello to Connie and gets introduced to Matt my gaze falls on a guy who looks like he's made for the pages of *Vogue*, or maybe something a little more rough and ready than that. His long brown wavy hair has been pulled back into a knot on the top of his head. His chiselled cheekbones create a gorgeously sharp shadow on his face, as does the light stubble of his beard. His outfit of boots, skinny black jeans, a black tee and thin red bomber-style jacket complete his effortlessly stylish look. Yet it's the tattoos I see poking over the neckline that leave me feeling rather flustered. I have an instant desire to see what they are. I might be inclined to say that I've fallen into the realms of being a wanton sex pest mere minutes after walking into this debauched club, but it's more to do with him and an intriguing energy he gives off. He's captivating. I have no doubt that he is an actual Adonis, and feel my jaw slacken at the sight of him.

I might even be dribbling.

'I'm Alastair,' he grins, revealing a northern accent. His dark eyes shine as he jumps up, greeting me with a kiss on the cheek. An actual kiss on the cheek, and not a pathetic air kiss.

Jesus wept!

'Lizzy,' I manage to breathe, while displaying something I'm hoping resembles a smile. I'm never like this. Soppy around guys, or, dare I say it, 'girlie'. But then I've not been single around a man this hot for quite some time. Maybe ever. It was different when I was in a relationship. I was secure in who I was and the relationship I had, which meant I could chat confidently; now I'm questioning myself and wondering if it's just me who's swamped with unexplained desire. This is going to take some getting used to. 'Connie and Matthew,' I say, continuing with introductions while gesturing behind towards my mates, hoping they'll help me save myself from becoming a complete tit.

'I'll get some more drinks sent over now you're all here,' shouts Jasmine over the music, even though it's clear the bottles of what must be vodka and a variety of mixers that have been placed beside our bed are still full. 'Have a good night.'

'Happy New Year,' Connie, Matt and I shout over to her as she walks away.

'I'm so sorry,' Natalia giggles, grabbing hold of my arm while covering her face with her other hand. 'I'm so embarrassed. I didn't realize it was going to be like this. The client is one I've had for a couple of years and he's always asking me to come here. I've always declined – mostly because clubs aren't really my thing.'

'Well, look at what you've been missing out on,' I laugh, gesturing around me. 'It's basically the coolest sex shop I've ever been in, but with a dance floor and glitter ball thrown in.'

'Oh God! Have you been to the toilets yet?' she gasps, this time her hand covering her eyes as though wishing whatever she's seen to be unseen.

'No,' I chuckle.

'Don't . . .' she demands, looking aghast as she shakes her head.

'Mentally scarred,' Alastair jokes, while putting his arm around her and protectively squeezing her.

Natalia laughs at the gesture and bats him away. For a second or two they look at each other with such admiration that it makes me wonder if I've read this right.

I glance at Connie and spot she's noticed it too. She catches me looking at her and raises her eyebrows at me. I know what she's thinking without her thoughts needing to be verbalized. She might as well be making a circle with one hand while poking a finger from the other hand through it.

Sex.

They're having it.

Surely.

Natalia did say they were only mates, and that the other friends in their group had all coupled off, leaving the two of them single and hanging out a lot more. But maybe single means slightly more than that. Perhaps they've got a little 'friends with benefits' thing going on. I'm not one to judge – if I were Natalia I'd definitely be reaping all the benefits I possibly could from *this* relationship.

'Best get comfy,' Connie sings, kneeling as she climbs on to the bed and grabs a pillow.

The rest of us follow, with Matt sliding in next to Connie on one side of me and Natalia and Alastair on the other. I suddenly feel like the third wheel on a double date. Or maybe I'm the fifth wheel – the one that's usually left in the boot untouched and unused.

I'm so glad I didn't try and squeeze into one of my old miniskirts for tonight. I would've spent the whole night worrying about flashing my foof. Not that anyone would notice here when there's so much naked flesh on show.

'What on earth is that?' Connie points.

The rest of us swivel our heads in time to see a stainless steel sink, complete with tap, being carried towards us by three members of staff. Sparklers branch out of it, making the whole thing light up.

'Everything's in the Kitchen Sink,' one of the barmen beams, looking impressed with himself as pillows are moved and it's placed right in the centre of our bed.

'What's in it?' I ask, amazed at the sight before us.

'Two bottles of champagne, two of vodka, and whatever else I could fit in,' he laughs, handing out two-foot straws to each of us.

'Thank you,' Natalia smiles while they're walking away. As soon as they're out of earshot her head spins across, looking at me worryingly. 'I'm going to be shit-faced after this.'

'I'll be lying down asleep on this in no time,' I laugh, rubbing my hand along the comfortable mattress we're all sitting on.

'I'm sure that's completely what they're here for,' smirks Alastair, twiddling his straw between his fingertips.

'Really?' I smile.

'Shall we?' asks Matt, tapping his straw against the stainless steel sink.

Our heads gather together as we dive into the pink liquid as one. It might look questionable, but it's deliciously fruity and bubbly. I pause to give myself a quick warning, knowing that I'm likely to just down a whole litre, forgetting how much alcohol is in it. Pace is key. A marathon not a sprint. I go in for some more . . . it's New Year's Eve, after all.

'This could be the best thing I've ever tasted,' says Connie, who's finally come up for air.

I can't help but giggle. I giggle at the absurdity of everything in this room, and how vastly different it is to everything that was in my life up until two months ago. I giggle so much I find myself laying back on the mattress and staring up at the stunning architecture above us, comparing it to this time last year when we were playing Trivial Pursuit with Ian's extended family, and I was bored out of my brains. There, I admit it. There were times when I was unfulfilled and tired of being with Ian. It wasn't all rosy. We were flawed.

Life has changed, but life under this majestic dome of purples, pinks, blues and reds is wonderful. Seeing people dance, talk and flirt is thrilling. The way people touch, look at and taste each other sends shivers through me, making me remember a time from before when I was the horny minx doing the seducing. Being surrounded by this room full of unrestrained indulgence, and people simply living without a single care is amazing.

I feel good.

I feel free.

26

Soon after the sink appears, out comes the food, and I'm so glad it does. I didn't even realize I was hungry until the sensational aromas started wafting their way up my nostrils. Steamed edamame, duck spring rolls, chilli salt squid, some sort of tempura crab roll, Thai prawn crackers and chicken gyoza – it's all spread around us. I don't know about everyone else, but I don't feel like I ever want to leave this bed, even if I have been wedged in between two couples for the last hour.

Minus all the rude things that are clearly going on around us (I'm pretty sure I saw an actual willy appear on the bed next to us a little while ago before its owner and his 'assistant' disappeared), there's no doubt in my mind that this is what heaven must look like.

The thought is confirmed when Sexy Al (I won't be calling him that out loud) passes me a tray with duck spring rolls on.

'Thank you,' I say, opting for the second one in on the plate, as that one looks more loaded and meaty than the rest. There's no point eating like a sparrow in front of him in a bid to impress. I don't believe in that crap anyway and something is clearly going on with him and Natalia, so I wouldn't want to go there even if I did feel like now was the right time to 'jump back on the horse'.

Being with someone else isn't something I've actually allowed myself to think about, but I know there will come a time when I want to. The thought of someone else even seeing me naked or sharing that intimate connection is crippling and heartbreaking – because a large part of me is still wrongfully loyal to Ian and considers it cheating, even though it's clearly not. Ian knew my body, he knew what I liked and how a quick nibble on my ear could get me going. More than that, no one else has seen me completely naked since I was eighteen. I owned my body back then and felt so utterly comfortable in it. But I've not got the body I once did. The legs are still killer, but I'm not as pert and seamless as I used to be. I don't feel so secure about it. Perhaps it's an age thing, or perhaps I've been comfortably in a relationship for too long.

That said, I have needs and haven't transformed into a nun just yet! I should probably be looking around to see what other fish I can tackle once I get my mojo back. It's not quite resurfaced yet, but, rather strangely, being in this atmosphere is helping coax it out of its current hiding place. I feel a yearning brewing and I'm hoping that energy isn't going to be targeted at the beautiful, yet obviously unavailable, specimen in front of me.

'I hear you're going to start working with Nat,' he smiles, placing the plate between us.

Natalia's helping Connie find the infamous sex toilet and Matt has gone off to try and call his nan ahead of the countdown – which clearly makes him the world's most perfect man. This means Alastair and I are alone with all the food and a sink that's still two-thirds full.

'Nothing's official yet. It's just been said in passing,' I say, delighted to hear she's been discussing it, but trying to stop myself from smiling so that I don't seem too keen and desperate. It's impossible, so I let a grin appear before popping a duck roll in my mouth and trying not to make too much of a mess. I'm not one to be strict about not eating in bed (Ian hated crumbs anywhere near the sheets) but this feels like we're pushing that relaxed way of living to the extreme.

'She's feeling you out,' Alastair says, matter-of-factly, in what I've discovered is a Leeds accent.

'Really?'

'Definitely.'

'There's no need, I'd love to,' I admit. 'She seems great.'

'She is,' he nods slowly, leaning towards the sink with his straw.

'How long have you known each other?' I ask.

'Since uni,' he says, taking a sip before sitting back up. 'There's a big bunch of us that are still super tight. It's good for all of us to have that unit here in London -- it can be a lonely place.'

'Natalia said you guys see a lot of each other,' I say, remembering her talk about them at Michelle's wedding. The hope is that innocently asking about the whole group will eventually lead to him telling me more about them as a potential couple.

'Yes. We have a weekly pub quiz team,' he says proudly.

'No way! I don't think she told me that!' I laugh. 'I didn't even think they existed any more.'

'Are you kidding me,' he gasps, pretending to be offended before breaking into a cheeky smile. 'We're actually very good too. Well, not all the time, but we hit a winning streak occasionally – it depends if we're all there, or if babysitters don't turn up.'

'You have kids?' I ask, surprised.

'God, no,' he declares, as though the mere thought of it is pure madness.

'I see . . . Well, I think I'd be rubbish at a pub quiz,' I say, even though I don't think that's necessarily true – I have watched every episode of *Friends* at least ten times (and still find them funny), am pretty clued up with 90s pop culture and retro celeb-based facts (for instance I can tell you what Paul Nicholls went on to do once his character Joe Wicks left EastEnders, or why the amazing Beppe di Marco was forced to leave the Square) and, perhaps more impressively, I can remember the names of most common birds (my granddad used to quiz me). I could start sharing the ways in which I am a fountain of knowledge, but I've simply become distracted watching his lips move. Lip-reading is a necessity because of the volume of the thumping music around us, but I'm aware that I'm drawn to them much more than I should be. They have a natural pout, with his peachy-coloured upper lip protruding a tad more than his lower one.

'I won't invite you along then,' he smiles, winking at me.

'So how long have you and Natalia been . . .' I ask, unable to finish the sentence and kicking myself for even starting it. I blame the wink.

'Been . . . ?' he frowns, the corner of his lips finding something amusing.

I shrug, and give a coy smile. I'm not going to say it.

'You do not want to go in there!' Connie chuckles as she and Natalia bounce back on to the bed and sort out their skirts so that they're sitting comfortably. 'There are dicks everywhere. Literally, pictures of great big throbbing hard-ons plastered over every surface, even the toilet seats.'

'It can't be that bad!' I shout over the music, cackling at the horror on Natalia's face; it's clear she hasn't found her second run-in with the bathrooms any easier to cope with.

'I'd have preferred lady bits in there,' Connie says, having given it some thought.

'Really?' asks Alastair with a grin. 'Then you'd love the men's loos! Fanny galore.'

'You mean Pussy Galore?' I correct with a smirk.

'Did you know she was a lesbian?' Alastair tells me, breaking away from the main chat.

'Really? But doesn't the film end with them kissing?' I ask as a memory of them doing so springs into my mind. My mum and dad used to watch James Bond films all the time, especially at Christmas, but I never took much notice of them. Either I'd be playing with my gifts from Santa or I'd be whining at them to turn it over so that we could watch *Miracle on 34th Street* for the millionth time, or perhaps a *Top of the Pops* special. Whatever the case, I'd clearly missed this bit of info when watching whatever Bond Pussy was in.

'Bond *cured* her,' he says, raising his eyebrows at me. 'That was the point of it.'

'Shut up!' I gasp.

'Ian Fleming wrote about it in a letter to someone,' he informs. 'It was the fifties though. The world was full of judgemental, narrow-minded idiots.'

'How'd you find out about this?' I ask, squinting my eyes at him.

'From a pub quiz,' he grins, wiping his hands on a napkin. 'I know a little about a lot.'

'You're a walking encyclopedia. A condensed version,' I laugh.

'You should hear what I've discovered about how they used to cure hysteria,' he says, loud enough for me to be able to hear, before picking up an edamame pod and popping it into his mouth, expertly sucking out the beans.

I'm grateful he's not looking at me, but it's enough to know he's aware that I'm still looking at him.

I go to reply, but nothing comes out. Instead I feel my cheeks flush. I know about hysteria. I remember hearing some actor talk about it when promoting a film on the subject. At some point in history, women with emotional tendencies used to be 'treated' by having their genitals massaged. This led to them having explosive orgasms. The thought of Alastair 'talking' to me about the subject is enough to cause a stir in a place that hasn't been stirred in this manner for quite a while, which isn't that great seeing as he's secretly dating my hopefully soon-to-be boss.

'They should've chosen boobs,' I say with great gusto, turning my attention back to Connie and Natalia. 'They're inoffensive and fun.'

'Then they could team up with a breast cancer charity!' declares Natalia, her face excited. 'You know, a cool one like CoppaFeel!. Then they could promote people checking for lumps and bumps while they're in there.'

'I'd be up for assisting,' smiles Alastair, amused by our chat. 'I'm always up for copping a feel.'

'You're so helpful,' Natalia laughs, putting her hand on her chest as her face drops into something more serious. 'Darling, the way you'd put yourself out for others is just truly admirable.'

'I know,' he shrugs, as though taking one for the team is a tough job.

'Everyone loves to see a good pair of tits, babes,' nods Connie thoughtfully while placing her hands on top of her own. 'I just don't want to see a stiffie. I don't need a bright red, throbbing cock staring at me while I'm trying to pee. I don't think that's too much to ask. I mean, why do they have to look so angry all the time?'

I look over to see Alastair chuckling into a bit of salted squid. I give him a playful shove and watch him collapse on to the bed before rolling off it.

'Sorry!' I voice, rising to my knees and looking over the bedstand, worrying I've hurt him.

He laughs as he pings up into standing, and walks off. 'Toilet break.'

'He's about to be greeted with a whole lot of fanny,' says Connie, causing Natalia and I to crack up.

'Oh, it's so good to laugh!' Natalia shouts, clutching her heart.

'Have you forgotten how?' I giggle, a giddiness washing over me.

'I don't make enough time for it. If it's not scheduled in . . .'

'That's so shit!' cries out Connie.

'I know, I know,' she sings, putting her hands over her eyes as though she's ashamed of how her life has panned out. 'Alastair always tells me that my priorities are wrong. He's even started pulling my phone out of my hands when we're together.'

Together. Everything she's just said literally screams the fact that they are indeed in an actual relationship. I hate to admit it, but my heart sinks at the confirmation.

'You're far too successful for your own good!' chips in Connie.

'It's hard not to run with opportunities when they arise, and I want to make sure I'm giving each client my best. Plus, I know how lucky I am. God, I hate moaning,' she frowns before grabbing a straw and taking a long hard suck of alcohol. Yes, she's doing impeccably well and has a career most people long for, but she's also got a lot of responsibility on her shoulders as a result. Our clients aren't anywhere near the calibre of hers, but even I struggle with their demanding ways occasionally, and have to really be on my toes to ensure they're satisfied with what I'm doing. It must be a lot for Natalia to tackle on her own. No wonder she appears to be so weighed down by it all.

'Right. I wasn't going to go here tonight because we're out in a friends capacity and you might find it weird, but seeing as you've brought up work stuff, I'll say it.' I pause for dramatic effect and to make sure I phrase the next few words in the right way. 'Hire me. You need me!'

Natalia looks up from the sink and straight at me, one side of her mouth rising into a small smile.

'You do!' nods Connie, eagerly.

'I've told you I do,' says Natalia, her eyes shining at me. 'I just haven't wanted to push it.'

'No pushing required!' I laugh. 'I know the business and love your work. It would literally be my dream to be working with someone as talented as you!'

'So you would want to work with me?' she asks, looking surprised as my praise makes her blush.

I feel like I've already dropped more than enough hints for her to see that I'm deadly serious, but clearly not.

'Here we go – leave her alone!' heckles Alastair, grinning as he jumps back on to the bed with ease.

'Shut it, stud muffin,' howls Connie, chucking a piece of food in his direction, before looking back at Natalia and me, her eyes narrowing so she can see us properly.

'Of course I do!' I say, turning my attention back to Natalia.

'I've given this a lot of thought,' she replies firmly, suddenly becoming less playful as she allows herself to go into work mode for a moment. 'I need someone to work with me. I don't mean a PA. I mean someone to take on the projects I can't do, or at least help manage the workload together. He's right,' she says, her head tilting at Alastair. 'Life's too short to be glued to my phone every second of the day.'

'That's what you're saying now, but you're forgetting about your control freak tendencies!' says Alastair.

Natalia takes a pillow from beside her and hits him with it.

'I need someone. I've looked you up and asked some of your clients for recommendations—'

'How?' I interrupt, confused.

'I did some digging, just like you have,' she shrugs nonchalantly. 'I know you're wonderful. Best of all, I know your talents are wasted where you are. You'll start falling out of love with interior design completely if you're not careful.'

'So you're actually giving me a job?' I say, my mouth dropping as I try to compute how easily this conversation has come about. I know she was thinking about it, but I thought I was going to have to jump through several more hoops that would see me hungrily elbowing other competitors out of the way.

'In theory!' she laughs. 'I have it all planned out to ask you properly next week but I'll email you an official proposal tomorrow.'

'New Year, new job!' shouts Connie, doing a little dance with her arms and head to show how excited she is. I love that she's here to witness this life-changing moment.

'Are you absolutely sure?' I ask.

'Read the details before deciding,' Natalia says, for the first time looking nervous over what I might say.

'I'd be bonkers to turn it down!' I say, even though

the sensible part of my brain is telling me to play it cool in case the pay is peanuts and not enough to cover my commute into town. Although will I still live out in Essex if I'm working in town? Or will I follow in Connie's footsteps, like she suggested earlier? What would I even be able to afford? There's so much to think about, and although I should probably be cautious, everything is telling me that this is the best thing that's happened to me in a long time. 'Who'd have thought I'd bagsy myself a job tonight!' I squeal, making Natalia laugh.

I sigh as the smile on my face grows even further.

Another part of life is about to change completely from where I was last year and this time there's something utterly wonderful about it. I suddenly can't wait for the New Year to arrive.

27

'Can we dance now?' Natalia asks, peering over the balcony to the crowd below who are bouncing up and down to Rihanna's 'This is What You Came For'.

'Yes!' shouts Alastair, jumping off the bed in one swift move, reaching out an arm for her. 'Coming?'

The three of us ladies climb off the bed in unison, giggling as we follow Alastair down two flights of stairs, grabbing Matt as we go, before passing more naked dancers and the sordid behaviour of people gyrating against walls, pillars and bannisters. Couples sucking each other's faces off for the last time this year. We then squeeze our way on to the crowded dance floor that's packed so tightly we're forced to part.

We're completely immersed with strangers. The bodies around me are sweaty, hot and barely dressed. Although part of me would like to run away in disgust, another part of me remembers a time when this was my life. Feeling the beat thump its way into my chest and shaking my body around in a way that I certainly didn't do at my sister's wedding with my parents and elderly Nan watching. Feeling alive in a completely different way. Feeling sexy, desirable and awake.

I feel less self-conscious than I imagine as I join in, moving my hips and waving my arms in the air. Despite all of the people gathered around me, no one is looking at what I'm up to. We're all one. All lost in the music.

I close my eyes and just feel, allowing myself to revel in the wonder the night has already brought with it.

Time passes but I can't stop, something inside tells me to keep going. I want to. I need to. My body is as sweaty as the next person's and I feel great for it. I feel like I could whip off my top and walk around in my bra, just like I did all those years ago. I stop myself from doing so, deciding that's one area of the list I don't need to revisit.

A familiar drumbeat kicks in over the current song, causing my mind to query whether it's what I think I'm hearing – but it is. 'Love Shack' blasts out of the speakers. This was the song that kicked off every night in Dukes back in Chelmsford and we'd go crazy for it. Wanting to share the moment with Connie, I open my eyes to find I'm no longer standing in the middle of the crowd, but have drifted over to the edge. Six feet in front of me is Alastair. He's not dancing or joining in with the rest of us, but is staring straight at me, causing me to stop in my tracks and look back.

His lustful expression sends a bolt right through me. Although it's quickly erased when he glances up to our dedicated area upstairs.

Natalia.

Just as I'm about to sigh to myself before jumping back into the music, two hands grab hold of me from behind and a body starts to grind its way into mine. I would think it was Connie if it weren't for the erect penis nudging me in the back. It's far from a pleasant experience so I instinctively jump away, off the dance floor and towards Alastair, who has just turned his attention back to me. I must look shocked or disturbed because the expression on his face is one of concern.

'You OK?' he asks, his face searching mine.

'Yeah.'

'What happened?' he prods, looking behind me and into the crowd and correctly guessing what's happened, his hand lightly resting on my arm protectively.

'Nothing!' I say far too quickly. The truth is, I'm fine. It just shocked me. I'd forgotten that side of club life when having my euphoric recalls. Good to know the perverts still linger. I'll be more prepared next time.

'Sure?' he asks, his dark eyes focusing back on mine.

'Where is everyone?' I ask, forcing myself to tear my eyes away from him.

'There you are!' shrieks Connie, bouncing over from the crowd with a beaming Matt close behind. 'Did you hear it? "Love Shack"?'

'Yes,' I laugh, loving that she was thinking of me in that moment too.

'Such a classic!' she grins, pulling me in and planting a kiss on my cheek. 'Where's Nat?'

'Oh, the boss turned up and wanted her to meet his wife,' Alastair says, again looking up to the top balcony. 'I'm going to the bar. I can't drink from that sink all night.'

'Beer?' suggests Matt, looking relieved that someone else has suggested it.

'Exactly.'

'I'm in,' Matt replies happily. 'Anyone want anything?'

'Yes!' I shout, feeling pleased with myself for remembering something else from the list. 'Archers! Archers and lemonade would be amazing. Thank you.'

'Well, hello to 2005,' Alastair laughs from beside me.

'I'll explain later,' I giggle, knowing how ridiculous it must sound.

'I look forward to it,' he smoulders, his lips twitching.

Argh, that face confuses me so much. I've not fancied someone like this in a decade, but I know I could ruin my chances of working with Natalia if she gets the faintest whiff of me lusting over her man.

As they walk off I turn to Connie to find her head cocked to one side and her eyebrows raised.

'Bugger off!' I shout.

She tilts her head back and lets out a booming laugh before grabbing my hand and pulling me back into the crowd for some more dancing. I don't resist and instantly start swinging my hips to a song that's telling me to move my body. I might not know the tune, but I happily oblige, this time staying with Connie and dancing together.

Just as we are perfecting the 'running man' move, a booming voice interrupts our flow.

'Ladies and gentlemen, this is your two-minute warning,' declares the DJ into his microphone while holding one hand to his headphone-covered ear to ensure he looks the part. 'We're about to welcome in the New Year!'

A flurry of activity ensues as half the people on the dance floor scurry away, dodging their way through the crowd to find the people they arrived with.

Connie and I stay close together. We're clasping hands as though we're pulling each other out of a horrific event, rather than being in a club and about to celebrate the arrival of yet another year.

Matt and Alastair are walking towards us by the time we're clear of the furore, both armed with drinks. Connie retrieves hers from Matt before flinging her arms around him and planting a kiss on his face. It's been absolutely years since I've seen her this affectionate with a guy; usually she's the one on the receiving end of PDAs and trying to shrug a boyfriend off or physically batting him away. It's lovely seeing her like this. She puts on this tough-nut front, but she's got so much softness to her really.

'Nat's not here still!' I say, turning to Alastair.

'She will be,' Alastair says, handing me my drink.

I take a sip and screw my face up at its sweetness.

'Is it all right?' Alastair laughs.

'Not quite as I remember.'

'What made you want to order it? Nostalgia?' he asks, looking genuinely interested. He's a listener. He's ridiculously hot and charming. He's taken. Taken by my soon-to-be boss. That's a line that's definitely not worth crossing.

'I have deep-rooted issues,' I say deadpan, stepping out of the way of a topless woman who's happily limping past with only one ridiculously high shoe on.

'You're not alone there,' Alastair comments, although I'm unsure whether he's referring to himself or the lady who's going to have a seriously sore leg in the morning from all the one-legged step-ups she's doing. 'Do you actually like New Year?' he asks, cupping one hand around his mouth to help me hear him as the noise in the room starts growing louder thanks to the excitement that's bubbling. I feel his warm breath on my bare shoulders and neck. Instinctively, I start to enjoy the sensation, then stop myself.

'When I was younger I did. I used to love it, I shout back, before thinking about when things must've changed for me. The last few New Years have been tough to swallow. Laden with possibility, hope and rejection. Each time the clock struck midnight and a new year began, I felt bruised and humiliated when a ring wasn't placed on my finger and I wasn't told I was starting the most exciting year of my life. This year, I don't have that particular worry. There is no ring on the cards, and no expectation that the clock striking midnight is going to offer me anything more than what is already in front of me.

'I've begun to realize that the whole thing is just a massive anti-climax,' he says, his mouth even closer to my ear, causing the warmth to turn to heat.

'Only just?' I laugh.

'Not really. I've actually felt this way since the Millennium.'

'Because we didn't all blow up?' I smile.

'Those computers weren't meant to be able to cope with the jump from 1999 to 2000. But they did. That was that. Every New Year's since has felt a bit lacklustre,' he shrugs, screwing up his face.

'I imagine it's hard to top the possibility of imminent death.'

'You are so on my page,' he grins.

'However, Will Smith did release an album called *Willennium*, that was totally worth celebrating,' I note.

Alastair stifles a laugh. 'I still have it.'

'You don't!' I say, my jaw dropping.

'No, but it was worth saying for that look on your face.'

'We're nearly there, everyone,' the DJ shouts, holding his hands wide in the air as he drops a drumroll over 'Can't Stop the Feeling!' by Justin Timberlake that's currently being faded out.

The volume of the crowd dims as an air of expectancy drops; we're all waiting to be shown the way into the New Year and the official countdown. 'Are you ready?'

'Yes!' the crowd shouts in reply, us four included.

'Then here we go! Ten!'

The room all join in as one. Each face gaily looking ahead at the balding DJ who looks ten years too old for the clothes he's in. Yet everyone in the room is captivated by him as the numbers start to fall.

Fingers lightly touch my elbow. I feel Alastair's body lean in to say something, I cock my head so I can hear better.

'It's a shame for the moment to pass without an event,' he whispers.

'You can't beat the world ending.'

'True,' he says, a hand finding its way to the arch of my back.

'What about Natalia?' I say firmly, my body tensing.

Alastair chuckles softly.

'We're best mates. Nothing else.'

'Really?' I ask, feeling relieved that I'm allowed to let myself experience the desire that's building inside me, unable to stop myself hungrily looking at his incredible lips.

I have no time to question him further. The hand on my back moves to my side and gives a tug so that I spin on the spot, stopping when our faces meet. The action startles me.

'Happy New Year!' shouts the whole crowd, while shiny confetti, balloons and streamers fall from the ceiling and float around us, sparkling majestically as they go.

We just stand there looking at each other while the mayhem around us grows, our noses mere inches apart.

'I have been warned to stay away from you,' he admits, his lips so near I can almost taste them.

'Why?' I frown.

He purses his lips to stop himself from smiling, leaning forward so I can hear him. 'Natalia doesn't like me dating people she works with, went to school with or generally knows in any sort of capacity.'

'Why? Because you're such a rogue?' I ask, putting my hand on his shoulder.

'It's not something I'm proud of,' he says, pulling backwards so I can see the sorrowful expression on his face.

'You're a heartbreaker,' I state, the clumsy way I lean in causing our cheeks to brush.

'I don't mean to be. I just haven't found the right person yet.'

I pull back and look at him. Do I even care if he's a player? Do I care if he causes a wave of destruction wherever he goes? I don't think I'm the right girl for him either, but my body doesn't care. It wants to experience the thrill of him.

'I've just got out of a long-term relationship,' I state, finally able to say the words. 'My heart is already torn to pieces.'

'I'm sorry to hear that,' he says kindly.

'No, you're not.'

'I am,' he says, trying to drop the smile on his oh-so-perfect lips.

'Happy New Year, sexy Al,' I laugh, cupping his jaw in my hands and bringing his face around to meet mine. My lips are on his in an instant. They're unfamiliar as they kiss mine back; the action sends a bolt through me.

Alastair suddenly bumps forward as though he's been struck.

'I told you not to fucking go near her!' shouts Natalia with a face like thunder.

'Nat, this wasn't me,' Alastair says, his hands releasing me so he can hold them up in surrender.

'It was me,' I laugh, covering my face as it screws up in embarrassment. Truth is, I didn't know she'd be this mad seeing as they aren't together. But it turns out she really doesn't like Alastair fooling around with people she knows.

'He's a total cock,' Natalia tells me before frowning at Alastair.

'Thank you,' he replies, bowing his head at her.

'He has a real issue with commitment,' she continues, raising her eyebrows at him, as though he's daring her to continue. 'I can't even remember the last time he officially brought a girlfriend into our group.'

'I'm not looking to be anyone's girlfriend,' I state. 'Not interested at all.'

'She just thinks I'm fit,' says Alastair as though it's an innocent comment, although he knows as well as I do that it'll wind her up.

'He never calls afterwards,' Natalia declares.

'Then I won't bother giving him my number,' I shrug.

'Really?' asks Alastair, his voice squeaking.

I nod and turn back to Natalia.

'Have I mentioned he's a massive cock?'

'Who has a massive cock?' shouts Connie, breaking away from her clinch with Matt to hear some juicy gossip.

'No. I *am* one,' corrects Alastair. 'And she's my best mate, so she should know.'

'See?' Natalia asks me.

I look back at Alastair, as though I'm sizing him up.

'He's not about to break my heart.'

'Good.'

'I have a feeling she's more likely to crush mine.'

'Can I just . . .' butts in Connie, looking very serious as she hands a bewildered Matt her glass of Prosecco. 'As Lizzy's best friend I feel I should represent her case here. I can confirm that she's not after a boyfriend. In fact, she won't even need a man soon enough thanks to her sister's Christmas present,' she adds, her fingers going up to the side of her head to make rabbit ears.

'Argh,' I groan as Alastair tries to stifle a laugh.

'She just needs a bit of oil in those joints. Someone to ride—'

'Thank you! That's quite enough!' I tell her.

'Very informative,' nods Alastair, squeezing my waist.

'Glad I could help . . .' nods Connie. 'She just needs a fantastic, out-of-this-world shag. Nothing else.'

'But I've got so much more to give . . .' he protests.

'Not necessary,' she interjects.

'Oh well, that's perfect then. As long as it's not going to affect us, I don't mind,' Natalia laughs, putting her glass to her mouth while waving her arm between the two of us. 'As you were.'

'Oh yay,' claps Connie.

'You're all crazy!' I scream, wondering how I got to the point in life where my best friend has had to negotiate the terms and conditions of sexual relations with someone else's best mate.

'Never a truer word spoken!' shouts Matt, who's been quietly observing the whole thing.

'Amen to that!' laughs Connie.

'Well, thanks for taking all the sexiness out of the hottest moment I've had this year,' I say. 'Now, let's get back on that dance floor! Now!'

I hold out my arm like I'm an army sergeant as I order them off to the square of enjoyment. Connie and Matt do so straight away, with Connie twirling under his arm as they go. Alastair and Natalia have a further stand-off first.

'Just don't hurt her. I need her,' she shouts, her finger waggling at him.

'He won't. I promise,' I say, taking her finger and pulling her with me as I turn and start shaking my hips to the music. 'Come on, you,' I shout at Alastair, smiling to myself as I see him following suit and catching me up.

'Hottest moment?' he says, his nose nuzzling by my ear.

'I said "this year". We're only a few minutes in,' I wink, giggling as I continue to lead us into the sweaty madness ahead.

28

'Where the fuck are you?' Michelle hisses down the phone.

'I've just handed in my notice,' I say, deciding not to add that Stephanie took my resignation so badly I've been forced into having an early lunch and am actually sitting on a bench by the river, in the freezing cold, scoffing down a Big Mac meal and half a dozen chicken nuggets – complete with a vanilla milkshake. Eating fast food is one thing, but actually eating 'in' McDonalds is quite the other. Order, leave, demolish, that's how I roll, and the only way I can avoid the guilt of eating it. Besides, despite the temperature, it's a beautiful winter's day with the sun shining brightly on the dark murky water, so it's been nice to sit and reflect on what has passed and what is about to start. Although Michelle's booming voice has put an end to that.

I've been over at her house a few times since New Year. We've been talking non-stop about Dad while stocking her freezer full of homemade meals in antici-pation of the birth. I say 'we' but really I've been doing most of the work while she puts her feet up and bosses me around. It's something she's very good at.

'Need something?' I ask.

'I'm in fucking labour.'

'Pardon? Now? The baby is coming right now?' I say, hastily shoving my empty wrappers into the brown paper bag and walking/skipping/tripping my way back up towards the high street. I won't be going back into work if that's the case. Michelle's only a few days before her due date, but I figured her baby would be just as stubborn as she is and would be at least a week late.

'Not right this second, you twat. I wouldn't be talking to you if a baby had its head out of my vag— Oh fuck,' she grunts, clearly holding her breath.

'You OK?' I ask, stopping in my tracks, while trying to breathe for her.

We've had a long time to prepare for and anticipate this moment, but hearing my sister having a contraction surprises me, making the whole situation more real. She's about to have a baby! I'm about to become an aunt!

'Am I going to be a good mum?' she asks when she starts breathing again, her voice now weepy and soft.

'The best,' I smile, wishing I could rub her back – although knowing I would not like to be in Stu's shoes right now. Michelle's difficult to deal with on a day-to-day basis; I can't even imagine how that'll escalate when she's passing a baby out of her lady garden.

'You would've been better,' she says sadly.

'Shut up,' I laugh, finding it ridiculous that she's comparing herself to me at this moment when she has far bigger things to be focusing on.

'It's true,' she says. 'You're the carer. You're more ready for this than I am. You're so together. That's why I hate you so much.'

'Michelle, don't be daft. I'm single and living in my childhood bedroom,' I remind her, sidestepping a bunch of schoolchildren who've congregated around a bench outside Debenhams to munch on their lunch, and puff on cigarettes at the same time.

'Very true. You fucked it all up,' she states, making us both laugh.

'I can't wait to see you as a mum,' I tell her, sincerely. 'You're the strong one.'

'I'm not,' she retorts.

It's true. I know she's not as strong as people think she is. I know she is the way she is as some sort of defence mechanism and that she would never truly want to hurt anyone, but she's still a force of determination and confidence. That's what makes her so great.

'Darling, out of everyone I know, there's no one else I'd rather have on my side in life; willing me on and supporting me. There's nothing you won't be able to tackle. Your little one is going to admire you so much. I'm sure they're going to look at you and think—'

'Elizabeth?' she interrupts.

'Yes?'

'Shut the fuck up.' I can hear the grin in her voice. It's not that she's ungrateful, but more that she's thankful that I've taken her out of her place of self-doubt and doesn't know how to respond.

'What do you need me to do?' I ask as I reach New London Road and anxiously wait to cross.

'You've already done it.'

'Is the midwife on her way? Is everything organized?'

I ask, wondering whether Stu has managed to fill the birthing pool in the lounge without causing it to flood.

'She's here.'

'OK. Well, I'll head home now.'

'It might be a while.'

'It's OK, I'll work from home today. Stephanie won't mind,' I say, although that's not technically true. I'm sure Stephanie would love to talk further about how she took a chance when she employed me, as I'd had no real experience. I'm sure she'd revel in repeating the fact she feels she's taught me all the tricks of the trade, so therefore I should be more loyal. I just think my sister having a baby is a great excuse to give us both some breathing space.

I haven't even told her about Natalia yet, I didn't think it was necessary this morning. I'm meeting Natalia in a fortnight (once she's back from a series of work trips in Milan, Dubai and Canada) to talk through the plan she sent over, but the offer alone has made me realize there are other opportunities that exist out of Home Comforts, and maybe, just maybe, staying in a job I've fallen out of love with is just the same as staying in a relationship purely because you're comfortable and don't want to rock the boat. If Ian could pull the rug from under both of us after ten years when our lives were so entwined, then I decided I could stop wasting my life in a job I get no real fulfilment from. Handing over that letter and uttering the words 'I'm really sorry, but I think it's time I moved on,' was a big step for me.

'So if you need anything, you know I'll only be just round the corner,' I tell Michelle, even though I know she's going to be in safe hands with Stu and the trained professionals.

'Just keep Mum there until I'm done,' she instructs. 'I know she means well, but I can't deal with her getting involved and offering around cups of tea like they're going to make the whole thing any easier. I don't want the faff.'

'If you insist,' I say.

'Don't say it like that, you're going to make me feel bad,' she grumbles.

'I didn't say it like anything!' I protest. We both know that if it were me in Michelle's shoes I'd be having Mum there with me, but we just have a different relationship. Not closer, just less intense than hers with Michelle. Mum winds Michelle up, whereas I love the fuss and effort.

A groan comes from the other end of the line as another contraction hits.

I wait for it to pass while I look around at shoppers going about their day-to-day life, completely unaware that a miracle is about to occur. I want to stop them and shout it in their faces, or maybe do a little song and dance number on the subject like we're in *La La Land*. Instead I nibble on my lip, smiling at the thought of what's to come, even though I'm aware of what Michelle is going to go through first. I'd say it's a small price to pay, but I don't think she'd be welcoming of my input right now.

She's wrong about me being more prepared or suited for motherhood, though. I might've agreed two months ago before we went to Dubai, but that's only because I yearned to be ready. It felt like the next step and the natural route for our lives to take, but now that path is way off in the distance after I achieve other goals that excite me. I know I'd like to reach motherhood at some point, but right now I'm happy watching her do it first. Plus, being second in this case takes the pressure off. It allows me insight into a world I've never seen before while preparing me for the reality of what'll hopefully happen to me one day.

'I'm going to head home and keep them all caged in,' I tell her, letting her know I'll take the task seriously so that she doesn't have to worry about Mum popping in and passing round an array of sandwiches. 'You just keep doing what you're doing. Breathe and enjoy.'

'Fuck off,' she replies with her usual air of affection.

'I hope it hurts like a mother fucker!' I state, my voice low.

'Bitch,' I hear, before the phone goes dead.

Now, obviously I hope my sister has a pain-free ride and that it all goes without a hitch and I know that she knows that too. But I also know my words will give her that extra bit of oomph to get through it. There's nothing like a bit of sibling rivalry to get you going.

It's not surprising that by the time I get home half an hour later, Mum, Dad and Ted are all sitting around the kitchen table with the home phone perched in the middle, alongside a pot of tea under a cosy and three open packets of biscuits. I imagine one thing that's really playing on Mum's mind right now is the fact that her selection of treats is part of the discarded leftovers from Christmas, and not specifically curated with this occasion in mind.

This isn't the time for a Rich Tea or Nice biscuit. It demands a Chocolate Hobnob, or Jammie Dodger, solid and dependable while multi-layered in their offerings.

'Are you literally going to be sitting around like this all day?'

'Until there's news, yes!' says Mum, not even tearing her eyes away from the cordless BT phone. It must be killing her not to be with Michelle right now.

I head upstairs to get changed into my comfies and when I come down ten minutes later they're still sitting in the same positions. The only sound coming from the room is either a rustle of a wrapper, the crunching of a biscuit, tea being poured from the pot or the slurping from their cups. If Michelle has a long labour, this is going to be tedious. I think I'd rather be with her where all the action is happening. No, that's not true at all. I'm safer here. We all are.

'Does this make you think back to when we arrived?' I ask Mum and Dad. I might as well start a conversation I'm going to enjoy hearing about.

'Oh, it does,' Mum smiles, looking up at me as she finally tears her eyes away from the phone. 'I was so nervous to meet you. I couldn't wait, obviously, but I was scared I wouldn't be enough. Your grandmother was amazing, and I didn't know if I could live up to that.'

It's funny how Mum's feelings of not being good enough echo Michelle's.

'You had nothing to be scared about though, did you,' Dad says, joining in while looking adoringly at Mum. 'You took to it like a duck to water straight away.'

'You say that, but then I used to escape to the loo and cry. Or I'd be feeding one of you in the middle of the night and sobbing all over you.'

'Why?' I ask, surprised by the confession when I've never known Mum to be anything but Wonder Woman and taking everything in her stride.

'All those hormones, I expect,' says Ted, taking Mum's hand and rubbing it with his own. I wonder what it must be like for him, never having had children of his own while Mum had this hugely significant part of her life that he didn't experience with her.

'Yes, it was that. But I also felt completely out of my depth. Everyone always told me I'd make a wonderful mother, and I completely agreed. Children loved me as much as I loved them. Having your own is a completely different situation though. You can't hand them back over at the end of the day and sleep. You can't slip to the shops on your own or have a bath without the worry of a baby waking from their nap and needing you.'

'It wasn't an easy time for you. Not with me working all the time,' Dad nods. 'You did it all on your own.'

'Most of it,' she agrees, picking up her teacup and cradling it in her hands. 'The guilt is the worst bit. Even now, I feel guilty for the fact that Michelle is about to endure childbirth, even though I had two wonderful labours with you girls. It's as though it's my fault that she's over there having to go through it.'

'You didn't force her into having a child, Mum.'

'You don't think so rationally when you're a mum. I don't anyway,' she says with a sniff.

'Do you wish you'd had kids?' I ask Ted, taking the focus off Mum.

'I used to,' he says thoughtfully, his forehead creasing. 'Sadly it never happened for me, but after I met your mum that void was filled. You and Michelle have been like daughters to me over the years, and that's more than enough for me.'

'Because we've been that awful?' I offer.

Ted laughs. 'I only got to know you girls from young adults and can honestly say you've been delights.'

'Slight stretch, but I'll take it,' I smile, tucking into the Rich Teas.

'That said,' he adds, 'I'm sure you were terrors when you were younger.'

'Michelle was!' I agree, nodding adamantly as memories of my little sister as a child flood into my thoughts. All the tantrums she screamed, the dinners she threw and the downstairs loo she managed to flood by blocking the sink with toilet paper. She really was a devious little thing when she wanted to be.

'Erm, you too!' adds Dad.

'That's not true,' I say, shaking my head at his muddled memory. Michelle was difficult, I was obedient and kind.

'It is,' laughs Mum. 'You could be just as bad as Michelle. Worse sometimes.'

'No! You're lying,' I gasp. I've always been good, that's why I get on with them both so well.

'It's true,' Mum says, rubbing my back while still laughing at my shock. 'You used to bite.'

'No!' says Ted, clearly as shocked as I am.

'Yes.'

'And you went through a phase of never letting us leave the house unless you were wearing green wellies and a pink tutu. Even in summer,' laughs Mum. 'Honestly, you'd throw the biggest wobbles if we said you couldn't.'

'You calmed down as soon as you met Connie,' says Dad, giving me a little nudge, as though I shouldn't worry about this hole in my childhood where I was evidently a madam.

'Well, not so much calmed down, but you had a bit more of a focus. You still had your moments, but your new friendship changed you.'

Interesting. If Connie and I ever fell out and decided to break up (I recently read in a magazine about 'friends' who've sat each other down to call off friendships due to having grown apart, or having a negative effect on each other) would I want to go back to before I met her and see who I was then? And find out the person I would've been if Connie wasn't in my life? Was I meant to be a green-wellied, pink tutu-wearing vampire? I'm guessing not. Actually, there is not one part of me that doubts the fact that the very foundations of my being and the core of who I am are largely down to knowing Connie – in exactly the same way that she is the Connie I know and love because she knew me.

People are meant to come into our lives and affect us. They're meant to challenge us and help us to grow. From the very first time you're cradled into your mother's bosom you're learning about human contact, love and devotion. Not every interaction will be quite as significant or powerful, but they'll push and pull you through life and help you grow and learn.

Ian was *always* going to change me. It was inevitable. Perhaps acknowledging that fact as a part of life is a huge leap towards accepting who I am today.

29

Michelle's living room looks like a bomb has been detonated in the centre of it and sent clothes, muslins, nappies, wipes and food wrappers flying everywhere. Empty mugs, cups and plates decorated with toast crumbs and splodges of honey have been stacked to one side of the coffee table in a bid to make some space, but they've failed to make their way into the kitchen. Books on labour, spare towels and a folded tarpaulin have been pushed into the corner of the room beside the sofa. They are no longer needed, but no one has found the time to find a home for them yet so this'll be a temporary holding until they're shoved into another tiny spot and forgotten about until (dare we say it) next time. Seeing as Michelle's house is usually spotless when she has visitors I'm surprised to find she's pretty calm about the disorder, especially when I can only imagine upstairs is even worse. But she doesn't even acknowledge it. Quite rightly, she doesn't care, and neither do I. Instead my attention is firmly on the miracle my sister spent nine months growing, who is now enjoying life 'on the outside'.

'I don't see what everyone makes such a fuss about,' she says, her hand down her top as she rubs a Vaseline-type substance on to her nipples. You think you see everything your sister can offer you, and there she is – giving you more.

'It didn't hurt?' I ask, tearing my eyes away from her massive boobs and focusing my attention on gorgeous and magical Duncan in my arms. My incredible little nephew, who I've already promised to spoil more than his mummy will probably let me.

He looks like me but with blond hair. Everyone's said it. I love that we're so similar and I'm sure it's deepened our bond.

This is the second time I've visited. We all came over first thing yesterday morning, as soon as Stu phoned to say baby Duncan had arrived. It was crowded and everyone kept hogging the baby, so I thought it would be best to come back today on my own so I can have uninterrupted cuddles while checking in on my little sister. For the most part she's seemed fairly upbeat so far, no baby blues here. Although she did cry when Stu said he was going to go down to the shops to get them some more milk and biscuits. You'd have thought he'd declared he was having an affair and leaving for Thailand the way she dissolved into tears. He didn't even flinch. Maybe he's found an even stronger sense of admiration for his strong wife now that she's pushed his son out of her nether regions.

'It was fine,' Michelle shrugs, wiping her hands on a tea towel before picking up her mug of tea for a slurp. 'I mean, it wasn't all sunshine, rainbows and unicorns – but it was, hands-down, the most amazing thing I've ever experienced.'

'You're joking?' I ask, having never heard childbirth

described in this way. It's usually portrayed as the most horrific event of all time. I've always thought it's a wonder why anyone does it more than once.

'Would you do it again?' I ask.

'Right now I'd say yes, but let's wait and see what the damage is to downstairs first. I did have a gander with a mirror earlier, not the easiest of tasks but I saw *it*. Very swollen,' she says, pulling a worried look in my direction. 'Stu might not want to come near me.'

'Michelle!' I choke, covering the baby's tiny ears.

'I'm only joking,' she says, leaning across while putting on a baby voice as she begins talking to Duncan. 'Mummy and Daddy will be back to bonking like rabbits soon enough.'

'Nice!'

'He'll have to put up with it if he wants a sibling or two,' she chuckles to herself, pulling a face at me before looking down at the newborn in my arms. The sight seeming to catch her off guard, she sighs and melts into the sofa, while her eyes soften as they fill with tears. 'He's so perfect.'

'He is. What do you wish for him?' I ask, enjoying seeing her in this gentler role. In all honesty, she's never been the most maternal person out there so I had worried about her natural instincts. This is probably what she was referring to on the phone during labour. But right now, sitting and watching her as she visibly pours love into her son from the other side of the sofa, it's clearly visible how much motherhood suits her. 'If you could grant him a wish, what would you ask for?' I repeat to the blank expression that's glaring at me.

'I feel like we're in a Disney film,' she says, screwing up her face in disgust. 'Are spinning wheels about to burn? Is he going to go live in a forest with three dippy fairies while harbouring a deep affection for wildlife? Should we tell him to be wary of poisonous apples?'

'Very funny,' I say, gently gliding my fingertip along his fine hair. 'And they were gifts in that film. Not wishes.'

'My Disney knowledge is not what it once was,' she mutters, taking another gulp of her drink.

I give Duncan a kiss on his tiny little forehead and start rocking, beginning to sing, 'Twinkle, twinkle, little st—'

'Nope,' interrupts Michelle, firmly. 'No!'

'No?'

'Can't you just be quiet for a bit?' she asks, exasperatedly. 'You keep bursting into song like you're Julie flipping Andrews.'

'Sorry,' I mutter, although I'm happy to acknowledge she's right. I have my first rehearsals with the choir tomorrow and am clearly excited as I keep musically erupting without even thinking.

A silence falls over us. There's no TV on for background noise, no music blaring out of the radio, just the sound of a clock ticking on the mantelpiece and Duncan breathing in and out contently. He's so beautiful. You often hear about the bond between a mother, father and their baby. I knew Michelle and Stuart would be in awe and love straight away, but I hadn't realized I'd get smacked with such all-consuming love too.

'Contentment,' Michelle says, taking me by surprise. It takes me a second to understand what she's talking about. The wish. 'That's all that matters,' she continues, moving along the sofa so that she's sitting next to me while looking directly at Duncan, as though she still can't believe that he's finally here. 'Money is pointless if all you ever want is more of it. A good job means nothing if you hate it. Life will always be a disappointment, no matter what you achieve, if you're longing for something else.'

'But dreams push you further,' I say, thinking of all the things I longed to do and be when I was younger and how they spurred me on to try things. The end of my relationship has given me another push, and I've loved rediscovering a thirst for new experiences.

'I'm not talking about not aspiring to achieve or settling for something that's less than you deserve,' Michelle explains. 'I don't want a lazy bum for a son. I just want him to look at his life every now and then and reflect on how lucky he is. He might never be the richest, the smartest or the most good-looking, but nothing comes from comparing. I want him to do things because he wants to do them, not because he feels like it's the right step to getting somewhere else. I hope he realizes that his life already contains some kind of wonderful and embraces it.'

'I'm sure he will,' I say, just as Duncan starts shifting in my arms, his mouth opening as he starts seeking out his next feed. 'You won't find anything in there, Mister!' I say, delicately passing him back to his mum. Having not held many babies in my life I'm clumsy and unsure, but Michelle seems confident and fearless.

'Come here, little man,' she says, unclipping her maternity bra and taking him to her boob. It's a fascinatingly intimate moment to witness, even if he is a noisy little chomper.

'Does it hurt?' I ask.

'Stings,' she admits, sucking in some air through her gritted teeth before visibly relaxing. 'Only at the start, luckily.'

'I guess that's something,' I say dubiously.

'One of my NCT friends has had a nightmare with it. Blisters, the lot.'

'Ouch,' I wince, as though my own nipples can feel her pain.

'Exactly. For me, this is simply not the sort of nipple action I'm used to, that's all. I'm all for a playful nibble or tug here and there, but this is something quite different,' she titters to herself before looking up at me, her eyes widening as though she's just remembered something important and can't wait to get it out. 'Mum says you've met someone!'

'What?' I say, laughing; this is not what I was expecting her to say. I thought she'd be talking more about her bruised and swollen fanny. 'How the bloody hell does she know?'

'Mum has ways,' she says, raising an eyebrow at me.

'Connie's mum!' I guess, knowing that Sue would've got the lowdown from her daughter straight away. I should be more surprised that it's taken this long to circulate and find its way back to me.

'You went home with him, apparently,' says Michelle,

unable to keep a smile from spreading across her face. I can tell she's desperate for details.

'I did,' I smile in return, thinking back to last week and how I didn't want the night to be over once the club had kicked us all out. I was on such a high I wanted it to keep going, so I jumped at the offer of going back to Alastair's even though Connie and Matt were heading home.

'And? Did you?' she asks, looking at me expectantly.

'A lady should never kiss and tell,' I state primly.

'I'm not talking to a lady, I'm talking to you,' she prods. 'And your reluctance to spill all speaks volumes, you big whore bag.'

'Actually. No. I didn't,' I say honestly. It's mean to stamp all over her hopes of some gossip and saucy behaviour when she clearly desires it so much, but I don't want an exaggerated version of the truth making its way back to Natalia via Stu and their mutual mates. That would be awful. I haven't even started my new job yet and don't want to annoy my new boss.

'Bit of oral?'

'No.'

'Hand job?'

'No!'

'Dry humping?' she pleads.

'No!' I shriek, laughing at the fact I've had to face the same line of questioning from Connie. She wouldn't accept the fact that nothing happened either. In fact I'm pretty sure she still doesn't believe me and instead thinks I'm just being coy about the whole thing.

'At least tell me there was a bit of fondling or nipple twitching,' Michelle begs, shaking her head at me with despair. 'He's a fucking Adonis. Please tell me you didn't miss your opportunity to let down that man bun and run your fingers through that gorgeous hair. Just the thought of his stubble nuzzling into my neck is enough for me to orgasm,' she smirks naughtily. Completely unfazed by the fact she has her newborn in hearing range and suckling on her breast.

'How do you know what he looks like?' I ask.

She gawps at me for a second or two. Her jaw drops, her eyes big and round as she realizes what she's said.

'Might've had a little Facebook stalk,' she shrugs, trying to bat the whole thing off in a totally unashamed way, although I see the tops of her cheeks reddening slightly.

I don't care. In fact, for the first time since deleting it, I wish I still had a Facebook account, purely because I too would love to perve over pictures of my non-shagging partner all day long. I debate asking Michelle to have a cheeky stalk now via her own account, but decide against it. Mostly because I know exactly how smug she'd be about it. 'This has to be a serious perk to Ian dumping you,' Michelle adds.

'Yes, I'm very grateful,' I say sarcastically.

'You were seriously punching above.'

'Thanks, sis.'

'So what did happen? I know you went to his place, so what went wrong? More importantly, what did *you* do wrong?'

'Flipping cheek!' I say, rolling my eyes at her before explaining. 'Yes, I went to his place, but we were with Natalia as well.'

'Weird,' she frowns.

'They're best mates.'

'She was cock-blocking,' she says bluntly, as though it's totally obvious.

'She'd just offered me a job.'

'She was still cock-blocking,' she repeats adamantly.

'I don't think so . . .' I say, thinking back to what happened when we got back to his trendy converted warehouse flat in East London. There was more alcohol offered around and a pizza was shared. It was a friendly gathering more than anything else. I didn't feel like Alastair was willing either of us to leave, and nor did Natalia seem pissed off that I was there. We simply weren't ready for the night to end. 'I wouldn't have slept with him that night even if we were alone anyway.'

Michelle laughs so loudly Duncan scrunches into a little ball. She places her hand on him for reassurance and soon enough he's going at it again, although she can't control her giggles.

'What?' I demand.

'Of course you would have shagged him, that's just what you're telling yourself to make you feel better about it not happening. Or to make you think you're a better human than you actually are,' she says, tapping my arm and pointing at the biscuit packet beside me, silently instructing me to pass it over. She continues as I do so. 'I'm sure you'd like to think you're prim and proper and a real credit to Mum and Dad, but if you were being really honest then you'd have to admit that all you really wanted him to do is bang your brains out.' And with that she takes a mammoth bite of her Chocolate Hobnob, looking rather pleased with herself as she munches away.

'You're probably right,' I sigh, remembering how charged and alive I felt that night. It wasn't solely down to meeting Alastair, but his attention certainly added to the confidence I felt. Since that night I've thought about him a lot while remembering the way he looked at me or kissed me. Each time I might as well have been back on that dance floor reliving it all again. My body has reacted in just the same way each time. Wanting him completely, longing for his touch. He's intoxicating, but of course he is. He's a self-confessed player. They're always the most charming because they've had limitless encounters to learn from.

'When are you going to see him again?' Michelle asks, her face full of hope.

'I don't know if I will,' I admit, aware of a sadness creeping over me as I say it.

'What?'

'He has a reputation,' I say honestly.

'Haven't we all?'

'I've just been dumped after ten years of playing the dutiful non-wife, so no,' I say with a dramatic sigh.

I can't see myself walking around Ikea and arguing over flat-pack furniture instructions with him or anyone else any time soon, but I realize it has been brilliant to move my attention away from Ian for a while.

Right now I'm not looking to find someone who's going to fill the void that he left behind in my heart and soul. I don't want to depend on another person to complete me because I now realize that people change and evolve. They always do. That makes them unreliable and unstable, no matter how much we'd love to think differently.

Perhaps I'm thinking too much like a woman who's had her hand severely burned by the flame, because despite these thoughts I know I had an unbelievable night. I loved everything about it. And yes, I loved the way Alastair made me feel sexy, proud and confident, but it simply irks me that it has taken someone else to coax out that side of me. It makes me uneasy.

I just want to get *me* back, and that's a task I need to do for myself and by myself. I don't need some man swooping in and saving me, because no matter how delightful that might sound it's not a realistic end to my problems. This isn't a fairytale and the story isn't going to end with me riding off into the sunset for my happily ever after. I thought I had that and it disappeared, so I'm not even sure I believe in them any more. Who knows, maybe Prince Phillip treated Sleeping Beauty awfully after he woke her up with a kiss. Maybe he kept using the fact he got ripped to pieces by rose bushes, and (probably) got burned by the fire-throwing dragon against her in arguments. Maybe he turned out not to be the man of her dreams and more like Joffrey in *Game of Thrones*, with a thirst for cruelty and torture. Maybe Aladdin was just a street rat and a thief. Maybe *The Little Mermaid*'s Prince Eric smelt of fish all the time. Maybe the ultimate one, *Cinderella*'s Prince Charming, was actually a sex addict with a wandering eye and that's why no one had been able to pin him down before. Even my favourite TV show *Friends* left me thinking Ross and Rachel finally got together after years of make-ups and break-ups – but what about Paris? What if it was all too much, or not enough? What if it didn't live up to the expectations they'd spent years building up? Then there's Bella and Edward, Pacey and Joey, Mickey and Minnie, and Leonard and Penny – their lives all continued after the last page or when the cameras stopped rolling, and none of us can predict what happened when we turned off the TV or shut the book. All I know for certain is that these tales have given me high expectations of what a man should be and possibly even moulded what I thought I wanted in life.

And this isn't me swearing off men and relationships or my desire to get married one day, just me recognizing the fact that now is not the right time to embark on anything serious with Alastair that could muddy the waters even further. I need to think about me and sort whatever is going on in my heart and head before I take on someone else's ego.

'I'm really not looking for a relationship, and from what I know he isn't either,' I explain eventually.

'So shag him instead,' she says flippantly.

I'm instantly aware of the flutter of excitement the thought sends through me. It's not as if he'd say no to the suggestion, and Michelle's right, things might've progressed that way if Natalia hadn't hung around.

'Trust me, I've thought about it. I don't want things to get messy with Natalia.'

'Hmmm . . . you don't want to upset things with the new boss who didn't understand you guys wanted to screw each other senseless?'

'You're so crude. Plus, you know her!' I remind her.

She shrugs in response and buries her head in her changing bag, pulling out more muslins even though Duncan hasn't moved for the last ten minutes.

'I don't know what I want right now, but I'm not ready for anyone else's problems to be added to my own,' I admit. 'It's probably a good thing we didn't exchange numbers.'

'What?' she shrieks, her head whipping back around.

'I promised him and Natalia I wouldn't earlier in the night, and then neither of us asked,' I say, remembering how we clumsily exchanged a quick peck on the lips before Natalia and I left. 'It's for the best, though. I don't want him getting in my head, not when I've finally started making some big plans.'

'Such as?' she asks doubtfully.

'I handed in my notice yesterday,' I say, delivering the line with pride. 'I bit the bullet and took a gamble. Even if the job with Natalia doesn't happen I needed to make a change and figured it was best to do it while I'm still at Mum's and not spending as much.'

'And?' she asks, not giving me the shocked reaction I was looking for. I thought resigning was a big deal. Clearly Michelle doesn't think so.

'And I was hit with a sense of possibility,' I share.

'So poetic,' she gently mocks.

'I think it's time to be a little selfish for a bit and put myself first.'

'Finally!' she shouts, raising her hands to the heavens as though her prayers have been answered at last.

'Michelle?'

'What?' she asks, gazing back to me while looking as perplexed as I feel. 'Stop being such a sap, Elizabeth. Don't be the dependable one making sure everyone else is happy all the time. Do *you*. Go chase your own contentment.'

'That's your wish for Duncan.'

'And you. Did you not feel enlightened and empowered when I said it? Was it too subtle that I was talking about you too? Well, that's not like me at all. Maybe motherhood *has* softened me,' she laughs.

'That's definitely not something you have to worry about,' I say, picking up a discarded breastpad and chucking it at her head.

'Good to know,' she says dismissively, eager to get back to helping me, her desperado big sister. 'You know, I don't know if you're going to find the answers you crave at the bottom of an empty bottle of gin, while having your brains shagged out of you by Alastair, or when you're innocently walking down the road and reflecting on the wonders of life. However, you've got to put yourself first and get rid of the shit!'

'Nicely put.'

'Am I doing a good job?' she asks, suddenly looking fretful, the atmosphere completely turning. 'At this,' she adds, gesturing towards Duncan.

The gear change from bolshie to fearful is sudden and dramatic, as though an emotion switch has been flicked.

'Marvellous,' I smile, without skipping a beat.

Michelle nods, nibbling on her lip as she looks back down at her son, her face full of worry. 'The midwife came earlier. She kept asking how I'm feeling.'

'That's her job.'

'Hmmm . . .' she ponders. 'Maybe she thought I wasn't doing it right.'

'You're doing it perfectly. Look how happy he is,' I say, pointing at the little bundle in her arms who's contentedly suckling on her breast. 'Are you OK?'

'I didn't realize it would be so hard!' Michelle says, her breath catching in her chest as she screws up her face and tries not to cry.

'Oh, Chelle!' I soothe, jumping across the sofa and throwing my arms around her, taking care to avoid squashing Duncan, who's now sleepily come off her boob and wanting to be winded. 'It's so new. It's going to feel overwhelming at times,' I offer, suddenly thinking about what a change the last forty-eight hours must be for her.

'Yeah. And I just haven't slept,' she says feebly, pulling her shirt together.

'Well, sleep. Now. I'm here to watch Duncan!' I tell her, getting up and holding out my arms for him.

In that second an almighty squelching sound erupts from Duncan's bottom. I look at his tiny frame in Michelle's arms to find his offerings have fired out of his nappy and squirted all up his back. His white babygro is now a shitty brown.

'That's gross,' I mutter, my nostrils flaring.

'Thank you so much for the offer,' my sister sings, on the verge of hysterically laughing and crying while handing over my nephew. 'I completely agree that it would be good to have a nap. Right now.'

'But . . . you . . .' I say, speechless, looking from her to him. 'You've just told me to stop being a sap and to start putting myself first!' I squeak.

'Yeah, but not when someone really needs your help,' she sniffs, staring at me with an imploring look on her face. 'We're family.'

I hesitate, knowing there's absolutely no way I can get out of this but not knowing where to start. I glance up at Michelle and notice she's now looking delighted at my bewildered expression.

'Changing mat, wipes and nappies are in here,' she grins, handing over the changing bag. She's lying back and curling her knees into her chest before I have a chance to protest. 'I don't need long. Ten minutes will fix me.'

I look down at Duncan to find he's pulling an expression that pretty much sums up my own reaction to the situation. This stinks.

After kissing his nose for the hundredth time today, I retrieve the essentials, place him on the changing mat and get on with the task.

Some people are worth being a sap for.

30

'I hope everyone has had a good Christmas and New Year!' trills Jodie from the front of the group. The pianist runs his hands up and down the piano, encouraging the stragglers to hurry themselves along so that the first rehearsal of the year for the Sing it Proud choir can finally commence. The church is freezing, but Jodie handed me my new branded t-shirt when I arrived and I am happily wearing it while try-ing to ignore the goosebumps that are prickling their way along my bare arms and sending a chill to my bones. The heaters that have been placed around the room haven't managed to take away the bitter bite from the air just yet, but seeing as the church has such high ceilings I'm guess-ing it'll take a while either to warm up, or for me to get used to it or turn blue and die of hypothermia.

I've been looking forward to my first official session with the group since watching them before Christmas. I've had a flutter in my tummy any time I've thought about it and have found myself singing at every opportunity – in cars, supermarkets, or simply walking down the street. There was even one awkward moment where I was walking to the station and thought I was completely alone, so decided to break into a bit of Taylor Swift's 'Bad Blood'. Five seconds later a teenage boy overtook me, flashing me a worried expression.

Tonight I arrived early, have mingled and made small talk and am now standing in the front row of the organized group feeling anxious but raring to go. Apparently it'll help me pick up the harmonies better if I stand close to Susan, the elderly lady I ended up speaking to when I came to watch before Christmas, as we're in the same vocal group — soprano. I guess that'll give me more confidence, although I'm not sure I'm going to be able to hear any noise that comes out of my mouth anyway. Having heard Susan carrying out her own pre-warm-up warm-up I'm astounded to hear she has a real set of lungs on her for one so tiny. The sound she creates is huge and powerful and travels down my eardrum at great speed.

'First up I want to tell you about a concert I've penned in,' continues Jodie with a clap, causing the rumblings of conversations in the room to cease. 'We didn't do a proper show this Christmas, and it was a complete oversight on my part. You all worked so hard, and while the emphasis within this group should always be about enjoyment there's a lot to be said for the thrill of a public performance,' she says, causing a stir of excitement from the group around me. Clearly they're all in agreement, however the thought fills me with fear. 'I was watching a programme over Christmas about loneliness during the festive period,' she continues loudly over the group to encourage them to keep listening. They obey quickly. 'It struck me that if the most magical time of year is the most lonely for some, then what is January? It has to be worse thanks to the weather turning more bitter and the reasons for people gathering together diminishing.'

'And the TV is showing a load of rubbish,' shouts Albie, Susan's husband. 'That doesn't help.'

'I'm sure,' nods Jodie.

'It's a very isolating time,' adds Susan.

'It's so true,' says an elderly lady standing at the end of my row. She shrugs her shoulders and looks around at the rest of the group. 'My son went back up to York with his family at the weekend. I probably won't see him again until Easter. I can't imagine what it would be like if I didn't have you lot.'

Even though the members of the choir are an array of ages it seems to me they rely on each other for support and are a real community. It's part of the reason I've been longing to come back. It's more than just singing through a few pop songs and getting our voices to gel as one sound. It's belonging to something; feeling part of a collective.

'I've spoken with the church and I want to turn the last session of the month into a real event for the community, inviting everyone around here along and getting them out of the house,' explains Jodie.

'Great idea!' enthuses a young blond man behind me who fiddles with his green-framed glasses as he talks. 'We can all bake cakes for it, too.'

'Better than a Christmas show,' adds someone else, as the group gets even more vocal and further suggestions are thrown out, like members offering taxi services with their own cars to help less mobile people get here and back.

I think of Michelle and the newborn whirlwind she's

currently in. We've spoken a lot since her emotional out-burst yesterday and she seems to be doing more than fine at the moment, but it's still a massive change for her. She's up all night with Duncan, so hugely sleep deprived and generally walking about in a haze. I imagine a couple of hours out of her pyjamas and mixing with adults who aren't Stu or her family would be a bit of a treat for her.

'It would be good to target new mums too, and make sure they know they can bring along their little ones,' I find myself saying out loud, feeling inspired by their plans.

'Definitely,' Susan bellows from behind me, making me jump. The rest of the group nod away, the excitement building. Having been lucky enough to watch this choir in action I know it'll be a special night for everyone who comes along.

Jodie beams at the crowd in front of her, clearly happy that her idea has been met with so much enthusiasm. 'If anyone has any song suggestions then please let me know by the end of tonight's rehearsal. We have only three weeks to put together a fab show, so let's pull out the golden oldies from previous sessions, but sprinkle them with extra magic.'

The pianist starts playing his scales again, prompting Jodie to look at us expectantly. Time to actually do a vocal warm-up.

'OK, let's go. Can I have an ee-ee-ee-ee-ee-ee-ee-eeeeee,' she sings, her voice rising and falling beautifully.

I take a deep breath and open my mouth in the same

way I've seen Jodie do and go for it. I'm surprised by two things: one, that I can actually hear myself over Susan, and two, by the sound that comes out of my mouth. And not in a good way. I sound like a boy going through puberty who's having to deal with his voice breaking. It cracks, crackles and dips between notes in such a peculiar way I think about miming. No, seriously. I could lip sync along quite happily and I'm sure no one would even be able to tell anyway.

I never used to sound like this. Fair enough, I never sang like an angel, but my parents have been going on about my 'lovely' voice for the last decade as though I threw away my chance of being the next Whitney Houston. Where's that voice gone? Or were they just humouring me when I was nothing more than mediocre?

Perhaps that's a bit harsh. I doubt they'd disillusion me on purpose. After all, almost every single dreadful contestant on *The X Factor* has a parent or two eagerly waiting in the wings for them, who genuinely believe their talentless child is the most gifted human being on the planet. Their unconditional love has not only left them blind, but deaf too. If I were to audition, Simon Cowell and Sharon Osbourne would be doing their best not to giggle their way through my audition before rejecting me and breaking all my hopes of popstardom. My mum would then come out and give the thoughtless judges an ear-bashing, but to no avail. They'd be forced to reiterate the fact that I shouldn't give up my day job – which would be disastrous as I technically don't have one right now. Cue more sob-story fodder.

The realization of this imagined scene leaves me deeply humiliated.

I squawk my way through the rest of the warm-up, feeling my cheeks redden and unable to look up at Jodie, even when she's telling us what the first song is. It's one of their favourites called 'I Will Follow Him', a song from the film *Sister Act*. I don't know it. Even with the lyrics in my hands I can't follow where we are in the song and I can't get to grips with the melody. My mind is all over the place; I can't think about anything other than how terrible I sound, so I try to be as quiet as possible so that I can't be heard. I do the same for the following two songs, willing the session to be over so I can scurry away and never come back.

When it's finally time for a break I sneak off to the toilet. My chin starts wobbling and despite telling myself that I'm being completely stupid, tears start streaming down my face. This is completely different to singing on my own in the shower, or in the car, where I can just let loose and do what I like. It's immediately evident that singing in a choir requires far more skill in terms of breathing, timing and, most importantly, gelling with everyone else. I'm shit at something I really hoped I'd be amazing at and that's a difficult pill to swallow. I am frustrated at myself for letting my brain get in the way of me having fun and embarrassed for my failings. Covering up my face with my arms I lean into the wall and try to calm myself down. I'm being an idiot.

'Lizzy?' I hear Jodie say softly from the other side of the cubicle door.

'Yes,' I say, trying to sound as bright and cheery as possible and failing. Instead I sound as though I've either suddenly contracted a severe cold and spent the last few minutes stuffing toilet paper up my nose, or been full-on ugly girl crying.

'You're doing brilliantly.'

I don't respond because I know she's lying. Instead my face contorts and screws up, as I try to ward off another sob that's threatening to escape.

'Lizzy?'

'Yeah . . .' I struggle.

'Want to come out?'

'Not particularly.'

'It's just me.'

I take a deep breath and wipe my eyes, shaking my body in the hope it'll shake my blues away, just as Taylor Swift recommends. It doesn't, but I realize I can't stay in here for ever.

I open the door to find Jodie leaning against one of the sinks, looking at me sympathetically. It's like we're back at school and hanging out in the toilets at loo break so that we can dissect the latest gossip: was Phillip Deyes touching Connie's boob really an accident (it wasn't, he absolutely meant to do it), had Daniel Durrant actually been stuffing socks down his pants in PE (he had), or had Tracey Perkins really touched Simon Clark's willy in the back of science class (apparently also true). The flashback makes me feel even more pathetic and a little sick for our younger selves.

I busy myself by going straight to the other sink and

washing my hands. Looking up at the mirror I see my eyes and lips are red and swollen.

'You *are* doing brilliantly,' Jodie says, pivoting round so that she's also facing the mirror above her sink, although I know she's still looking at me.

'I can't sing,' I say matter-of-factly.

'You can.'

'I can't even hold a tune. Everyone else is amazing.'

'They've been doing this a long time but the majority of them would've felt like you at the start.'

'Bet they didn't cry in the toilets,' I reason, wiping my eyes on the cuff of my jumper.

'A couple did. It's a huge deal for people to be taken out of their comfort zones,' she admits, drawing in a deep breath through her teeth. 'Singing isn't something we do as adults unless you're in groups like this. I don't audition people to be in this choir because I want people to see that singing is about so much more than rigidly banging out the correct notes.'

'You're a choir. Of course you want that! You want it to sound good,' I argue, placing the backs of my wrists into my eye sockets to stop tears from streaming again. A few seconds later I look over to see her still staring at me.

'Perfect notes aren't everything,' she says, shaking her head. Her face changes suddenly, as though considering something. 'The odd moment of divine sound is more than enough to please me for a lifetime.'

'See?'

'But it's the cherry on top of an already delicious bowl of ice cream, and it's not why I started this group,' she protests, banging her fist into her hand passionately. 'I could've auditioned and turned people away who couldn't hit a top C or hold a note for thirty seconds before perfecting a vibrato finish, but I didn't want that. How do you feel when you sing?' she asks, bringing her hands into a prayer position. She points them at me before placing them under her chin as though she's begging or praying.

'Out there I feel like I'm letting everyone down,' I admit.

'Forget out there for a minute,' she tells me, gesturing to the door separating us from everyone else. 'What's your favourite song at the moment? What do you belt out in the shower?'

'"Fix You" by Coldplay,' I say, able to answer without giving it too much thought. Ever since I first heard that song (and then experienced it in motion in an episode of *Lost*) it's called to me. I sing it in the shower with my eyes closed. Sometimes as I sing it, I'm promising I'm going to put myself back together, and other times I'm imagining I'm in a stadium singing it for the crowd with their lighters swaying in the air (I know it's all iPhones now, but it's not quite as magical) and everyone singing along. It's euphoric and anthemic.

'And how do you feel when you're singing that song into your bottle of shampoo?'

'Great,' I admit, smiling despite myself as I think of my wonderful shower performances.

'Because you're not thinking about it, you're just doing it.'

'I guess. Plus, the acoustics in there are fab,' I remind her.

Jodie laughs. 'Sing it Proud is about a bunch of people coming together to celebrate their love for singing. It's about taking confidence from each other and should be an extension of what you're already doing in the shower. When people come through the door I want them to escape whatever is going on in their everyday lives. I want them to just be focused on the music in their hands, the sound of the piano and the emotion they feel when they open their mouths and tell the story of the song.'

'I sounded like a cat being strangled,' I admit, cringing at the memory.

'I was standing in front of you and I can tell you that you categorically did not, but I saw your face looking deflated and knew something was up,' she tells me. 'Can you remember why you loved singing back in school?'

'I was a bit of a show-off?' I offer, thinking back to my Girls Can Too girlband days with knicker-flashing Connie. I might've only been seven years old when our success peaked with a performance of Bananarama's 'Love in the First Degree' in assembly, but I remember feeling incredible when the applause erupted at the end. I can still remember the grins Connie and I flashed each other as we soaked up the admiration.

'You are funny,' Jodie smiles, placing her hand on my shoulder. 'When you're a kid you don't worry so much. I didn't, anyway. I didn't care what people thought but I knew how good singing made me feel. Singing is entertainment, it's also an emotional outlet for whatever you have gurgling away inside.'

'Do you think I'm overthinking it?'

'I don't know what's going on in your head, but in the last few months you've overcome far worse than a community choir,' she says, raising her eyebrows at me and pursing her lips. 'I can't force you to be in this group, and really don't want you to be here if you feel uncomfortable.'

'Are you kicking me out?'

'No! I'm trying to make you see that everyone out there is on your side.'

'Sorry, I'm being a twat,' I say, sighing at the stupidity of me sobbing in the loo of my local church.

'No, you're not, but please remember that it's *just* singing,' she says, gently rubbing my shoulder and smiling at me in the mirror. 'I'm going to go back in for the rest of the rehearsal, but take your time and come out when you're ready to have another bash at it.'

'Thank you,' I say.

I still feel foolish as she walks out of the door, but at least I feel less alone. Perhaps I wasn't as bad as I thought I was. Or maybe it actually doesn't matter as long as I'm enjoying it.

I take a few deep breaths and wait for my face to appear less blotchy. When I'm finally convinced that people won't notice I've been having an emotional meltdown in the toilets, I rejoin the group who are now putting down their paper cups and getting back into their previous positions, ready to go again.

I catch Albie's eye as I pick up my sheet music. He winks. I smile. It's enough.

'The next song we've not done for a few months because we sang it to death at the start of last year, but I know you all love it and so will our audience,' Jodie says, passing a new set of music to a woman at the end of the row to pass around.

I laugh when I see the chosen song.

'Fix You'.

It's time to pretend I'm in my shower.

31

As I have no job or commitments to tie me down, I offer to meet Natalia in town. This is obviously the right thing to do, as she's hopefully going to be offering me a job. In a further attempt to impress her I've been through my wardrobe millions of times, trying to figure out what to wear. Aside from the items I bought for New Year's Eve, everything in there is still black – a further reminder that I need to go to the flat and sort out my clothes – but I've not been able to work up the courage to go back there yet. The thought alone causes me to grimace. So I've put on my best black jeans, black cable-knit woolly jumper and black ankle boots. To liven it all up I've pinched a leopard-print coat from Michelle along with a light-brown cashmere scarf.

I might look the part but I'm nervous, because I know this meeting isn't going to be as straightforward as I would've hoped. Having read through Natalia's email I initially squealed with delight because it's clear she really does need someone to work alongside her. My heart skipped at the thought of it being me in that role, but then something started niggling away at me and I've not been able to shake it off since. Those thoughts are still very much present when I walk through the front door of Soho House's private members' club in Dean Street and am faced with three girls staring at me from behind a large podium of a desk.

'Hello, can we help?' one of them asks, flicking her luscious blonde hair over her shoulder. The fact they don't mistake me for one of their members confirms my suspicion that I stick out like a sore thumb.

I nervously mumble something incomprehensible in reply.

'Pardon?' she asks, her high-pitched voice piercingly jarring as she leans in.

'I'm Lizzy Richardson,' I say, swallowing hard, not sure why I'm so nervous.

'Here to see . . . ?' she prods while I gaze gormlessly at her.

'Natalia Wood!' I practically shout.

'Great,' she chimes, plastering a forced smile across her face. 'Please sign in,' she asks, handing over a pen while sliding a big black folder in my direction.

Putting pen to paper I start writing.

'Wait,' I apologize nervously. 'That's not my name. I put Natalia, that's the person I'm seeing, not me. I'm Lizzy.'

The three girls look at me suspiciously. Now they definitely know I'm a novice in these parts. Girl One places her hands back on the folder and swivels it around so they can all inspect my error.

'Up these stairs, room on the left,' Girl One says without even looking up from the mess I've made.

I scuttle up the grand wooden staircase quick enough to ensure they can't change their minds. I'm in. Even though I feel like I don't quite belong here, I feel a thrill at being allowed in to this exclusive London club. It's literally like a house, albeit the home of a billionaire who can afford this huge building in the heart of Soho. At the top of the stairs I ignore what looks like the main room in front of me, which I note has been painted a vibrant rust and filled with gorgeous leather and heavily textured armchairs and sofas, and turn to my left to find somewhere even more pleasing on the eye. Mustard-coloured walls, elegant and simple 70s-inspired wooden furniture and a green floral-patterned sofa of dreams, which I instantly know to be a William Morris creation. If I could freeze time and live here, I would.

I spot Natalia sitting in a comfy armchair, her perfectly manicured fingers frantically scribbling into a notepad as she waits for me. I feel unusually nauseous, so take a deep breath and step towards her.

'You're really early! I mean, *I* aimed for early, but you basically opted for the day before,' I nervously ramble, placing my hand on her shoulder.

She turns to me and laughs while getting to her feet, opening her arms for a hug. She looks divine in a spectacular orange knitted midi dress, which accentuates her petite yet curvy frame. I'd look like a sack of potatoes in it; despite going on a few runs I've not curbed my heartbreak-and-Christmas diet of shoving all food within eyesight straight into my gob.

'I finished at Selfridges a little while ago and had some work to be getting on with,' she explains, looking around the swanky room at the other guests who are chatting away in little clustered groups of twos, threes and fours. 'It's just a blessing mobiles are banned in here. It gives me a good excuse to go off radar for an hour or two.'

Following her gaze, I think I recognize someone from a huge British girl band, but I can't be sure and it'd be super uncool of me to look at her for any longer than I already have. Even though there's no chance I'd ever go over and talk to her, just knowing we're in the same place gives me a sense of pride and excitement for the future. I wouldn't see her in McDonald's in Chelmsford, or grabbing a quick bucket of deep fried chicken. Times are changing.

'How have you been?' Natalia asks, sitting back down and gesturing at the armchair next to her. 'Come, take a seat.'

I start to do as she says and notice the atmosphere between us is unfamiliar. The last time I saw her was New Year's Day and we were both leaving Alastair's flat. I looked a state – like I'd had my first night out in a long time and had certainly made the most of it. Which I had. There was no way I could prise my feet back into my heels so I'd pulled out the flats I'd cleverly stowed away in my bag (after managing to resist them the whole night). I was still hobbling thanks to a few numb toes, my hair looked like a bird's nest, my make-up had melted off and my clothes had pizza and Archer's stains down them. Natalia, on the other hand, had looked radiant – as though she'd spent the evening skipping through calming meadows of wild flowers, surrounded by magical unicorns. We may have been completely shattered, but we were experiencing the buzz that delirious exhaustion from a night out provides. Now there's an air of professionalism in the way Natalia holds herself. Her back is a little straighter, and her shoulders are pinned back an inch further. She still seems as lovely as ever, but there's something authoritative about her now. She's in boss mode, which I can't help but find intimidating.

'Can I get you a drink, Ma'am?' a waitress asks as soon as my bum has found the seat.

'Tea, please. English breakfast,' I clarify, knowing they probably serve a whole host of loose, exotic posh types and I won't know how to work the strainer. I just want the normal one. Nothing fancy.

The waitress smiles knowingly and leaves.

'Forgive me for diving in,' Natalia pre-warns, adjusting her position on the chair and rearranging the fabric of her dress before looking up at me with great expectancy. 'What did you make of my proposal?'

'Ha! Do you know how long I spent waiting for one of those?' I ask, laughing at her choice of words.

It takes a second or two, but eventually Natalia understands what she's said and laughs too, the atmosphere instantly becoming more relaxed. She chuckles into her coffee while keeping her eyes on me.

'I read it and I loved it,' I admit. 'It's exactly what I want to be doing.'

'Amazing,' Natalia beams, the palm of her hand excitedly tapping on the table between us. 'So when do you want to start?'

'I've got the job?' I ask slowly, absorbing the moment that sits heavily on my heart.

'Of course,' Natalia grins. 'I said as much the other night.'

'I still didn't think you meant it though . . .'

Finding her enthusiasm infectious, I can't help smiling back at her, but realize I'm about to make the right decision for me, and that's not necessarily going to be the right one for her.

As Michelle has instructed, I have to stop being the sap.

I take a deep breath and twiddle with my fingers, then look up at the woman whose work I truly admire, knowing I'm potentially about to disappoint her. 'Natalia, you know I'd love to work for you. I would literally have begged for a job with you if you hadn't asked me first. In fact, I think I practically did anyway,' I laugh, thinking back to our chat in the club on New Year's Eve.

'That's good to know,' she replies, putting down the coffee cup before running her hands along her thighs and cupping both her knees.

'And I really do want to work for you,' I say, placing my hand on my heart to highlight my sincerity. I have to show her how serious I am about that before I can tell her what else is on my mind. 'Really, truly, I couldn't think of anyone I'd rather work with – your passion and dedication are so clear and I admire all you do.'

'Why do I feel like there's a *but* coming on?' she asks, looking curious rather than deflated, interested rather than angry.

'Because there is,' I say, letting the realization settle. Her surprised expression mirrors my own.

'A couple of months ago my life took an unexpected turn into a dead end,' I say, repeating the words I'd found myself nervously putting together on the train on the way here. 'Ever since then I've been on this massive journey to reverse myself out of that crappy spot and find out who I am, or who I was meant to be if my ex and I hadn't joined forces and moulded into one entity. I've been looking at clues and second-guessing everything, but really I just need to give myself time to take opportunities now that I've only got myself to think about. I've not had that in ten years,' I exclaim, pausing as my tea is brought out and arranged in front of me at a snail's pace. Neither of us fills the gap in the conversation. As soon as the waitress is gone I continue. 'Even this, sitting here with you and having your incredible offer of a job, would've been carefully discussed and considered by me and Ian. We'd have had to think about how the change would affect us as a couple and the life we shared. We'd have had to contemplate moving somewhere between our two jobs, or I'd have had to plan the commute from our existing flat and see whether it was something I could handle. I'd have had to make sure Ian understood that working for such an acclaimed company would mean him getting less of my time. I'd have had to preempt what that might mean for us and whether it would cause any problems.'

'Well, I'm glad we didn't meet before you broke up then,' Natalia cuts in, looking bewildered.

'That's relationships, though,' I shrug.

'Putting someone else first? Maybe that's why I've been single for so long,' she suggests with a slight pout.

'Or why you're such a success! I have to say, on reflection, I think I put his needs before my own too much. It should've been far more equal than it was,' I admit. 'But we aren't here to talk about my ex.'

'We aren't,' she agrees, bowing her head and willing me to continue – or probably get to the point a little quicker. After all, she has a million places to be right now, I'm sure.

'I know I want to work for you. I know how much I would absolutely love being a part of your team and getting my teeth stuck into some of your projects,' I say, stopping and taking a deep breath. 'That said, I need to get away and take some time for me that isn't spent living at my mum's in my childhood bedroom. I need to go away and explore. There are places I've always wanted to see and I need to do it now before committing myself to another chapter in my life. I need to be selfish and make things just about me for a while. I know you gave me the nudge to do it, but leaving Home Comforts seems to have given me the perfect time to stop and think about the things I need to do for me before I can continue giving so much of myself over to others.'

'So where do you want to go and for how long?' she asks, her face not giving away how she's feeling about my plans.

'I've always wanted to go to Thailand. I thought I'd visit Bangkok and then do some island-hopping before working my way down to Malaysia, Indonesia and then taking a bit of a tour of Australia and New Zealand.'

Natalia's jaw drops, causing my heart to sink. 'That's quite a trip.'

'I'd like to do what I can within three months,' I gulp.

Natalia purses her lips and looks down at the grey-carpeted floor between our feet. A small frown line has found its way on to her forehead as she contemplates what I've said.

I hold my breath in suspense, wondering how she's going to reply. I thought about emailing her with all of this as I knew I'd be able to write it more eloquently than I could verbalize it, but I reasoned that words on a screen could be taken in the wrong way. She might think I was saying a polite 'thanks, but no thanks' to the job offer, and I didn't want that to happen.

Natalia looks up at me and starts nodding. 'I couldn't be more supportive of what you're planning if I tried,' she shrugs, a smile creeping across her lips.

'Really?'

'Absolutely. I agree with you. Now is the time for you to do this. If it wasn't my company, or if you were Connie, say, I'd be actively encouraging you to take that time. As your friend, and boss,' she says, lingering on the word with a sparkle in her eye. 'I'm someone who wants the best for you. I think I'd be a fool to do otherwise because it's only when you feel fulfilled and happy that you'll be able to give me your focus and dedication to ensure you're producing your best work. I have my heart set on you purely from how you spoke about what we do when we first met. It was so impassioned and heartfelt. Plus, you had no idea what I do. Usually people find that out and try to impress me with their knowledge of designers or materials, but it means nothing. It's vacuous knowledge with no soul or thought.' She pauses and squints at me, her shoulders rising and falling as she lets out a sigh. 'I think you're worth the wait.'

'Thank you,' I say, feeling a weight lift from my shoulders, making me realize how much this chat was hanging over me. If she'd told me there was no way I'd have a job when I got back then I'd probably have fallen straight back into being a people-pleaser and told her I'd stay put. Now any trepidation I feel is targeted towards the actual trip and getting everything organized.

'I think it's a very brave move,' praises Natalia.

'I'm not sure about that. Part of me wonders if I'm being completely idiotic. I'm not exactly eighteen years old and on my gap year before I start taking life more seriously. I should have it all figured out by now.'

'Well, don't listen to that part!' Natalia giggles. 'It sounds like you have a firm understanding of what you want, and that's brilliant.'

'I'm not sure I do,' I say, batting away her compliment. 'Doing a bit of exploring is something that's been niggling away at my brain but I haven't wanted to focus on it. I didn't want to feel like I was meekly running away from my problems,' I say, knowing the main reason I didn't give it any real consideration when I was sitting in my room writing lists on my past self versus my present self was because it felt too much of a cliché. The wait has made me take the leap purely for my own desire to see more of the world with nothing to tie me down. I really do feel it's now or never – or at least not for a very long time.

'I'm sure people would understand if you did,' she reasons.

'Running away wouldn't have solved anything though, would it?' I say, deciding to finally pour the tea that's been stewing since the waitress left. I add a splash of milk and a spoonful of sugar before taking a sip, watching as the pop star from earlier saunters past, presumably going to the loo. A trail of her exquisite perfume wafting over us, floral, fresh and sweet, with undertones of vanilla. It's a far deeper scent than anything I'd be able to find on the high street. It literally screams 'I'm famous!'

I glimpse at Natalia and find that she's clocked her too.

'Is she . . . ?' I whisper, leaning in conspiratorially and making sure she's completely out of earshot. I'm pretty sure she is who I'm thinking of. She's been all over the *Mail Online* lately though due to her breaking up with a huge boyband member.

Natalia gives me a wink in response, confirming my suspicions.

'Ooooh . . .'

We have a little giggle together.

'So, when do you think you'll leave?' Natalia asks, grabbing a notepad from her bag, the pen hovering over the page, waiting for details. 'More importantly, when will I have you back here with me?' she asks, her eyes flicking up at me.

I smile at the thought of it actually happening as I place the delicate china cup back down in front of me. 'As soon as possible. I have a choir performance I'd really love to do in a couple of weeks, and then I'm off.'

'OK . . .' she nods while scribbling, as though she's mentally calculating what it'll mean for her, which is essentially a new member of staff who won't be actually working with her for another four months.

'It's scary thinking about it,' I say, taking a breath.

'I'm sure it is!'

'Joining a choir is one thing, but leaving everything I know, my whole support system, and flying across the world to somewhere new is a huge deal,' I realize, the reality of not seeing my family for months really hitting home. Baby Duncan might be rolling over by the time I'm back, Dad could've found a boyfriend or Michelle might've become a nicer person and joined a hippy tribe – all these things are possibilities and I'd miss the transition, but they'd happen regardless of me being here. None of them have tried to convince me to stay, or even said they'll miss me. They've all simply championed my plans with nothing but joy and optimism. 'That said, I'm twenty-nine in a couple of months and I'm not getting any younger. I need to do this now while I still have only my own happiness to think about.'

'Before you meet someone else who might stop you from going off whenever you feel like it?' she asks, raising an eyebrow at me. 'Like Alastair?'

'Well, no, maybe not him, but yes,' I flounder, not really wanting to lose focus by talking about him. 'I guess so,' I shrug. 'This trip has to be all about me, and not what I'm potentially missing out on,' I explain. When I was younger travelling used to be something you did for fun – one big, crazy, wild adventure to see you off into adulthood and stability. Now, as someone who's going to be travelling later than most people I know who either jetted off straight after A-levels or university, it's about something else entirely. It's all about me, having a deeper understanding of myself and the world around me. It's a peaceful waltz for one, rather than an action-packed rave surrounded by strangers.'

'Well, I know Alastair will be gutted,' she says in a way I can't read. I think of Michelle calling Natalia a cock-blocker, and wonder if this is a ruse to get more information out of me, or a genuine statement. Mentioning her best mate twice in the space of ten seconds certainly feels like the conversation is being forced upon me.

'I don't know about that,' I say uneasily, aware of my heart constricting as I think of him, which is ridiculous because we only had that one night together and even then, it was just a bit of fun really.

'He really likes you. Trust me.'

'I'm sure he's liked a lot of girls over the years,' I say, attempting to brush the thought away. 'I'm just going to pop to the loo.'

'Left, right and all the way down,' she informs me, totally unperturbed by my scatty reaction.

'Thanks,' I mutter, getting up from my seat and walking out, doing my best to avoid the situation entirely.

Turning into the main room I saw earlier I bump

straight into the brunette pop star. She tuts, scolding me for being so careless even though she wasn't paying much attention either. Regardless, I go to apologize but the bitchy look on her face stops me.

I pivot and continue with my hunt for the loo, smirking at the fact pretty Miss Pop Star is now walking around with a strip of toilet paper stuck to the bottom of her shoe.

Serves her right.

32

I couldn't visit London without arranging to meet Connie for a drink once she finished work. Three glasses of wine later, and we're strolling along the South Bank, finishing off McDonald's burgers and enjoying being together.

Festoon lighting is hanging from the trees above, casting a beautiful reflection into the Thames beside us. In the daytime it usually looks murky, green and somewhat disease-ridden; as if it would kill you instantly if you were unfortunate enough to fall in, but right now it looks magically romantic as it sparkles and glistens. We hear a busker with a guitar up ahead, his enticing Scottish accent clear through the poetic words he's singing. The moon above is big and bright in the clear dark sky. It's freezing cold and, even though there are a few dozen commuters or tourists milling around us, it feels strangely tranquil – as though we're in our own little world.

'I can't believe you're actually going!' Connie says sadly, throwing her empty wrapper in the bin before taking hold of my gloved hand and grasping it in both of hers, as though she's keeping hold of me so that I can't leave.

'It'll fly by,' I tell her, stuffing the last mouthful of burger into my gob while screwing up my face as if to say I don't even want to go on the trip of a lifetime I'm planning, which I'm aware is a complete lie. Now I've told Natalia, I'm more excited than ever about the prospect of getting on that plane to the other side of the world with nothing but me and the bag on my back.

'For you it will, when you're swanning around the world in your khaki harem pants. It won't for me!' she argues, before sighing heavily and blowing a deflated raspberry through her naturally plump lips. 'Can you reactivate your Facebook now? Just so you can keep us up to date with where you are?'

'No. Absolutely not,' I declare, firmly against the idea. 'I don't need everyone who's ever had eye contact with me knowing what's going on in my life. I'll text you what I'm up to. I might even be able to WhatsApp you some pictures when I find some Wi-Fi.'

'Hmmm . . .' she says dubiously, still clutching my hands. 'It's just like when you left for uni,' she barely mutters, causing my heart to ache for her.

'Except I won't meet a guy and drop off the face of the earth,' I promise her, knowing how much I'll miss her. Even though we probably only see each other once a week, we still call each other a lot and it'll be weird for both of us not to have that contact.

'You'd better not,' she snorts, elbowing me in the ribs. 'I'd come chasing after you this time and demand you came home. In fact, I'd fucking drag you back myself.'

'Probably for the best. You'd have saved me a lot of heartache if you'd done that last time,' I joke, putting my arm around her and pulling her body into mine.

Perhaps the biggest shock from my break-up with Ian

is learning that Connie felt she lost me when he came along and dazzled me with all his enticingly mysterious ways and long luscious hair. I realize that's what she was getting at when we had our tiff before Christmas. I was young, foolish and totally self-absorbed when we started dating. Nothing existed outside the bubble of us and I closed myself off from the other people I loved, not because I'd stopped caring but rather because there was this new and exciting relationship that I'd become intoxicated by. Plus, I was living away from home for the first time and making the most of not having Mum and Dad know where I was every minute of the day. It felt rebellious. Now I realize how wonderful it would have been to have let in that group of fantastic people who wanted to know, and actually cared about what I was up to, as well as having the fab (turned out to be not so fab . . .) boyfriend in my life. I will no longer be dismissive towards people I adore. A partner should be an added bonus to my life, not the centre of it . . . or maybe just off-centre so everything sits a little more equally.

'How are things with Matt?' I ask, knowing that if New Year's Eve was anything to go by then she's well and truly smitten.

'Really good,' she says, practically singing the words.

'He seems great,' I admit. At no point have I ever thought anything different, although the call to his grandma while we were out partying was the moment I knew he was a serious keeper. Far more than the good looks and the dazzling smile, it highlighted his caring side. Even *I* fell in love with him after that.

Wait!

I look at Connie, who's uncharacteristically silent, and see she's got a humungous grin on her face. The term 'ear to ear' doesn't even cover the sight I am seeing. It's practically face-splitting-in-two material.

I gasp, tugging on her arm and pulling her around to face me. I cup her chin in my hand and pull it gently towards mine, looking at her closely.

'You're in love!' I exclaim, my jaw dropping.

'I might be,' she says bashfully, backing away from me to giggle into her scarf while grabbing my arm and pulling me along so we keep on the path ahead of us.

'Shitting hell!' I mutter, making her light giggle grow into a fully fledged guffaw. 'I don't even know who you are right now. What happened to my straight-talking, ball-breaking best mate who writes about all the losers of the world on her super-successful blog? She's turned soft!'

Letting out a loud cackle, she stops walking, bending over in two and grabbing hold of her knees as her whole body starts to shake. She's lost the plot. Love has actually turned her crackers.

'Connie?!' I squeal, thoroughly enjoying this new side of her and finding myself infectiously joining in. Over twenty-five years of friendship and she still never ceases to surprise me.

'Sorry,' she breathes, dissolving further into hysterics. 'It's not even funny . . .'

'It's hilarious!' I correct her, struggling to get my words out.

Passers-by stare as though we're up to no good, but we don't care. If anything it goads us on further, highlighting how silly we're being. It feels great. The laughter takes over completely, so much so that a stitch punches me in the side. It could be the burger I've scoffed, or it could be the fact I've not laughed like this in a long time and my muscles simply aren't used to being pummelled in such a manner. Whatever the reason, it forces me to calm down and attempt to get a grip.

'Oh, Con!' I sigh, wiping away my tears while trying to catch my breath, my hand rubbing at my side as the discomfort subsides. 'You're so funny.'

'I've been trapped by the flipping love bug, haven't I?'

'It's adorable,' I say, putting my arms around her shoulders and giving her a big hug. 'I'm proud of you.'

We squeeze each other. We used to hug like this a lot when we were younger, but grew out of it at some point. It feels so comfortable, like a pair of worn-in jeans.

'Well, it was going to happen some day, wasn't it,' she smiles, breaking away from me. 'The dream was always that some guy would come along and sweep me off my feet with his greatness. I just didn't think such a man existed.'

'Have you actually said it out loud to him yet?'

She nods and lets out another giggle. 'Obviously he's just a guy—'

'Good observation,' I interrupt.

'But he's a bloody superb human. I want him in my life always. He makes me feel . . . amazing.'

'God, you make me sick,' I grin.

'Tell me about it. I make myself gag these days.'

A group of rowdy lads begin cheering and shouting animatedly at each other as they exit a nearby bar. Without saying anything we loop our arms and start walking in the opposite direction.

'Well, how's that for timing,' I say, largely to myself.

'What? You suddenly becoming footloose and fancy free just as I get firmly removed from the most-shagged list?'

'Connie!' I laugh.

'True. I can still count on four hands my sexual encounters . . . oh wait, that's not right,' she says when her hands are out in front of her. She shakes her head free of the maths that's confusing her. 'Anyway, you were saying?'

'I was going to finally take you up on your offer,' I say.

'Which one? There have been many!'

'Of getting out of my mum's and staying with you for a while.'

'What, when you get back?' she asks excitedly.

'It would only be for a bit while I wait for the flat to sell and find somewhere new.'

'In London?' she shrieks. 'You're moving to London?'

'It's not a million miles away from Essex. I think I'd cope,' I giggle, her excitement building my own. 'I never meant to move back to Essex after Sheffield, anyway. I planned to be here, living life on the edge somewhere trendy. While I fear my trendy days are behind me—'

'They aren't!'

'—I'd still love to try it.'

'Yes, Lizzy!' she shouts, happily stamping her foot on the ground and punching the air. 'It's going to be brilliant! I'm actually jealous that you're going to experience it all for the first time. Living here is so different to visiting once or twice a month.'

'Well, that's my plan.'

'And you have to stay with me. I would absolutely love that!' she says, squeezing my arm.

'You have a proper boyfriend now,' I remind her.

'And?'

'And you aren't going to want me there being your third wheel.'

'Fuck that! Matt would be the third wheel,' she retorts with a big grin. 'Let him feel awkward.'

'It won't be for long.'

'It can be for as long as you like. How much did we talk about living together when we were growing up?' she asks, stopping to buy some roasted nuts from a guy standing on the pathway. With two cups of roasted sweetness in our hands we walk a little further and then lean on the stone wall by the river. 'Remember when you got back from your family holiday in Cyprus?'

'I suggested moving over there for a summer,' I say, realizing that before any boyfriends came along to tempt me otherwise, Connie had always been my ideal flatmate. Living somewhere away from our parents and having as much fun as we wanted was the ultimate dream.

'You didn't just suggest it, you got in touch with a load of bars to see if they had any vacancies for us,' she reminds me.

'It was all going so well until our mums found out,' I tut.

'Remember the family meeting they ambushed us with?'

'Yes!'

'Us and our parents sitting around your living-room table getting a right rollicking while Michelle pissed herself in the hallway . . .'

'She was always such a cow,' I say, finding it funny now, although at the time I didn't speak to her for three whole days. She didn't care though. She said she quite enjoyed getting away from me and my nasally whiny voice.

'Please come stay at mine. I want you to.'

'Only if you're sure.'

'Definitely . . . there's not enough nude Bananarama dancing in my life for my liking.'

'Well, I think I can fix that!' I chuckle, placing a nut in my mouth before spitting it straight back out. 'Fuck me, that's roasting.'

Connie cracks up.

33

As Stephanie didn't want me to work my two weeks' notice in case I stole her fascinating clients (she can keep them), I've found myself joining Mum at her weekly yoga class in the hall where I used to have Girl Guides. I'm pretty good at yoga and have done a fair bit in the past, but Mum is the youngest member in attendance in this class. By about twenty years. I'm not ageist in the slightest, but I keep being dragged out of my zone thanks to the elderly man beside me breaking wind whenever he moves. Literally; even extending his arm seems to unlock an air bubble of gas that he can't help but unleash into the world. I can block out the long trumpet sounds but the lingering smell is horrendous. Being engulfed by the stench of rotten eggs while trying to perfect the Triangle Pose is not where I want to be in life.

'That was brilliant,' Mum claps at the end of the class, sighing blissfully as though she's just spent a week in a health retreat in Thailand. 'Honestly, I think something like this would do the world of good for Michelle.'

'She's just had a baby.'

'She'll be up to it soon enough.'

'Maybe,' I shrug, although I doubt Mum will get Michelle anywhere that focuses on finding your inner peace. Michelle lives for the chaos, and if she were to come along she'd have a thing or two to say to Mr Trumpy Pants.

Following Mum out of the hall I retrieve my phone and see that it's silently ringing, and that it's Natalia who is calling.

'Just got to get this, Mum,' I say, swiping my thumb across the bottom of my screen. 'Hello?'

'Lizzy!' she chirps, sounding thrilled I've picked up.

'You OK?' I ask.

'Yes, yes, yes, all good,' she sings. 'I have a favour to ask.'

'Oh?'

'Are you busy this afternoon?'

'If watching *Gossip Girl* in bed constitutes busy then yes. If not, no,' I say, aware that I'm about to lose my afternoon date with the delectable Chuck Bass.

'Would you be able to travel into town?'

'Definitely,' I say, looking over at Mum who I can tell is desperately trying to listen in on what Natalia is saying.

'Great start!' she trills. 'I need you to buy lots of sweets. Not for me, of course.'

'Sweets?' I repeat, feeling instantly deflated that I'm not being called in to do something of value.

'Sounds bizarre but it isn't really,' she says, speaking quickly. 'I've just finished a total refurb for a new client and we have an area of the hallway that's been decorated with old-fashioned sweet-shop jars which they want filled. The family are meant to be moving back in in less than three hours and they're expecting everything to be complete. The delivery van containing my sweets order has broken down and so they won't be getting here today.'

'Oh dear.'

'While I'm here finishing off the final touches would you be able to run to a Costco or something?' she says, sounding awkward as she asks.

'Of course!' I laugh. 'Email me the details and I'll head off as soon as I can.'

'Thank you!' she breathes, the relief audible as she hangs up.

As soon as I'm back home I quickly change out of my workout gear and into jeans and a jumper. Normally I would hate the idea of not showering after doing a class, but I barely broke a sweat. My main concern would be particles of an elderly man's trumps sticking to my clothes, but I've got a job to do and not long to do it, so I dowse myself in Ghost Deep Night, grab Mum's car keys and run out of the door. If I'm going to be laden with sweets there's no point in bothering with the train. I just have to hope there's no traffic and somewhere to park at the other end.

As expected, Natalia has already sent over her shopping list and where I have to go afterwards. It turns out the closest Costco to me is in Grays, but that's a bit of a detour if I'm driving to Chelsea afterwards so I end up heading into London and going to one on the way. It all goes smoothly. Everything asked for is sourced (as well as a gallon of white wine because it was so reasonably priced), so before long I'm travelling through the posh borough of Chelsea and Kensington with the sweet smell coming from the thousands of penny sweets on the back seat giving me a sugar rush. Literally my jaw aches just from sitting so close to them.

'You're an absolute star!' Natalia says, opening my boot before I've even had a chance to park properly so that she can pull out the two-hundred flying saucers, cola bottles, caramel bonbons, marshmallows, jelly beans, aniseed balls, banana splits, liquorice sticks, shrimps, black jacks and Catherine wheels as quickly as possible. Parking restrictions don't appear to apply when a wealthy client needs his sweetie shop set up. I jump out and help carry the heavy bags inside, running up the front steps behind her.

Having not had time to take in my surroundings when I was pulling up I stop as soon as I've taken a foot inside the house. Tall ceilings automatically lead my eyes upwards, enabling me to see the vast scale of the space. A warm grey has been painted on the walls, leaving it bright but inviting. Monochrome Victorian tiles with an ornate detail have been laid on the floor, leading to a cantilevered staircase that travels from one side of the hallway and loops up and around, creating a beautiful spiral further than I can see, teasing me with how many floors this insane place might have. A slightly flecked striped runner, which gives hints of pastel pink, green, blue, red and turquoise on top of a neutral grey grounding, has been used on the stairs, with lavish African blackwood showing either side. The beading and spindles have been painted white while the handrail is a contrasting jet black, helping to really accent the swooping of the carpentry in the design. It's the making of a Pinterest board from heaven.

'Oh my God!' I find myself saying, so in awe of the sight

in front of me that my feet forget how to function properly. I have to shuffle them along the pristine tiles to get to the 'sweet station', a nook in the corridor, which is in fact bigger than any sweet shop I've ever been into and lined from floor to ceiling with a beautifully crafted white unit. Tall rows of chunky shelves have been topped with an elegantly tapered cornice. There's even a flipping sliding ladder to ensure all sweets will be in reaching distance. The floor is covered with rows and rows of footed bonbon jars, which, once filled and placed on the awaiting shelves, will ensure this spot looks like something from *Charlie and the Chocolate Factory* – albeit with a lot more taste.

'This is bonkers,' I say to Natalia, who's already ripping into the plastic bags and tipping the goodies I've bought into glass jars that are covering the floor.

'I know. Everything else is done. The decorators and electrician have left,' she says without stopping. 'They aren't going to be long.'

I take the memo and get on with it. Sweets to jar then on the shelf, sweets to jar then on the shelf, sweets to jar then on the shelf . . . The task is repeated over and over, the repetitive action becoming therapeutic as we beaver away in silence.

We both jump when Natalia's phone starts ringing, the noise catching us by surprise. I look over and see it's Alastair. I watch as she spots it too and sighs before switching it to silent. His call seems to have irritated her.

'Everything OK?' I ask, not meaning to pry but feeling my question is warranted thanks to her clear emotional shift.

She gives a little cough before getting to her feet, taking her glass jar and placing it on one of the shelves. 'He knows it's an important day,' she grumbles, but not in the way that tells me he was being friendly and thoughtful by wanting to speak to her.

'Oh? Perhaps he's forgotten, or something's happened,' I say, although I've no idea why I'm sticking up for him. Maybe they've fallen out over something and he's genuinely been a cock and deserving of her wrath.

'It's you,' she says, looking at me with her arms crossed.

I stare back. The word 'cock-blocker' appears in my mind in big, bold, black letters. I blink it away.

'He knows you're with me,' she adds.

I shrug in response, picking up the glass jar I've just filled with jellied rings and passing it to her. She takes it and pops it next to the one of chocolate mice she's just arranged, speedily moving on to the next jar to fill.

'He keeps badgering me for your number,' she says, ripping into a packet of flying saucers and tipping them in. The sound of them landing against the glass fills the silence that's fallen between us.

We continue with our task, keeping our heads down as we do so. My mind isn't on the fact that her fit mate wants to get in touch with me, but rather her reaction to it. I don't like the murky feeling it creates between us, but seeing as I've done nothing wrong I'm not sure what to do. She's the one who keeps bringing the situation up though, so maybe it's something that needs to be addressed. He's her best mate so won't be going anywhere, and I'm going to be working for her in a few months.

'Do you want me to give it to him?' she eventually asks as we continue to sort through the bags, the distraction helping make the awkward conversation less intense.

'Do you want me to want you to give it to him?' I ask, looking up at her just in time to catch a frown line appear. She definitely didn't want me to that night, and the fact he didn't ask for it regardless was probably a blessing in disguise. I was disgruntled about it at first, but a couple of weeks have passed and I'm over it. I don't see the point of him having my number now when I'm off next week.

'He likes you,' she says matter-of-factly.

'I'm sure he likes a lot of girls,' I retort.

'He's not *that* bad,' she says, the wobble in her voice suggesting she doesn't fully believe her own statement.

'You weren't saying that the other night,' I remind her, another reason why I'm so confused by the whole thing. She was actively against us hooking up from the start, then she relaxed when she realized it was never going to be anything more than fun. This was followed up by her not leaving us alone to have said 'fun', and then telling me that he likes me and wants to get in touch with me, while clearly being hacked off about it. I'm not entirely sure what to make of her conflicting actions.

The other part of the confuddlement is my own feelings towards Alastair. Yes, he's a charming, beautiful man, but after having some serious shit fall on me from a great height not so long ago, I don't need new dramas in my life. I'm not willing to let someone knock my confidence again when I'm still trying to claw it back. I'm not ready to have my broken heart shattered into even tinier pieces that might never be able to be pieced back together again, not even by all the King's horse and all the King's men. I don't want to be left as a heap of shards alongside bloody Humpty Dumpty . . .

In all honesty, I'm scared. Scared of being back out there in the dating game, terrified of being exposed and horrified at the thought of being rejected. I'm just at the point of learning to accept who I am. I don't want to fall for someone like Alastair who probably changes his mind as soon as he's added that coveted notch.

I don't know how to do single. It's terrifying knowing I'm back out there and on the market, ready to be sized up and compared to the next ripening fruit next to me on the shelf. I'm not ready and the thought is deeply upsetting, because I don't know when I will be. But then I think of New Year's Eve and how the encounter with Alastair made me feel, and how I've replayed it in my mind since. I feel deeply deflated at the thought of that being it, of not experiencing any more of him.

Yet, the idea that we meet people at certain points in our lives for a reason has been playing on my mind. Perhaps Alastair was meant to help me out of the fog and ignite that spark of fun within me without it being made into anything else? Maybe placing too much of anything more serious on to it would be a huge mistake anyway. Or maybe, just maybe, I shouldn't allow memories of him to be clouding my thoughts when I have great things to look forward to.

'He's a complete swine when he wants to be, that's

completely true,' Natalia confirms, while wrestling with the lid of a tub of multi-coloured sweets. 'That's why he's so infuriating. He'll make a terrific boyfriend when he finds the person that has him hooked. I know it.'

'I'm really not looking for a boyfriend,' I remind her.

'Husband?'

'No!' I say, even more confused by her. 'And that's a terrible sell.'

'He likes you.'

'You must hate that,' I say, gathering up the empty bags and clearing the floor before glancing at my watch. We really don't have long until the owners arrive.

'Why'd you say that?' she asks, sounding genuinely intrigued.

I turn and raise an eyebrow at her. She can't think I'm that dumb not to notice something is going on.

'OK,' she says, holding her arms in the air, as if to confess. 'I'd rather he didn't have a crush on someone I plan to have a long and healthy working relationship with.'

'And also because you have a thing for him?' I ask, knowing I'm pushing my luck but wanting to just get it out there. If the two of them are meant to be together then I'd rather she realized that and got on with making it a reality while I was away travelling. At least that would mean I could come back and avoid more of this nonsense.

'I'd be lying if I said it wasn't something I've thought about over the years.'

'Oh shit,' I say, surprised by the feeling of disappointment her words stir. Part of me clearly didn't believe my suspicions.

343

'But only because all our other mates are in places that we aren't,' she says quickly, her face turning red. 'I think I've mentioned it before. It's a hard thing to get your head around when people you've known your whole adult life start growing up and leaving you behind.'

'But you run your own highly successful business,' I point out, finding her worries more than surprising seeing as I envy everything she's built up and managed to achieve. 'People worship you! You're more together than anyone I know.'

'Oh, bless you,' she says with a sigh, checking over our sweet-shop creation now that all the jars have been filled and displayed, twisting and shifting them so that they sit perfectly in uniform. 'I know you're new to the single life, but it's tough to see the people you love tackling new stages in their lives when you're still waking up alone. Priorities change, and even though I know they'll always love me, and would hate to know I feel this way, I have found myself sliding down their list in the pecking order. I've dedicated myself to my work, but it's come at a personal price.'

'When was your last date?' I ask, realizing we haven't had this chat yet.

'I can't even remember, it's been that long. I don't have time to socialize and meet people. I really don't,' she shrugs, stepping away from our handiwork and turning to scrutinize it once more. 'It's been a comfort to have Alastair by my side, but I dread the day he turns up with an actual girlfriend. A girl that he cares about. My comrade leaving me behind too would be crushing.'

'You know, even when I was in a relationship I had those worries. Everyone was overtaking me,' I tell her, fascinated by how similar our insecurities would have been even though we would've thought we were in such different situations. 'It worried me so much I became obsessed by it. I didn't want to be left behind and so preoccupied with what everyone else was doing. Always looking longingly outwards rather than contentedly inwards.'

'Wow. You've hit the nail on the head there,' she says, shaking her head in disbelief. 'I don't want Alastair to be my boyfriend. I never have. I honestly mean it when I say he's great, but it would literally be like sleeping with my brother – and that's too *Game of Thrones* for my liking. I'm no Cersei Lannister.'

'Eeesh,' I laugh, screwing up my face at the thought. 'So you've not made a pact that you'll get married or have a kid together if you're still single in a few years?'

'Absolutely not!' she says, looking aghast. 'Which is a shame, because those genes would be . . .'

We both start giggling like little girls and I'm so relieved to have this all cleared up now, rather than letting it fester into something it really isn't.

'Oh god. They're going to be here in ten minutes,' Natalia says, snapping back into professional mode. 'I should have another run around before they do.'

'I'll leave you to get on with it, but it looks amazing!' I say, gesturing to the stunning display.

'Let's hope they think so,' she says, looking genuinely worried rather than fishing for compliments. 'And thanks for your help today.'

'Not at all. It's great to see your work,' I say, feeling even more excited about the prospect of coming back and getting my teeth stuck into a project like this with her. It's funny how, for a long time, work had been something I endured and my relationship with Ian was something I hooked all my dreams and ambitions on. Now it's entirely different. This is something I want completely for me. It's not an event to brag about online in an attempt to display the fact that someone else clearly valued me more than I ever did myself. It feels great to have taken back control of my own life, even if it is a daunting prospect. Living with Connie, being in London and eventually moving into my own place, while working in such amazing buildings, is literally beyond any other plan I could've had for myself at this point. Sure, it might not feel like that when I'm downing Baileys at two in the morning and having my thoughts turn to an emotional mush – but I'm getting there!

'I'm glad you like it,' Natalia says, gathering her phone and notepad, her eyes scanning her way down a scribbled 'to do' list. 'Certainly helps when the budgets go into the hundreds of thousands and beyond.'

'Shut up!' I say, picking up the rest of the rubbish and starting to walk towards the door. 'Oh, how the other half live!'

'Yep,' Natalia nods, moving with me and squeezing a rogue bit of plastic into my bag of rubbish as we go. She opens the door for me and pulls me in for a hug. 'Thanks again.'

'I loved it. I can't believe we didn't even eat one!'

'Cameras everywhere,' she whispers.

'No!' I gasp, wondering if I did anything embarrassing like pick my nose or pull my knickers out of my butt (turns out they're always hungry).

'So, in all seriousness, should I give him your number?' she asks, holding on to my hand.

I look at Natalia for a second or two as I mull it over.

'No. Thanks, but I'm not ready yet,' I say, the sadness that drifts into view making it evident I'm talking with my head and not my heart. 'Maybe one day.'

'He's going to be heartbroken.'

'I'm sure he'll get over it,' I laugh. 'Right! Good luck!' I chime, bouncing down the stairs while feeling uplifted, empowered and in control of the direction my life is heading. It seems there's so much to look forward to at last, and it's that thought that leads me to skip to my car with a big grin on my face.

Before getting into the driver's seat I whip out my phone to find a text message from Ian. I groan before opening it.

34

It feels like it's been years since I was last here in my heartbroken, zombified state, wondering how on earth the walls around my supposedly perfect life had totally crumbled and taken all of my purpose and self-worth with it.

This time there are no memories being stirred as I stare at the front door of the flat. It's just a door, albeit a very nice wooden one, and one that I was happy to walk through every day. But I'm not hankering for that life any more. Even though that's the case, I'm apprehensive to go inside now, knowing that it might be the very last time I do.

We got an offer today, which was thankfully for the asking price, so no discussion was necessary. As Thursday nights are when Ian goes to spin class, I figured I should use the opportunity of him being out to head over and round up some clothes that aren't black which might be good for travelling. I also need to dig out my old backpack and anything else that might be useful. If the sale goes through as planned then it'll complete while I'm away and I won't have another chance to come back. Now that I'm feeling in a better place than I was, it's worth seeing if there's anything else I want to take with me and box up so that it's not chucked away like I was tempted to before. Dad has told me to put everything to one side so that he and Mum can do the boxing and lifting later on, although the thought of them running into Ian is a frightening one. God knows what they'd both say to him, but thankfully I won't be here to find out.

I put the key in the lock and turn it. As I push it open I'm instantly hit by an incredibly familiar smell. It's one I can't describe other than to say, it's of my flat. Ex-flat. I shut the door behind me, take off my shoes, ignore the sentimental key bowl on the side, and go through to the living area.

'Shit!' I blurt as soon as I walk through the doorway and spot Ian sitting on the sofa in his gym gear with his head bowed, his hands clasped together and raised up to his mouth. He flinches at my reaction.

'Sorry,' he says, standing up, his face looking pained. 'I couldn't go.' He seems so nervous I can't help but feel for him.

'Why not?' I ask, hearing a mixture of emotions in my own voice – surprise, fear, concern and anger, it's all there.

'You being here while I headed out . . . it felt cowardly not to be here,' he says, reaching his arms out towards me.

'Some would say decent,' I say, unable to stop myself spitting the words out.

'Would you?' he asks, his eyes begging me to be more understanding, or at least willing to listen.

'Depends what you're here for,' I breathe, feeling my jaw tighten.

'Nothing!' he says with possibly a bit too much punch than he should've done. He's not about to start begging for me back. Well, there's a relief . . .

'I just want to sort out my things,' I say, looking around the flat that's more immaculate than ever.

'I know . . .'

He's here when he said he'd be out. It's as though he has purposefully trapped me into being here at the same time as him. I should be angrier than I am, but the truth is there's something strangely comforting about seeing him. When I walked off at the airport (while whispering champagne-fuelled expletives as I went), I was so charged and grief-stricken. It's sad to think that after ten years of being completely entwined, that was our last moment together. I wasn't looking for something more meaningful then, I haven't been looking for more since, but seeing him now and not hating every fibre of his being and recognizing he's still the man I loved for so long, draws me in. I owe it to the memory of us to round this off in such a way that I can look back at the memories we shared with something other than pain, anger and disappointment. I don't want to reach indifference, but a fondness would be nice.

'How have you been?' I ask.

'Good. Fine,' he says with a shrug, the right side of his mouth giving the tiniest of smiles. 'You?'

'Great,' I nod.

'Oh!' he says, genuinely shocked that I'm not dwelling or struggling. It occurs to me that he thinks I'm either lying in a bid to do the whole 'I'm so over you' thing or that he's surprised that I'd admit I'm coping in a moment in which we should both seem gravely downtrodden at the way in which we both failed our relationship. 'Good to know,' he adds.

'I'm going travelling,' I share.

'You always wanted us to do more of it,' he remembers, looking impressed.

'If it weren't for your work we could've done,' I say, thinking about how much I used to whitter on about different countries for us to explore, only to be reminded about his commitments at work (which always seemed to be less accommodating than my own) and the fact it would be virtually impossible for him to be granted a substantial amount of time off.

'True,' he nods.

'I've got a new job too and am moving to London,' I say with pride while wondering why I'm telling him – but of course, I'm telling him because he knew everything there was to know about me for so long, just as I did about him. It's the most natural thing in the world to want to share it with him.

'Right,' he nods, raising his eyebrows while pursing his lips for several seconds. I guess it is a lot to take in. I've completely overhauled my life.

'You?' I ask.

'Same,' he nods, looking dazed and somewhat hurt. 'Same as in I'm still living the same life I was. Nothing's changed.'

'I'm not in it,' I argue, stating the obvious. 'That's quite a dramatic change right there.'

He looks speechless at my blunt words, his jaw hanging in a dumbfounded manner as he grapples for something to come out of it. Nothing comes. Instead he sadly nods his head as he concedes to my statement. However, proving him wrong on the matter doesn't make me feel particularly good.

'How was your holiday?' I ask, wanting to steer us away from the place it's clearly so easy for me to go. It's not how I want this to pan out – not that I've had much time to think about what I do want to come from this. Not once have I thought about what I would do if I ever had to see him again. It was something I wanted to avoid at all costs.

'Fine,' he tells me, looking bashful about it. 'I just went to Tenerife with Mum and Dad.'

'I saw her,' I say, aware of something in me softening. I don't know what I thought his holiday would consist of, but it wasn't sitting with Mummy and Daddy Hall at dinner. But then, it's Ian. He wasn't going to be out clubbing with a bunch of eighteen year olds or ending up getting smashed with the lads. I should've known that, but then I'm not sure whether any of the things I know about him are accurate any more.

'She said. Phoned me straight after,' he says, giving a feeble laugh that's led more by pain than humour. 'If she could've grounded me for life she would've done.'

'I got that impression.'

'She liked you,' he says matter-of-factly. 'Loved you even.'

'I'm glad someone did,' I laugh, before an awkward

silence lands between us. I hate it being like this. 'Do you want a drink?'

'Yes!' he says without a beat being skipped. 'Crap. I've not got anything in,' he says, genuinely looking crestfallen. Which is a good job as I would've taken it as an excuse that he'd rather not.

'Mum's car is outside,' I say, holding the keys out to him. 'There's a whole gallon of wine on the back seat.'

'A gallon?'

'And it's white,' I declare.

'I don't mind white,' he shrugs.

'Are you joking?' I laugh incredulously, as though he's just said the funniest thing I've ever heard.

'What?' he asks, looking befuddled by my reaction.

'*White* wine.'

'Yeah . . .' he says slowly, his voice looping in pitch.

'You're a total wine snob,' I remind him.

His face cracks into a proper smile for the first time since I walked through the door. 'I can be a bit picky,' he acknowledges, becoming bashful as he covers his face with his hand.

'A bit? What happened to drinking only red and organic?' I say, unable to hide the humour in my voice.

'That was after we went to Bordeaux for the weekend, remember?' he asks, although I'm unlikely to forget the trips we took in which I was convinced he was going to propose. We were staying in a remote chateau with an adjoining vineyard for three nights. The whole trip was based around food and wine, and although we'd make sure we'd get in a morning run, the rest of the time we were more relaxed than ever. I was thrilled because we'd managed to accidentally time it to coincide with the family of the house harvesting the grapes and turning it to wine. I assumed Ian knew about it all, to be honest, and expected a big rock to show itself as a flipping toe-ring as I diligently squelched the fruit with my bare feet. 'Great weekend,' he recalls. 'And we never got a hangover no matter how much we drank, remember?'

'True . . .'

'Purely because of the lack of chemicals!' he reminds me. 'Seeing as the shop up the road started stocking a few organic wines a little while after, it made sense to go for one of them, right? Drinking it has always made me think of that special weekend.'

'Really?' I ask. Wondering how I had not linked these two events. Or maybe I had at the time but not remembered all these years later. It was a sweet gesture, not him being a picky arsehole.

'Yes,' he proclaims. 'Although, fair enough, I do prefer red. It's more full-bodied and giving. I get a metallic aftertaste with white that stays in my mouth for longer than it should.'

'Well, in that case, would you like some headache-inducing, aluminium-tasting, selfish wine in the colour you dislike?'

He laughs.

I can still make him laugh.

He takes the keys from my hand and makes his way out of the front door, leaving me standing in the middle of the home we once shared together, with the weird sensation of being comforted by someone I once shared so much with, but have since lost so much because of.

I close my eyes and take a deep breath.

As lovely as this is, it's not why I came here.

I go to the cupboard underneath the kitchen sink and pull out a roll of black bin liners, which I carry with me to the bedroom. I open my wardrobe to find everything is neater than it was when I left, with all of my holiday clothes having been washed and put away (although not in their correct places). It looks great, but really the neat piles are home to chaos. PJs mixed in with holiday shorts, or t-shirts mixed in with jumpers. Still, it's all mine and, thankfully, hardly any of it is black.

I pick up the piles of folded, fresh-smelling clothes, and start gently placing them inside the bags. Unlike last time when I didn't want to take anything away with me, I load the bags with as much as they can hold before either placing them by the door (they'll be coming with me tonight) or at the bottom of the cupboard they've just come from (they'll be waiting for Mum or Dad to rescue them). I want it all.

'Here you go,' Ian says coming into the room, carrying two glasses filled to the brim with white wine. He holds one of them out to me.

'Thank you,' I say, taking it and having a gulp, its sweetness making my eyes water. 'Eesh, that's really not the best.'

'It's all right,' he says, although I notice the triangles of his nostrils expand and flare ever so slightly as he takes a mouthful.

'Not your organic red,' I muse, putting the glass down on top of our chest of drawers. Opening the drawer beneath it, I find my underwear and swimwear all neatly displayed like everything else. I'm really not going to sort through all of this in front of Ian, even if he was the one who laid out my knickers and bras in this orderly fashion. Instead I just scoop it all into a bag. I'm alarmed to see a few thongs lingering at the very back of it. I can't remember buying them, if they were ever worn, or Ian's reaction to them if I had.

Ian scoots past me awkwardly and goes towards the bed.

'This is weird,' he sighs, gesturing at bags I've managed to surround myself with in the five or so minutes since he's been gone. 'Seeing you do this.'

'Not going to pack itself,' I shrug. 'And you'll be doing the same soon.'

'Yeah . . .'

I'm on socks now and although I have no qualms sorting through the hole-ridden material in his company, I'd rather not. Another bag is opened for my possessions to be shovelled into.

'I've missed you,' he says quietly.

'That's inevitable, I'm afraid,' I joke, managing to laugh while my insides weep.

'You're right,' he says, a sadness in his voice. 'Although this time apart has made me realize I've been missing you for a long time. Not purely since Dubai.'

I look up at him. He's on his side of the bed with all four of our pillows plumped up behind him. He holds the glass against his chest while his eyes are fixed on the ceiling above him.

'I thought I hated you, like you said in your message,' I say, thinking back to the stupidity of my Christmas Day communication and what I woke up to the following day. 'Although it wasn't for dumping me.'

'No?' he asks, his sorrowful gaze finding my own.

'Well, maybe. You were waving a diamond ring in my face at the time. It was very confusing and cruel.'

'Don't. It's not even funny,' Ian says, covering his face in horror, his hand making his voice muffled. 'I have nightmares about how badly I dealt with the situation. I talk through all the things I should've said but didn't.'

'Well, I've recently discovered hindsight is actually a total bitch so I wouldn't torment yourself,' I advise him, almost stumbling on my words while opening the last drawer to find some 'sexy time' outfits I'd completely forgotten about.

'What do you hate me for then?' Ian asks, clearly not noticing how much I'm blushing. 'Surely that's the worst thing I've ever done to you.'

'I said I thought I did . . .' I remind him, shutting the drawer and sitting at the end of the bed by his feet. I look up at him, his eyes staring back at me and willing me to continue now I've started. 'I thought I hated you for changing me.'

'Huh?' he asks, looking genuinely shocked.

'Yeah . . .' I nod, frowning as I hear it said out loud. 'But you didn't. Not intentionally. You were just very clear and direct about your likes and dislikes, whereas I realize I've always been too eager to please.'

'You think I overpowered you?' he asks.

'I thought maybe your decisiveness did,' I shrug, pondering his words. 'I wanted to please you and you always seemed so sure of what you wanted, so when I started looking back on our time together all I could see were the parts of me I'd compromised on. All the little, tiny bits of me I'd given up in order for you to be happy.'

'You're painting yourself to be some weak follower,' he frowns, sitting upright so that our bodies are much closer. 'You have never been that.'

'No. I know I was looking at the whole thing in such a skewed way,' I admit, speaking more quickly as the realization comes flooding in. 'I've grown up. We grew up together. I was bound to stop doing things I enjoyed when I was younger, and to change my views and tastes.'

'I've changed too,' Ian exclaims. 'At least, I should bloody hope I have!'

'Exactly!' I say, pleased he's agreeing with my point. 'I would've always changed in those ten years. It's an inevitable fact. I've been trying to discover who I would've been if you weren't in my life – but that's an impossible task. There would've always been something or someone there to have some sort of an effect.'

'True,' Ian nods, taking a sip of his wine.

'I like the person I am right now, and there's no denying that I am the person I am this very second because of you,' I declare with confidence and belief. 'I don't regret the person I am. I'm sad she's been hurting so much, but she's not a total disaster.'

'She really isn't,' Ian agrees.

'Exactly!' I almost shout again. 'She's ambitious, brave, funny and kind . . . and, thanks to you, she also has quite an eclectic taste in music, film and literature,' I joke.

'You really are quite a catch,' Ian smiles, taking my hand and squeezing it tightly.

'I'm just not *your* one.'

Ian sighs.

'I'm sorry.'

'I know you are. And thank you.'

There's no anger or animosity towards one another, and there's absolutely no regret that we found each other all those years ago. There's only gratitude that we've reached this point. Now we can say goodbye, knowing we wish each other nothing but happiness and fulfilment.

35

'My tummy is full of knots!' Susan whispers to me with a worried look on her face, which probably echoes my own expression.

We're standing in one of the side rooms of the church along with the rest of the Sing It Proud choir. Some of the audience have been picked up and brought in to sit alongside other members of the community who've managed to walk or drive here themselves. Wine, coffee, tea and hot chocolate have been served, and we're now able to hear their buzz of conversation as they natter amongst themselves, hopefully enjoying being out of the house and having something different to do with their evening.

Now that we've juggled logistics and our audience has gathered, it's time for us to get ready. The fact we're actually about to put on a show is becoming more real by the second.

It's comforting to know that Susan is as nervous as I am, although it's also slightly disconcerting at the same time, as I assumed she'd have her shit together as a choir veteran and would be taking this in her stride. Learning she's worried isn't doing much to calm the bazillion butterflies that are currently flooding through my body at great speed – they're not even sticking to the usual boundaries of being in my tummy. They're everywhere, even in my fingertips and toes; my entire being is pumping with pure adrenalin, aware that I'm about to do something I've not done in years.

'Are you still panicking?' Albie asks his wife, as he takes off his black winter coat and places it over the back of a wooden chair. 'It's us lot standing in a church singing a few songs we know inside out to a bunch of people we want to cheer up. It'll be fun. Let's give them all we've got.'

Susan breathes out a long sigh. 'You're right,' she tuts.

'Can I have that in writing?' he chuckles, his hand reaching out to hers.

'Have you got any family in?' I ask, the question making my nerves build further as I picture the lot out there, looking aghast at my pitiable attempt at singing, especially poor Mum and Dad. I'm pretty sure they're expecting me to sing the whole thing solo with these guys only pitching in as my backing vocalists. 'I couldn't stop mine. They're all coming and making a night of it. They've been for a curry first.'

'Sounds great,' Albie says, looking at Susan with a flicker of concern on his face.

'We have some friends from the community club coming,' she nods, smiling brightly, although I can see a watery shine in her eyes. 'But no family. No. Our son sadly—'

Jodie claps her hands together to get our attention, interrupting whatever it is Susan is about to tell me. I notice Albie put his hand protectively on the small of her back. She dips her head at his touch. It bounces slightly, as though she's nodding at something he's said. She takes a breath and pulls her head up. She's smiling, or at least trying to.

'How are you all feeling?' Jodie asks, standing on a chair, so animated that she suddenly seems like she's a CBeebies presenter.

The rest of the choir all cheer in her direction.

'Good!' Jodie nods. 'You've done the hard bit. Working out your harmonies is the tricky stuff, this is the pay-off!' she tells us all. 'Right, are we ready?'

'Yes,' they all shout.

'Yes,' I whisper, blowing air out of my mouth and clapping my hands together in a bid to steady the apprehension I'm feeling. Like Albie said, what do I really have to be scared of out there? It's only singing in front of people who care for us.

'Let's do this!' shouts Marie, an elderly lady who lives around the corner from Mum. I regularly see her singing in the fruit and veg aisle in Budgens, so I wasn't too surprised to see her as part of the choir when I joined.

'Come on then,' Jodie says, waving her arm in the direction of the door as she climbs down from her pedestal and leads the way.

The atmosphere is charged and expectant as we shuffle into the room in single file, causing lots of hushing and whispering from our audience. I'm aware of the room being full even though I don't look up to take in their faces. My focus is on getting in position, which is now on the second row between Susan and Nicola, a young woman who's just rejoined the group after having a baby. I'm thrilled not to be in the front row any more. Firstly, because it means Susan is now at a much kinder volume on my ears, and secondly because I feel I'm cuddled and empowered by the rest of the choir all around me, rather than right at the front, exposed and alone.

The music starts. Just for tonight the pianist has been joined by a guitarist, drummer, cellist and violinist. They're a bunch of his mates (all locals) who were happy to give up their free time to be a part of the evening. We haven't been able to rehearse together yet, so the sound of a guitar strumming our intro of 'One Day Like This' while Fiona at the end of my row takes the opening two lines as a solo is new to my ears. It causes a thrill of delight and fire to surge through me.

I look up and see Jodie looking at us all, her face alive and bright as her hands jump along to the beat, ready to bring us all in together. My heart jumps in my chest as I take a deep breath and open my mouth, becoming one with the group as we sing the song I first saw them perform last month – the one that moved me to tears. It's just as emotional now as I deliver it to others. I don't take my eyes off Jodie. I'm immersed in the sound being created around me, loving the way my voice blends in with those of my new friends and the impassioned joy that's seeping from each and every one of us.

As I start to relax I allow myself to take in the faces behind Jodie. People of all ages are crammed into the church's pews, some are even standing along the back and down the sides. Everyone's eyes are on us as they cradle their drinks in their hands, clearly captivated by our performance. I spot a woman put an arm around the elderly man next to her, another man taking his wife's hand as she kisses the head of the toddler on her lap, and a young couple bashfully smiling at each other. We're inspiring these emotions. It's pretty magical.

It doesn't take me long to spot my family and Connie and Matt at the end of a row two-thirds of the way up the church. Mum, Dad, Ted, Connie, Matt and Stuart are all smiling back at us, their grins reflecting those of the choir. However, I can see that Mum and Dad are both visibly crying too.

Michelle, on the other hand, notices that I've clocked them all sitting there and pulls a comical face of disinterest at me, tapping her hand against her open mouth as though yawning, before breaking into a grin of her own and winking.

It strikes me that I'm really going to miss the bitch when I leave in a few days' time. I'm going to miss all of them so very much.

Movement from the back of the church catches my attention. A quick glance lets me know that Natalia has come along. I hadn't even told her where tonight's concert was being held so it's a pleasant and thoughtful surprise. I force myself to refocus my attention back on our musical supervisor.

Before long the song finishes to rapturous applause and we're flying through the rest of our numbers: Christina Perri's 'A Thousand Years', 'Somewhere Over the Rainbow' from *The Wizard of Oz*, John Legend's 'All of

Me', Bob Marley's 'One Love', Michael Jackson's 'Earth Song', 'Climb Every Mountain' from *The Sound of Music*, and Pharrell Williams' 'Happy'. Each song creates a different reaction from our audience; a reminiscent sigh, an excited cheer of surprise that we're attempting to perform it. They feed off what we're giving them, but their response and attention pushes us to deliver even more and give them our very best.

It whizzes by in a flurry of exhilaration and soon we're waiting for the introduction to the final song. The piano starts with gentle percussion splashing over the top. When the violin begins creeping in with the melody a chill runs down my spine.

'Fix You'.

From behind me Albie starts singing the first verse, his gravelly, experienced voice giving a greater depth and meaning to the words of regret, loss, failure, desperation, pain, love and longing. I know this song inside out, but hearing him sing it right now moves me more than I'm expecting it to. A lump forms in my throat. He's married, happily so far as I can tell, but I can't help but feel he must be drawing on something real from his own life as he sings the lyrics with so much feeling. I know I shouldn't but I sneak a peek at Susan beside me and see tears streaming down her face.

Their son.

Even though I don't know the whole story I know enough to see she's hurting. I search out her fingers and grab her hand, squeezing it tightly. She takes a big intake of breath as she pats my arm with her spare hand. We never really know what others are going through or have been through. Sometimes even the happiest of souls can be the ones suffering the worst pain.

When we all join in I feel like we're singing this for each other, about each other. We all have our difficulties, our struggles and heartache. They're a part of our story. They have a part to play in the people we become, but they don't define who we are.

When we're devotedly singing a promise of leading someone home, of giving someone their life back and putting them together again, I can't help but think of what I've been doing for myself over the past few months.

I never would've thought I would be capable of coming out of the fog of heartache and turning my life around so drastically. I thought this new life was going to be nothing more than a consolation prize. A downgrade on what could've been.

It's true; sometimes you don't know what you've got until it's gone. But you also don't know what you're made of until all you thought you knew and wanted is stripped away from you.

The song builds with all the instruments coming in and multiple harmonies being sung, the words ringing out loud and proud. It's clear each of us is loving every single second of it.

And then we all fade away, leaving just Albie and the piano to finish the number.

The audience are on their feet before he's even sung the last note.

36

'Oh, come here, you!' Connie chirps, throwing her arms around me and squeezing me tightly, which nearly causes me to spill my glass of precious red wine. Yes. Red. It turns out I, like Ian, prefer red wine over white in the colder months – it really is far more inviting and warming as it slides down your gullet. 'That was flipping amazing!' Connie continues with a huge grin on her face. 'You were great!'

'Thank you,' I say, feeling bashful at receiving praise without the other choir members with me to accept it.

'I'm going to miss you so much,' she says, refusing to release me from her grasp.

'You're going to be seeing plenty of me when I get back,' I remind her, talking into her hair while aware of the excited grin on my face, my stomach flipping at the thought of getting on a plane in just two days' time.

'I can't wait!' she tells me almost humping me as she jumps up and down.

I love that Connie's as excited about it as I am. We won't be living together for very long, and I know we'll be in her flat rather than one we might have found together – so it'll probably be like I'm there having a sleepover rather than it being a home for me. However, it'll give us a taster of what living together years ago could have been like, and a taster is sometimes better than the real deal. I'm sure I'm totally annoying to live with, as is she, but we won't get stressed or agitated with each other because it's only short-term. Plus, we'll have to make the most of it before it's over. I've no doubt she'll be taking the plunge and moving in with Matt by the end of the year. Although, as with my situation, you never can tell what's going to happen in life. Maybe he'll grow two heads, we'll discover he has a secret wife living in Norfolk, or he'll simply change his mind after playing the devoted boyfriend for long enough. I sincerely hope not. I've never seen Connie as happy as she's been in the last few months. It's been a wonder to see.

'Who's the silver fox with the voice?' she asks, looking around the room.

'That would be Albie,' I smile, taking a sip of my drink. Now the performance is over the adrenalin has kicked in and I'm buzzing even more. I need something to take the edge off and calm me down. 'Married to Susan, the woman I was standing next to in the choir,' I add.

'Well, he's a dream, as are you!' she beams.

'Thank you,' I say bashfully.

'Hello, slappers!' Michelle whispers loud enough for only us to hear, making us jump as she pinches our bums.

'We're in a church,' I hiss, which only makes her chuckle filthily. 'And don't you have to have some sort of sex life to be one of those?' I ask, aware that the only action I've had since becoming single was the steamy session with Alastair on New Year's Eve. And that didn't even lead to us having sex, although now I really wish it had.

'Well done,' she says, giving me a kiss on the cheek. 'I couldn't even fake disinterest. It was ace.'

'Thanks!' I say, unable to hold back a frown. She never praises me without a catch so I brace myself for what's to come.

'What I want to know is, who's the hottie and can you introduce me?' she asks, eagerly leaning in.

'What is it with you two?' I exclaim, shaking my head at them both.

'Albie,' Connie states with a knowing tilt of the head towards Michelle, completely ignoring my look of disapproval. 'I've already asked.'

'I'll fight you for him!' says Michelle, and I've no doubt she means it.

'Married,' Connie states, pursing her lips together and almost looking like she's enjoying delivering the bad news.

'Fuck,' she says, having the decency to look apologetic as soon as the word is out.

'As are *you*,' I remind her.

'Bloody wedding vows! Always ruining my fun,' she groans. If it weren't for the cheeky glint in her eye, I'd wonder if she was being serious.

'Darling, Stuart's looking for you,' Mum informs Michelle as she comes over and gives me a hug, then turns back to my sister while continuing to hold on to my arm, patting it lovingly. 'He thinks Duncan needs feeding.'

'He always needs feeding when he's with him,' Michelle grunts, the annoyance almost steaming out of her nostrils. 'Why can't he fucking grow a pair? And I don't mean balls, because baps are far more hardcore than those droopy fellas. No, I literally want him to grow some rock-hard leaky boobs that Duncan can suck the life out of every second of the day. You'd think he'd let me have just five minutes away . . .' As her voice cracks with emotion she stops and closes her eyes, screwing her face up as she takes a breath.

'You OK?' I ask softly, placing my hand gently on her shoulder. Michelle can usually go one of two ways when she's like this and being offered sympathy; crumble and cry (which I obviously do not want) or turn her anger towards me, which will inevitably lead to her ripping my face off (again, I obviously don't want that. I like my face).

'It's been a long day,' she sighs, trying to pull herself together and attempting to smile back at me. It's been a few weeks since the last emotional wobble in her living room. Since then she's appeared to be on top of everything and brushed off my attempts at finding out how she's really doing. All I can do is ask. It's up to her to allow herself to be honest about what's going on. 'Duncan didn't sleep well last night, and I think I only got one solid hour,' she admits.

'Oh, love,' Mum sighs, her face full of concern.

'Sounds painful!' winces Connie.

'It's fine,' she says, although the way her chin wobbles tells us it's really not fine at all.

'You should've said!' I say, daring to move my hand from her shoulder and take hold of her hand. 'You know I would've come over today and let you go back to bed for a bit.'

'You really are the shittiest sister,' she tells me, quickly regaining her steely composure and standing a little taller. 'Now, I'm not allowed to swear in this bloody place, but can I go get my tits out?'

'Absolutely! Just pull up a pew!' I chime over-enthusiastically as I gesture to the empty rows surrounding us. After all, the main reason for tonight is getting people to connect with others in the community. I'd love for Michelle to be relaxed enough to start up conversations with strangers and maybe even meet some new mum friends in the process. 'Although there are also a few side rooms if you want some privacy,' I say, suddenly remembering that this is her first public outing with Duncan and there's a possibility she'll be finding this all overwhelming, no matter how much she wants to be here.

'I'm out of the house, Lizzy,' she states, looking at me with an aghast expression on her face. 'I'm not about to go hiding me and my knockers. It's been a while since I offended anyone other than you lot. I need my fix.'

'Couldn't agree more,' nods Connie approvingly.

'*You* know!' Michelle says to my best mate, as though their shared desire to wind people up is something I couldn't possibly understand. Quite frankly I'm not sure I do get them and their love of 'bantz'.

'Fair enough,' I shrug, relieved that Michelle seems chirpier, even if it is in response to the mere possibility of inflicting discomfort on others who are small-minded conservatives. Although I have to state that I will be flying straight to her aid if anyone does so much as look at her in a disapproving way.

'I'll come with you. I could do with a wee,' Connie says, sliding her arm through Michelle's and walking towards Stuart. He looks hysterically anxious as he peers into the pram at a wailing Duncan, while Matt stands beside him appearing equally clueless.

'He hasn't even picked him up!' I hear Michelle exclaim as they go.

'God, they're useless,' tuts Connie, shaking her head.

'I don't know why she doesn't say she's struggling,' Mum sighs, shaking her head as she watches Michelle pick up an inconsolable Duncan.

'Because she's proud like you?' I offer, much to her surprise. 'Can you imagine having to hold your hands up and say you're finding something difficult? Worse than that, ask for help?'

'Yes, I can. I didn't want to tell a soul about your dad after he left. I couldn't admit that his honesty left me feeling like I was drowning,' she says, shaking her head vigorously at the mere thought of it. She stops and notices what she's said. 'Ah. Fair point. Too much like me. That's why we bash heads occasionally.'

'Mum, *everybody* clashes with Michelle!' I giggle. 'Constantly.'

'She knows what she wants, that's all,' Mum says defensively, never having been one to talk about Michelle in a detrimental manner – something I know is the same when it comes to Michelle talking about me, too. Mum's the one to calm any tension between us, not build it. She's always longed for us to refer to one another as best friends.

'We've just got to keep an eye on her but try not to

interfere,' I say to Mum, knowing how much Michelle goes on the defensive whenever she feels people are trying to tell her what to do – which definitely happens when it comes to anything about Duncan. She won't listen to me because I'm not a mum and so simply couldn't understand, and she won't let Mum even give suggestions on things like winding positions without barking at her for trying to take over. 'You know what she's like.'

'I do,' she nods. 'Oh, and well done, darling,' she says, rubbing my arms again. 'What an absolute treat! And what a turn out! I've seen people here I've not seen in years. Bev and Gill who both used to work in the florist, Joan who used to be on reception at the doctor's, and then Jonathon who delivered our post for decades. So many faces I recognize,' she muses, clearly delighted to be seeing them all.

'That's great!' I say, looking around the room to see dozens of people talking and laughing exactly as we'd hoped they would.

'Not seen some of them since before me and your dad split,' she notes.

'Oh?'

'We've had a couple of awkward chats,' she says with a grimace, looping her finger along the collar of her cerise woollen jumper – a colour I've always loved on her.

'A couple?' laughs Dad, instantly joining in with the conversation as he and Ted walk over, both looking a little red faced and flustered.

'They just don't know,' shrugs Mum regretfully.

'I guess not everyone knows the ins and outs of our lives,' I say.

'You say that,' says Dad, putting his hand on Ted's forearm while waggling his index finger between them both. 'But Mrs Summer from Rye Walk just asked how long we'd been dating.'

'Us!' chimes in Ted.

'No!' I gasp, finding it difficult to suppress a guffaw. 'Word's out, Dad!'

'Hallelujah!' Dad states, raising his hands as if he's praying.

'I think it has been for a while, to be honest, love,' Mum says.

'What? How did everyone else suspect when I knew nothing?' I frown, before remembering how Michelle found out and realizing that it probably sent rumours soaring through the village. Seeing as I was in a bubble of my own at the flat and hardly came back to the village, it's not too surprising that I wasn't aware in the slightest. 'Oh . . . well, at least there's no more hiding, then,' I smile.

'Sing it proud? More like gay and proud,' Dad says loudly, causing a few people to look over and smile politely.

One woman who I don't recognize turns to a friend standing next to her and, probably louder than she means to, exclaims, 'I told you so!'

I can't help but giggle.

'Slightly worrying that the wrong news is out and circulating through the gossip mill, though,' Dad grimaces. 'Sorry, Ted,' he says apologetically.

'I'm flattered,' Ted smiles bashfully, the red of his cheeks deepening.

'Don't be getting any ideas!' Mum says, playfully

pulling Ted towards her and away from Dad's grasp. 'I've already lost one husband.'

We laugh at the unusual situation we're now all so used to being in. The absolute truth might not be out there but over time it will be, and that's got to be a relief for all of them, not just Dad. Their close bond never needed explaining anyway, but at least it now makes more sense to outsiders looking in.

'We met your new boss just now,' says Ted, looking around the room to see if he can spot Natalia, who I realize I haven't seen since she wandered in late.

'Oh yes!' says Mum with a big grin on her face. 'She loves you!'

'What a fascinating woman,' nods Dad approvingly. 'She's fluent in Italian, French, Spanish and Russian.'

'Really?' I question, understandably impressed. There's so much I'm yet to learn about my new friend.

'And she was talking to a very handsome chap,' trills Mum.

'Not Albie again?' I laugh, wondering if every woman in my life is going to be falling at my new friend's feet now they've had the pleasure of hearing him sing.

'I don't think that was his name, dear,' Mum says distractedly, waving at someone behind me. 'Here they are.'

I turn to find Natalia looking as pristine and pretty as ever, although she looks uncharacteristically agitated. I only have to move my gaze to the left slightly to find the source of that emotion.

Alastair. The man-bunned, tattooed wonder I've not been able to stop thinking about.

My tummy flips in response.

'Hi!' I say, the word getting lost in my constricting throat.

'That was incredible!' Natalia says to me, grabbing my shoulders and pulling me close so she can hiss in my ear, 'I'm so sorry.'

When we part she flashes me a regretful glance.

'Alastair,' I say, turning to him, caught off guard by the fact that he's even more good-looking than I remember. Especially now in his skinny jeans, white tee, camel-coloured boots and sheepskin coat. He's like a winter's dream and I have to resist the urge to slide my hands under the layers of his clothing and throw my own body against his inviting chest. Instead I find myself rooted to the spot, not moving while gawkily gawping at him.

He must sense my hesitation as there's a grin on his face as he places a hand on my waist and leans in to kiss me on the cheek. 'What a brilliant night,' he says sounding sincere, leaving me with a lingering and inviting whiff of his familiar aftershave.

'Thanks . . . I would introduce you to my family but it appears you've met them,' I say, looking awkwardly around the circle we're all standing in.

'I have,' Alastair grins again, nodding to each of them as they greet him warmly.

The fact that he's here uninvited should be creepy, but my insides are too confused, too chuffed, too touched to protest.

'Alastair was telling us all about your night together,' says Dad, shaking his head in disbelief. 'Sounds saucy.'

My mouth drops. Surely not.

'Clubs have changed a lot from when we were younger,' Mum thankfully adds, raising her eyebrows in dismay.

'Oh,' I say, trying to recover from my overreaction. 'Yes. Shocking,' I say, matching their reactions. I'm not about to tell them I thoroughly enjoyed it all and ruin their good opinions of me.

'Definitely the best New Year's I've ever had . . .' says Alastair, looking straight at me, the loaded statement catching me by surprise.

'Wouldn't recommend the club, though,' Natalia says sweetly to my parents, mercifully pulling the attention away from me and Alastair as it takes a second or two for me to tear my eyes away from his gaze.

'No, doesn't sound my cup of . . .' Mum stops talking midsentence and starts squinting between Alastair and me. I can literally see the realization hit her. Alastair is not my new boss's man, but the man Connie's mum told her I'd spent all of New Year's Eve getting jiggy with.

'Darling!' she says, looking over my shoulder again at something she's supposedly seen across the room. She manically pats Ted on the arm. 'Is that Vanessa leaving? We should grab her before she does. It's Dennis's birthday party next week and I need to find out if she wants dark or milk chocolate put on top of the profiteroles I'm making. It will be a disaster if I get it wrong.'

'OK,' says Ted compliantly, eager as ever to do whatever she asks.

'You should come too,' she says to Dad, her eyes shooting daggers at him.

'Really? I don't think I—' Mum's continuous glare halts him. 'Oh yes! You're right. I should see if they've had any more thought on that reading they wanted me to do,' mumbles Dad, glancing at me sideways before going after them.

'Back in a bit,' Mum cheerily calls over her shoulder.

I look from Natalia to Alastair, while Natalia looks from Alastair to me, and Alastair looks just at me. We stand silently, yet loudly. I've no doubt Natalia is inwardly screaming after being ambushed into coming by Alastair, while I'm wondering what on earth I should say and why I'm so happy to see him. On the flip side, Alastair's probably cackling away inside – the only one of us to be fully prepared for our being face to face again.

'Oh sod it,' Natalia says, with no enthusiasm or drive, her voice monotone and robotic. 'I've not seen Stu yet. I should probably go say hello to one of my oldest friends.'

She can't even look at me as she swivels and goes towards Stu and Michelle who are now standing talking to another baby-holding couple.

I look at them imploringly, willing one of them to come back and rescue me, but of course, no one does.

37

'Fancy seeing you here,' Alastair says, unable to control the smile on his face from growing even wider now that it's just us left standing together.

'Fancy that,' I say, raising an eyebrow at him.

'Want to go for a walk?' he suggests.

I hesitate. I'm safe here, surrounded by my family and new and old friends, but I also don't really want to be having this conversation in plain view of everyone else. I have to agree that it would be good to have some privacy away from my biggest fans, who are currently pretending to chat amongst themselves but are actually just staring at us rather unsubtly.

'All right,' I say, grabbing my puffy North Face coat from where I dumped it earlier and guiding us out into the frosty winter air. Following the street lamps, I walk around the side of the church and lead us past the small playground where I used to play when I was younger.

Apart from the odd bit of chatter or laughter travelling across from the crowd we've just left at the church, it's quiet. It's a still night, with just a hint of a cool breeze tickling the branches of the trees around us. The sky is clear and black, allowing me to see the twinkling of stars above.

Sitting down on a bench on the dimly lit pathway next to the park, I take in the peacefulness of it all and instantly regret it. This would be easier on my feet. I'd be freer and able to put more of a distance between us, but now I'm committed. I'm not trapped, but acutely aware of my desire for him, and how conflicted that makes me. I sigh at the romance of it all, realizing it's been a long time since I've experienced feelings like this.

'It's been four weeks,' Alastair says gently, sitting down next to me, the bench wobbling as he does so. I look over at him to find he's not looking back. Instead he's taking in the view in front of us as he twiddles his fingers. The heartthrob beside me who is known for his expert and confident flirting skills seems surprisingly nervous. 'I've been thinking about you.'

Suddenly the air surrounding us is expectant, charged and thick, as though something is going to happen. Some big, monumental life moment, and I can't cope with the thought of it.

'Sorry, Alastair,' I hear my own voice regretfully yet decisively saying. 'It's so sweet of you to come all this way and support me, but – and I've already said this to Nat – I really can't have some guy flouncing into my life and complicating things.'

'You can't,' he agrees, sounding more supportive than deflated.

'I've got a plan,' I carry on, reminding myself what I've been working towards in these last few weeks as I tell him. It's not been easy to pick myself up off the ground and move forward, but I have and I'm hugely proud of the decisions I've made. 'I'm going travelling, and I don't want my feelings for that being muddled.'

'And they shouldn't be!' he argues rather too adamantly.

'Exactly,' I say, confused as to how I've found myself nodding along with him when it was my point to make. 'I want to enjoy it and not feel like I'm being pulled between two places or like I have a choice to make.' I stop, deciding to bite the bullet and just get it out there. 'I like you. I really like you. We had an amazing time on New Year's Eve, but right now my life isn't about *that*.'

I take a deep breath, happy that my thoughts are out there, but also apprehensive about how this guy who I've only met once is going to reply to my rebuff. I'm not rejecting him, it's more the thought of having anyone in my life right now that fills me with fear for what could be – a bunch of 'what ifs' when what I really want is to be able to spend the next three months living completely in the moment.

'Well, this is awkward,' he coughs, shuffling his body, his knee accidentally grazing my leg and startling me. 'I'm actually just here to see my aunt . . . She's in the choir. Tall blonde lady. I was as surprised as you are to find us both here,' he declares, glancing at me sidelong.

I want the ground to swallow me up, which is hardly surprising as I've just acted like he's here to sweep me off my feet and fireman-lift me all the way to his great white stallion of a horse so that we can gallop towards the sunset in each other's arms, chasing after our happily-ever-after ending together.

'Oh,' I manage to mumble as the heat of embarrassment floods through my entire body. 'I'm so, so—'

'Slight lisp,' he interrupts.

I think through all the ladies in the choir, not sure I've noticed any of them having a lisp. But then there's also the fact he's from Leeds, and I don't seem to remember any blonde woman with an accent either . . .

I pause in my frantic scramble to get out of the hole I've dug myself into and look at him. The world is a small place, but can it really be *that* small?

'Maybe I've not met her,' I say, unable to hide my suspicion as I turn to him and study the finer details on his face to see if I'm right.

His upper lip twitches, something he must be aware of as he quickly pouts and relaxes in a bid to regain control of it. The lip twitch has gone, but now he seems to have something in his throat as he gives a feeble cough to clear it.

'You must know her,' he swallows, putting a hand over his eyes before continuing. 'Has a wooden leg and a pet raccoon? Drives a pink moped?' He turns to me, cocking his head to one side as a delicious smile starts climbing its way across his lips.

'Very funny,' I say, relieved that my earlier spiel isn't quite as embarrassing as I'd feared.

We sit in silence for a few moments, each looking out at the beautiful view of the park which is lined with trees that have been growing their roots here for decades, possibly centuries.

'I'm sorry for turning up unannounced but you're not on Facebook,' he says by way of explanation, looking over at me with an incredulous expression. 'I mean, who isn't on Facebook these days? And then no one would give me your number. They said you wouldn't let them.

Connie, Matt, my best mate – even your sister, who I managed to find through tagged wedding photos, said I wasn't to contact you.'

'Must've hurt,' I say, wondering when he and Michelle started talking. Judging by her reaction to his profile I'm sure she was thrilled when his name popped up in her inbox. I imagine it's kept her highly entertained during the delirious night feeds.

'I've never had someone I like not want me to get in touch before. It's never happened,' he admits, his words matter-of-fact rather than arrogant. 'I'm glad I finally tracked you down. I was going to start going to coffee mornings and fetes next.'

I laugh at the thought of it.

'Will you let me take you on a date?' he asks, his voice naturally low and bewitching.

'Have you not been listening to a word I've said?' I groan. 'I'm going away.'

'Then let me treat you to a goodbye date,' he suggests with a shrug, as though it's a perfectly innocent suggestion.

'I'm going away,' I repeat, standing my ground.

'Yep, heard that bit loud and clear . . . but you like me,' he smiles cheekily. 'You *really* like me. You said so yourself.'

His persistence makes me chuckle.

'I'm going through a bit of a thing and it's complicated,' I explain.

'Michelle told me,' he nods, his eyes looking at me with tenderness, as though he completely understands my woe.

'She did?' I ask.

'Yes,' he nods. 'I totally get it. You're completely right. This is your time to get out of here and do whatever it is you want to.'

'That's what I've been trying to say . . .'

'I respect that wholeheartedly. I don't want to be complicating things or stopping you from having an amazing experience away. That's not who I am,' he shrugs. 'I think it's admirable.'

'Thank you,' I say, nibbling on my lip, not entirely sure what's happening.

'I just wanted to see you before you went.'

'OK . . .'

'Shit,' he says, shaking his head. 'I've met you once. *Once.* There is no pressure from me, although I understand that me being here tonight might give off those pressure vibes . . .'

'It has the potential,' I admit.

'I should've asked for your number that night,' he says regretfully. 'I don't know why I didn't.'

'Even if you'd asked I promised Natalia I wouldn't, anyway,' I smirk.

'True,' he says, considering the thought. 'But I think you would've done. And not because I think I'm amazingly smooth and can get whatever I want – but because you like me and I like you. It's that simple,' he stops to flash me a bashful smile.

I return the look because I can't help but do so. It spills out of me.

'I don't say that, by the way. Ever,' he continues. 'But then I don't feel it either. You're not going to be here for a while, so I had to see you. I'm not here to interfere with your plans, but I want you to know that when you're back I would very much like to take you out for a drink, or pancakes, or to the cinema, or to the zoo – whatever you fancy,' he says, rhythmically tapping his palms against his thighs.

'You'll have moved on by then,' I tell him, wrapping my coat around me a little more in a bid to keep out the frosty air.

'I doubt it,' he says with an exasperated sigh, breathing into his hands.

'Fine,' I tell him with a defiant nod. 'But I'm not giving you my number or going back on Facebook. There'll be no time wasted with me waiting for your call or wondering why you've not responded to a message. I do not want to even think about you until I've landed back at Stansted Airport and am ready to think about what I want from the future.'

'Got it,' he says.

'And even then, you'll be a fleeting thought,' I add.

'Obviously.'

'A casual flicker of a thought that I'll brush over and forget about for at least a week or two . . .'

'Steady on,' Alastair says, amused, holding his palms in the air to stop me getting even more carried away. 'I get the point.'

A giggle flies out of my mouth, catching me off guard. 'Sorry,' I say, instinctively placing my hand on his thigh to give further weight to the apology and ensure I haven't actually offended him.

He puts a hand on top of mine.

We sit staring down – at his thigh, my hand, his hand, as though it's the most fascinating, alluring and compelling sight we've ever come across. The way my breathing becomes heavy in my chest you'd be forgiven for thinking it is.

'It was only one night,' I eventually mutter to myself, echoing what he said earlier.

'Maybe it only takes one night,' Alastair says so quietly I almost miss the words.

I take a deep breath and remove my hand, which now feels as though it's been placed into a roaring hot fire.

'I'd best get back. They'll be waiting for me,' I say, looking towards the church which, by the sounds of it, is still a hive of activity.

'Yes,' he says, jumping to his feet.

I join him in standing and am wracked by hesitation. Suddenly realizing that if I don't do something right now I'm going to spend the next three months regretting it anyway – and therefore thinking about him regardless of my resolve.

'Fuck it,' I say as I practically jump on him, wrapping my arms around his neck as I place my lips upon his. I breathe as much of him in as I can and I love every single second of him wanting me back.

I pull away, my head light and my chest pounding, unable to look away from Alastair, who looks happily taken aback at what's just happened.

Laughter spills out of me uncontrollably, the sound reverberating around the park and gloriously bouncing its way back to me.

'One for the road,' I say bashfully, taking Alastair's fingertips in mine and pulling him back up the pathway to the church.

I don't need a special someone in my life to complete me, and I know I'm going to be learning all sorts about myself and the world over the next three months, but maybe it's OK to admit that I need all kinds of people around me to make me feel whole. Mum, Dad, Ted, Michelle and baby Duncan, Connie and Natalia, all my new friends at Sing it Proud, and Alastair – they all bring out different sides of me, whether that be ambitious, brave, funny, sexy, loving, caring, silly or dedicated. Allowing all of those parts to shine is surely the only way I will ever feel content and happy. I will forever be working on my progress list, and that's life. I'm not meant to be who I was yesterday, last year or a decade ago. Changing isn't a weakness or something to be ashamed of. Evolving can only be seen as a success. Allowing people in will always be the making of me, whether for better or worse.

I'm lots of things, and just as different experiences along the way shape me into the person I am at one given moment, so too do the people I encounter. And that's got to be some kind of wonderful.

Epilogue

Three months later

I take a breath, my backpack firmly on my shoulders, having recovered it from baggage claim. It was pink when I left, now it's a murky purple thanks to the dirt that's attached itself and followed us on our travels.

Have I found myself? Did I ever think that was truly possible? Surely not. We are ever changing. The second you think you've got a grasp of your true self the situation alters and you have to start solving the puzzle once again.

I am at peace with who I am in this exact moment. I can't predict what'll happen tomorrow, or who'll be standing through these doors when I step into arrivals at Stansted Airport and how that might, or might not, affect who I'll be tomorrow or in ten years. But I can accept myself for who I am, and allow myself to explore without having too many expectations.

I spent so long focusing on something that wasn't real. From now on, all I ask of myself is to home in on the now and realize that that is all that matters. The here and now.

A young couple walk past me. As if their blinding rings aren't the biggest giveaway, a huge sticker on the woman's gold suitcase declares they're 'Just Married'. Honeymooners, coming home with their tanned skin and blissfully loved-up expressions.

Good for them, *I think to myself with a wry smile, before peeling my eyes away and focusing on the doors in front of me.*

Not my story.

I can't stand here for much longer. It's time to head through them and see what the moment holds.

One more breath.

In.

Out.

Calm.

Let's go.

Acknowledgements

Writing a book can be a lonely experience. I can be sitting in my office for up to twelve hours a day with nothing but a packet of Chocolate Hobnobs to keep me company. That said, this book is a team effort and there have been many wonderful people who've cheered me on along the way! So, let's get thanking!

Hannah Ferguson, there's a reason you're always listed first. I would not be doing this if you hadn't seen my potential all those years ago. Thank you for being the right literary agent for me, and always replying to my worried emails with your super-relaxed energy! Thanks to the teams at Hardman & Swainson and The Marsh Agency for supporting us both.

Maxine Hitchcock, what a joy it's been to have you editing this book. Thank you for doing so in such a calm and supportive way. Ellie Hughes, Claire Bush, Nick Lowndes, Fiona Brown and the various teams at Penguin Random House who've shown me nothing but love and support – you're all brilliant!

Rebecca Boyce, Claire Dundas, Sophie Gildersleeve and everyone at James Grant for being the absolute best management team around. Thank you for encouraging me to keep reaching beyond what I ever imagined would be possible. I can't wait to see what we get up to next!

The readers – YOU! I can't thank you enough for

making my dream of being an author a reality. Without you buying my work and asking for more there'd simply be no books. This is all on you!

A big thanks to my great friends who never put pressure on me or make me feel crap for disappearing each time I have a book to write. Katy, Emma, Charlie, Savannah, Lauren, Karen, Bex, The Hoppers, The Handy Crew and all the other kind and thoughtful special mates I've made – life has changed for all of us, but I love watching your lives unfold. I'm so proud to call you my friends!

I would not be able to physically sit at my desk each day if the Fletcher/Falcone troops didn't gather around and look after the boys/us. Bob and Debbie, thank you for pouring so much love into the boys and making the fact I have to work a little bit easier on my heart. Dad, you really are the wisest man I know. Mum, you really are the nuttiest woman I know. Giorgie, Chickpea and Miss Summer Rae, how lucky are we to have you guys – trashy TV, food and wine. Thanks for keeping us sane and giving us a bit of normality. Mario and Becky, I can't wait to see what the next few years have in store for you both. Debbie B – thanks for your continued kindness and love! Carrie, you're such a talented soul with so many strings to your bow.

Tom, Buzz and Buddy. Well, the book is in and you've finally got your wife/mumma back. Tom, thanks for juggling this parenting malarkey with me and being as work-obsessed as I am. How lucky are we to do what we love and have two adorable boys to call our sons? Yes, the six a.m. starts aren't pleasant, and we could probably do without all the wailing and senseless meltdowns, but the smiles and laughs make those moments more than worthwhile. Thank you for being my partner in crime and making me belly laugh on a regular occasion. Date night soon?

Buzz and Buddy, you two are perfectly imperfect and I will spend my entire lifetime loving every single thing about you. Thank you for being my driving force and my biggest inspiration. I love you!

He just wanted a decent book to read ...

Not too much to ask, is it? It was in 1935 when Allen Lane, Managing Director of Bodley Head Publishers, stood on a platform at Exeter railway station looking for something good to read on his journey back to London. His choice was limited to popular magazines and poor-quality paperbacks – the same choice faced every day by the vast majority of readers, few of whom could afford hardbacks. Lane's disappointment and subsequent anger at the range of books generally available led him to found a company – and change the world.

'We believed in the existence in this country of a vast reading public for intelligent books at a low price, and staked everything on it'
Sir Allen Lane, 1902–1970, founder of Penguin Books

The quality paperback had arrived – and not just in bookshops. Lane was adamant that his Penguins should appear in chain stores and tobacconists, and should cost no more than a packet of cigarettes.

Reading habits (and cigarette prices) have changed since 1935, but Penguin still believes in publishing the best books for everybody to enjoy. We still believe that good design costs no more than bad design, and we still believe that quality books published passionately and responsibly make the world a better place.

So wherever you see the little bird – whether it's on a piece of prize-winning literary fiction or a celebrity autobiography, political tour de force or historical masterpiece, a serial-killer thriller, reference book, world classic or a piece of pure escapism – you can bet that it represents the very best that the genre has to offer.

Whatever you like to read – trust Penguin.